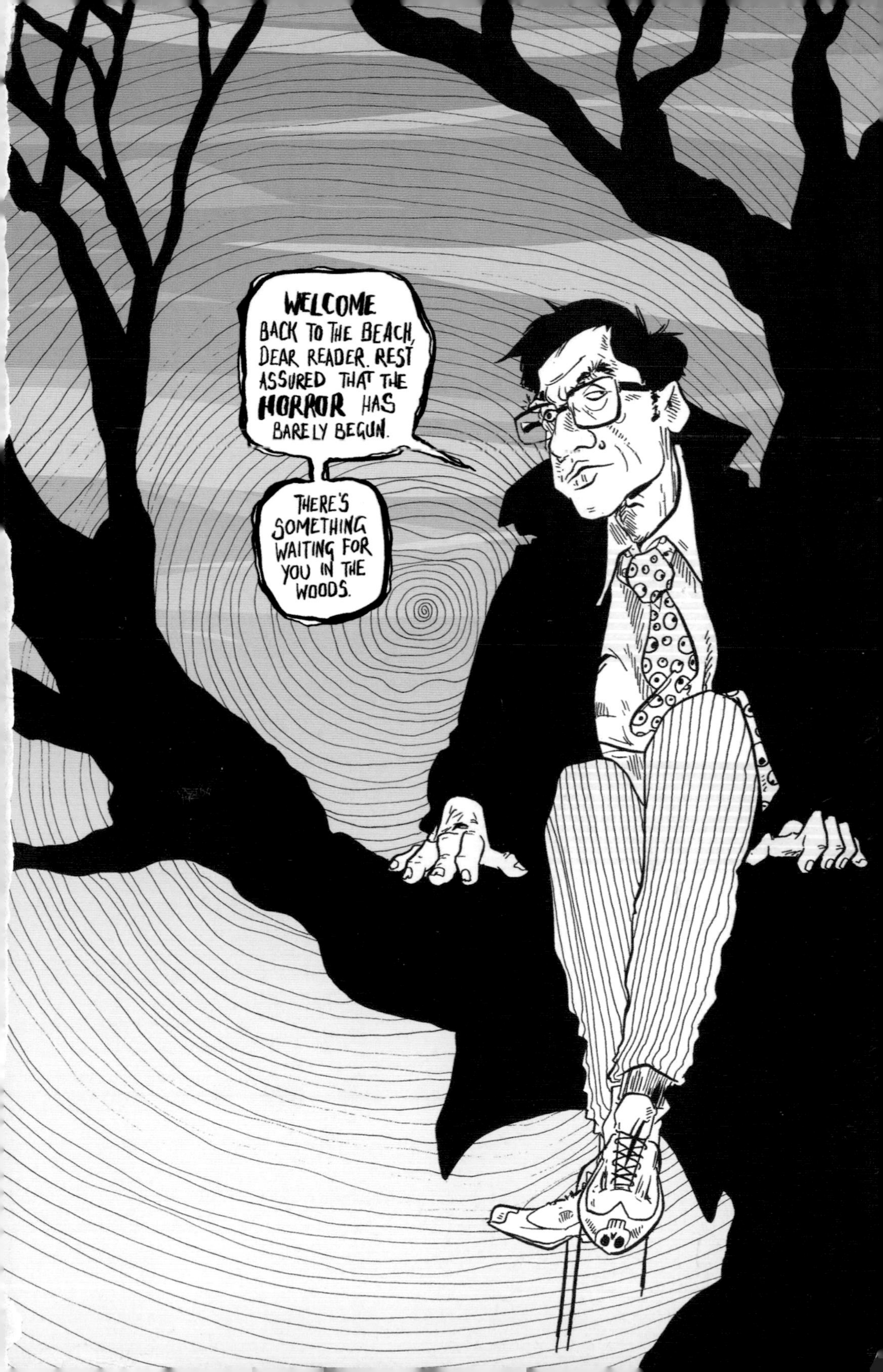
WELCOME BACK TO THE BEACH, DEAR READER. REST ASSURED THAT THE HORROR HAS BARELY BEGUN.
THERE'S SOMETHING WAITING FOR YOU IN THE WOODS.

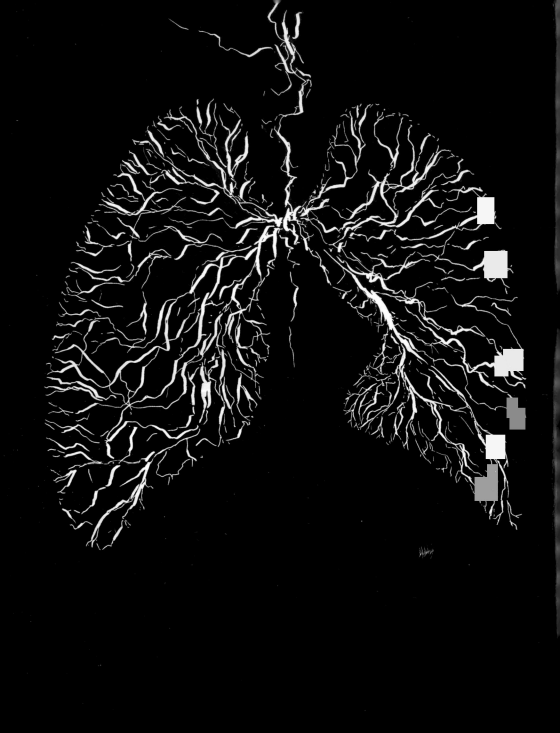

BLACK SAND BEACH

DO YOU REMEMBER THE SUMMER BEFORE?

BY RICHARD FAIRGRAY

PIXEL
INK

For Gizella

PIXEL ▌INK

Text and illustrations copyright © 2021 by Richard Fairgray
All Rights Reserved
Pixel+Ink is a division of TGM Development Corp.
Printed and bound in January 2021 at Toppan Leefung, DongGuan, China.
Book design by Richard Fairgray
www.pixelandinkbooks.com
Library of Congress Control Number: 2020944067
Hardcover ISBN 978-1-64595-004-2
Paperback ISBN 978-1-64595-003-5
eBook ISBN 978-1-64595-072-1
First Edition
1 3 5 7 9 10 8 6 4 2

Do You Remember the Summer Before?

PREVIOUSLY

Dash West had been dreading having to spend all summer at his family's ramshackle beach house at Black Sand Beach, convinced that even with his best friend, Lily, there it would be unbearably boring. But after just a week in the house with his cousins, there hasn't been a second to be bored.

Mysterious whispers calling Dash to the abandoned lighthouse, a glowing snake monster in the basement, and Lily almost being replaced by a creature who was definitely not a cow are just the beginning for these kids.

Dash was convinced that he hadn't been to Black Sand Beach for years, but if that were true, then why was his journal from last summer in the basement of the lighthouse? It's pretty clear that he was there, because even that glowing snake monster remembers him.

What clues can last year's journal offer?

What happened to Dash to cause him to forget?

Why did he really change his name to Dash from Harry-Gilbert?

How much darkness is really seeping through from the beach at the edge of the world?

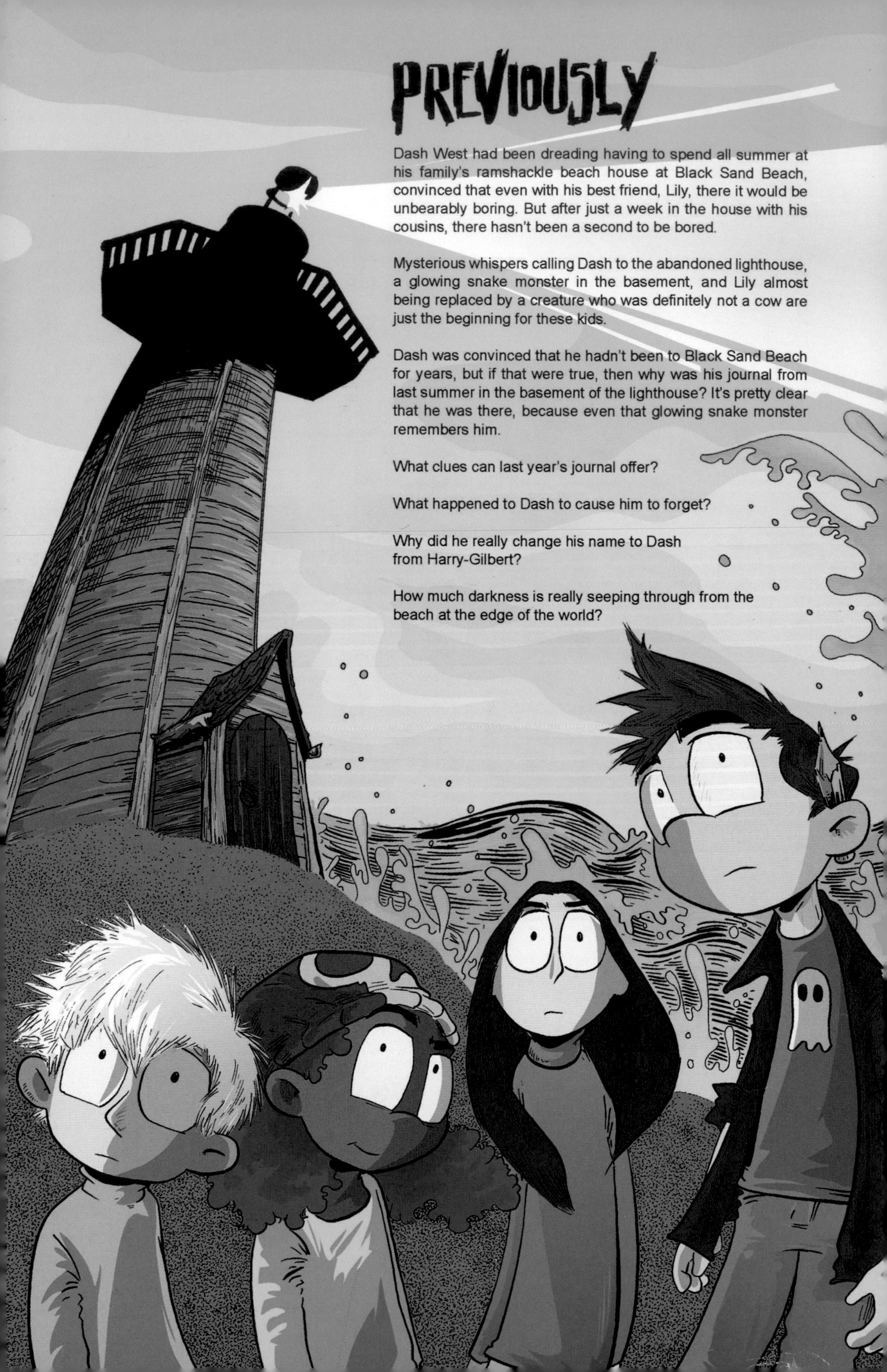

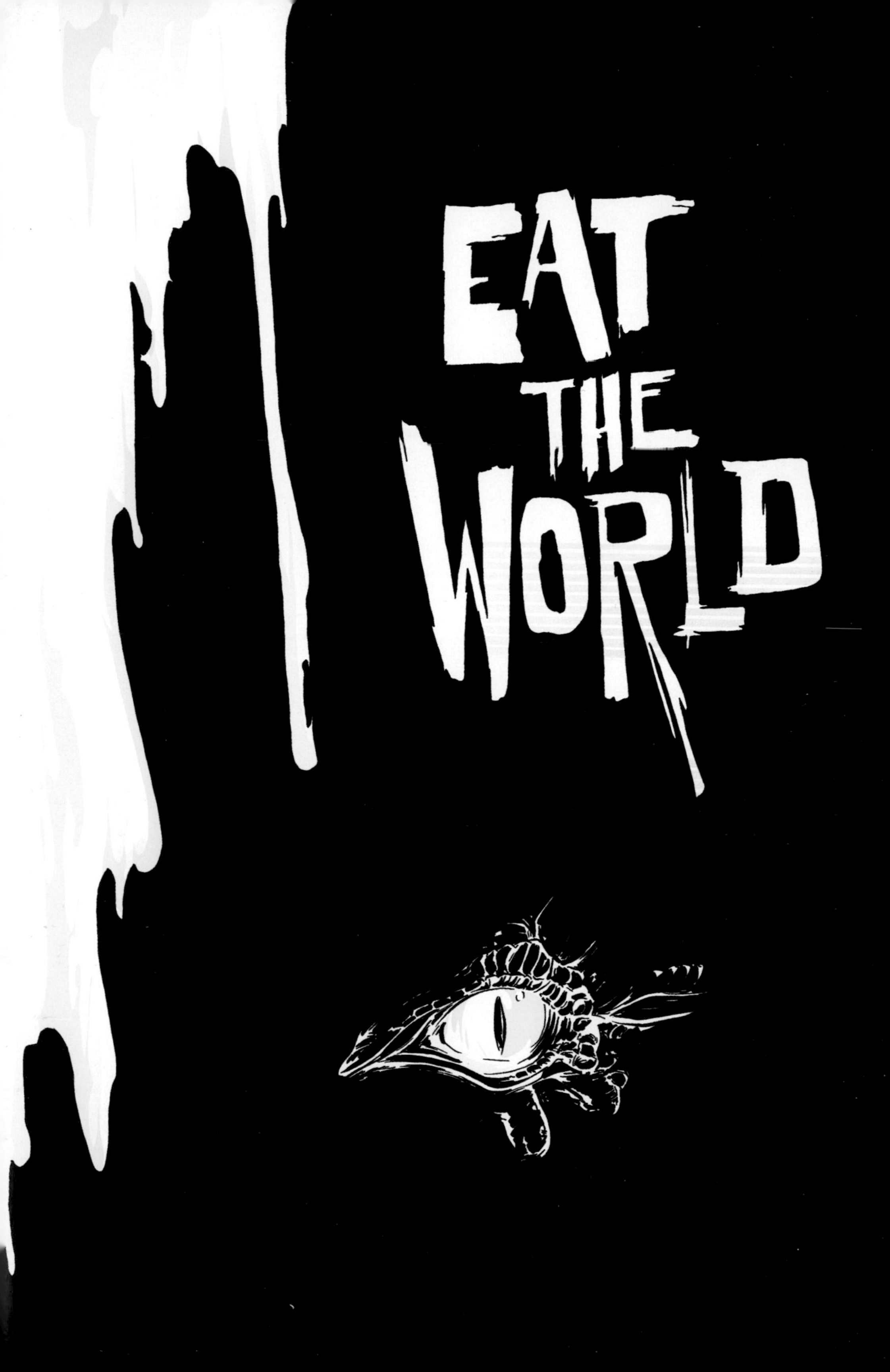
EAT THE WORLD

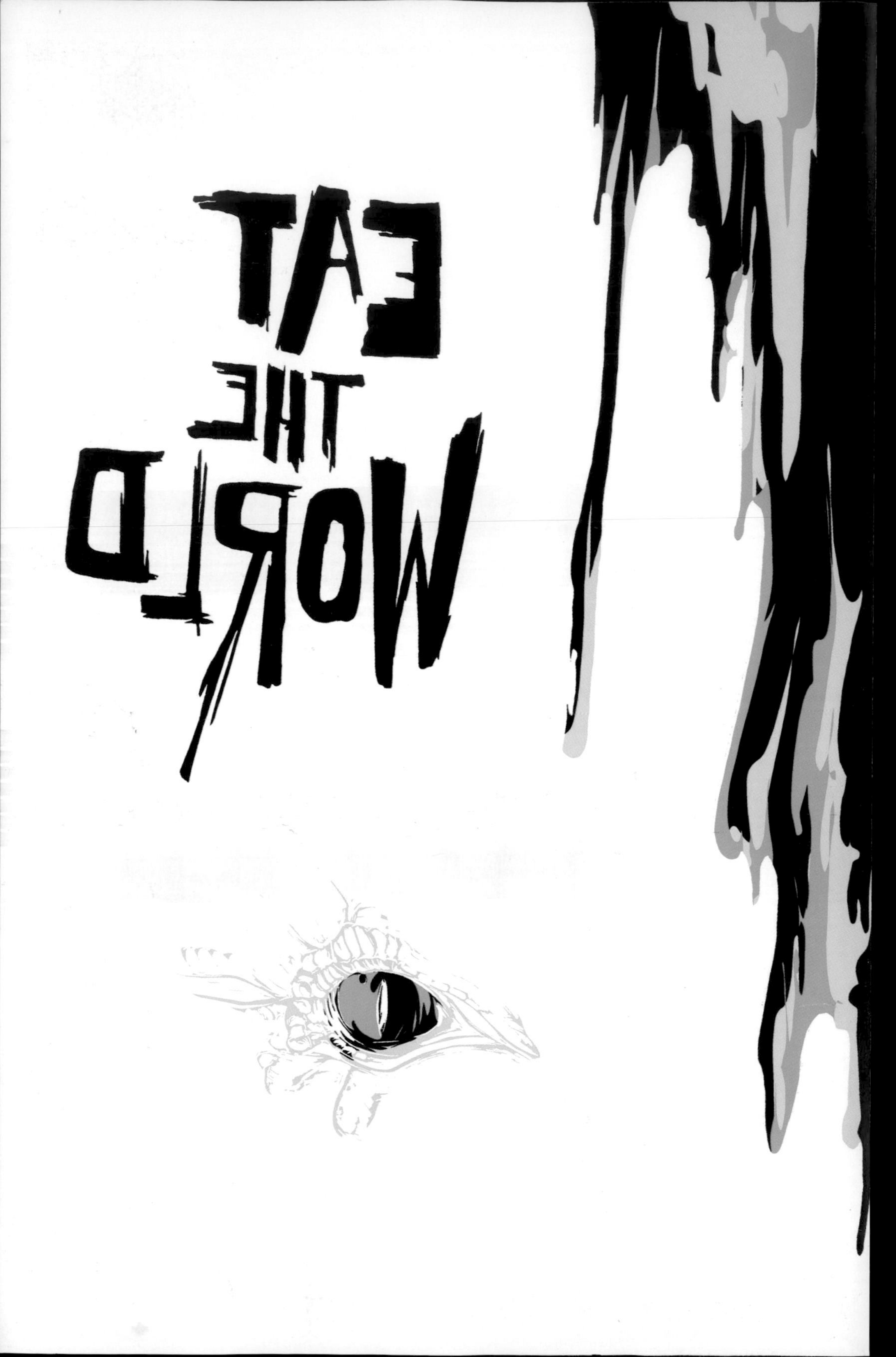
EAT
THE
WORLD

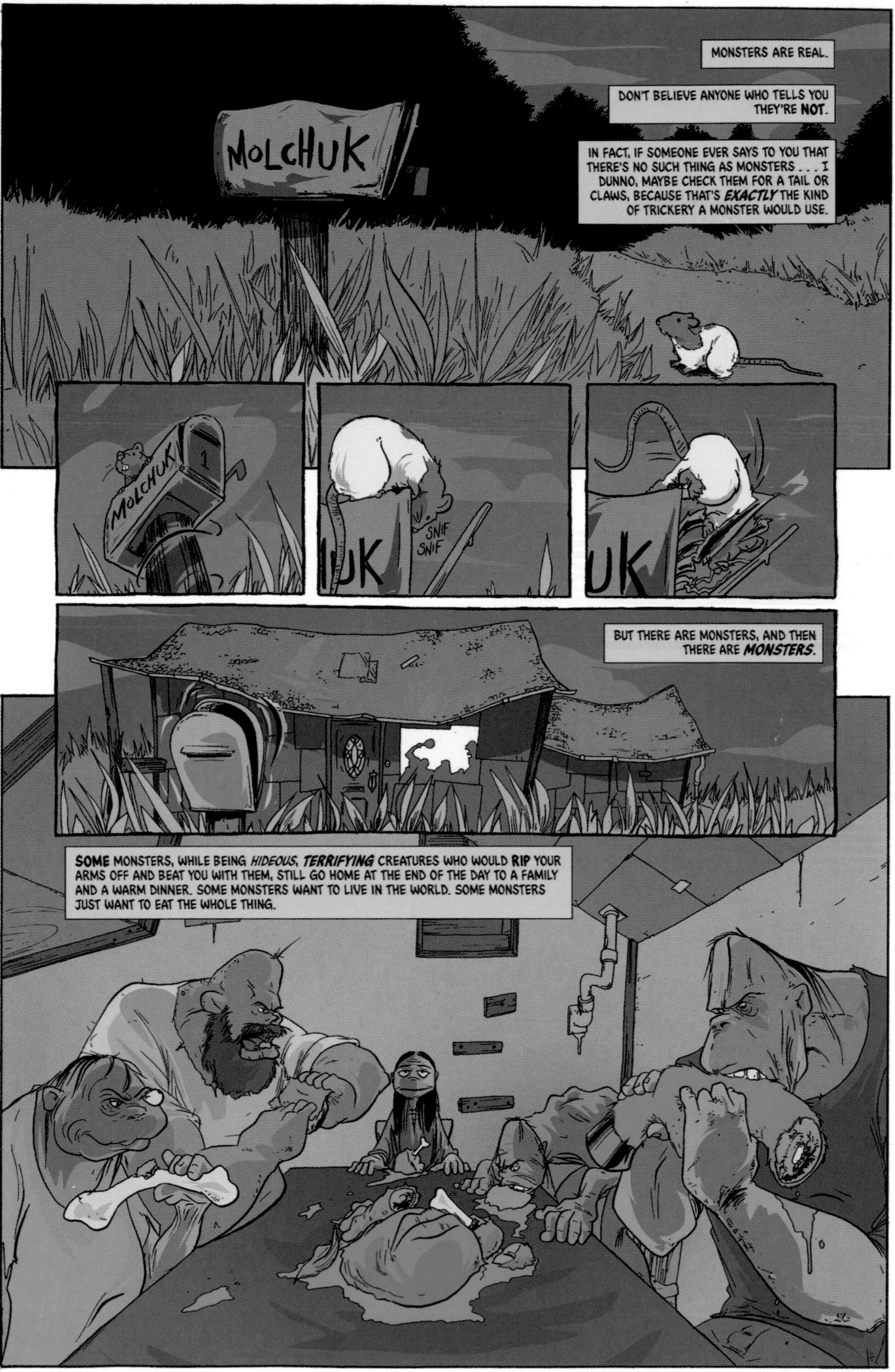
MOLCHUK
MONSTERS ARE REAL.
DON'T BELIEVE ANYONE WHO TELLS YOU THEY'RE **NOT**.
IN FACT, IF SOMEONE EVER SAYS TO YOU THAT THERE'S NO SUCH THING AS MONSTERS . . . I DUNNO, MAYBE CHECK THEM FOR A TAIL OR CLAWS, BECAUSE THAT'S ***EXACTLY*** THE KIND OF TRICKERY A MONSTER WOULD USE.
MOLCHUK
1
SNIF SNIF
BUT THERE ARE MONSTERS, AND THEN THERE ARE ***MONSTERS***.
SOME MONSTERS, WHILE BEING *HIDEOUS*, ***TERRIFYING*** CREATURES WHO WOULD **RIP** YOUR ARMS OFF AND BEAT YOU WITH THEM, STILL GO HOME AT THE END OF THE DAY TO A FAMILY AND A WARM DINNER. SOME MONSTERS WANT TO LIVE IN THE WORLD. SOME MONSTERS JUST WANT TO EAT THE WHOLE THING.

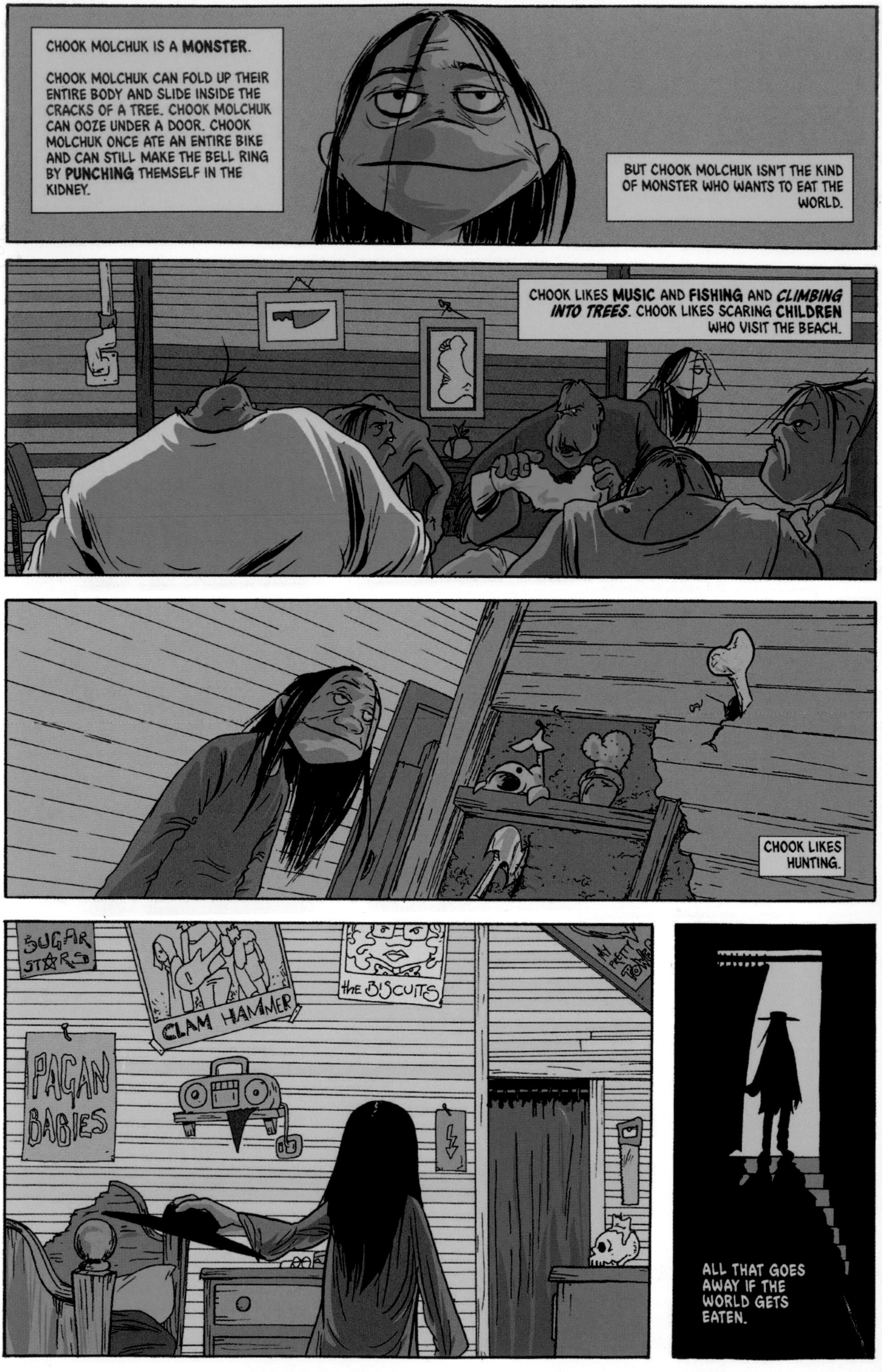
CHOOK MOLCHUK IS A MONSTER.
CHOOK MOLCHUK CAN FOLD UP THEIR ENTIRE BODY AND SLIDE INSIDE THE CRACKS OF A TREE. CHOOK MOLCHUK CAN OOZE UNDER A DOOR. CHOOK MOLCHUK ONCE ATE AN ENTIRE BIKE AND CAN STILL MAKE THE BELL RING BY PUNCHING THEMSELF IN THE KIDNEY.
BUT CHOOK MOLCHUK ISN'T THE KIND OF MONSTER WHO WANTS TO EAT THE WORLD.
CHOOK LIKES MUSIC AND FISHING AND CLIMBING INTO TREES. CHOOK LIKES SCARING CHILDREN WHO VISIT THE BEACH.
CHOOK LIKES HUNTING.
SUGAR STARS
CLAM HAMMER
the BISCUITS
MY PRETTY POWDER
PAGAN BABIES
ALL THAT GOES AWAY IF THE WORLD GETS EATEN.

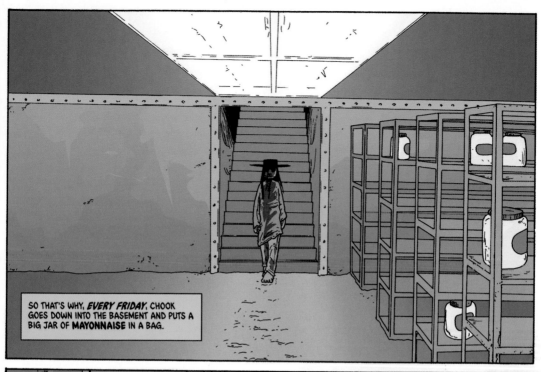

SO THAT'S WHY, *EVERY FRIDAY*, CHOOK GOES DOWN INTO THE BASEMENT AND PUTS A BIG JAR OF **MAYONNAISE** IN A BAG.

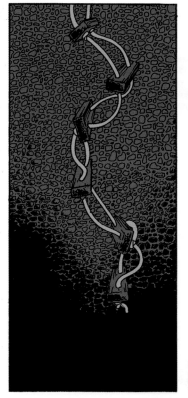

THEN CARRIES THAT BAG . . .

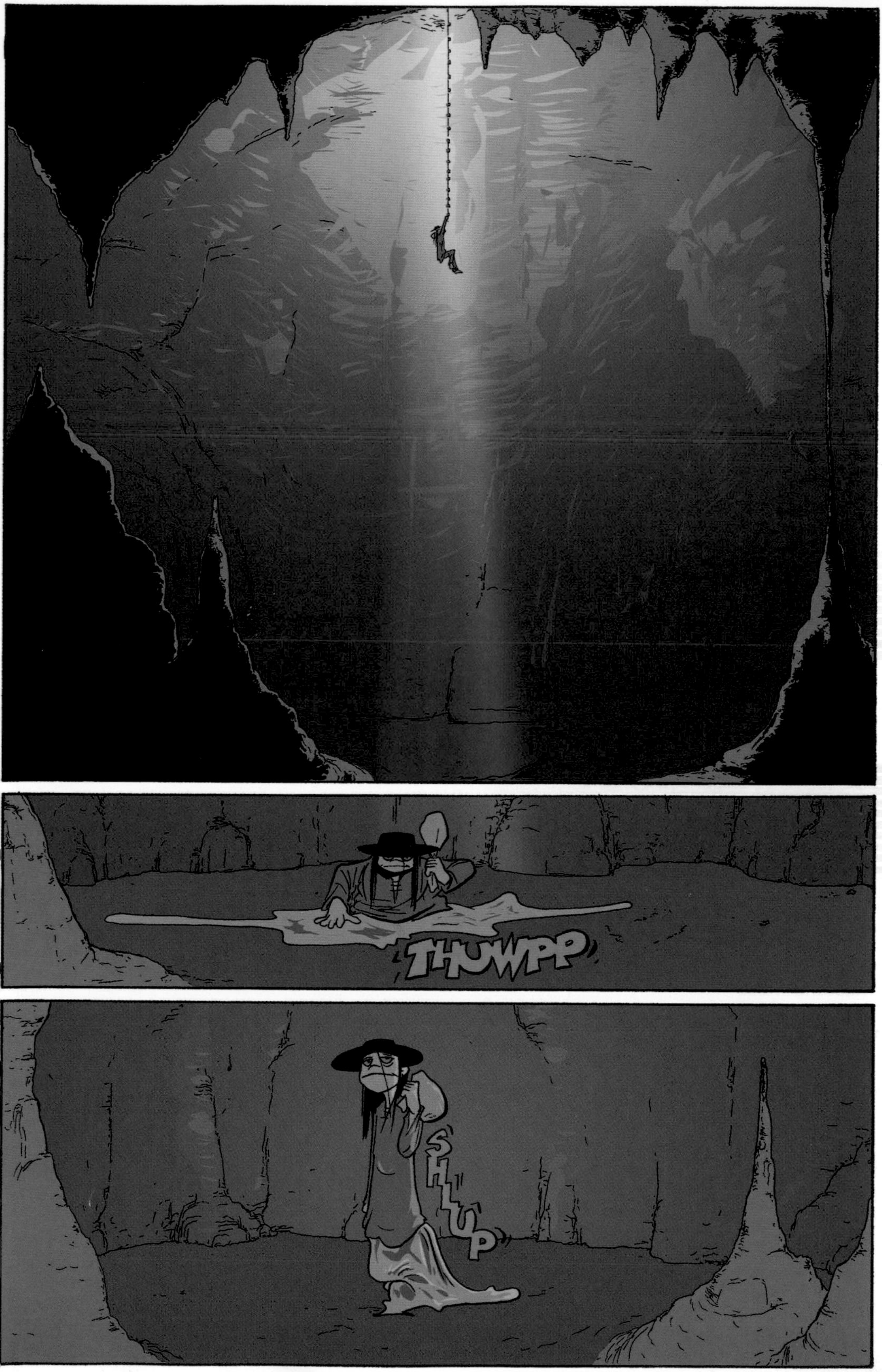
THUWPP
SHLUP

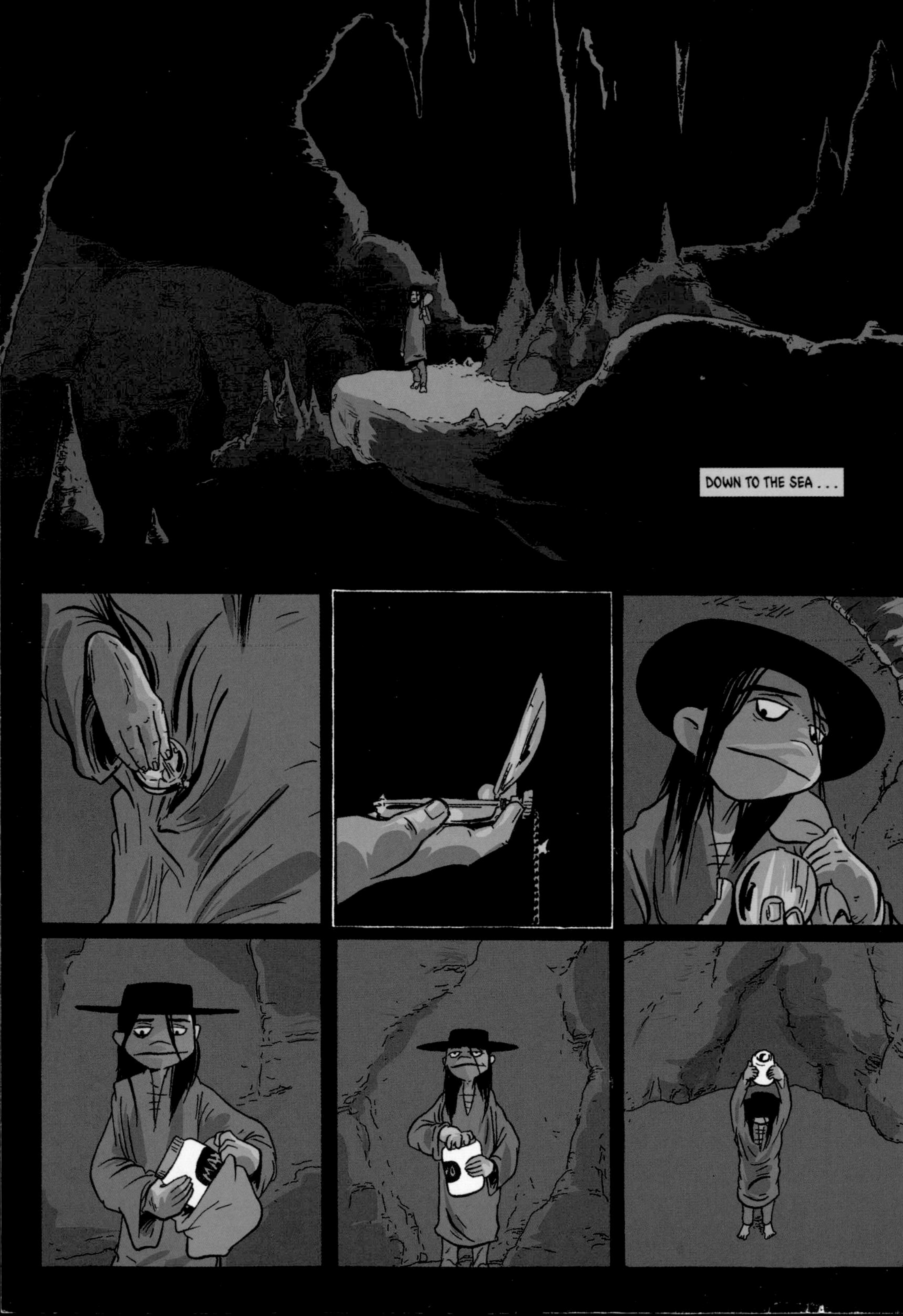
DOWN TO THE SEA . . .

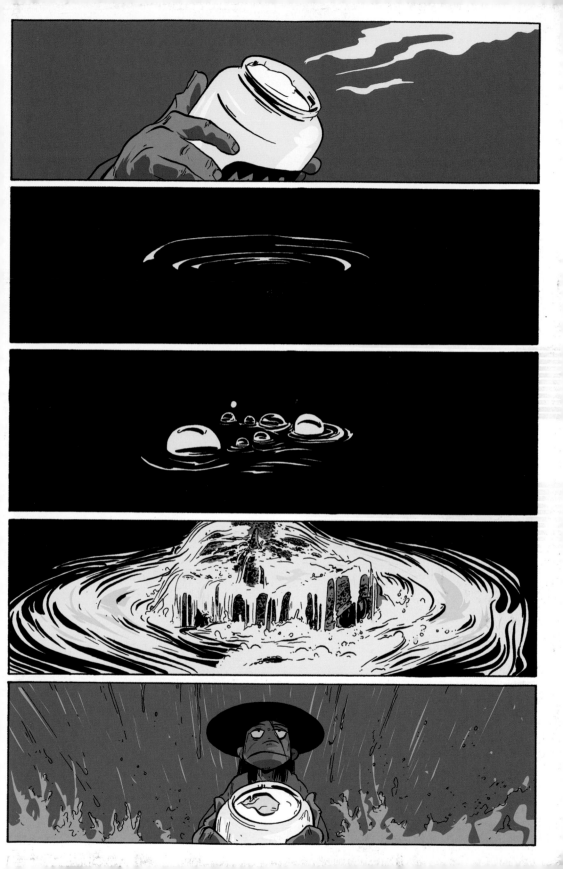

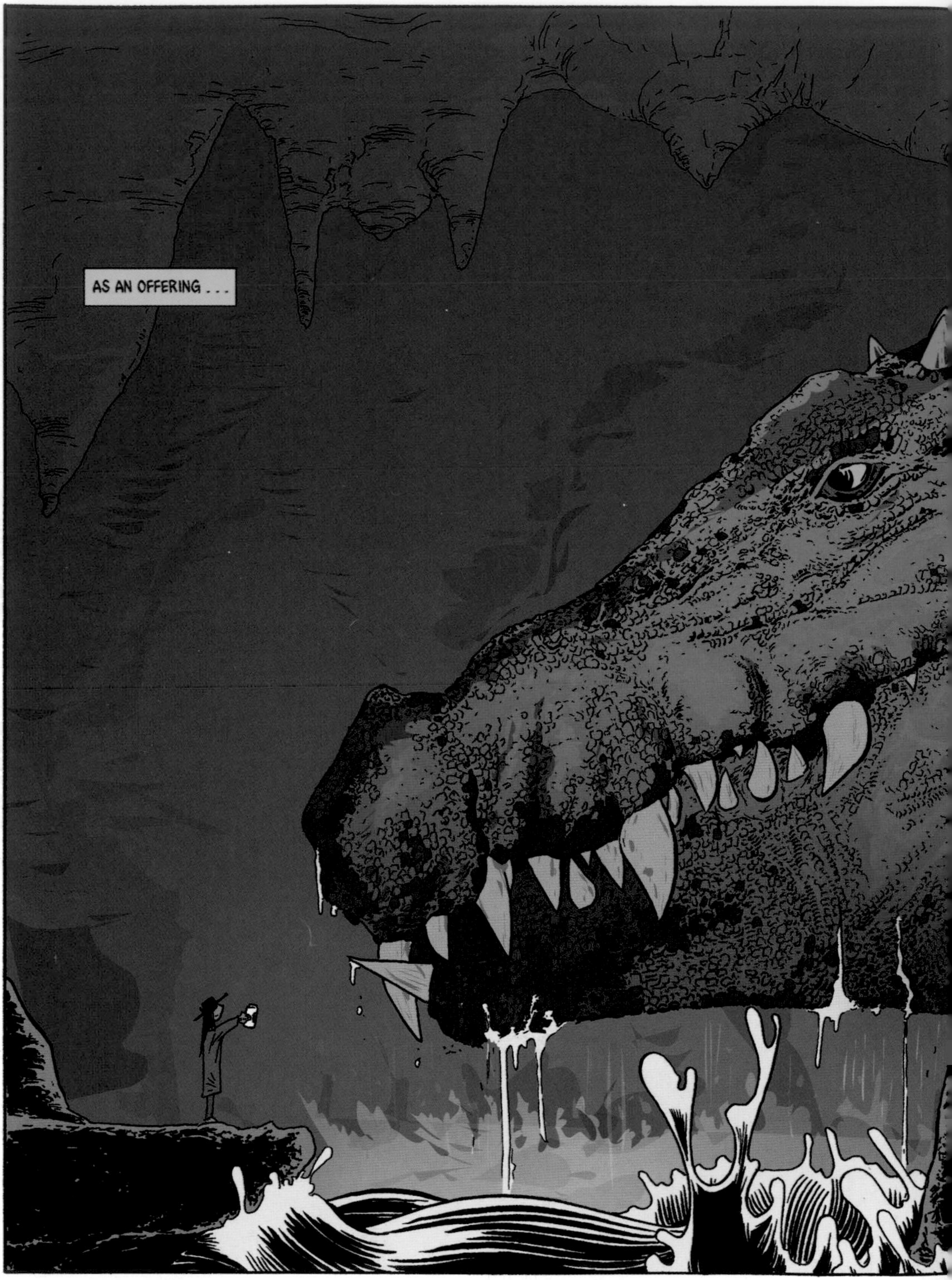
AS AN OFFERING . . .

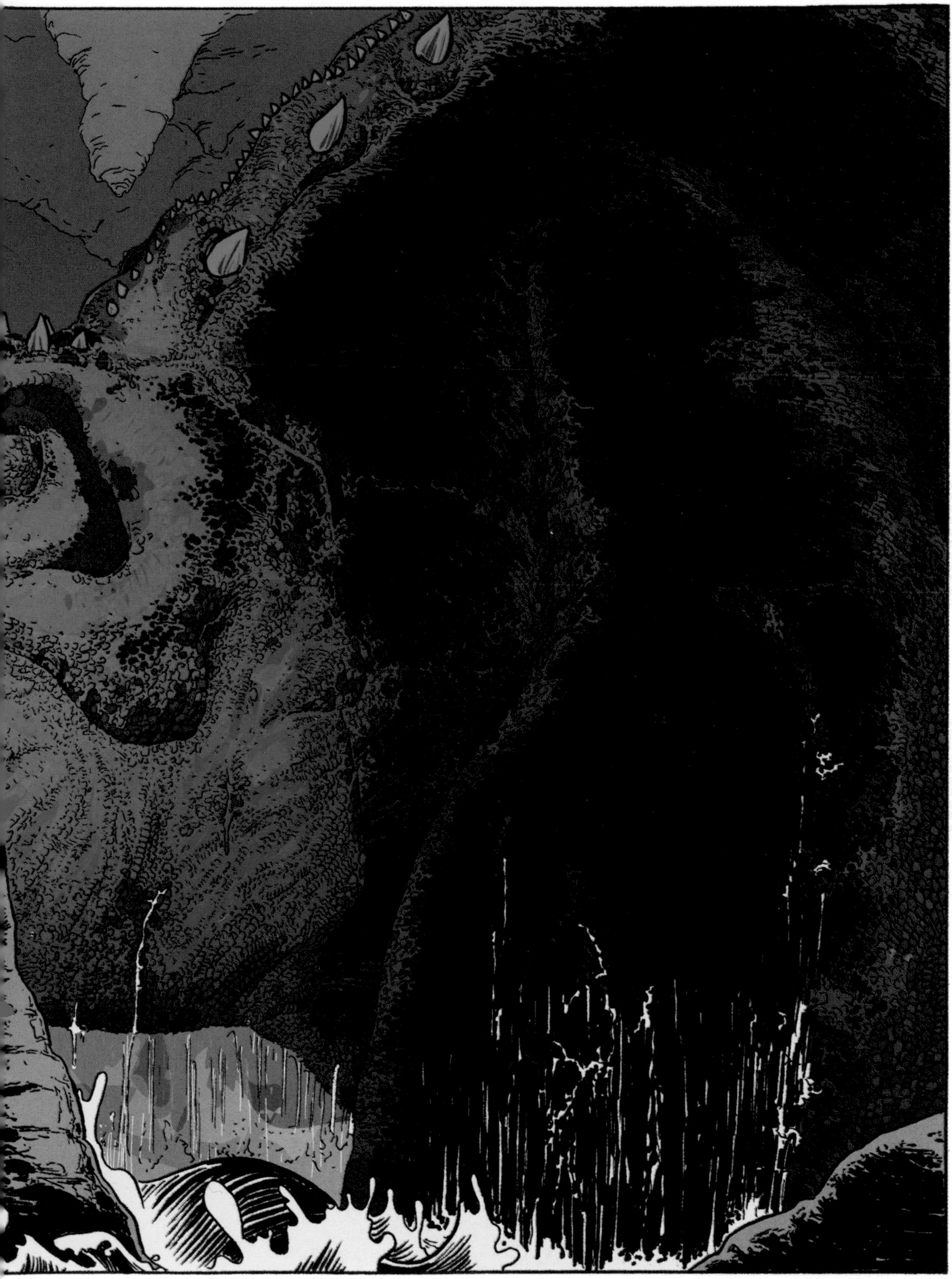

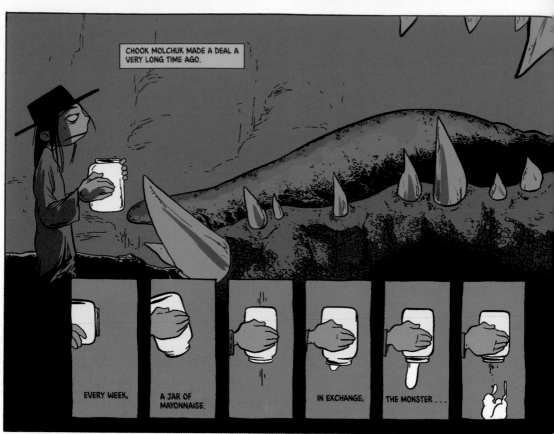

CHOOK MOLCHUK MADE A DEAL A VERY LONG TIME AGO.

EVERY WEEK,

A JAR OF MAYONNAISE.

IN EXCHANGE,

THE MONSTER . . .

DOESN'T COME ASHORE.

THE MONSTER DOESN'T EAT THE WORLD.

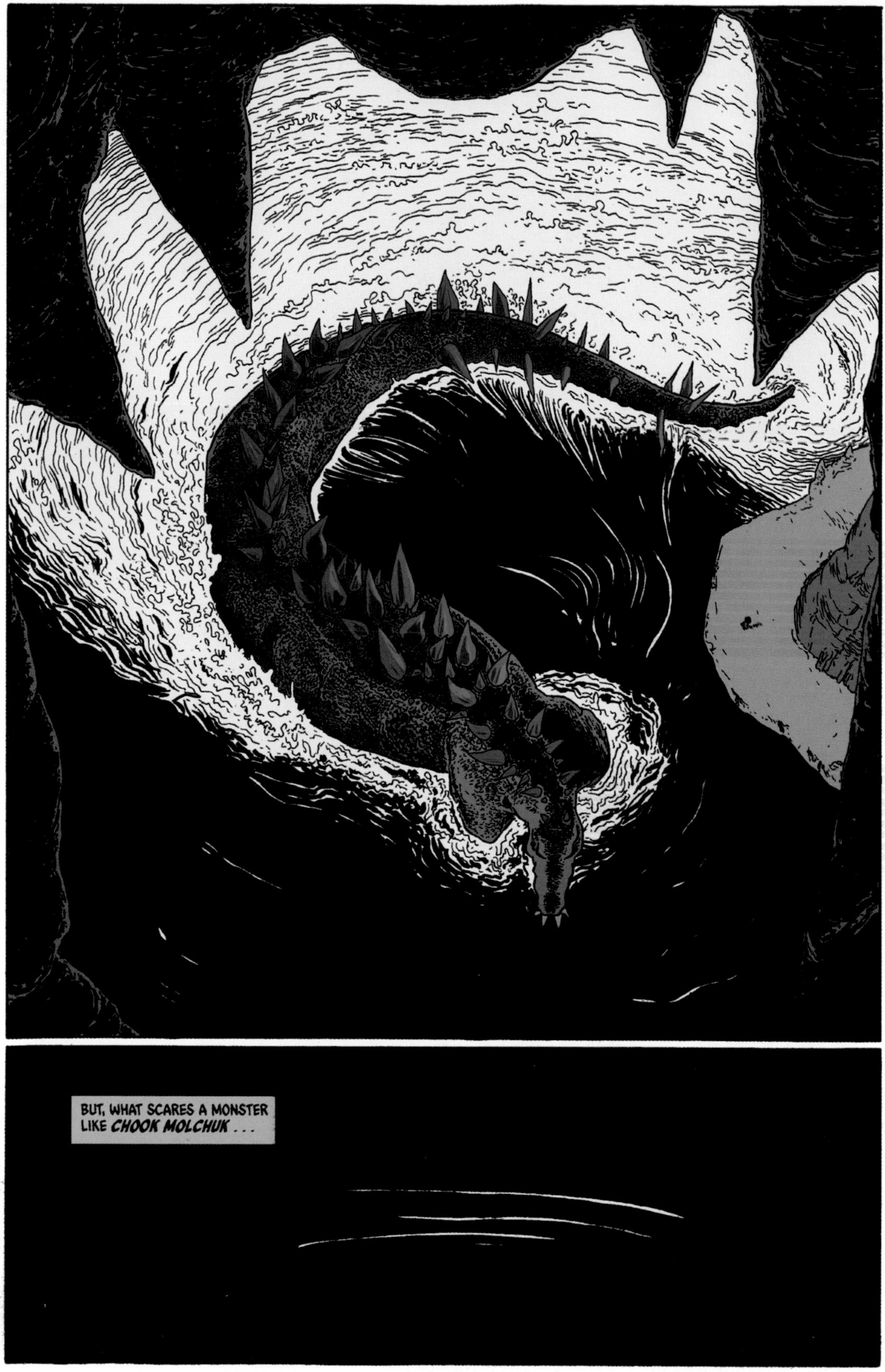
BUT, WHAT SCARES A MONSTER LIKE *CHOOK MOLCHUK* . . .

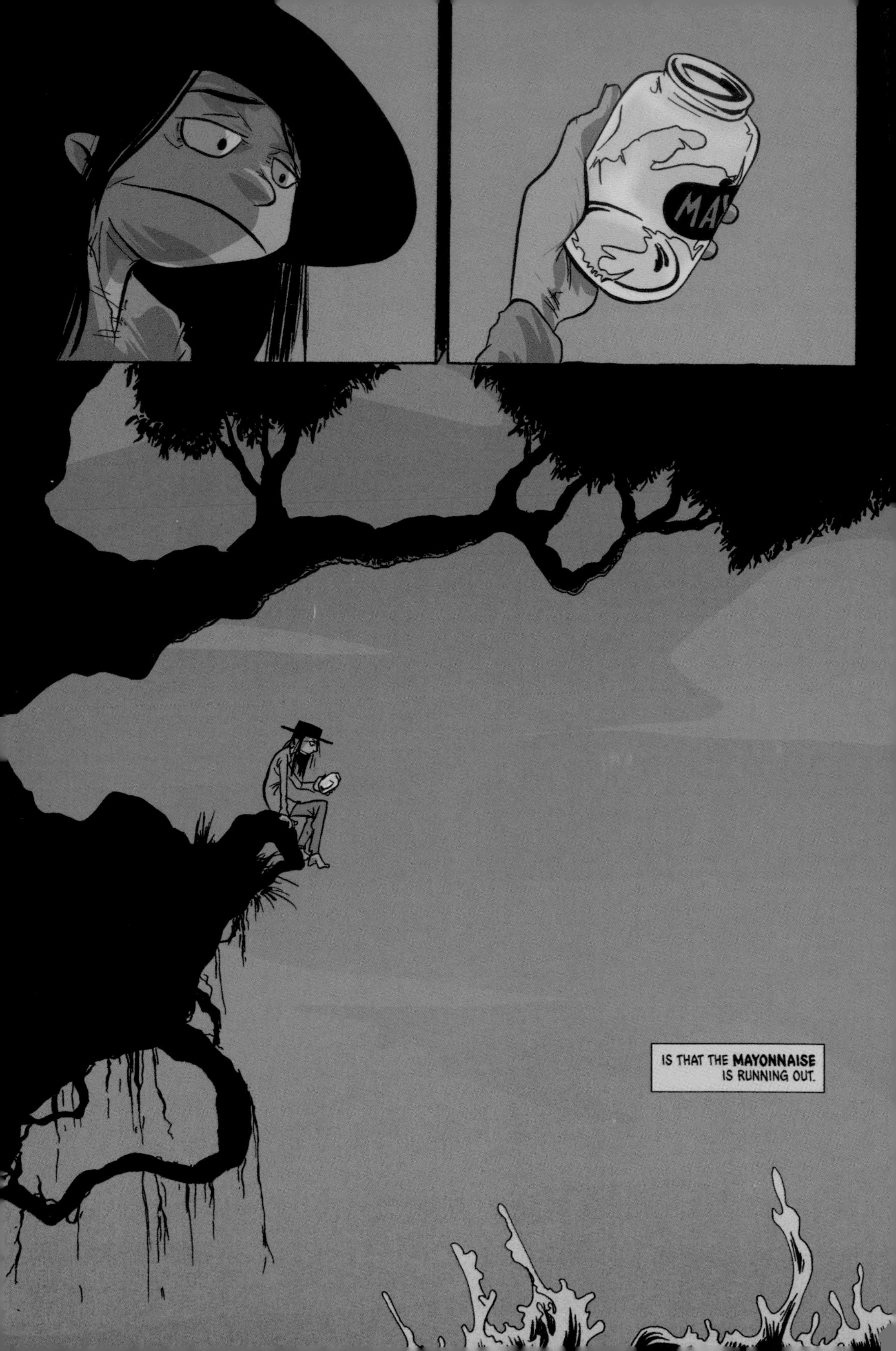
MAY
IS THAT THE MAYONNAISE IS RUNNING OUT.

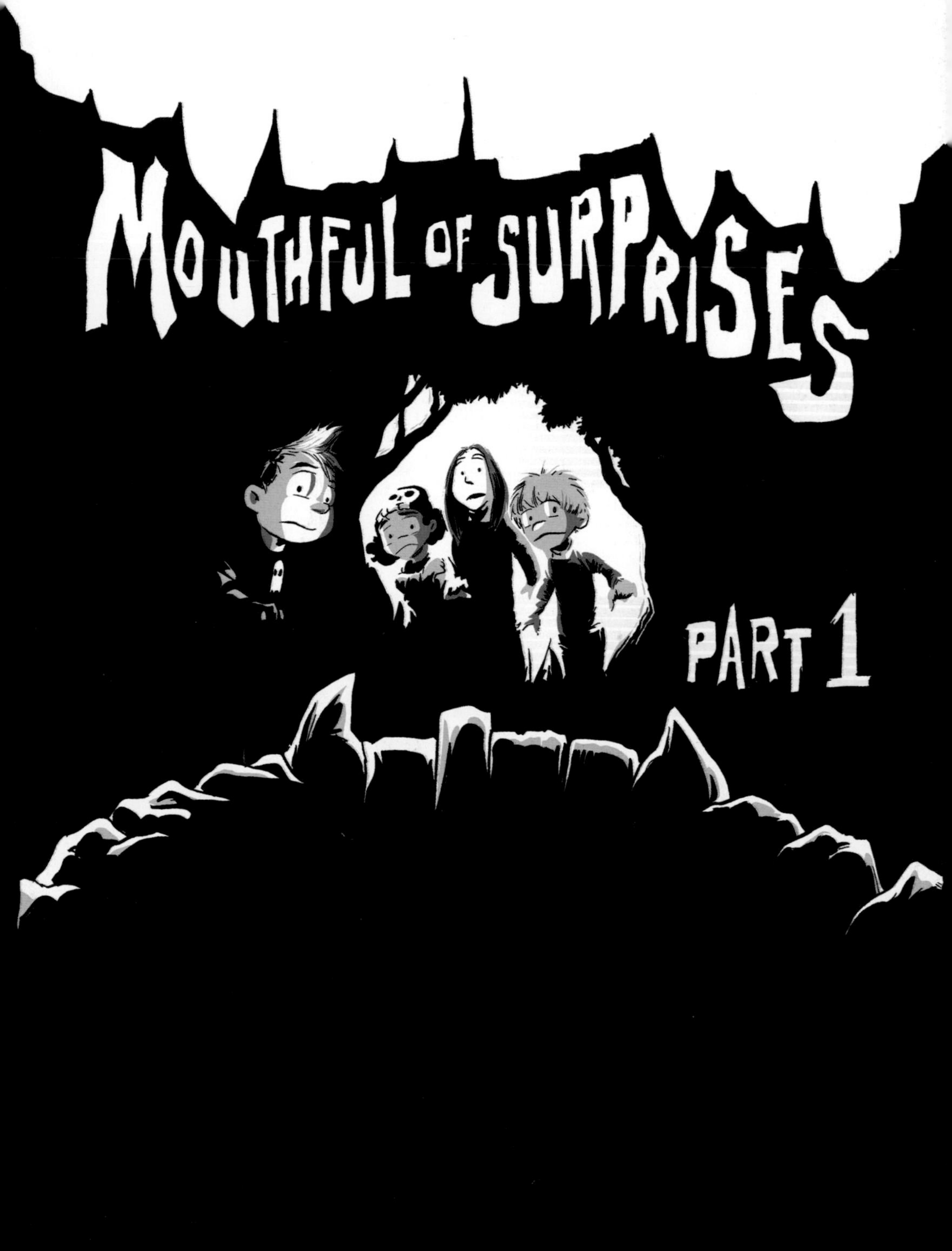
MOUTHFUL OF SURPRISES
PART 1

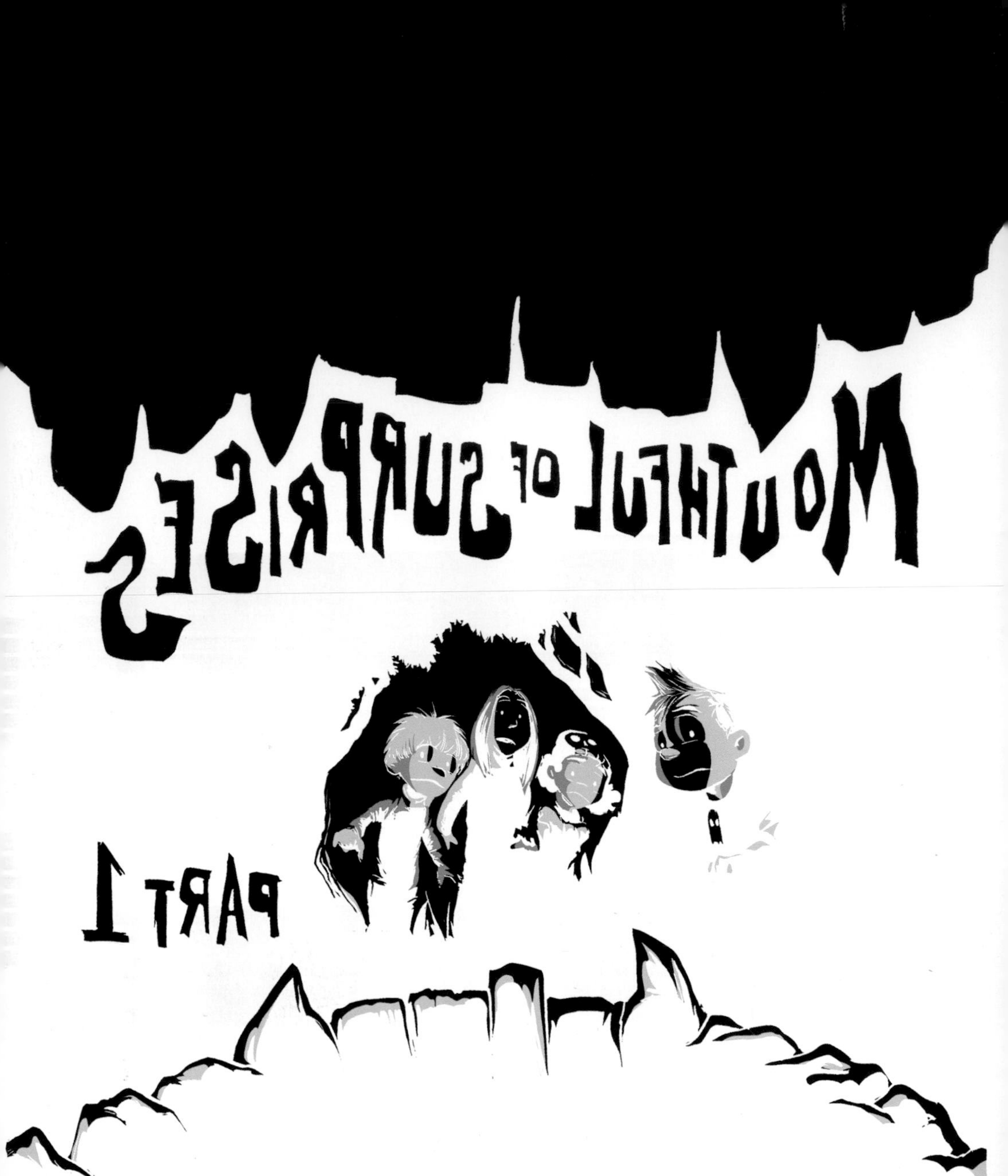
MOUTHFUL OF SURPRISES
PART 1

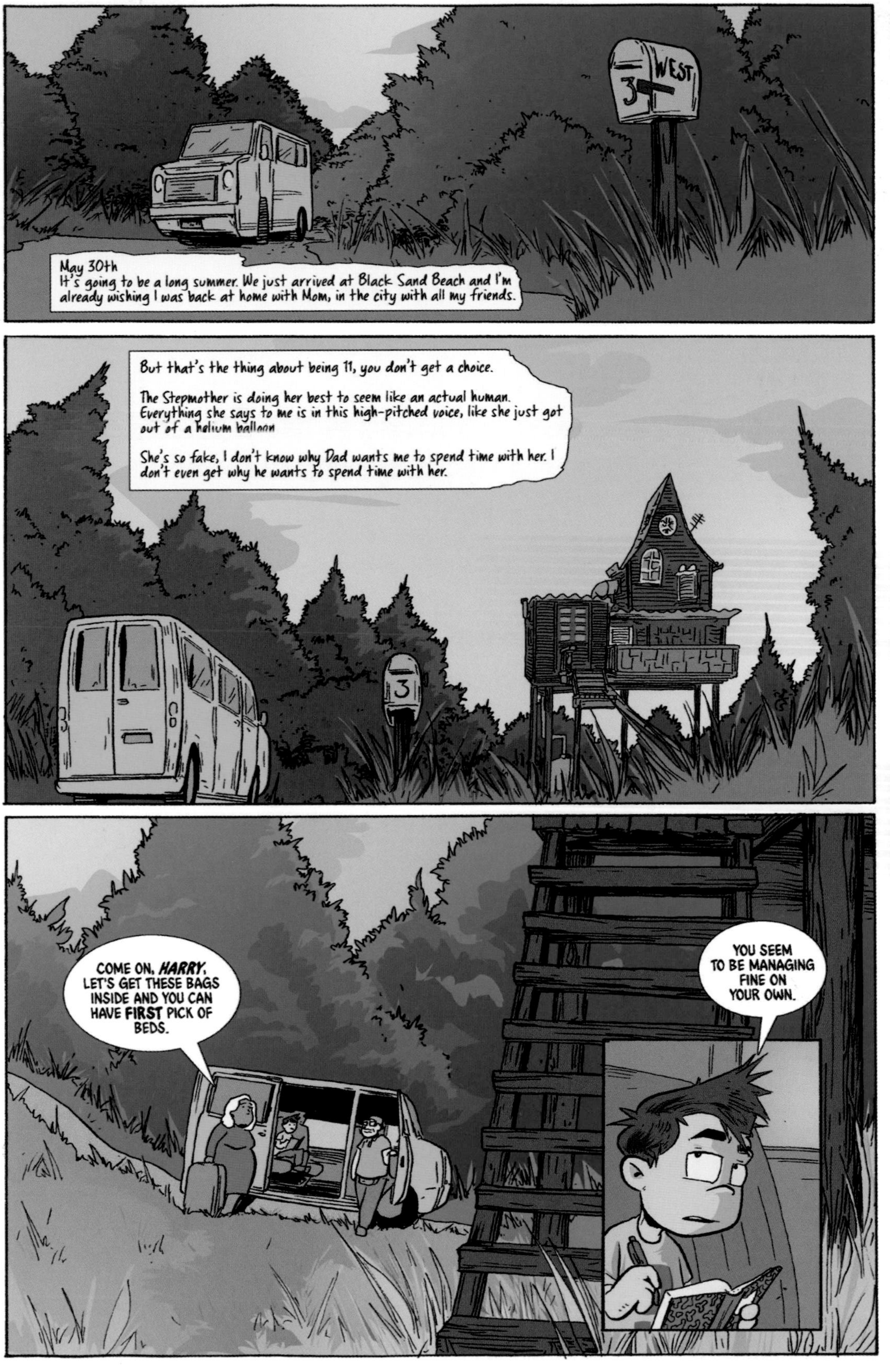

WEST
May 30th
It's going to be a long summer. We just arrived at Black Sand Beach and I'm already wishing I was back at home with Mom, in the city with all my friends.
But that's the thing about being 11, you don't get a choice.
The Stepmother is doing her best to seem like an actual human. Everything she says to me is in this high-pitched voice, like she just got out of a helium balloon
She's so fake, I don't know why Dad wants me to spend time with her. I don't even get why he wants to spend time with her.
COME ON, HARRY, LET'S GET THESE BAGS INSIDE AND YOU CAN HAVE FIRST PICK OF BEDS.
YOU SEEM TO BE MANAGING FINE ON YOUR OWN.

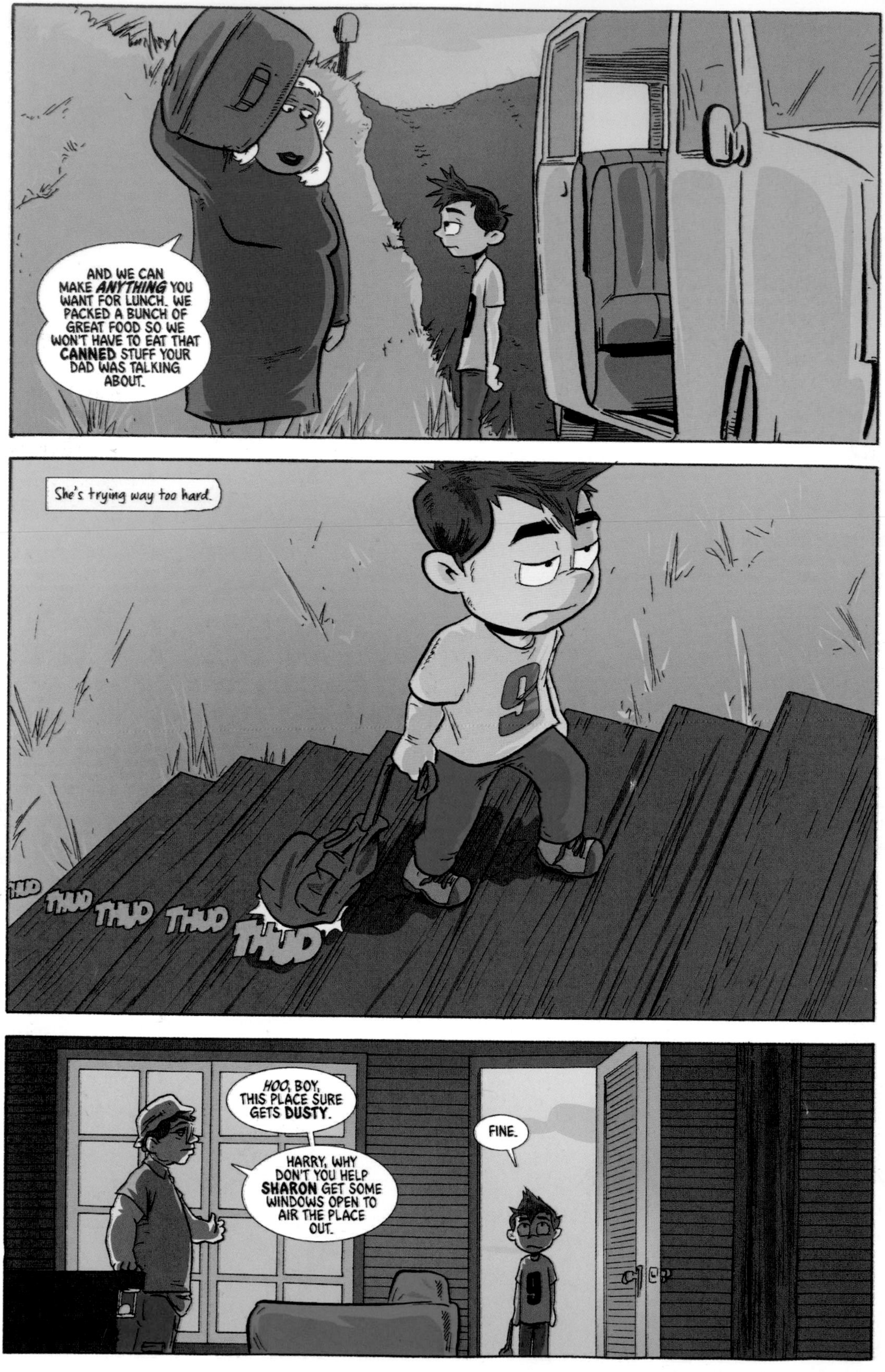
AND WE CAN MAKE ANYTHING YOU WANT FOR LUNCH. WE PACKED A BUNCH OF GREAT FOOD SO WE WON'T HAVE TO EAT THAT CANNED STUFF YOUR DAD WAS TALKING ABOUT.
She's trying way too hard.
THUD THUD THUD THUD THUD
HOO, BOY, THIS PLACE SURE GETS DUSTY.
HARRY, WHY DON'T YOU HELP SHARON GET SOME WINDOWS OPEN TO AIR THE PLACE OUT.
FINE.

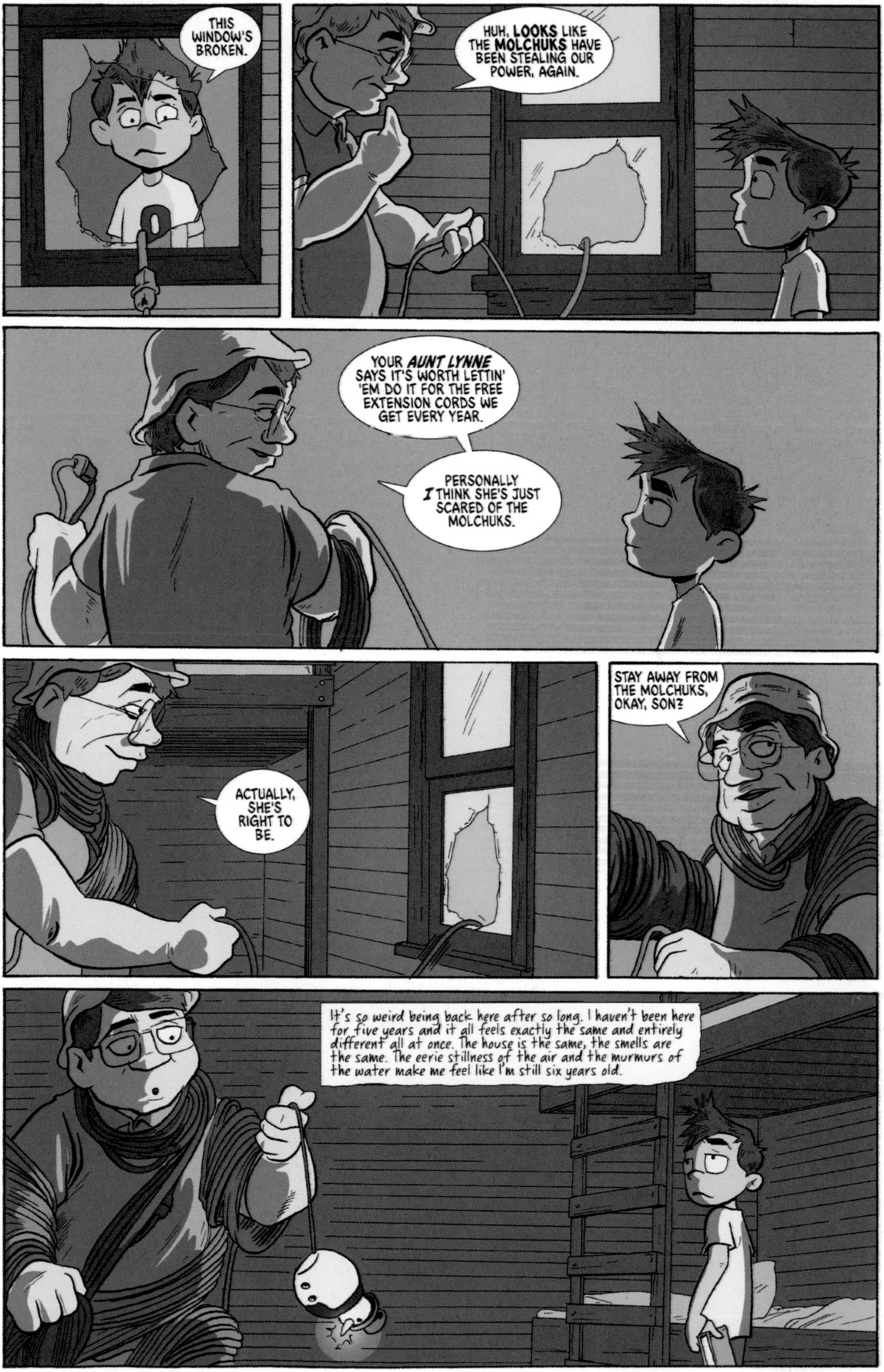
THIS WINDOW'S BROKEN.
HUH, LOOKS LIKE THE MOLCHUKS HAVE BEEN STEALING OUR POWER, AGAIN.
YOUR AUNT LYNNE SAYS IT'S WORTH LETTIN' 'EM DO IT FOR THE FREE EXTENSION CORDS WE GET EVERY YEAR.
PERSONALLY I THINK SHE'S JUST SCARED OF THE MOLCHUKS.
ACTUALLY, SHE'S RIGHT TO BE.
STAY AWAY FROM THE MOLCHUKS, OKAY, SON?
It's so weird being back here after so long. I haven't been here for five years and it all feels exactly the same and entirely different all at once. The house is the same, the smells are the same. The eerie stillness of the air and the murmurs of the water make me feel like I'm still six years old.

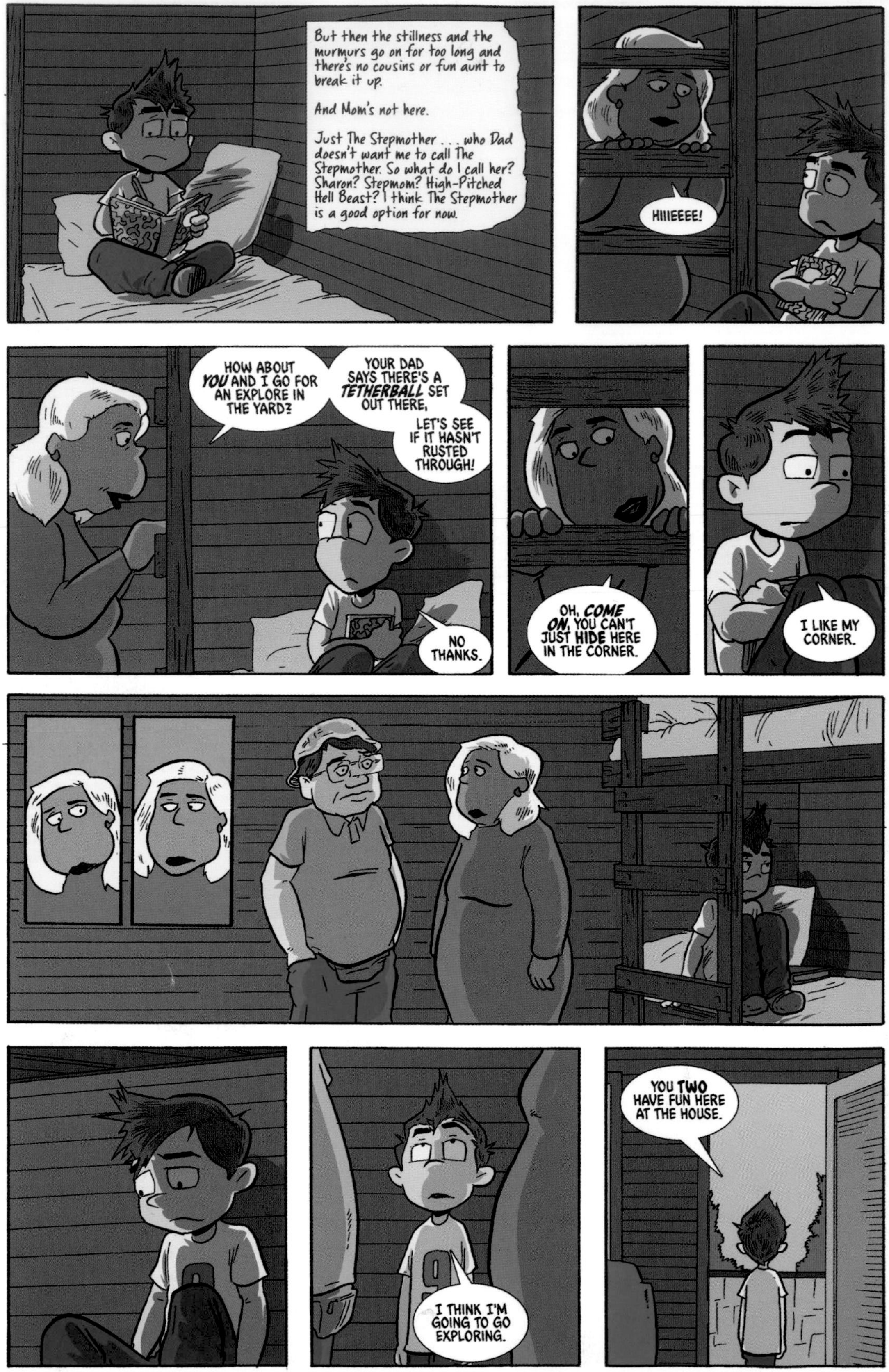

But then the stillness and the murmurs go on for too long and there's no cousins or fun aunt to break it up.
And Mom's not here.
Just The Stepmother . . . who Dad doesn't want me to call The Stepmother. So what do I call her? Sharon? Stepmom? High-Pitched Hell Beast? I think The Stepmother is a good option for now.
HIIIEEEE!
HOW ABOUT YOU AND I GO FOR AN EXPLORE IN THE YARD?
YOUR DAD SAYS THERE'S A TETHERBALL SET OUT THERE.
LET'S SEE IF IT HASN'T RUSTED THROUGH!
NO THANKS.
OH, COME ON, YOU CAN'T JUST HIDE HERE IN THE CORNER.
I LIKE MY CORNER.
I THINK I'M GOING TO GO EXPLORING.
YOU TWO HAVE FUN HERE AT THE HOUSE.

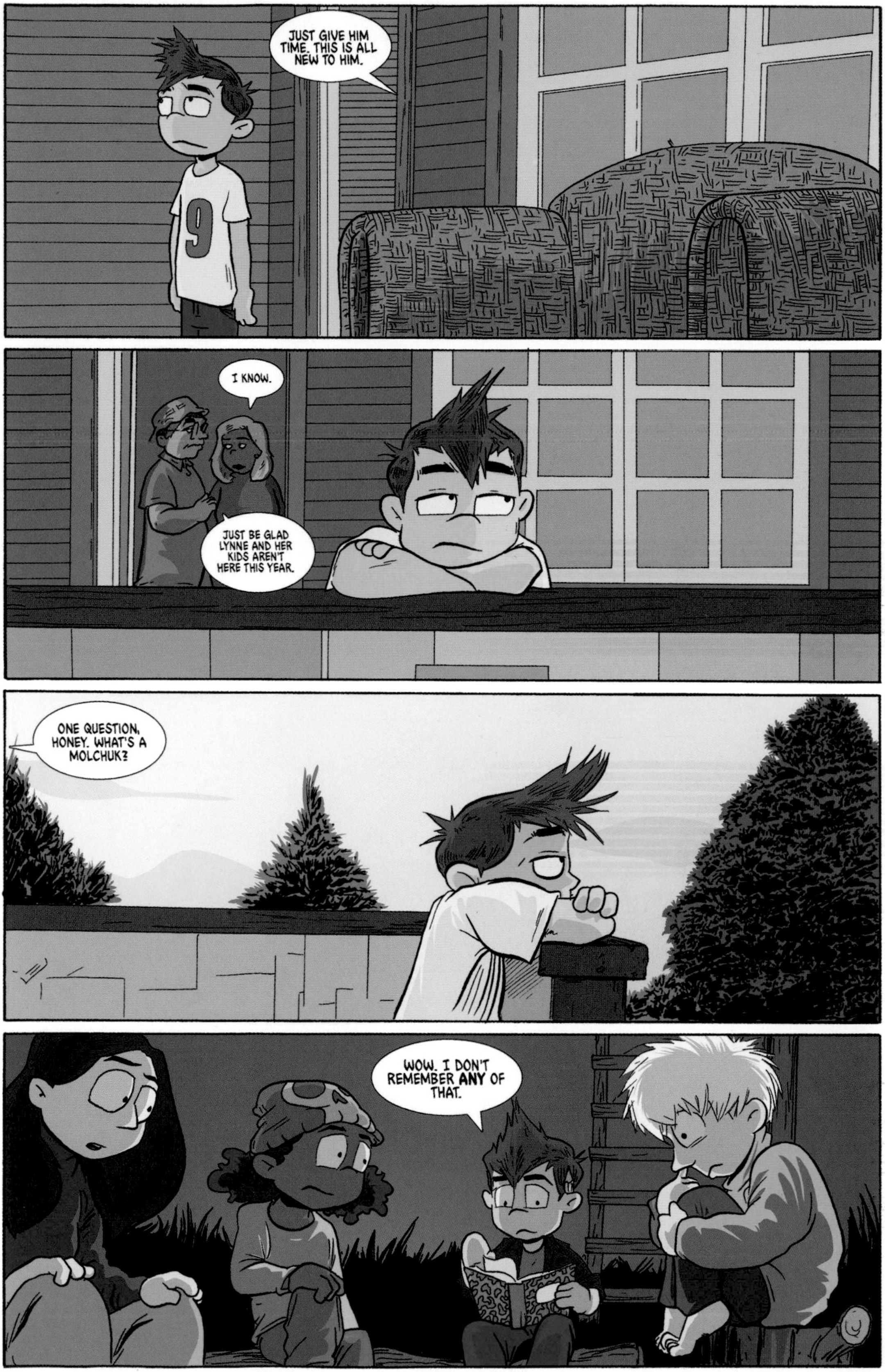
JUST GIVE HIM TIME. THIS IS ALL NEW TO HIM.
I KNOW.
JUST BE GLAD LYNNE AND HER KIDS AREN'T HERE THIS YEAR.
ONE QUESTION, HONEY. WHAT'S A MOLCHUK?
WOW. I DON'T REMEMBER ANY OF THAT.

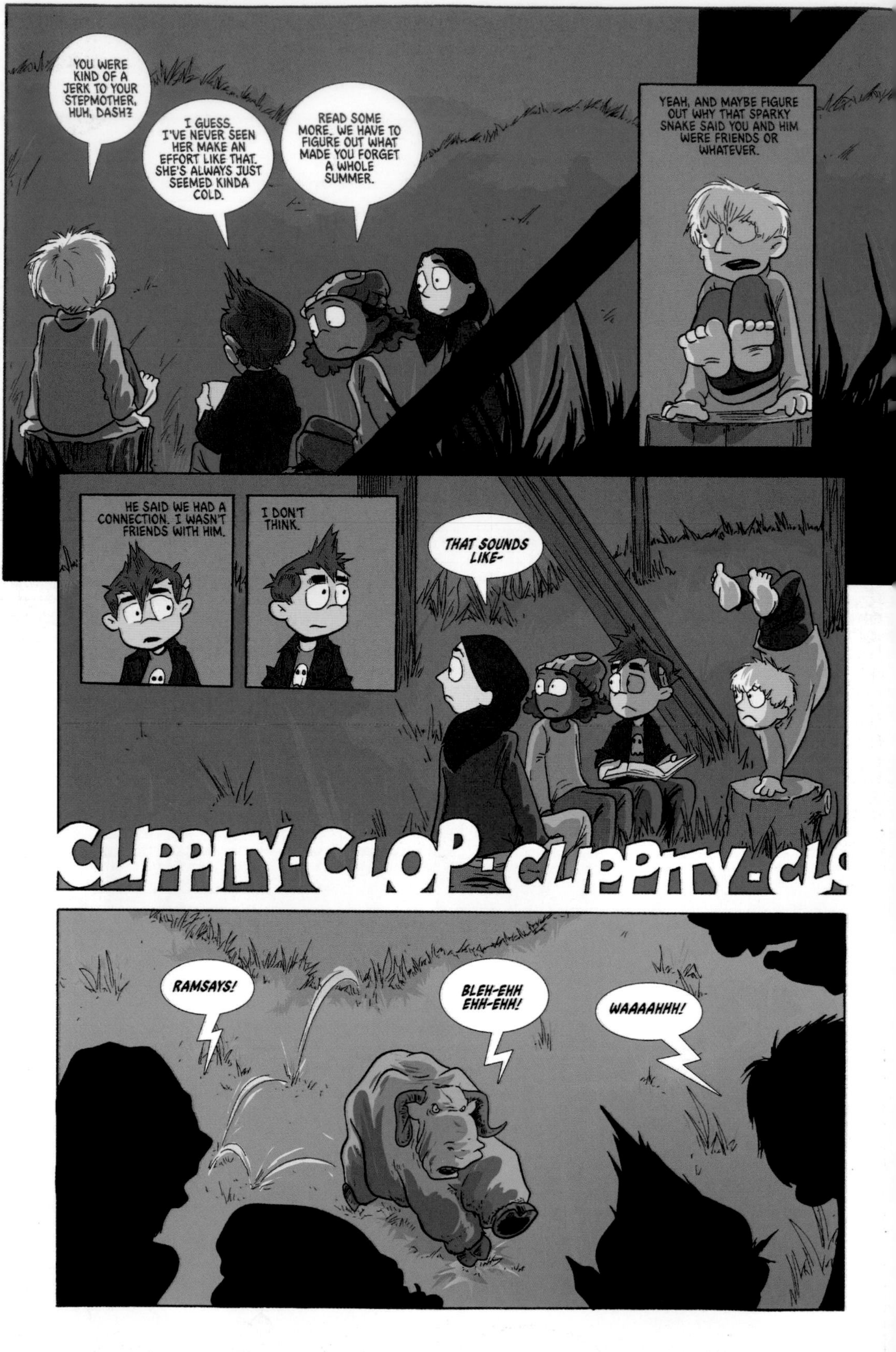

YOU WERE KIND OF A JERK TO YOUR STEPMOTHER, HUH, DASH?
I GUESS. I'VE NEVER SEEN HER MAKE AN EFFORT LIKE THAT. SHE'S ALWAYS JUST SEEMED KINDA COLD.
READ SOME MORE. WE HAVE TO FIGURE OUT WHAT MADE YOU FORGET A WHOLE SUMMER.
YEAH, AND MAYBE FIGURE OUT WHY THAT SPARKY SNAKE SAID YOU AND HIM WERE FRIENDS OR WHATEVER.
HE SAID WE HAD A CONNECTION. I WASN'T FRIENDS WITH HIM.
I DON'T THINK.
THAT SOUNDS LIKE-
CLIPPITY-CLOP-CLIPPITY-CLO
RAMSAYS!
BLEH-EHH EHH-EHH!
WAAAAHHH!

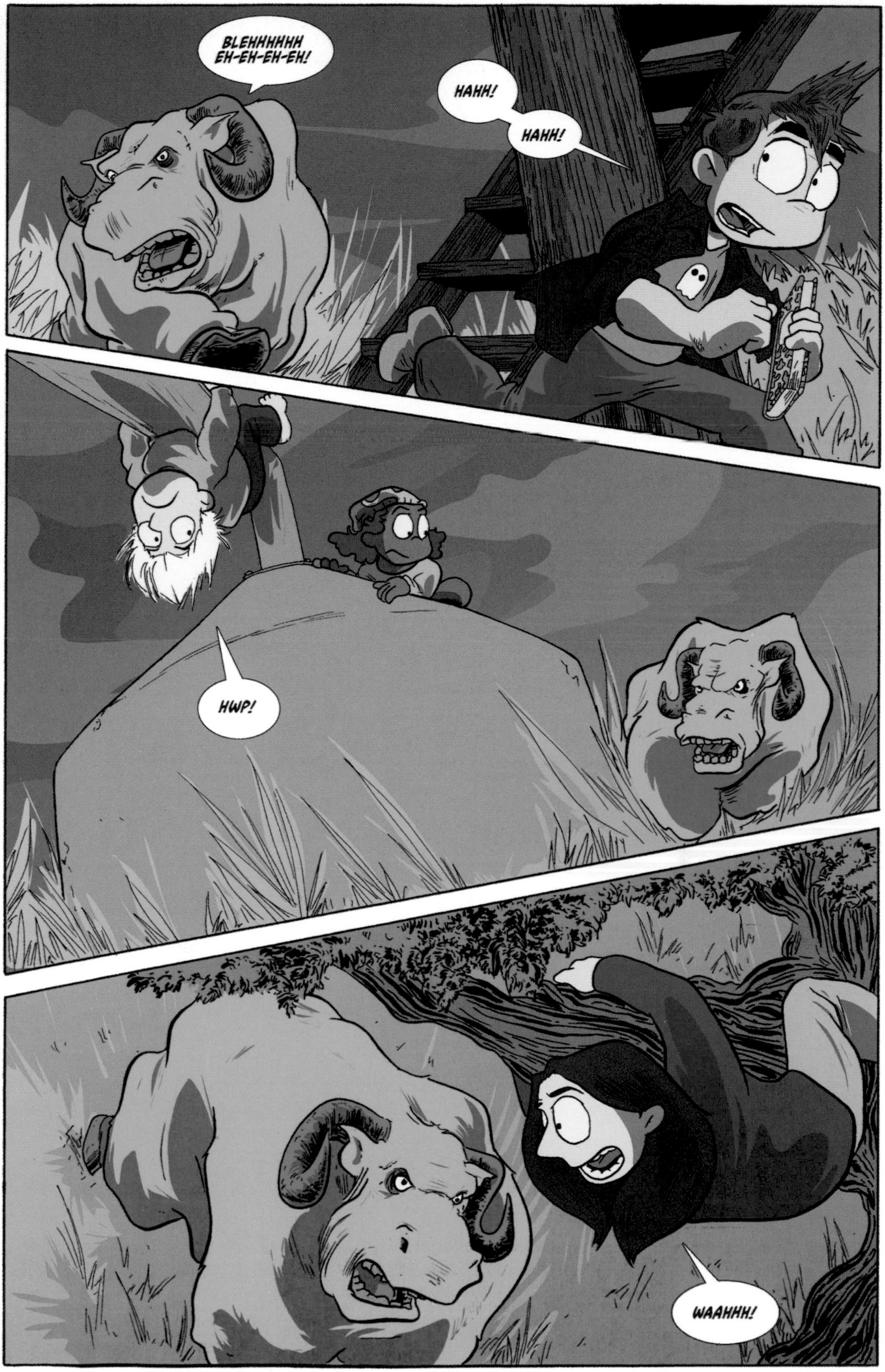
BLEHHHHHH EH-EH-EH-EH!
HAHH!
HAHH!
HWP!
WAAHHH!

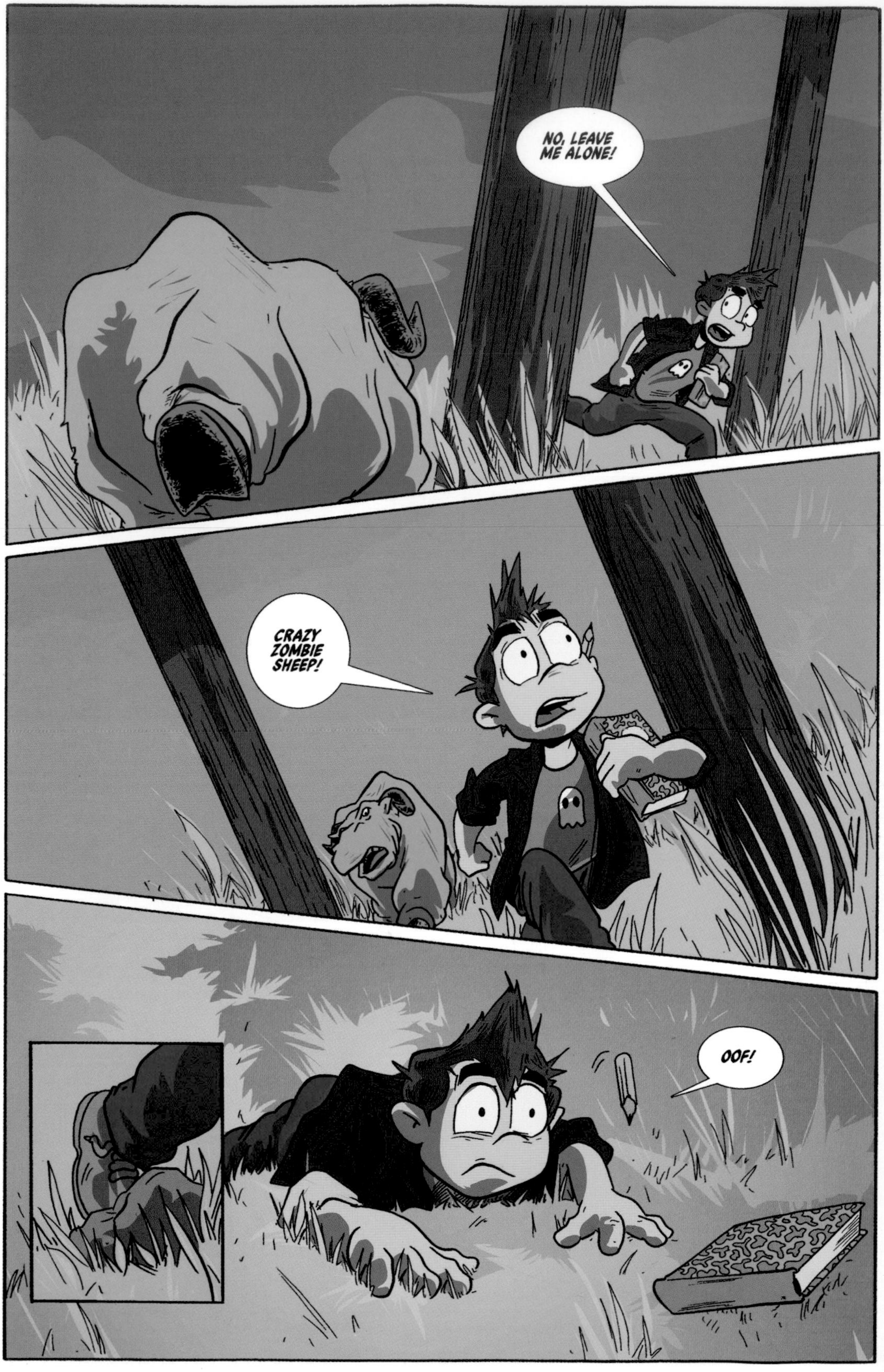
NO, LEAVE ME ALONE!
CRAZY ZOMBIE SHEEP!
OOF!

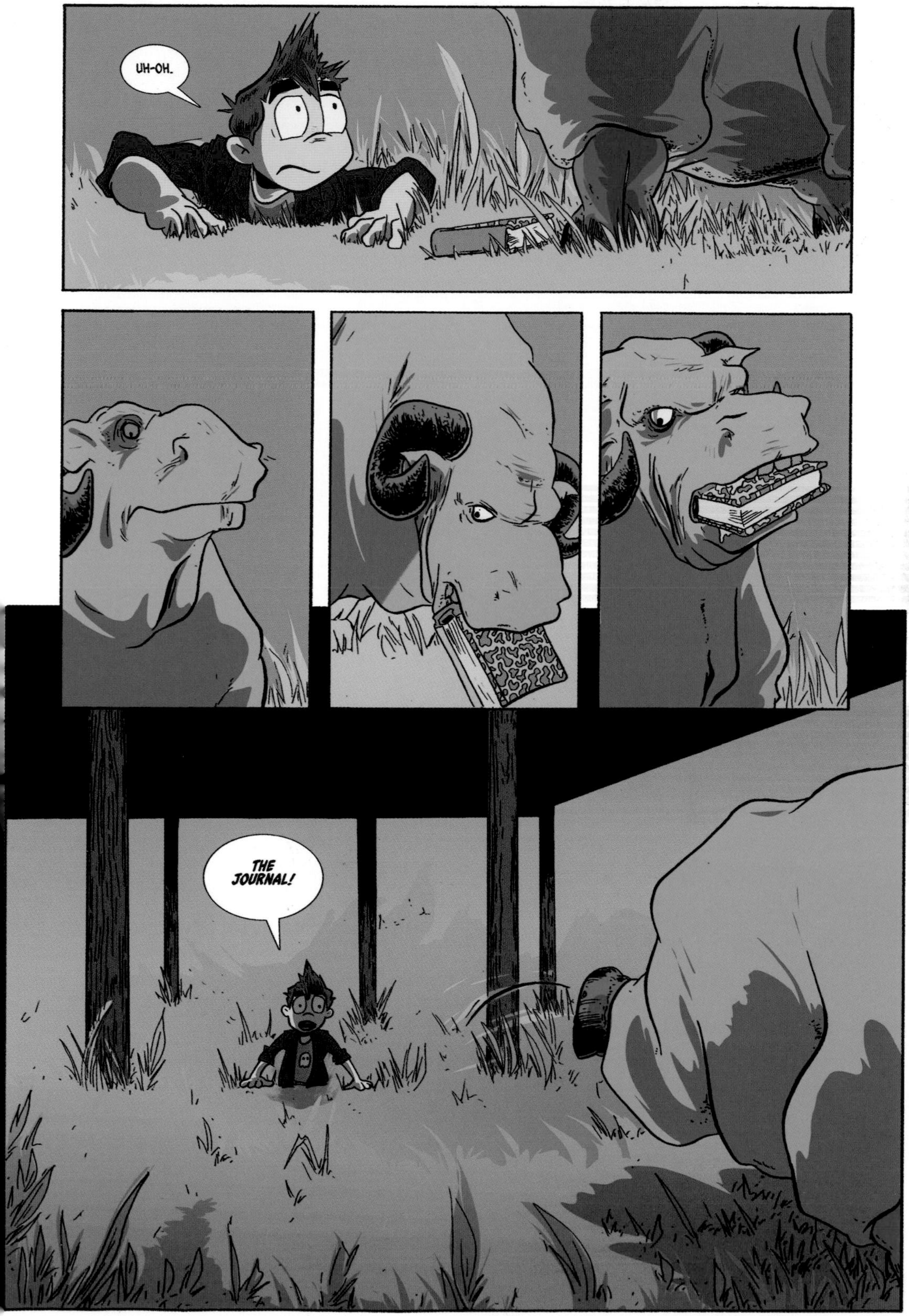
UH-OH.
THE JOURNAL!

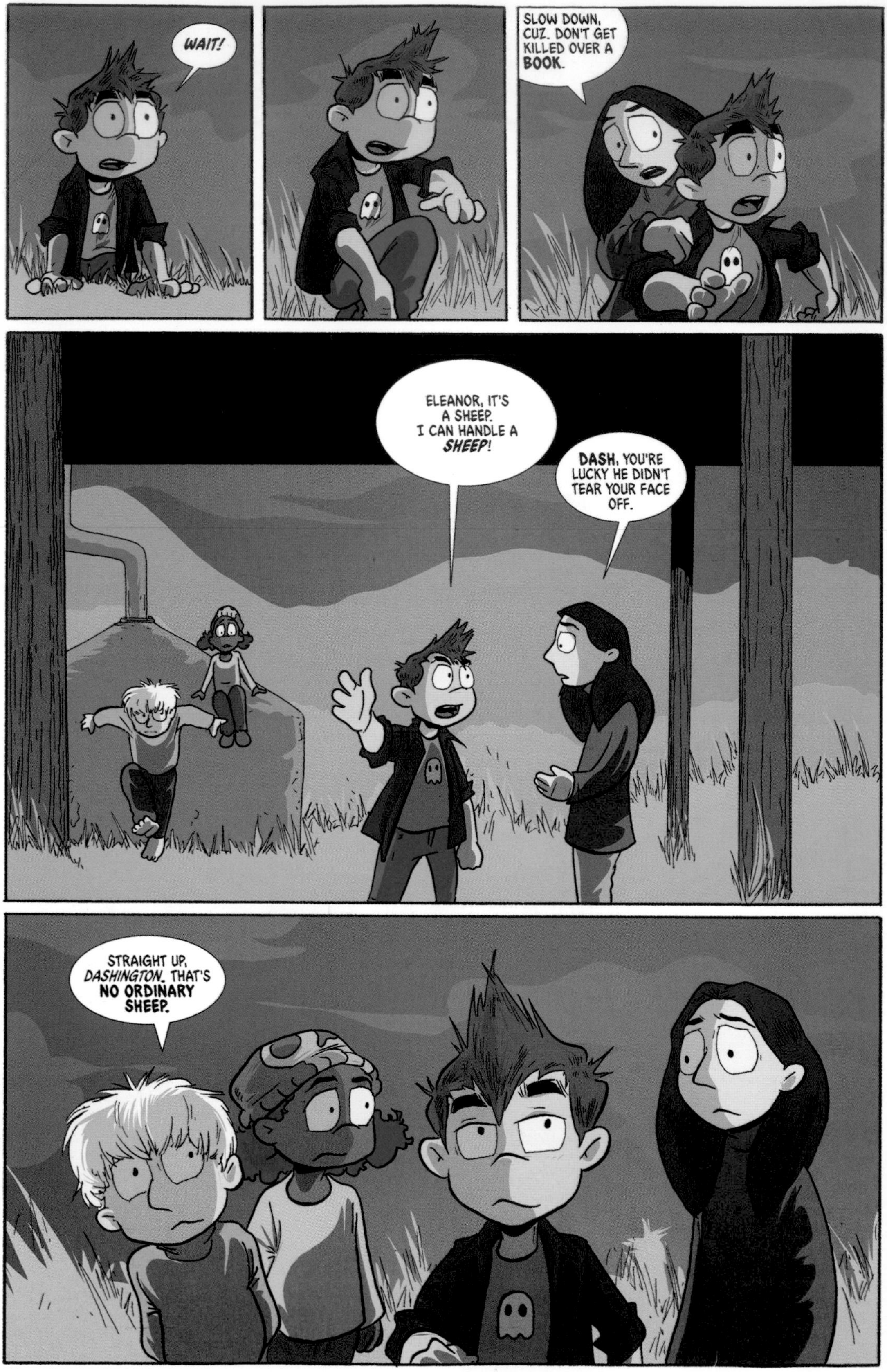
WAIT!
SLOW DOWN, CUZ. DON'T GET KILLED OVER A **BOOK**.
ELEANOR, IT'S A SHEEP. I CAN HANDLE A ***SHEEP***!
DASH, YOU'RE LUCKY HE DIDN'T TEAR YOUR FACE OFF.
STRAIGHT UP, *DASHINGTON*. THAT'S **NO ORDINARY SHEEP.**

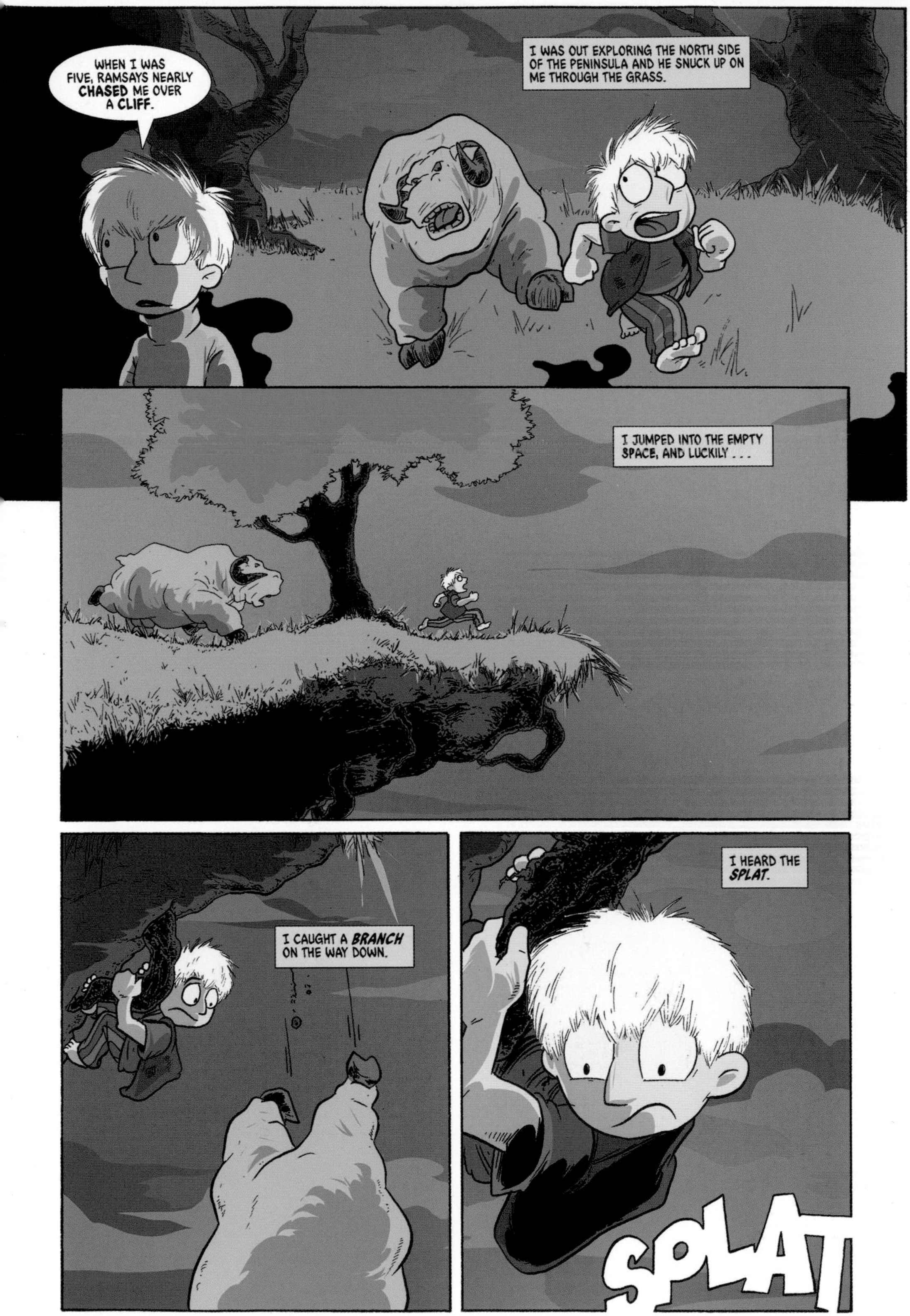
WHEN I WAS FIVE, RAMSAYS NEARLY CHASED ME OVER A CLIFF.
I WAS OUT EXPLORING THE NORTH SIDE OF THE PENINSULA AND HE SNUCK UP ON ME THROUGH THE GRASS.
I JUMPED INTO THE EMPTY SPACE, AND LUCKILY . . .
I CAUGHT A BRANCH ON THE WAY DOWN.
I HEARD THE SPLAT.
SPLAT

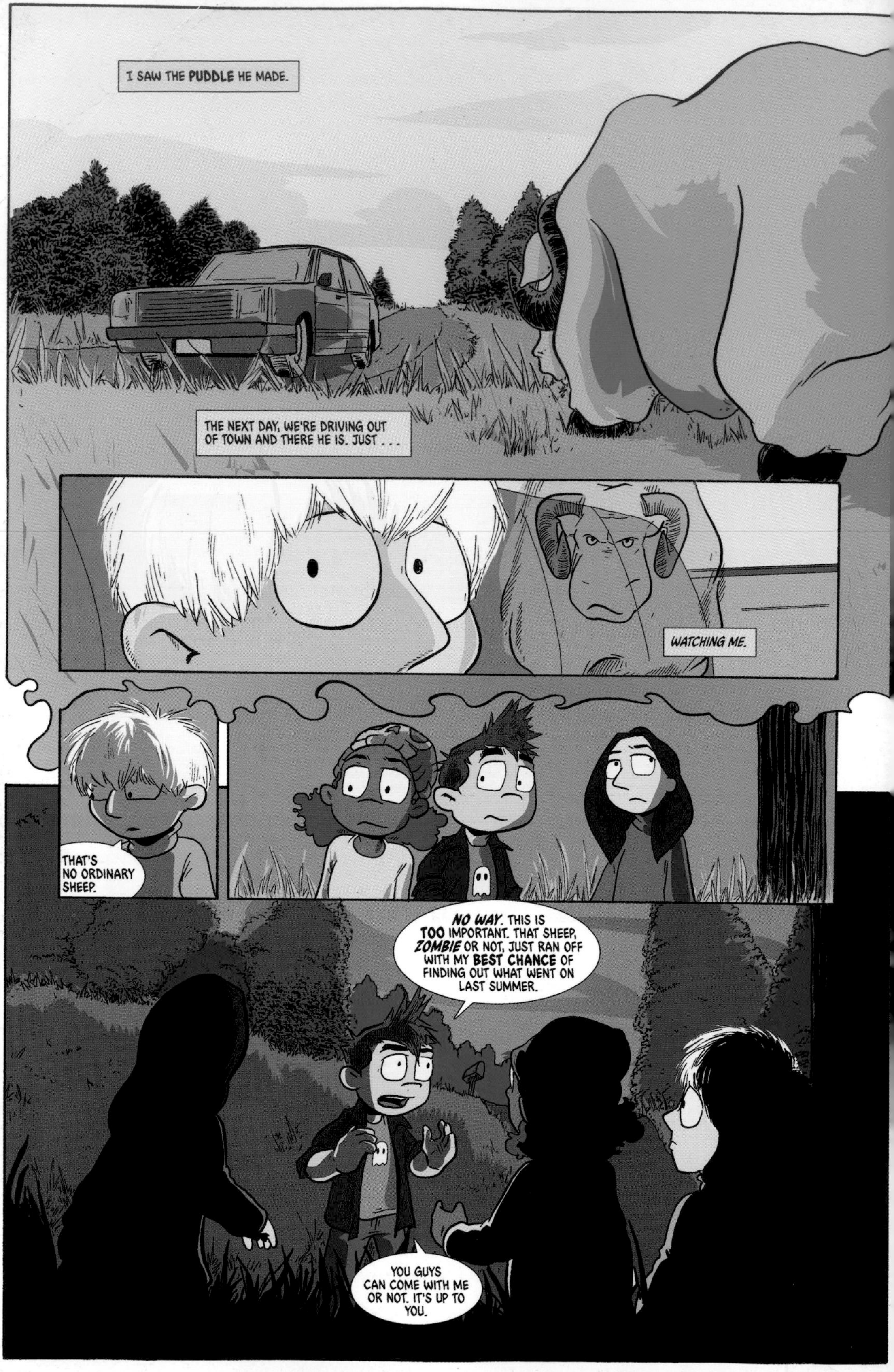

I SAW THE **PUDDLE** HE MADE.
THE NEXT DAY, WE'RE DRIVING OUT OF TOWN AND THERE HE IS. JUST . . .
WATCHING ME.
THAT'S NO ORDINARY SHEEP.
NO WAY. THIS IS **TOO** IMPORTANT. THAT SHEEP, ***ZOMBIE*** OR NOT, JUST RAN OFF WITH MY **BEST CHANCE** OF FINDING OUT WHAT WENT ON LAST SUMMER.
YOU GUYS CAN COME WITH ME OR NOT. IT'S UP TO YOU.

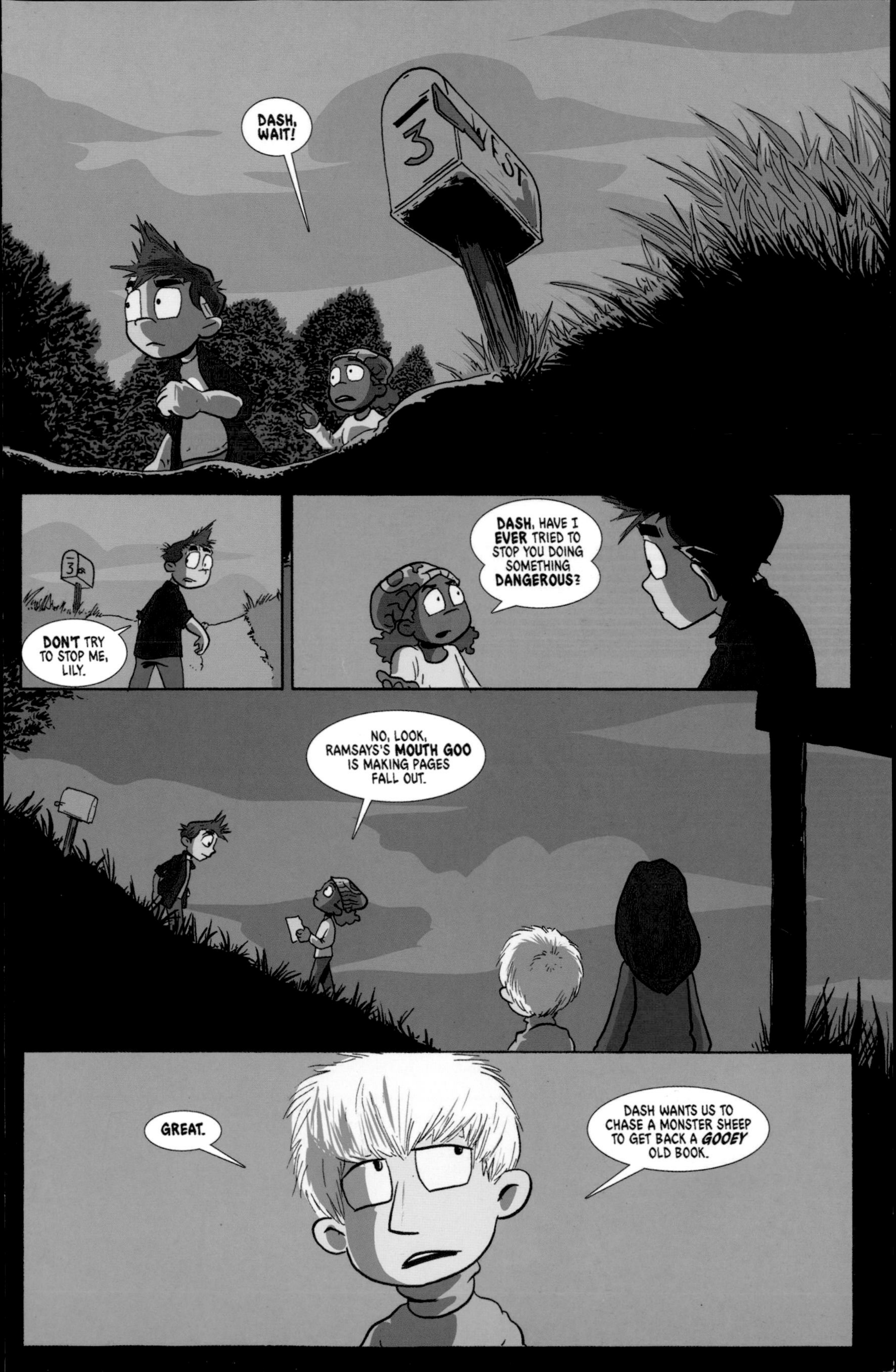

DASH, WAIT!
3 WEST
DON'T TRY TO STOP ME, LILY.
DASH, HAVE I EVER TRIED TO STOP YOU DOING SOMETHING DANGEROUS?
NO, LOOK, RAMSAYS'S MOUTH GOO IS MAKING PAGES FALL OUT.
GREAT.
DASH WANTS US TO CHASE A MONSTER SHEEP TO GET BACK A GOOEY OLD BOOK.

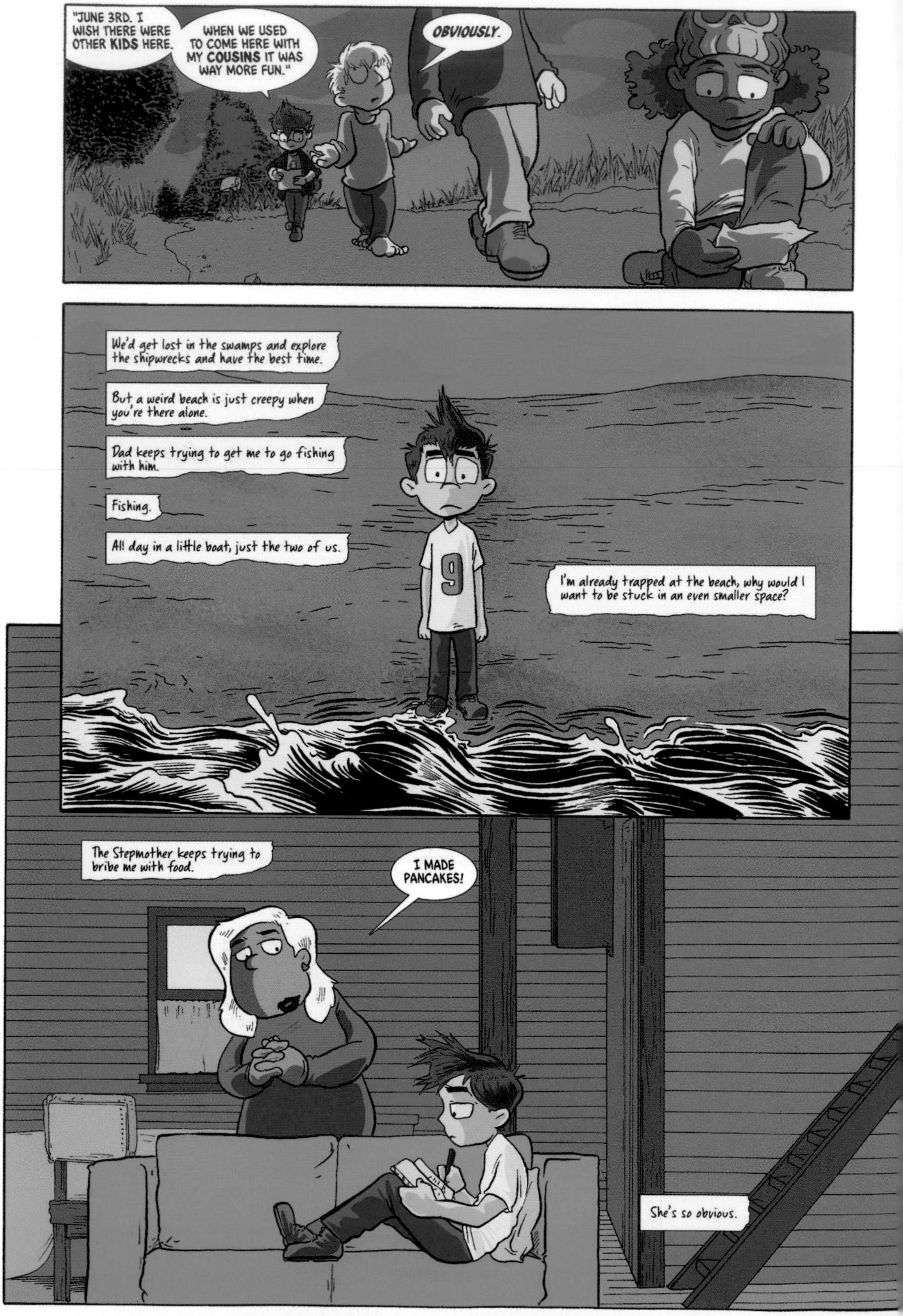
"JUNE 3RD. I WISH THERE WERE OTHER KIDS HERE.
WHEN WE USED TO COME HERE WITH MY COUSINS IT WAS WAY MORE FUN."
OBVIOUSLY.
We'd get lost in the swamps and explore the shipwrecks and have the best time.
But, a weird beach is just creepy when you're there alone.
Dad keeps trying to get me to go fishing with him.
Fishing.
All day in a little boat, just the two of us.
I'm already trapped at the beach, why would I want to be stuck in an even smaller space?
The Stepmother keeps trying to bribe me with food.
I MADE PANCAKES!
She's so obvious.

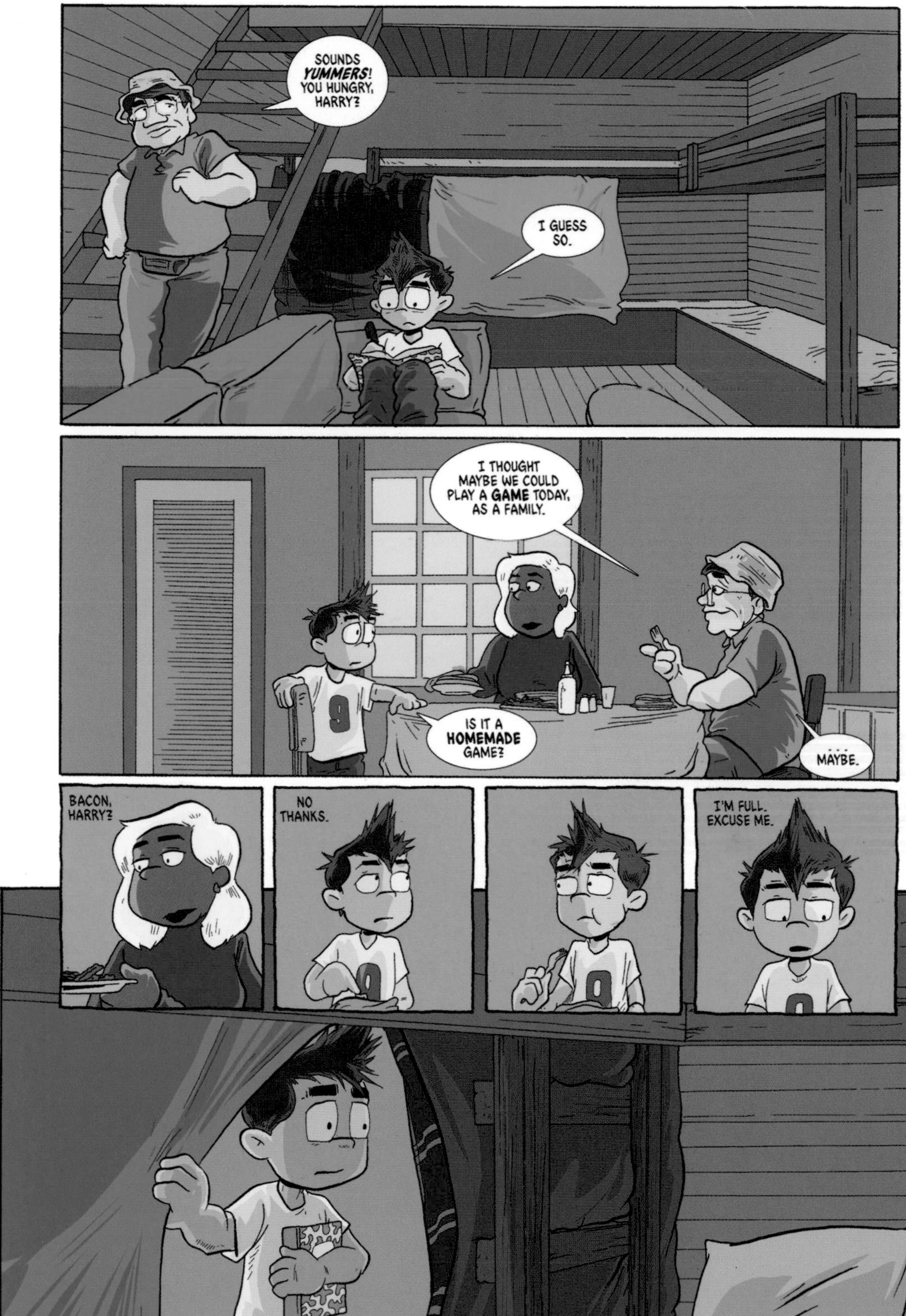
SOUNDS YUMMERS! YOU HUNGRY, HARRY?
I GUESS SO.
I THOUGHT MAYBE WE COULD PLAY A GAME TODAY, AS A FAMILY.
IS IT A HOMEMADE GAME?
... MAYBE.
BACON, HARRY?
NO THANKS.
I'M FULL. EXCUSE ME.

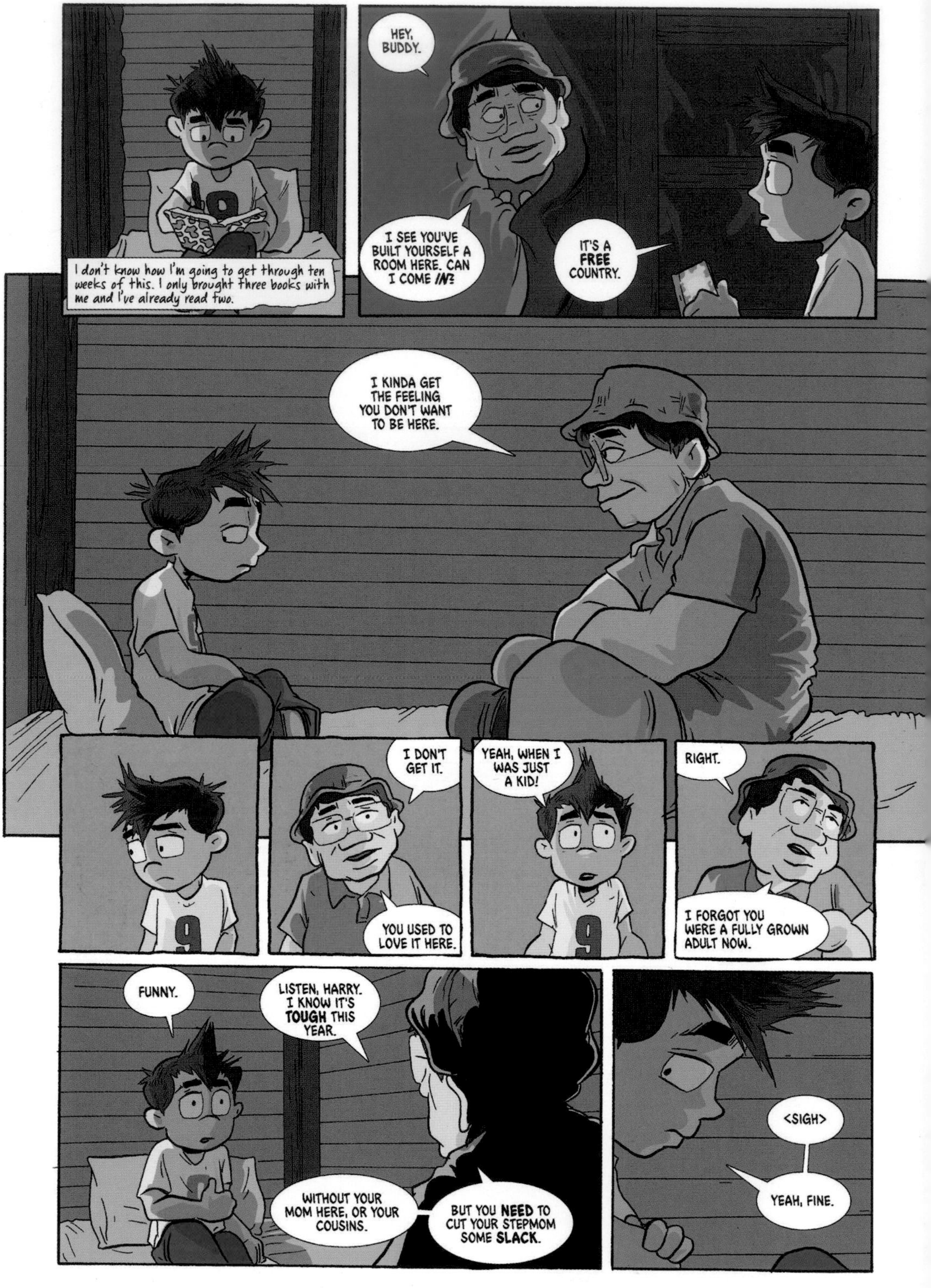
I don't know how I'm going to get through ten weeks of this. I only brought three books with me and I've already read two.
HEY, BUDDY.
I SEE YOU'VE BUILT YOURSELF A ROOM HERE. CAN I COME IN?
IT'S A FREE COUNTRY.
I KINDA GET THE FEELING YOU DON'T WANT TO BE HERE.
I DON'T GET IT.
YOU USED TO LOVE IT HERE.
YEAH, WHEN I WAS JUST A KID!
RIGHT.
I FORGOT YOU WERE A FULLY GROWN ADULT NOW.
FUNNY.
LISTEN, HARRY. I KNOW IT'S TOUGH THIS YEAR.
WITHOUT YOUR MOM HERE, OR YOUR COUSINS.
BUT YOU NEED TO CUT YOUR STEPMOM SOME SLACK.
<SIGH>
YEAH, FINE.

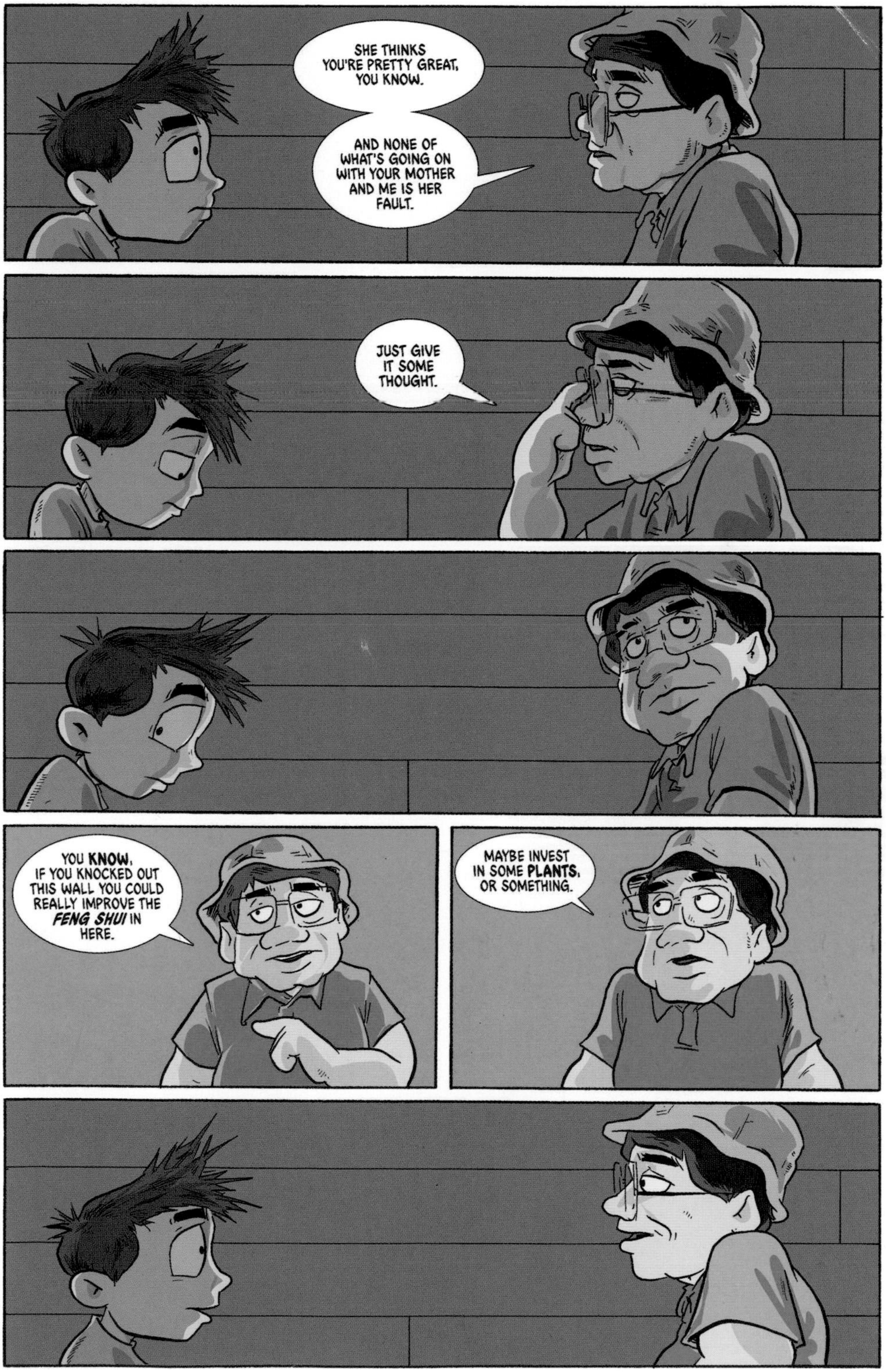
SHE THINKS YOU'RE PRETTY GREAT, YOU KNOW.
AND NONE OF WHAT'S GOING ON WITH YOUR MOTHER AND ME IS HER FAULT.
JUST GIVE IT SOME THOUGHT.
YOU **KNOW**, IF YOU KNOCKED OUT THIS WALL YOU COULD REALLY IMPROVE THE ***FENG SHUI*** IN HERE.
MAYBE INVEST IN SOME **PLANTS**, OR SOMETHING.

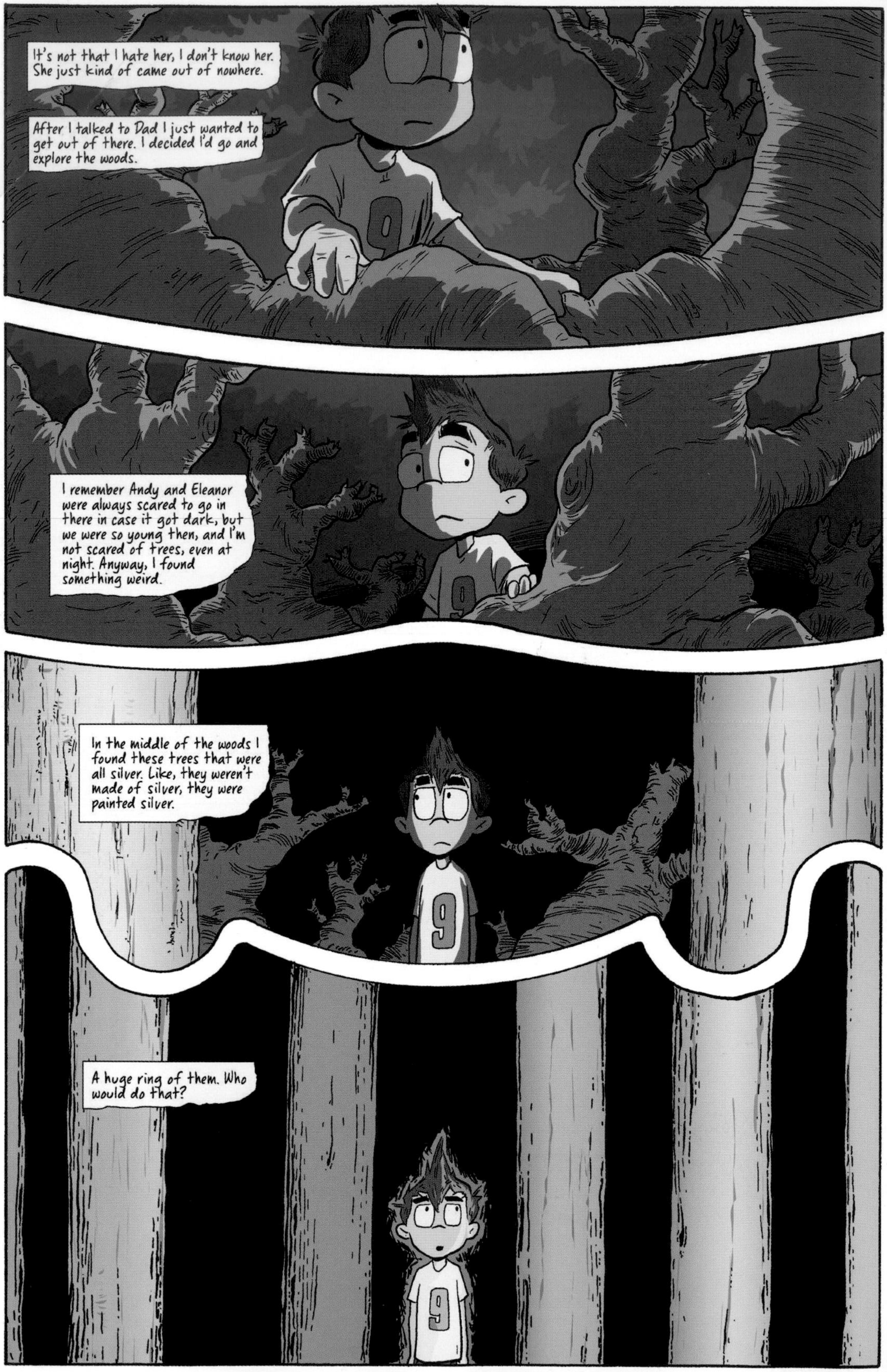
It's not that I hate her, I don't know her. She just kind of came out of nowhere.
After I talked to Dad I just wanted to get out of there. I decided I'd go and explore the woods.
I remember Andy and Eleanor were always scared to go in there in case it got dark, but we were so young then, and I'm not scared of trees, even at night. Anyway, I found something weird.
In the middle of the woods I found these trees that were all silver. Like, they weren't made of silver, they were painted silver.
A huge ring of them. Who would do that?

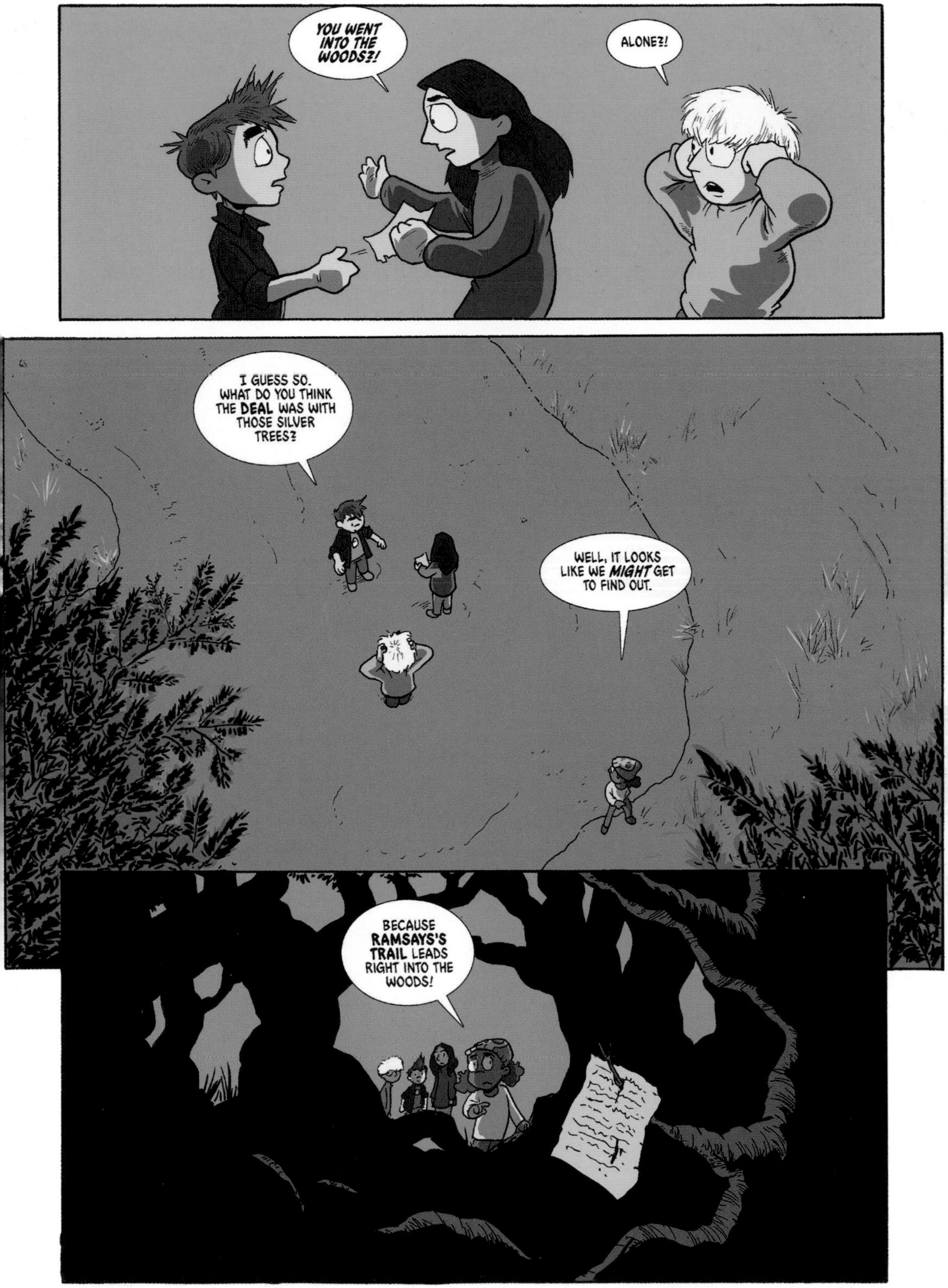
YOU WENT INTO THE WOODS?!
ALONE?!
I GUESS SO. WHAT DO YOU THINK THE DEAL WAS WITH THOSE SILVER TREES?
WELL, IT LOOKS LIKE WE MIGHT GET TO FIND OUT.
BECAUSE RAMSAYS'S TRAIL LEADS RIGHT INTO THE WOODS!

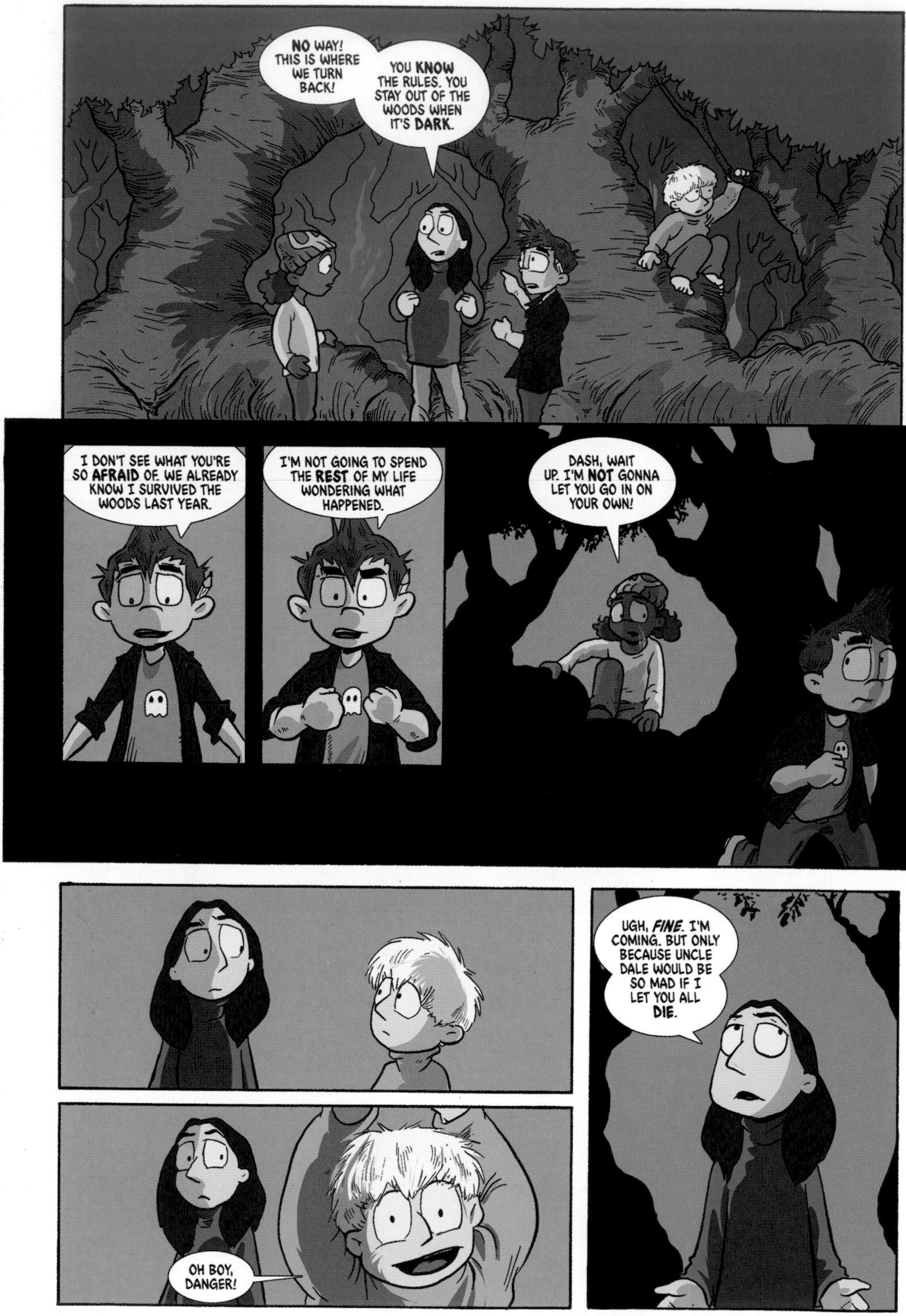
NO WAY! THIS IS WHERE WE TURN BACK!
YOU KNOW THE RULES. YOU STAY OUT OF THE WOODS WHEN IT'S DARK.
I DON'T SEE WHAT YOU'RE SO AFRAID OF. WE ALREADY KNOW I SURVIVED THE WOODS LAST YEAR.
I'M NOT GOING TO SPEND THE REST OF MY LIFE WONDERING WHAT HAPPENED.
DASH, WAIT UP. I'M NOT GONNA LET YOU GO IN ON YOUR OWN!
OH BOY, DANGER!
UGH, FINE. I'M COMING. BUT ONLY BECAUSE UNCLE DALE WOULD BE SO MAD IF I LET YOU ALL DIE.

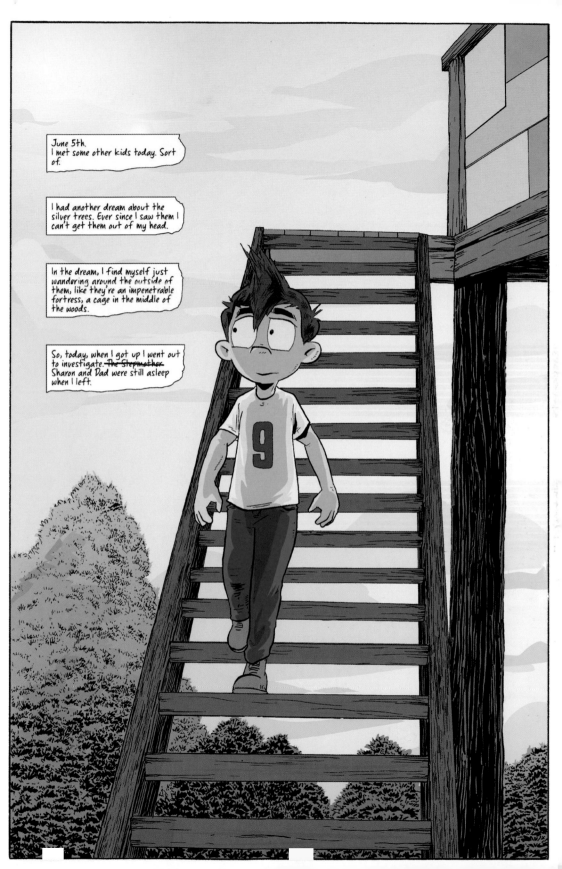

June 5th.
I met some other kids today. Sort of.

I had another dream about the silver trees. Ever since I saw them I can't get them out of my head.

In the dream, I find myself just wandering around the outside of them, like they're an impenetrable fortress, a cage in the middle of the woods.

So, today, when I got up I went out to investigate. ~~The Stepmother~~ Sharon and Dad were still asleep when I left.

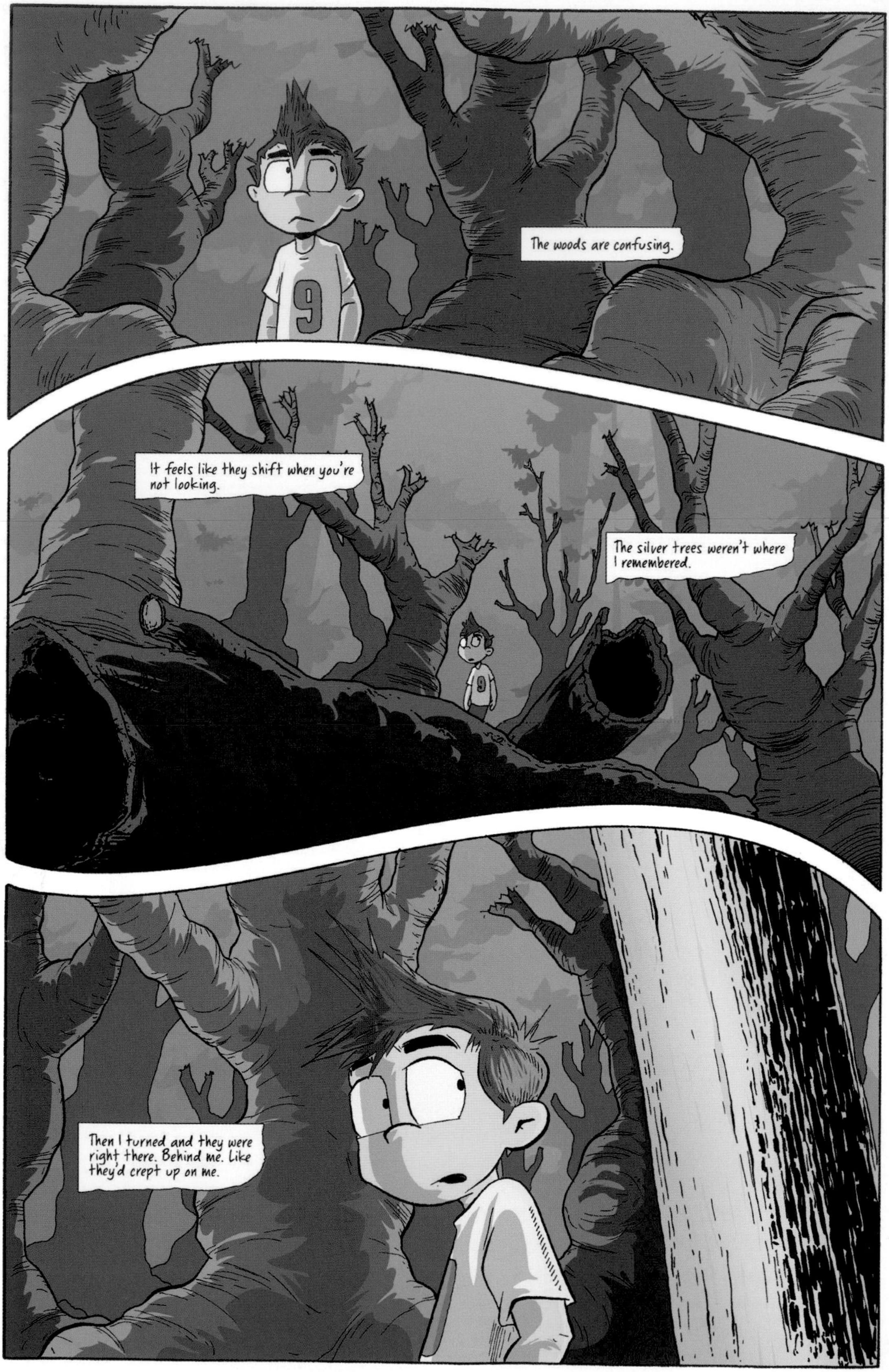
The woods are confusing.
It feels like they shift when you're not looking.
The silver trees weren't where I remembered.
Then I turned and they were right there. Behind me. Like they'd crept up on me.

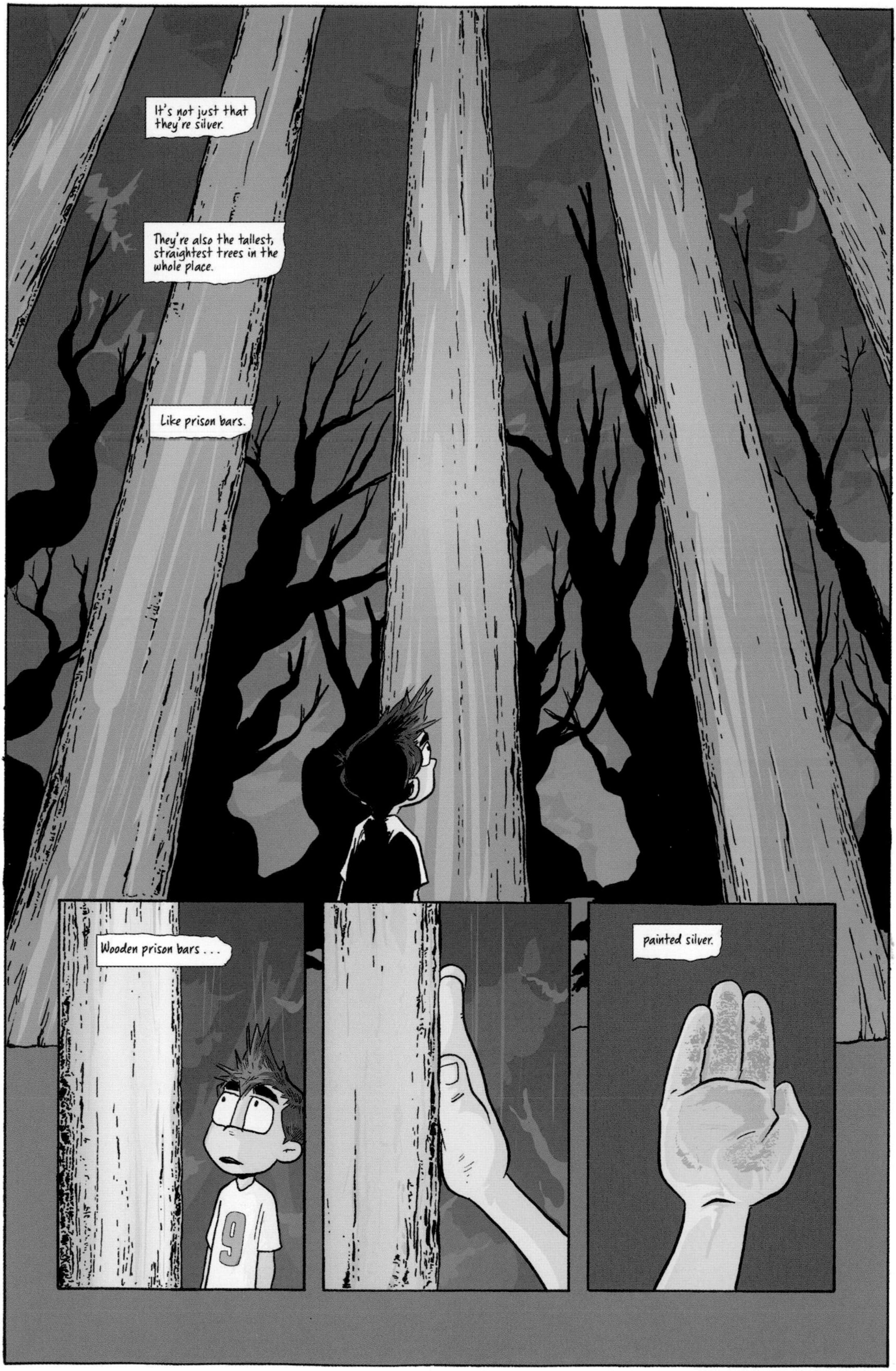
It's not just that they're silver.
They're also the tallest, straightest trees in the whole place.
Like prison bars.
Wooden prison bars . . .
painted silver.

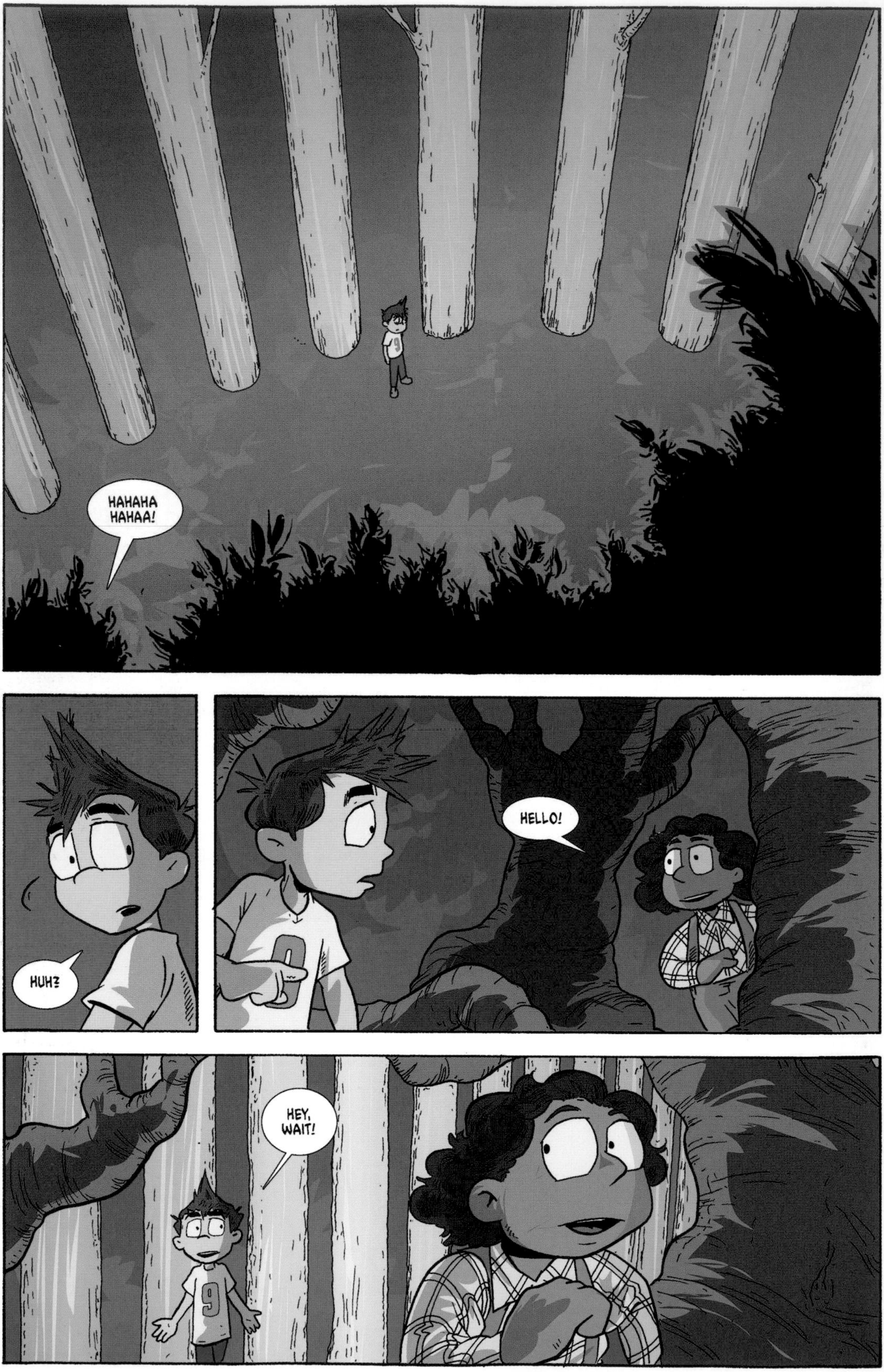
HAHAHA HAHAA!
HUH?
HELLO!
HEY, WAIT!

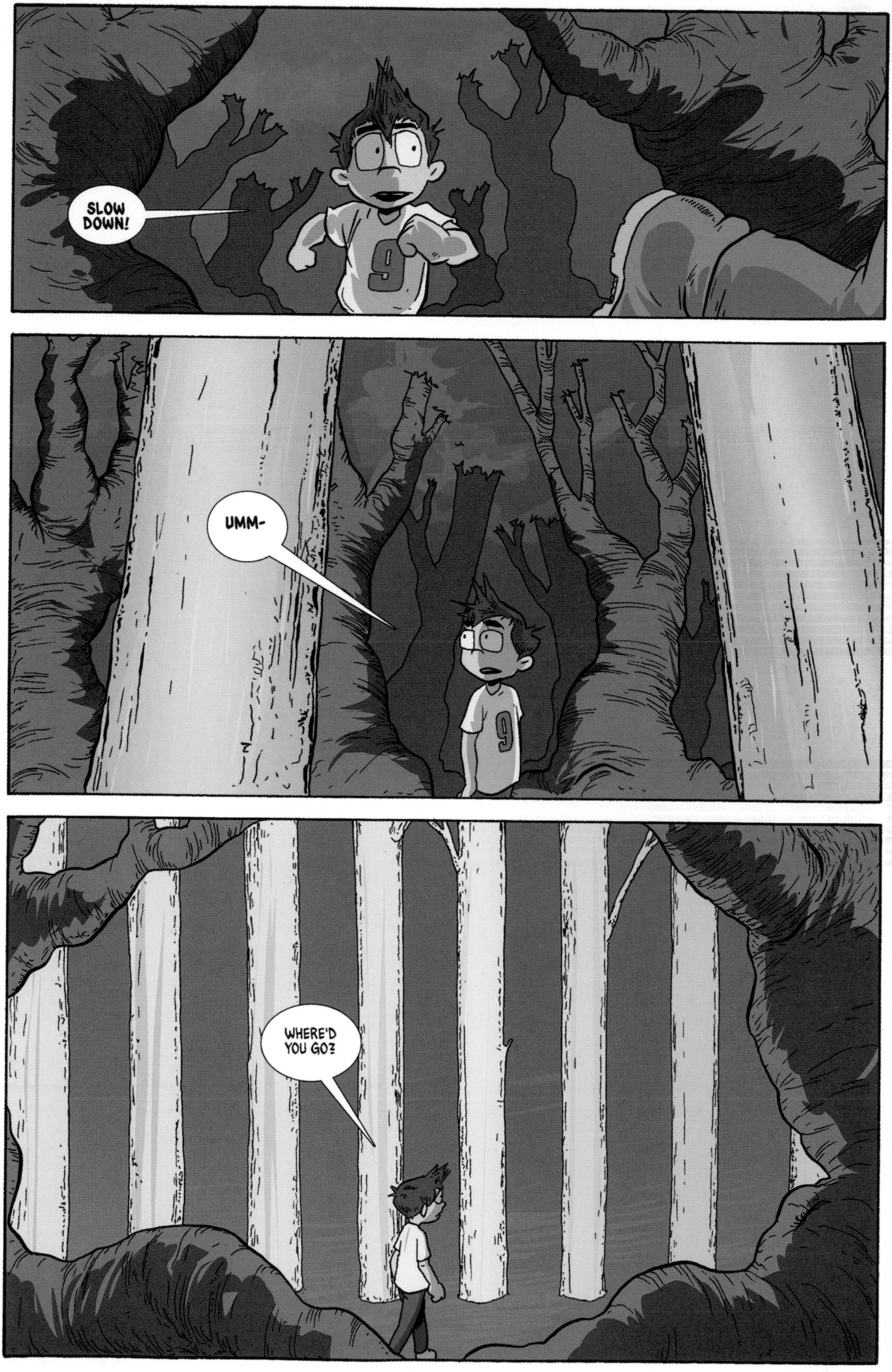
SLOW DOWN!
UMM-
WHERE'D YOU GO?

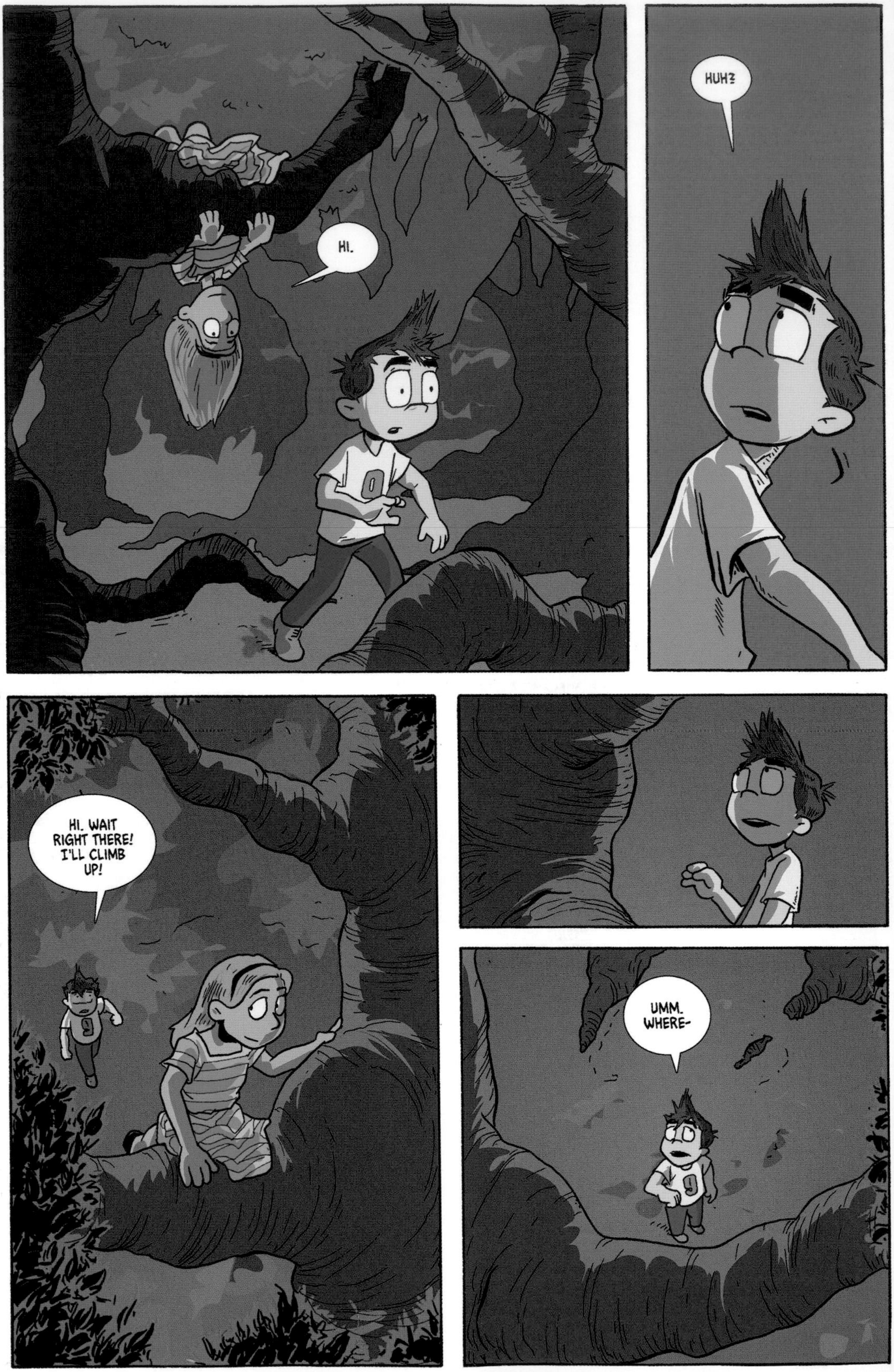
HI.
HUH?
HI. WAIT RIGHT THERE! I'LL CLIMB UP!
UMM. WHERE-

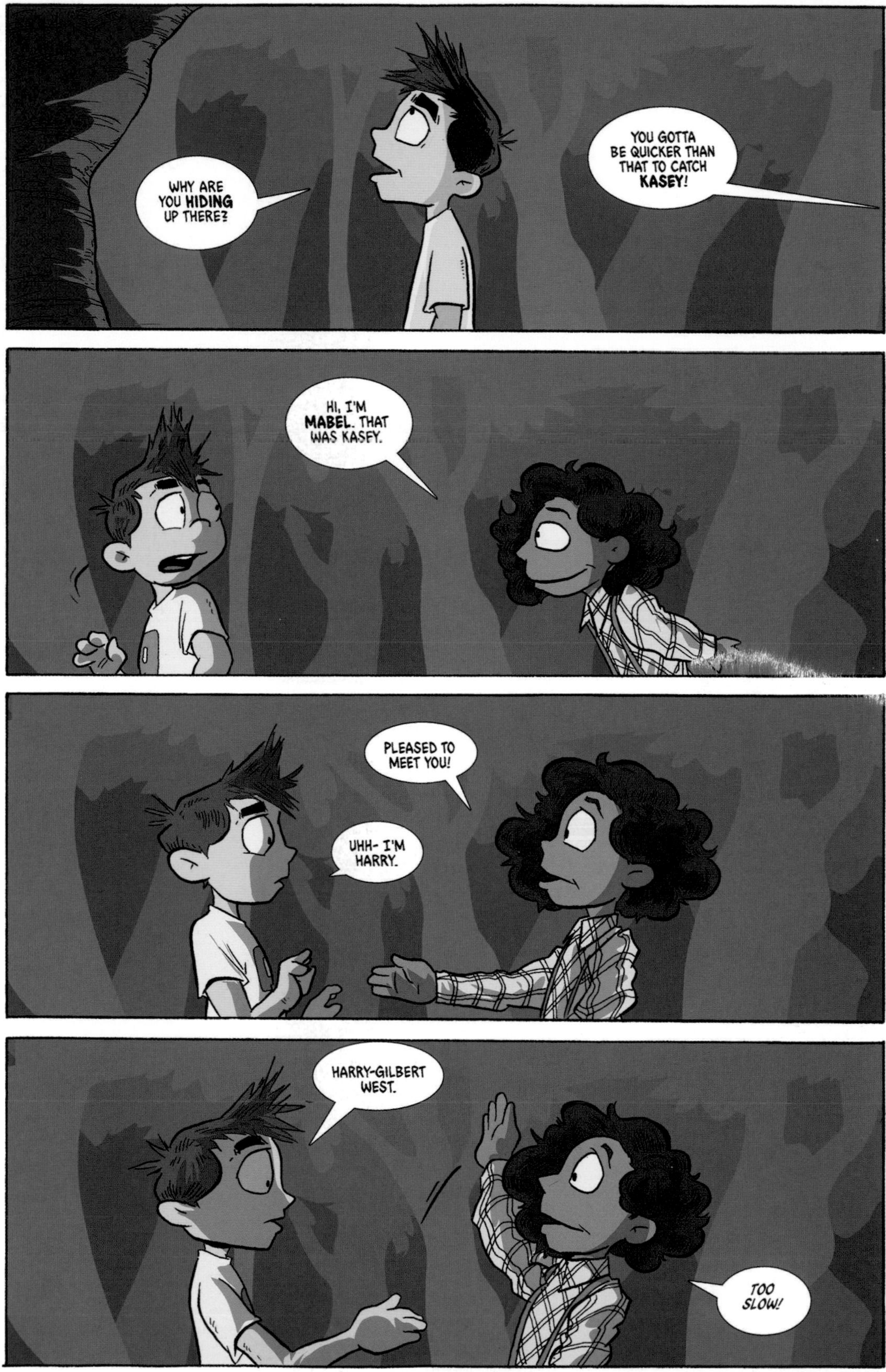
WHY ARE YOU HIDING UP THERE?
YOU GOTTA BE QUICKER THAN THAT TO CATCH KASEY!
HI, I'M MABEL. THAT WAS KASEY.
PLEASED TO MEET YOU!
UHH- I'M HARRY.
HARRY-GILBERT WEST.
TOO SLOW!

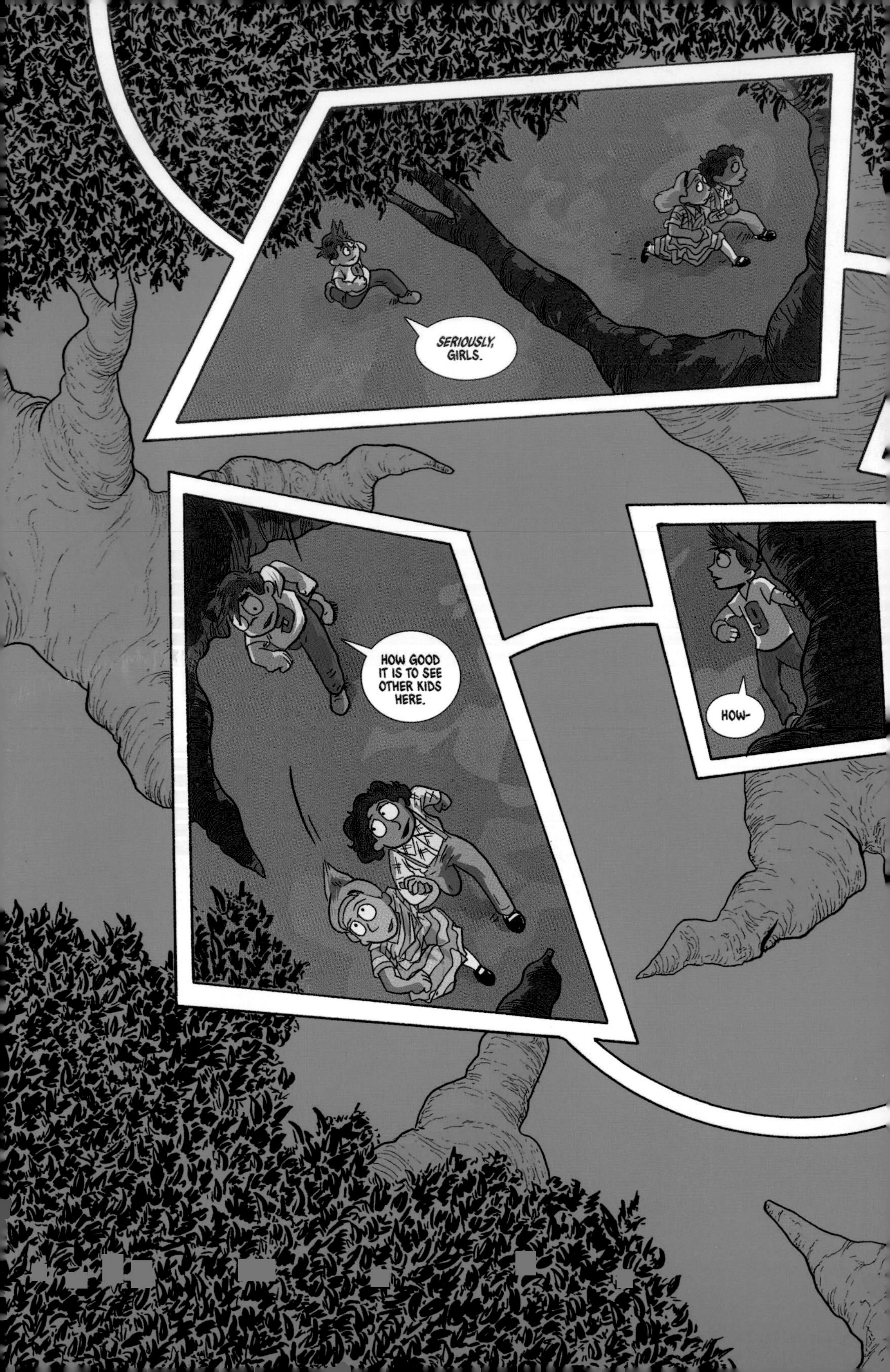
SERIOUSLY, GIRLS.
HOW GOOD IT IS TO SEE OTHER KIDS HERE.
HOW-

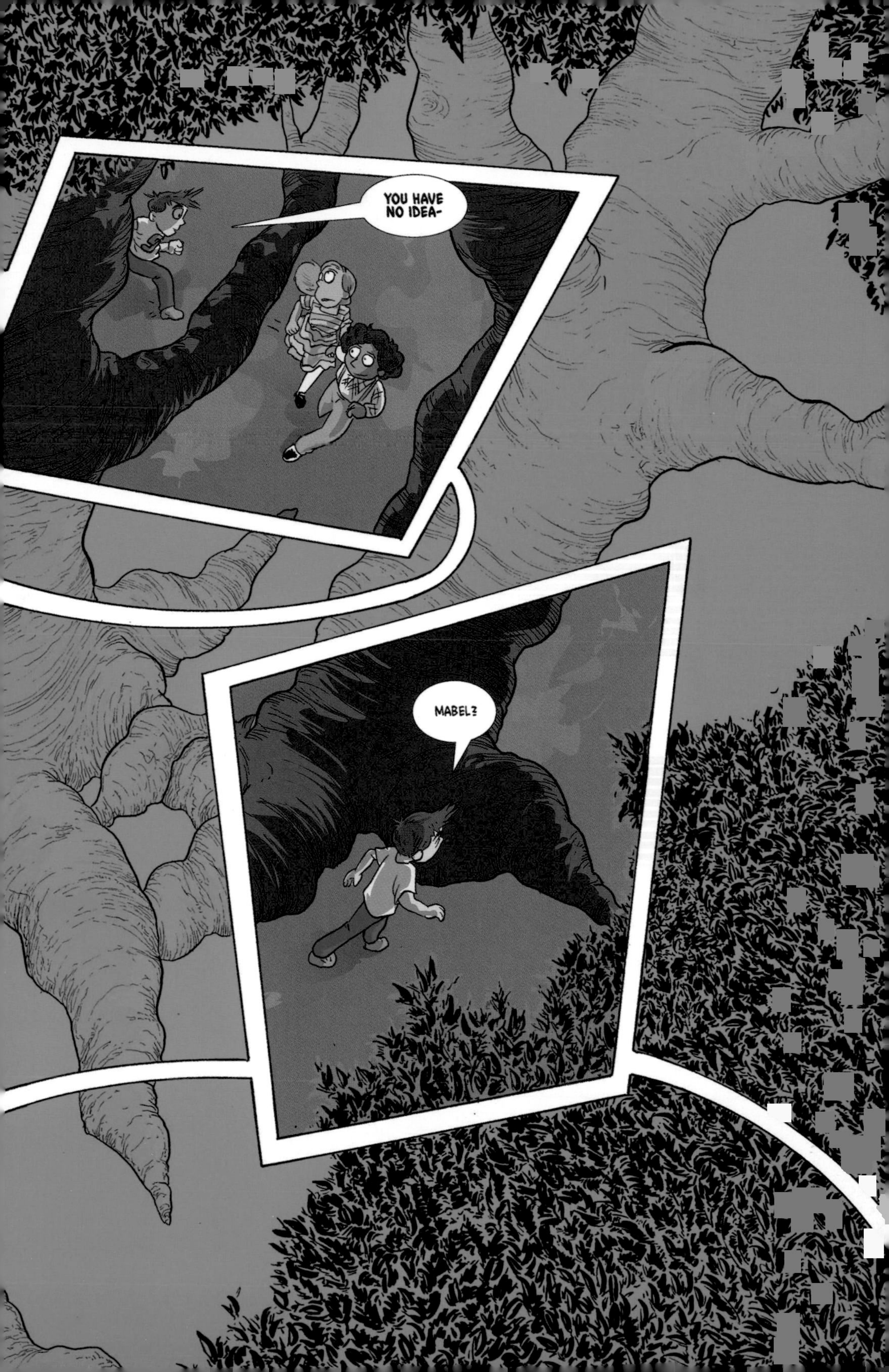
YOU HAVE NO IDEA-
MABEL?

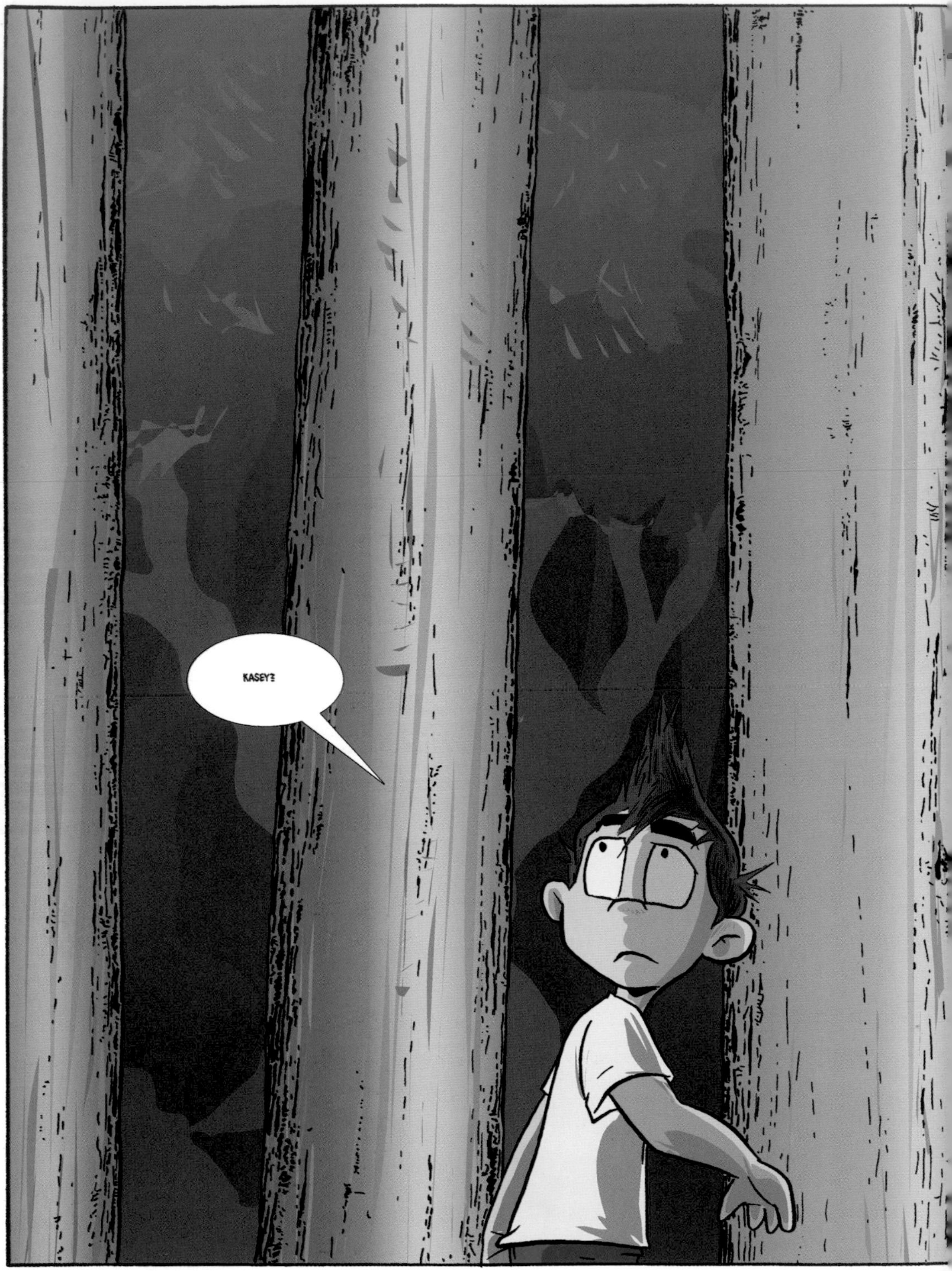
KASEY?

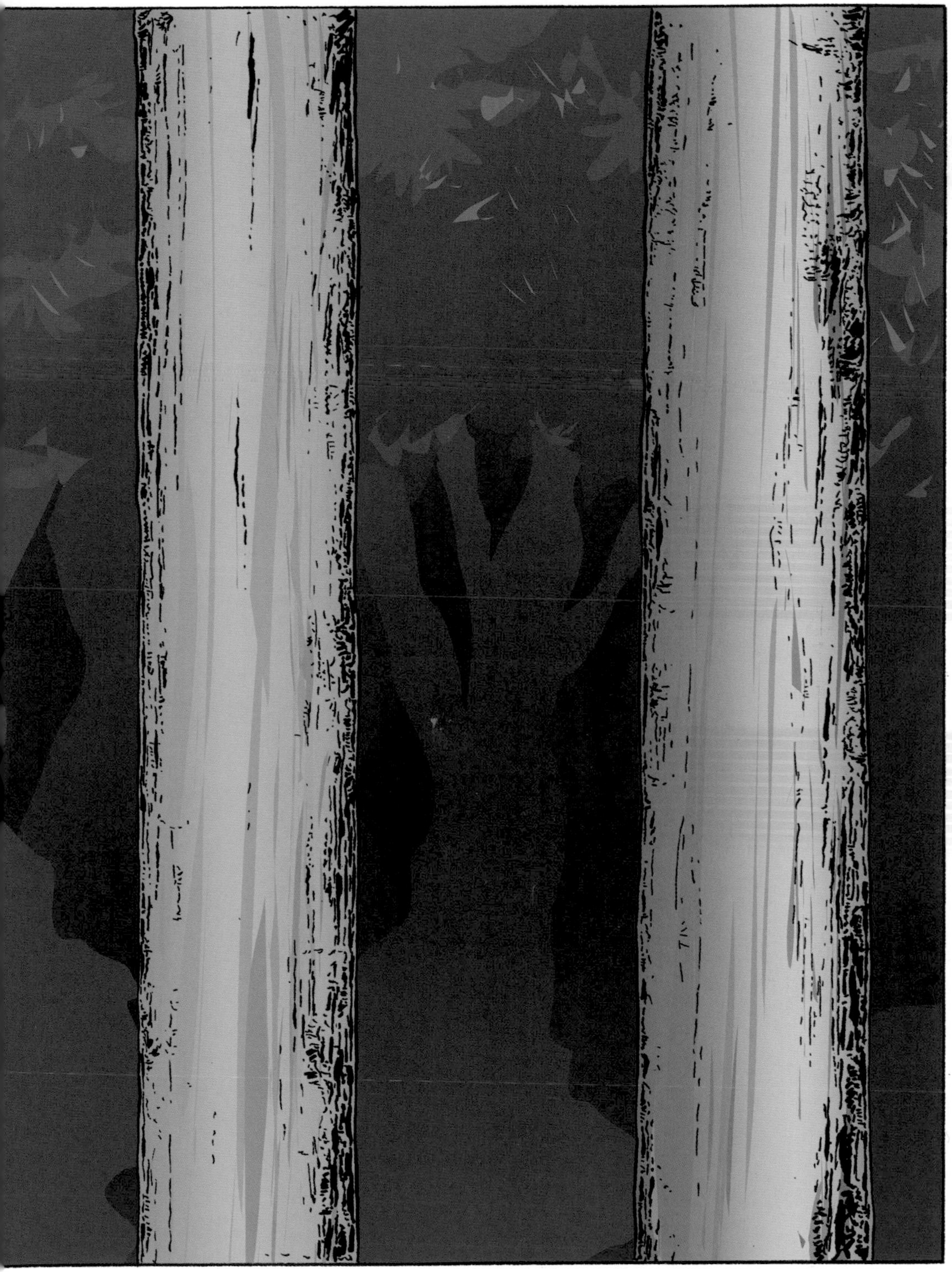

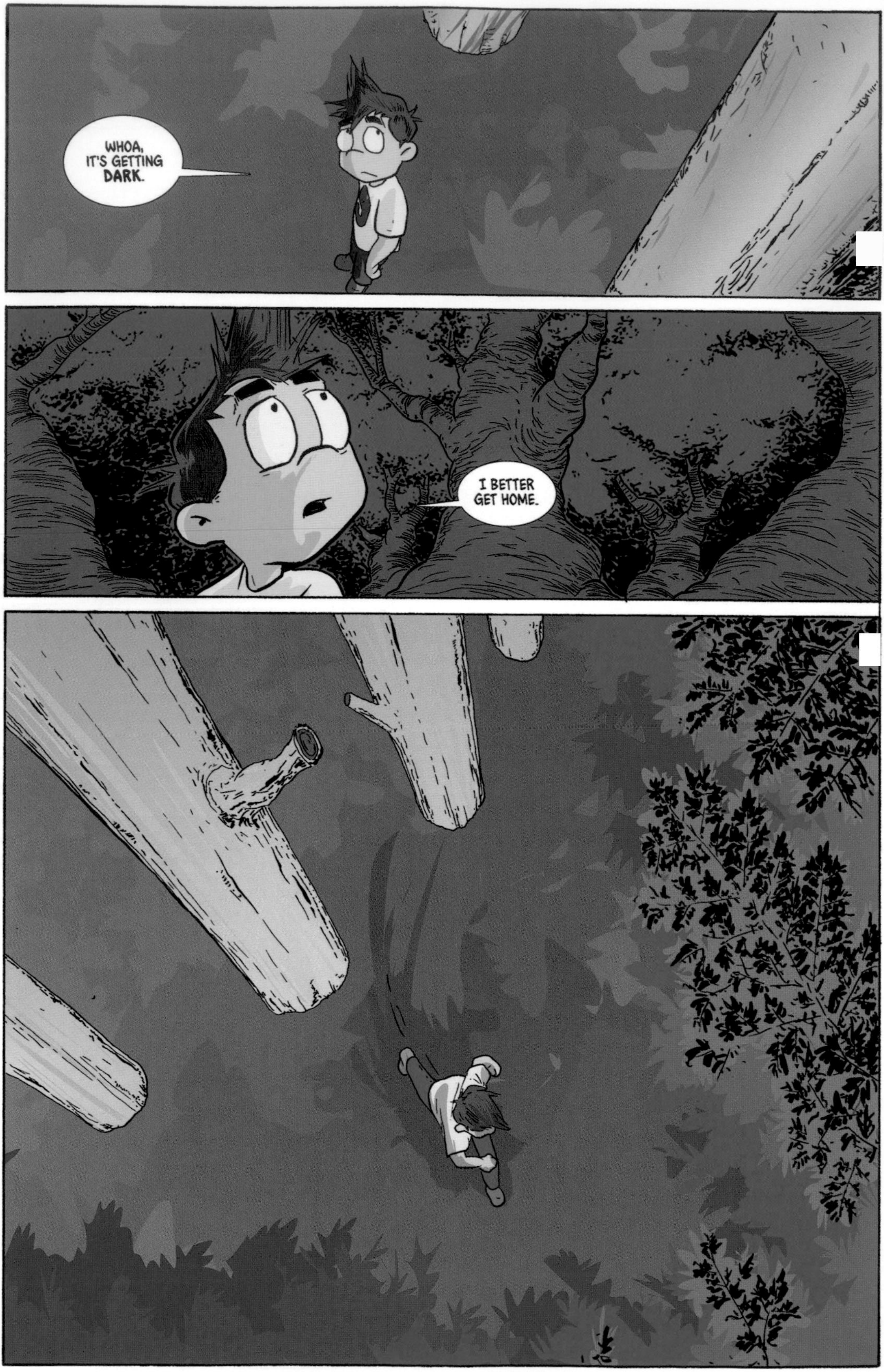
WHOA, IT'S GETTING DARK.
I BETTER GET HOME.

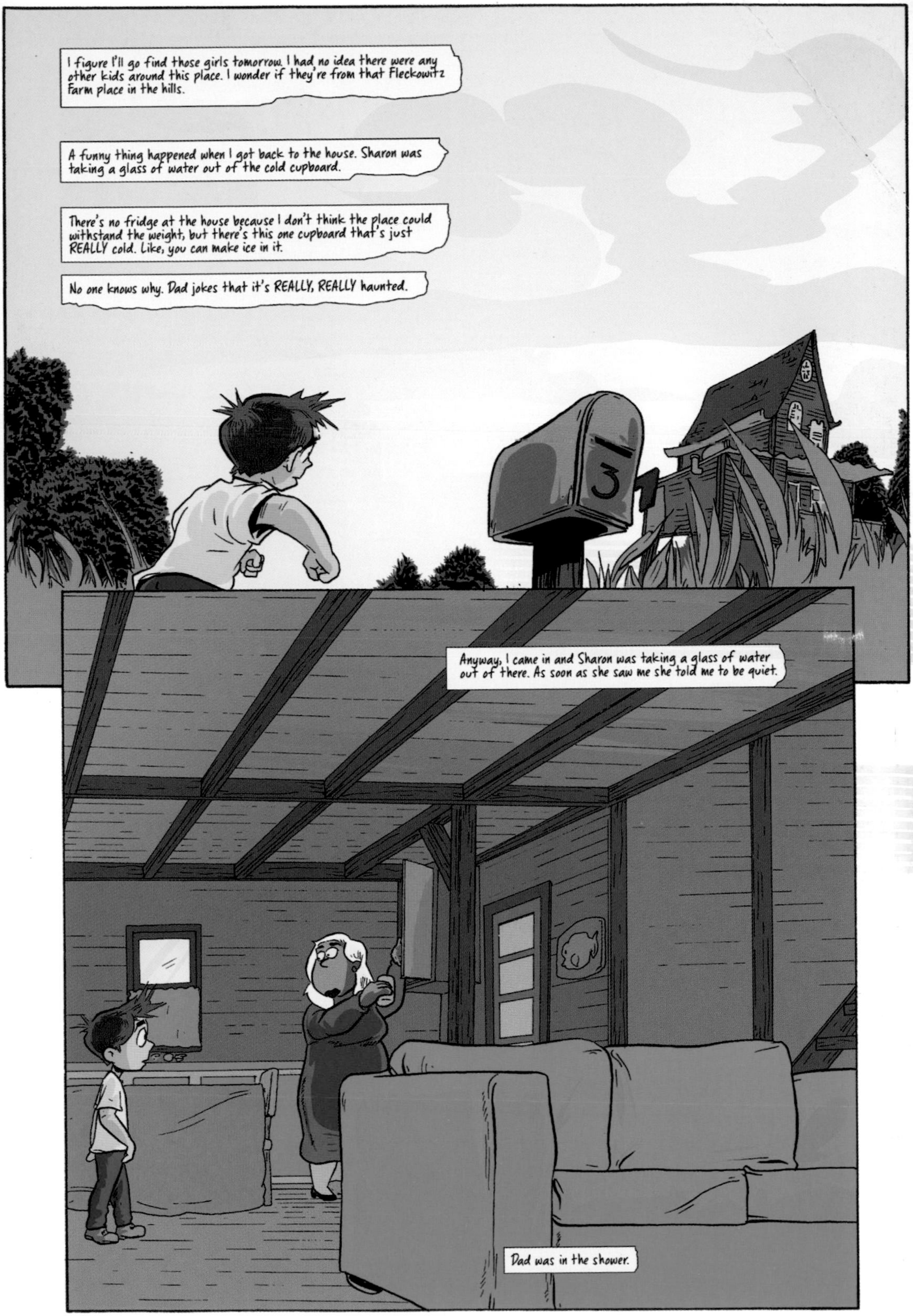
I figure I'll go find those girls tomorrow. I had no idea there were any other kids around this place. I wonder if they're from that Fleckowitz Farm place in the hills.
A funny thing happened when I got back to the house. Sharon was taking a glass of water out of the cold cupboard.
There's no fridge at the house because I don't think the place could withstand the weight, but there's this one cupboard that's just REALLY cold. Like, you can make ice in it.
No one knows why. Dad jokes that it's REALLY, REALLY haunted.
3
Anyway, I came in and Sharon was taking a glass of water out of there. As soon as she saw me she told me to be quiet.
Dad was in the shower.

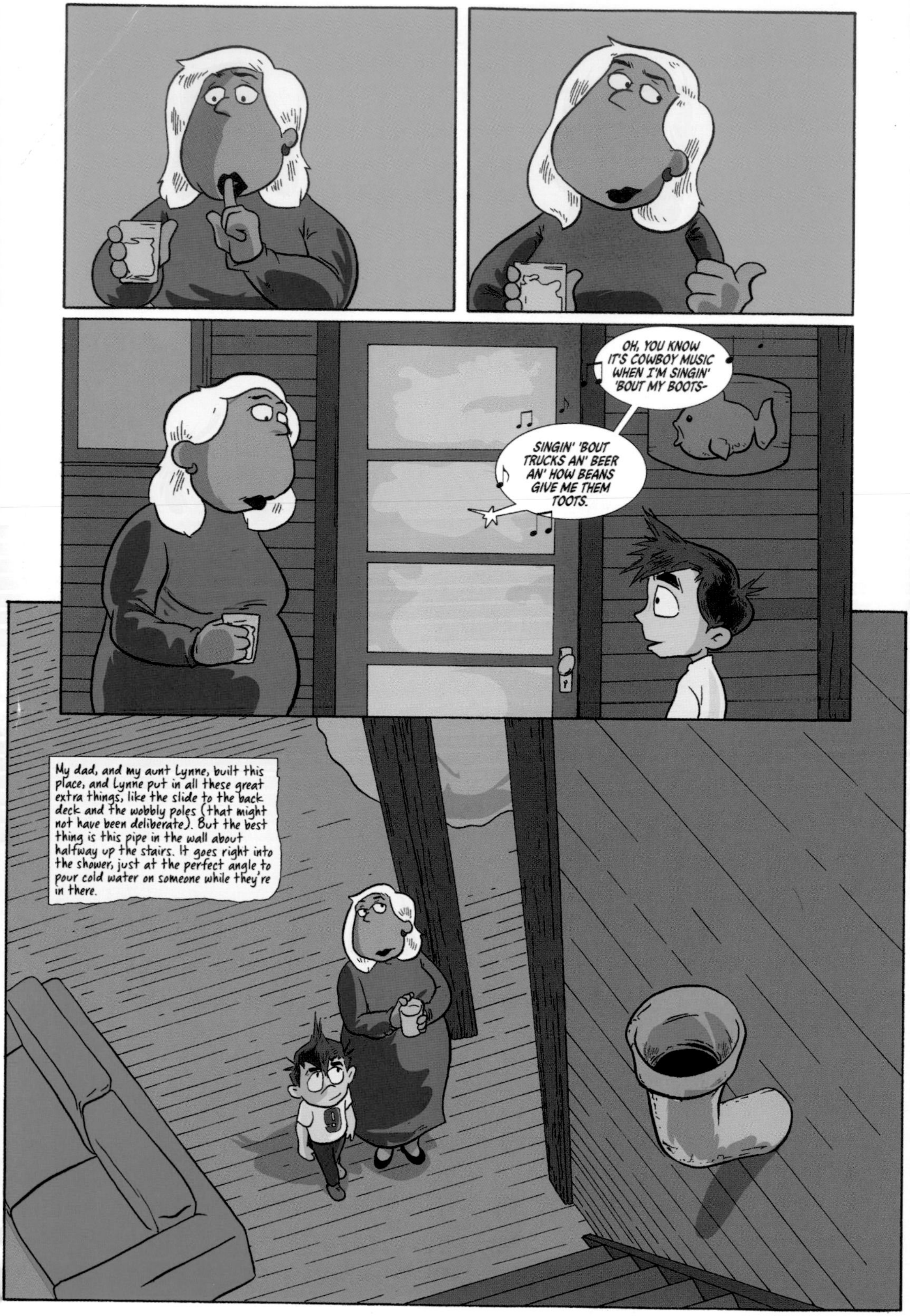
OH, YOU KNOW IT'S COWBOY MUSIC WHEN I'M SINGIN' 'BOUT MY BOOTS-
SINGIN' 'BOUT TRUCKS AN' BEER AN' HOW BEANS GIVE ME THEM TOOTS.
My dad, and my aunt Lynne, built this place, and Lynne put in all these great extra things, like the slide to the back deck and the wobbly poles (that might not have been deliberate). But the best thing is this pipe in the wall about halfway up the stairs. It goes right into the shower, just at the perfect angle to pour cold water on someone while they're in there.

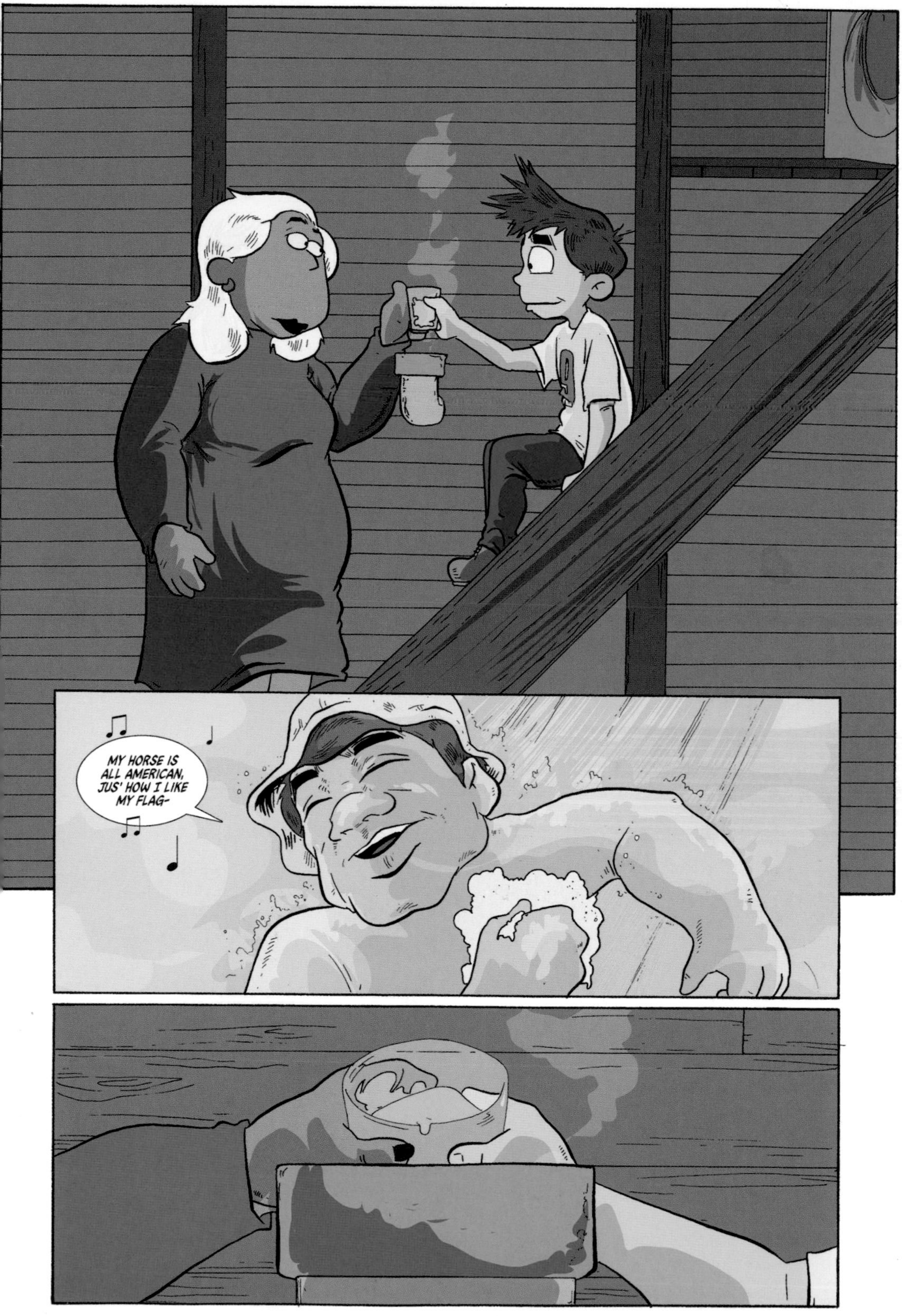
MY HORSE IS ALL AMERICAN, JUS' HOW I LIKE MY FLAG-

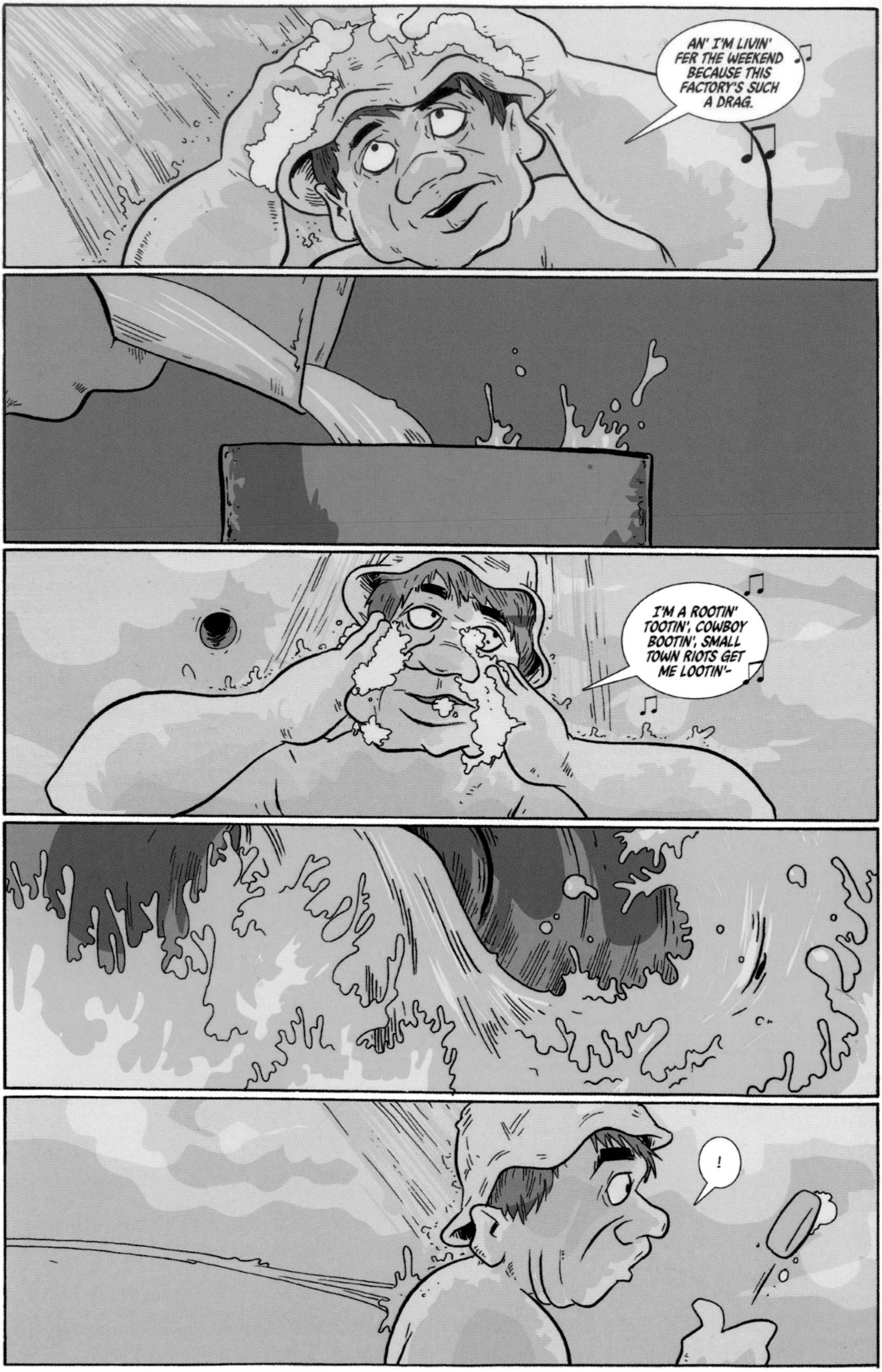
AN' I'M LIVIN' FER THE WEEKEND BECAUSE THIS FACTORY'S SUCH A DRAG.
I'M A ROOTIN' TOOTIN', COWBOY BOOTIN', SMALL TOWN RIOTS GET ME LOOTIN'-
!

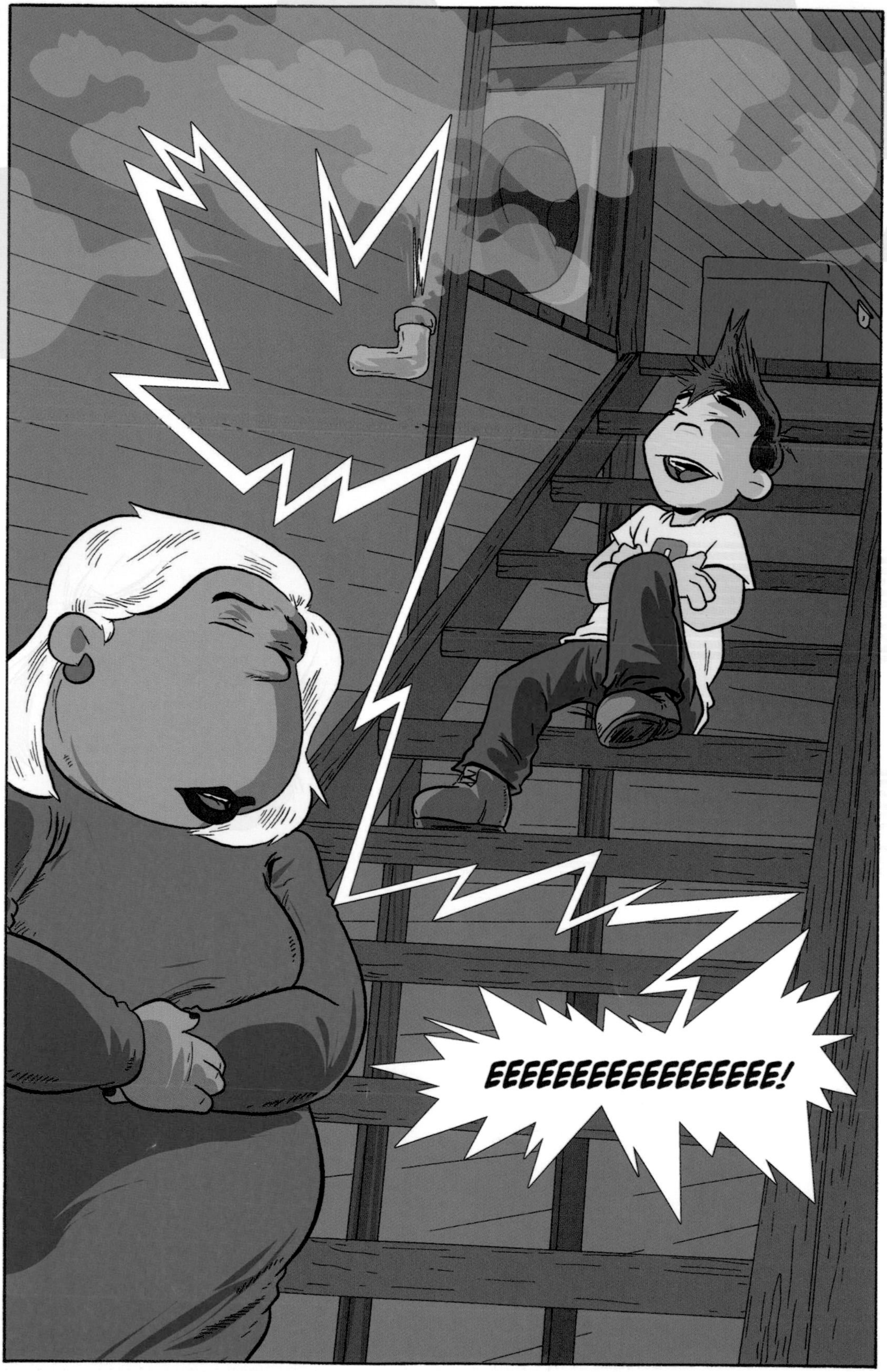
EEEEEEEEEEEEEEEEEE!

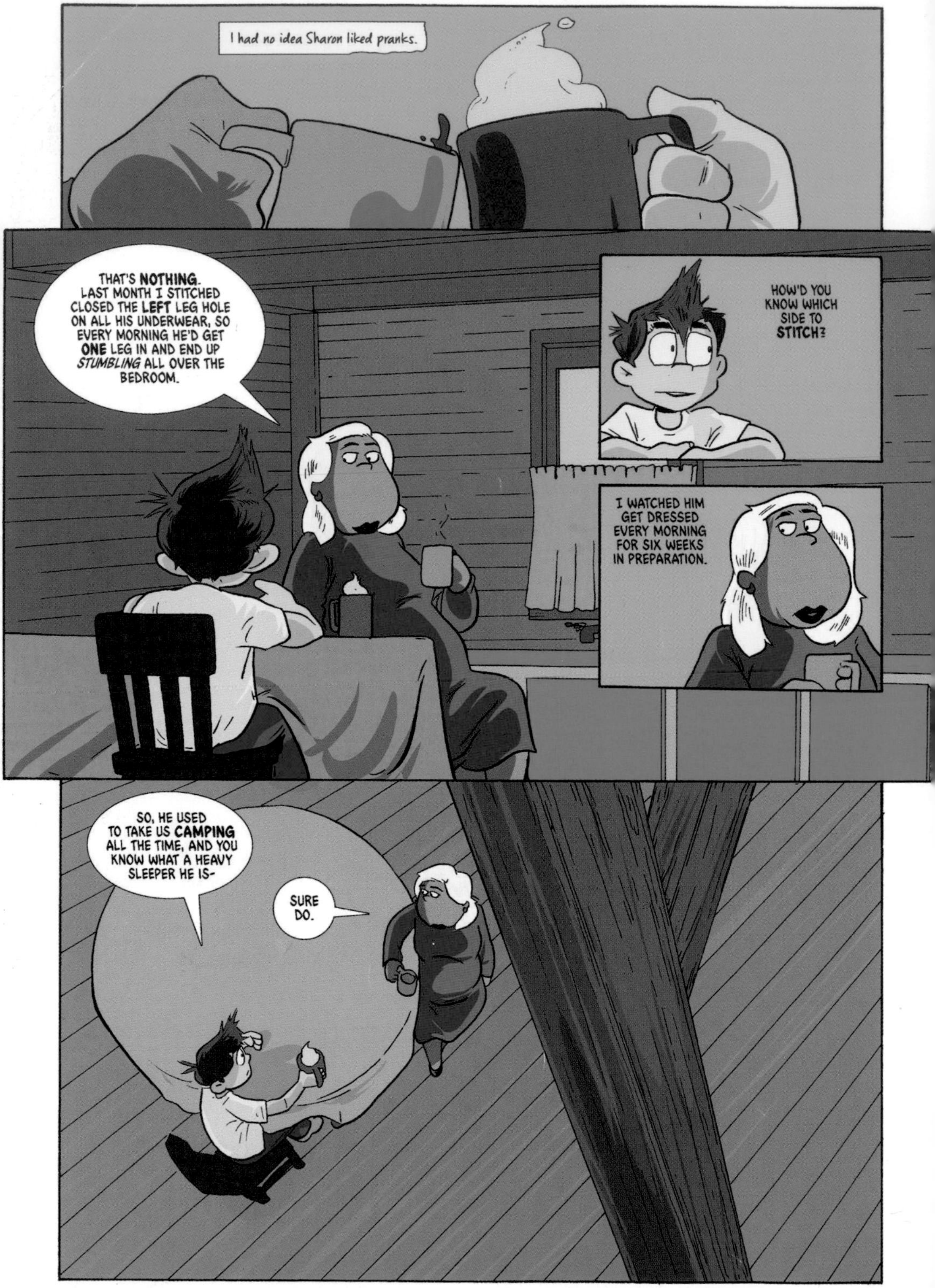
I had no idea Sharon liked pranks.
THAT'S NOTHING. LAST MONTH I STITCHED CLOSED THE LEFT LEG HOLE ON ALL HIS UNDERWEAR, SO EVERY MORNING HE'D GET ONE LEG IN AND END UP STUMBLING ALL OVER THE BEDROOM.
HOW'D YOU KNOW WHICH SIDE TO STITCH?
I WATCHED HIM GET DRESSED EVERY MORNING FOR SIX WEEKS IN PREPARATION.
SO, HE USED TO TAKE US CAMPING ALL THE TIME, AND YOU KNOW WHAT A HEAVY SLEEPER HE IS-
SURE DO.

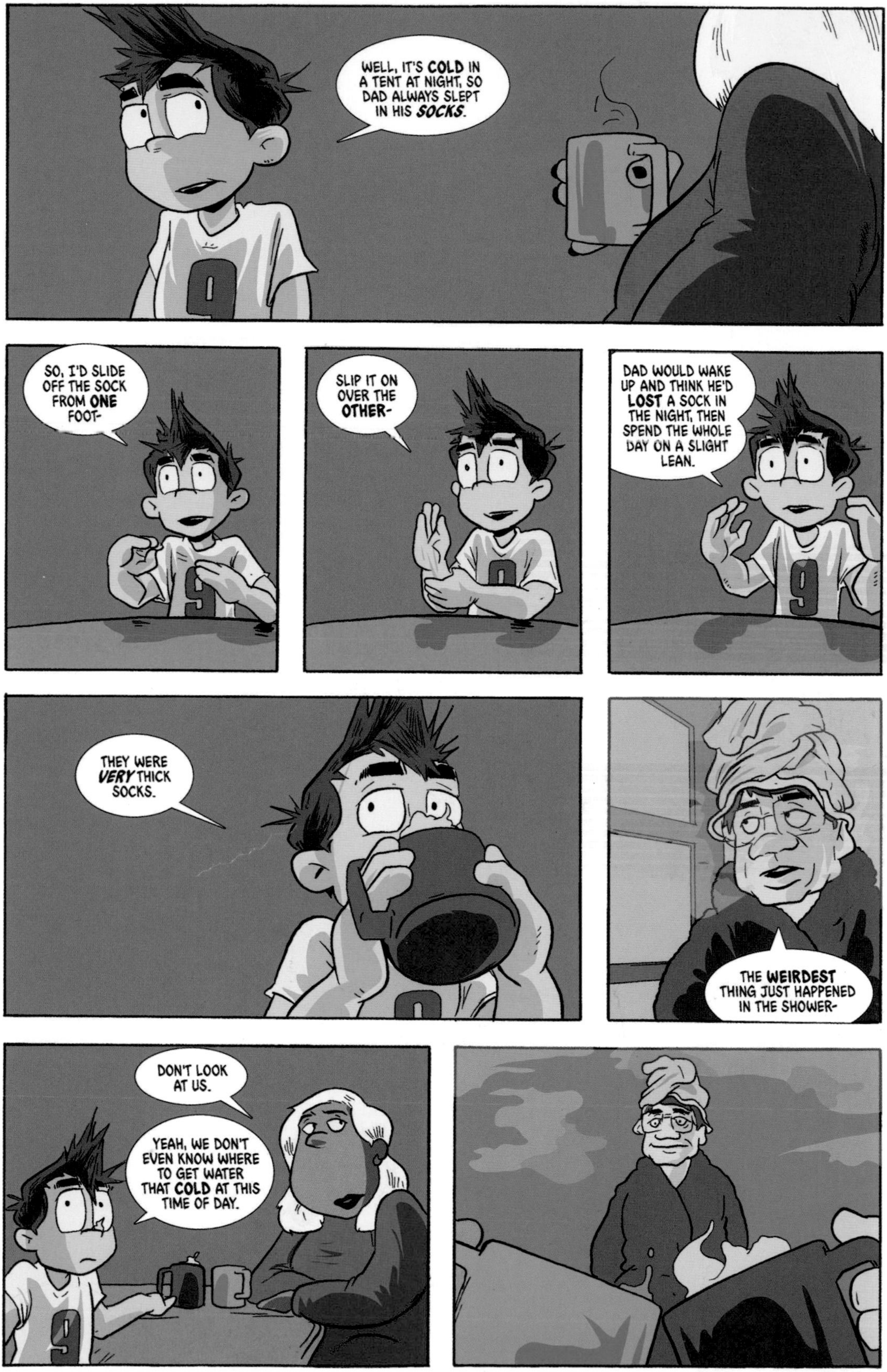
WELL, IT'S COLD IN A TENT AT NIGHT, SO DAD ALWAYS SLEPT IN HIS SOCKS.
SO, I'D SLIDE OFF THE SOCK FROM ONE FOOT-
SLIP IT ON OVER THE OTHER-
DAD WOULD WAKE UP AND THINK HE'D LOST A SOCK IN THE NIGHT, THEN SPEND THE WHOLE DAY ON A SLIGHT LEAN.
THEY WERE VERY THICK SOCKS.
THE WEIRDEST THING JUST HAPPENED IN THE SHOWER-
DON'T LOOK AT US.
YEAH, WE DON'T EVEN KNOW WHERE TO GET WATER THAT COLD AT THIS TIME OF DAY.

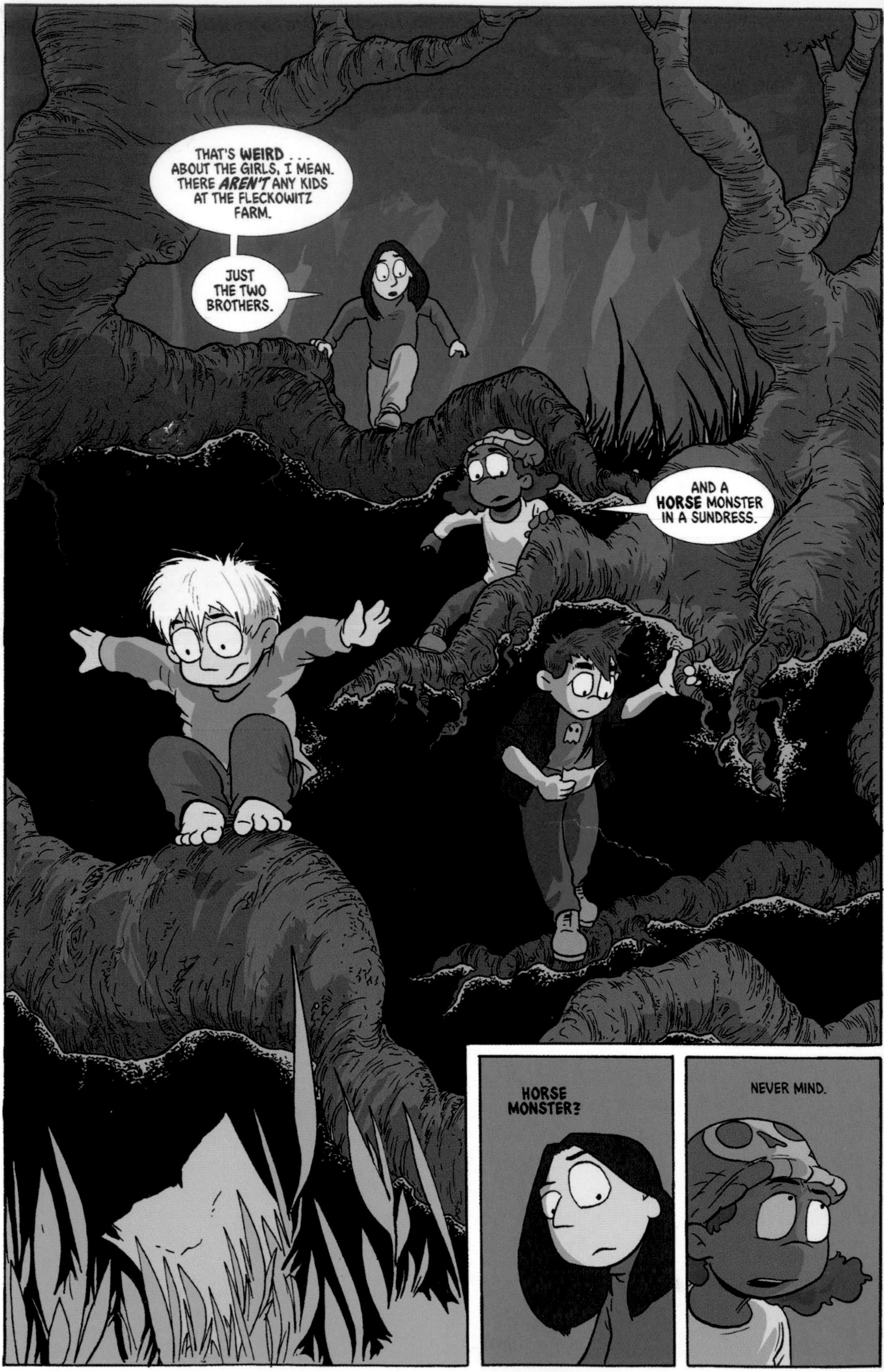
THAT'S WEIRD . . . ABOUT THE GIRLS, I MEAN. THERE AREN'T ANY KIDS AT THE FLECKOWITZ FARM.
JUST THE TWO BROTHERS.
AND A HORSE MONSTER IN A SUNDRESS.
HORSE MONSTER?
NEVER MIND.

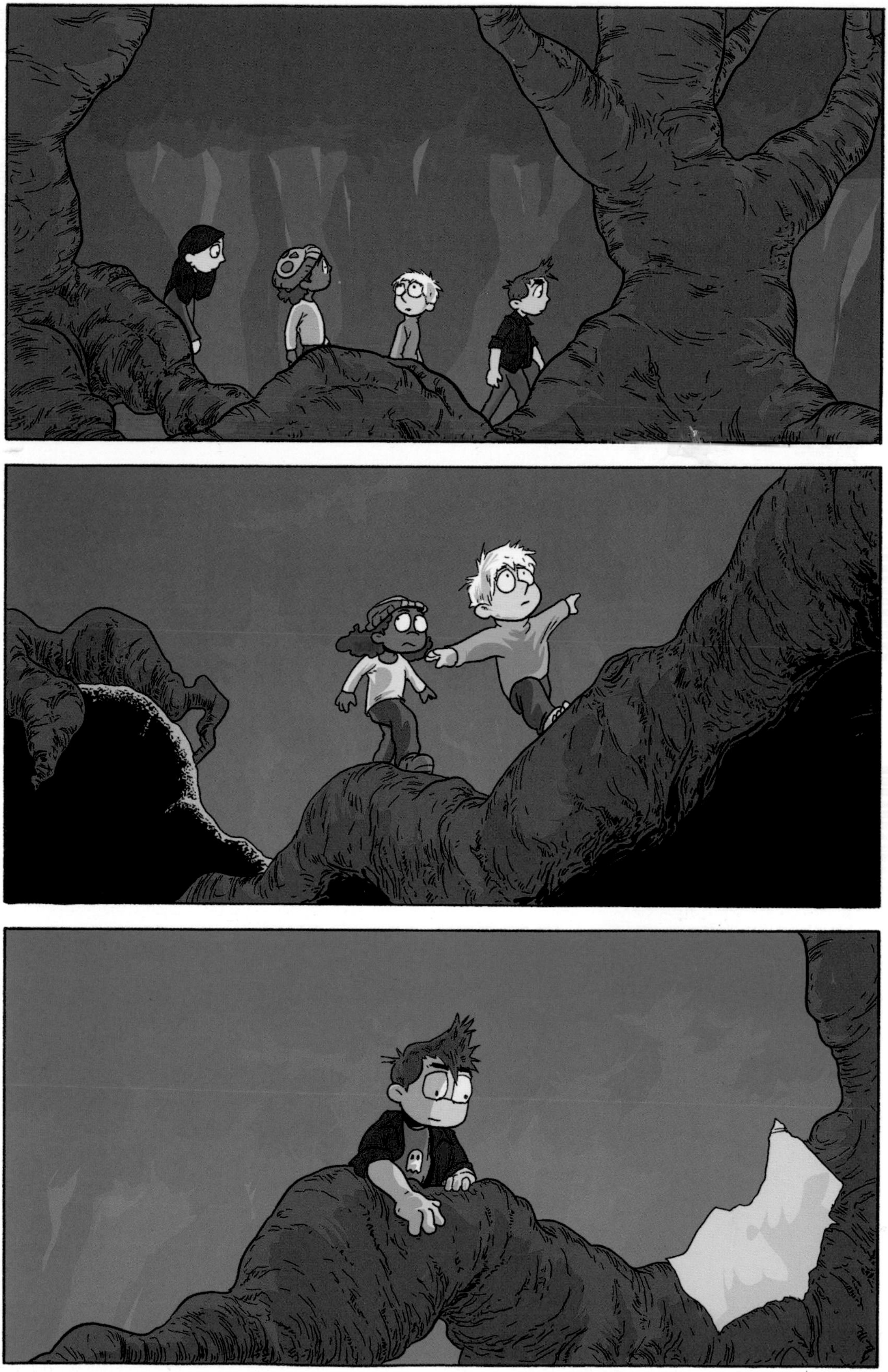

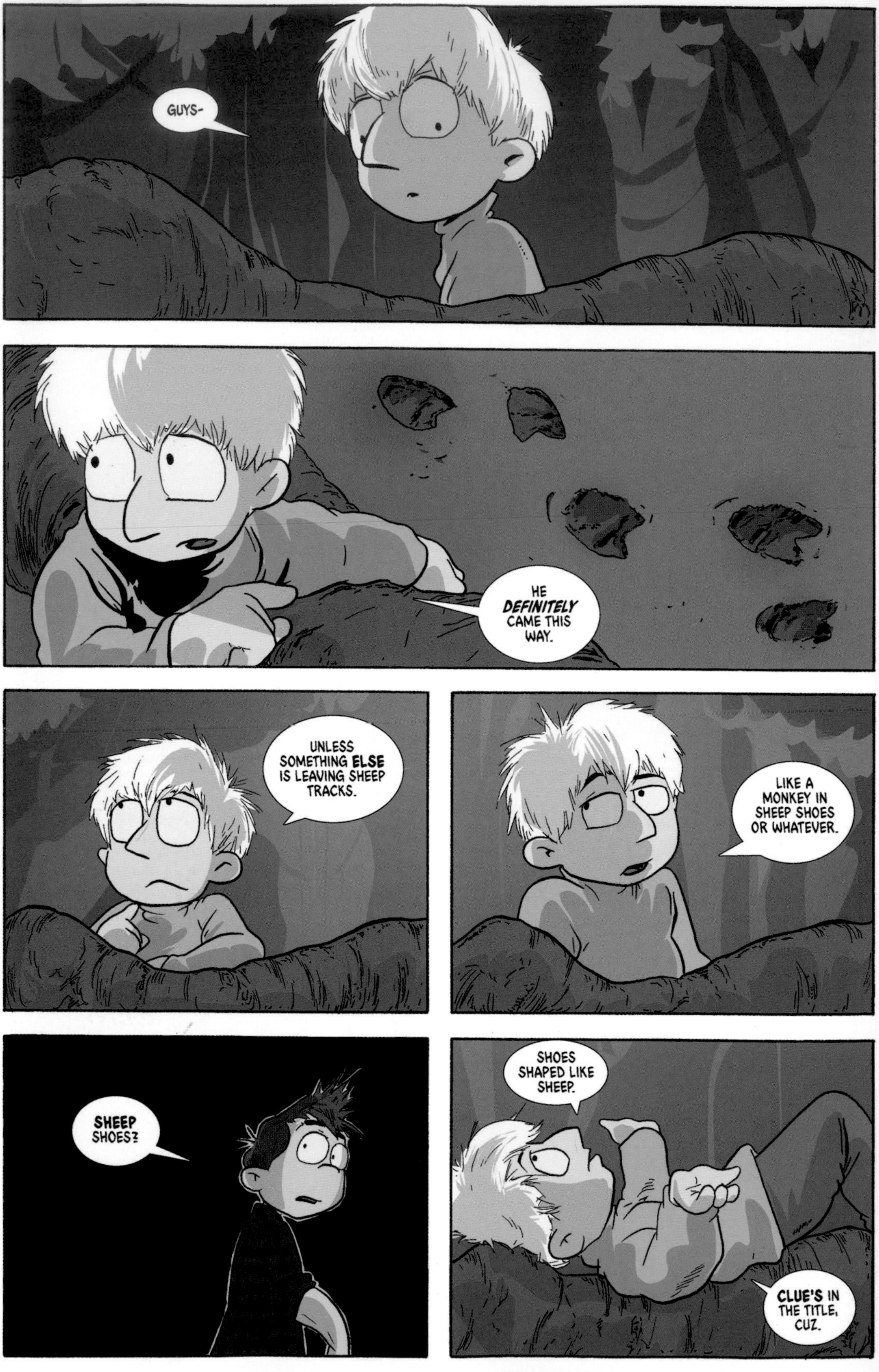
GUYS-
HE DEFINITELY CAME THIS WAY.
UNLESS SOMETHING ELSE IS LEAVING SHEEP TRACKS.
LIKE A MONKEY IN SHEEP SHOES OR WHATEVER.
SHEEP SHOES?
SHOES SHAPED LIKE SHEEP.
CLUE'S IN THE TITLE, CUZ.

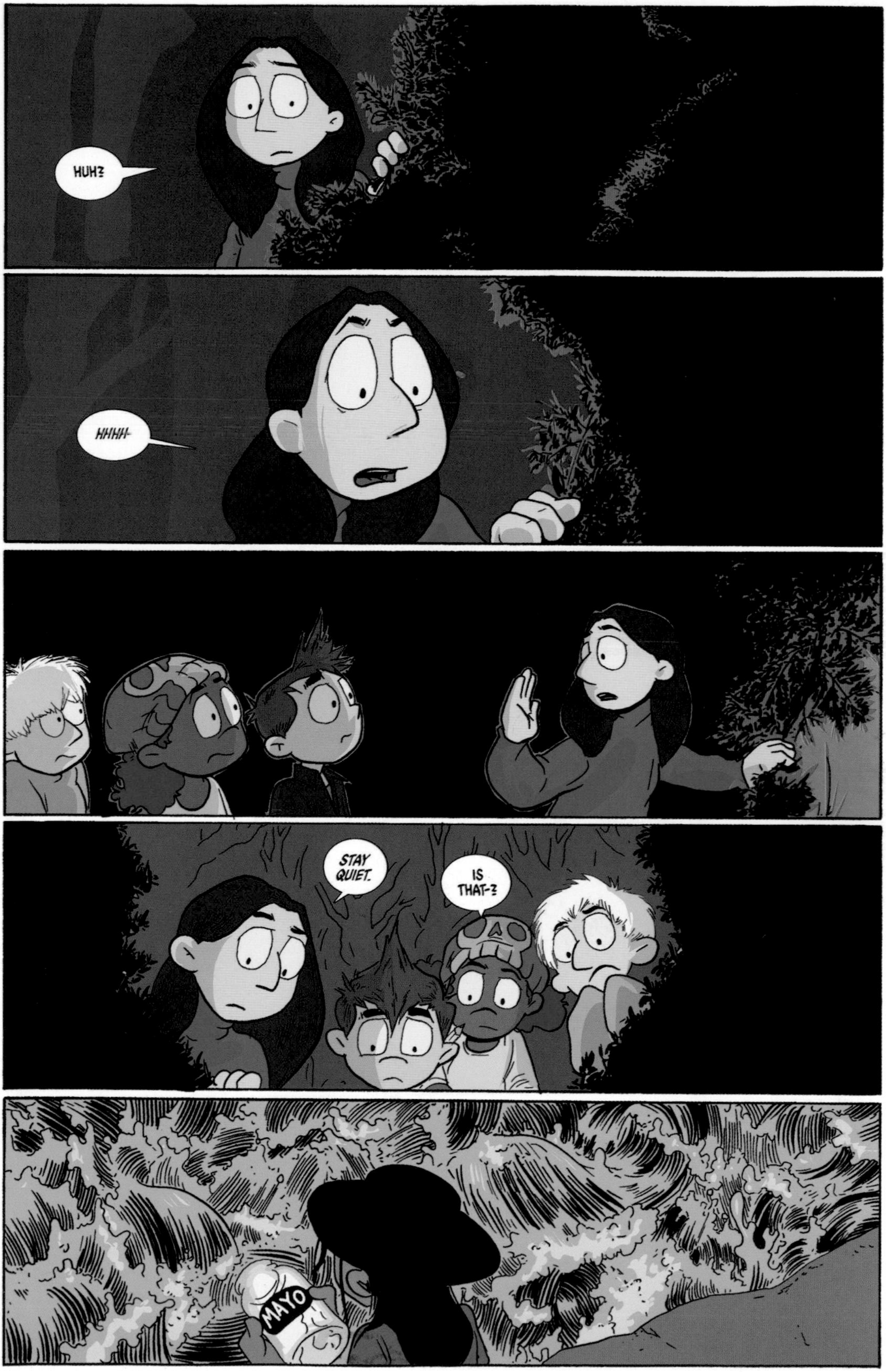
HUH?
HHHH-
STAY QUIET.
IS THAT-?
MAYO

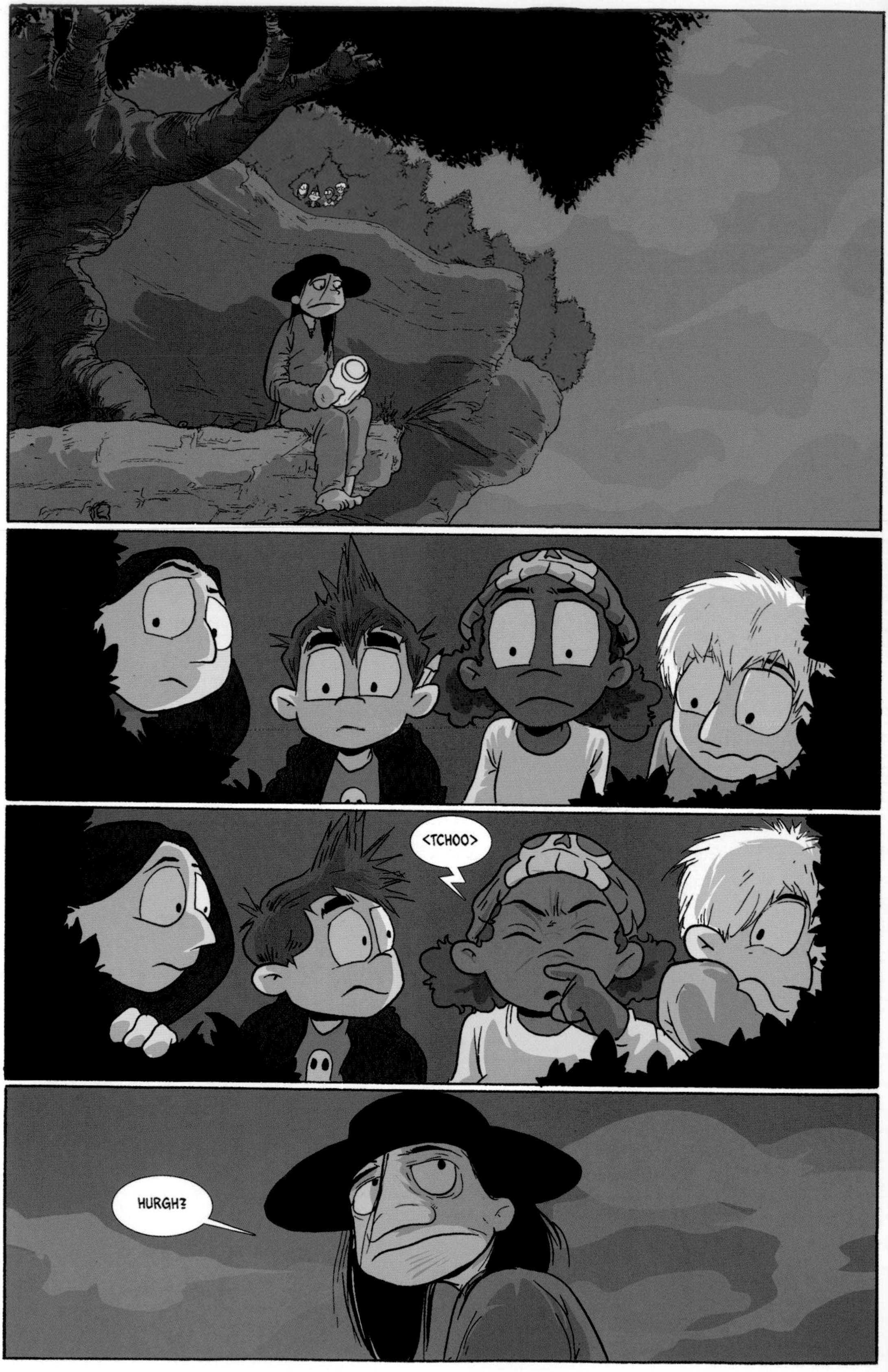
<TCHOO>
HURGH?

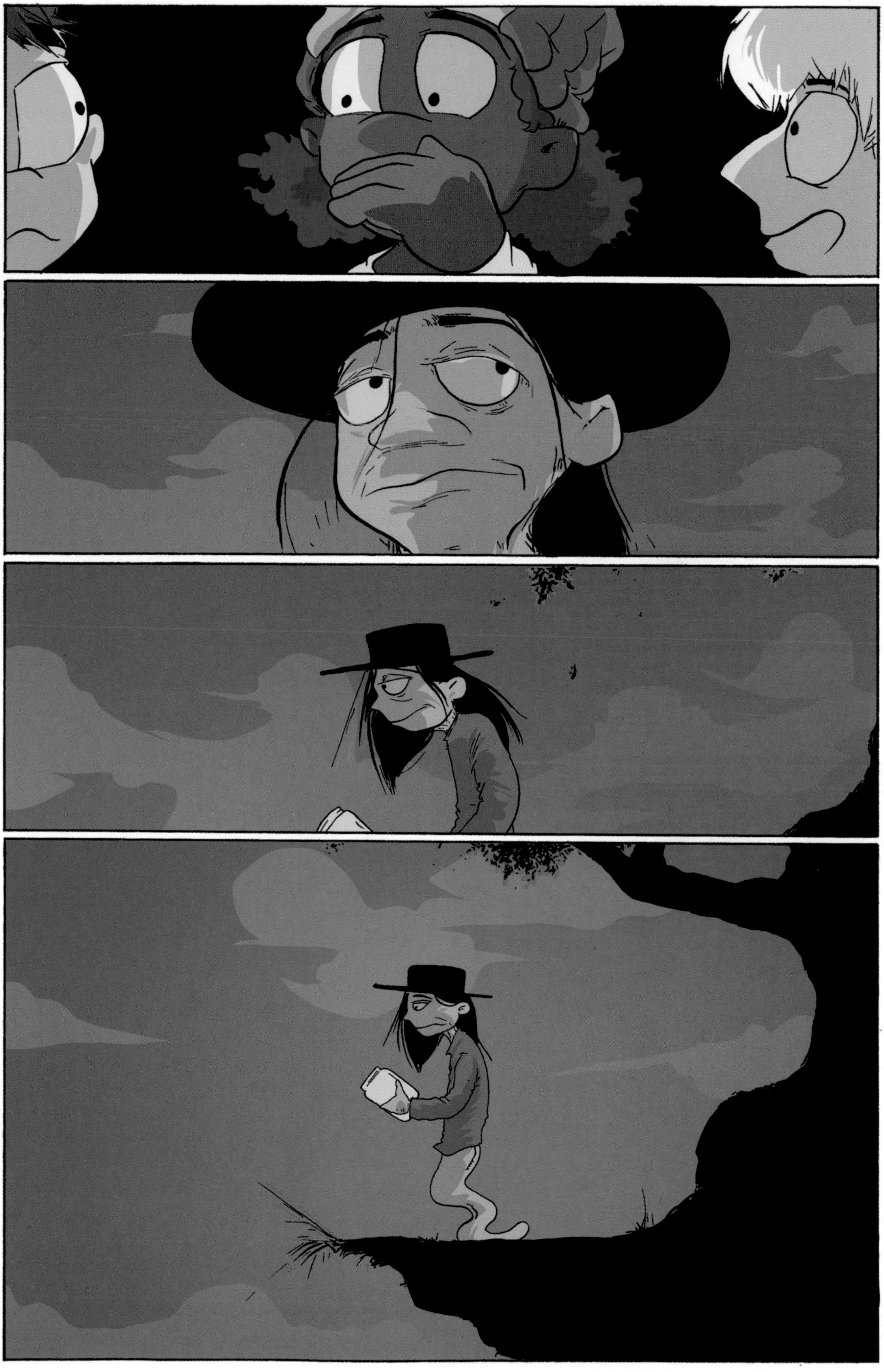

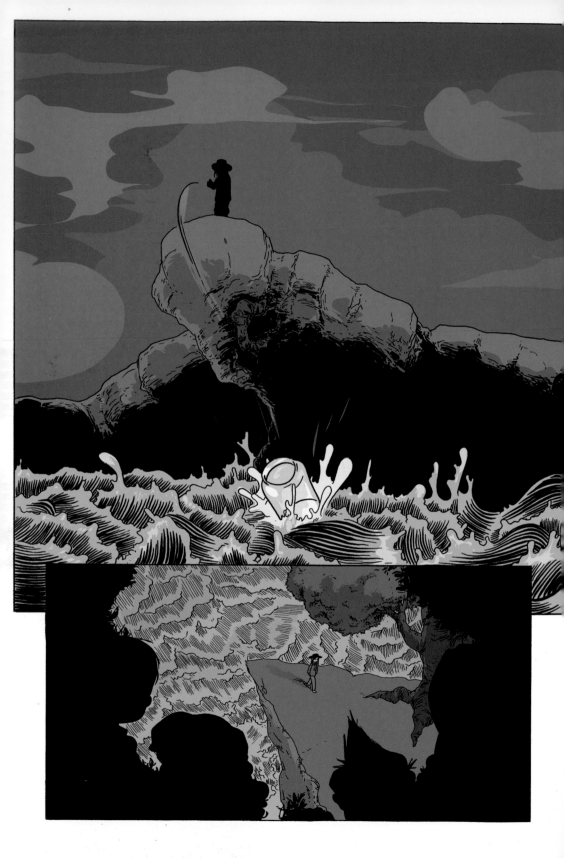

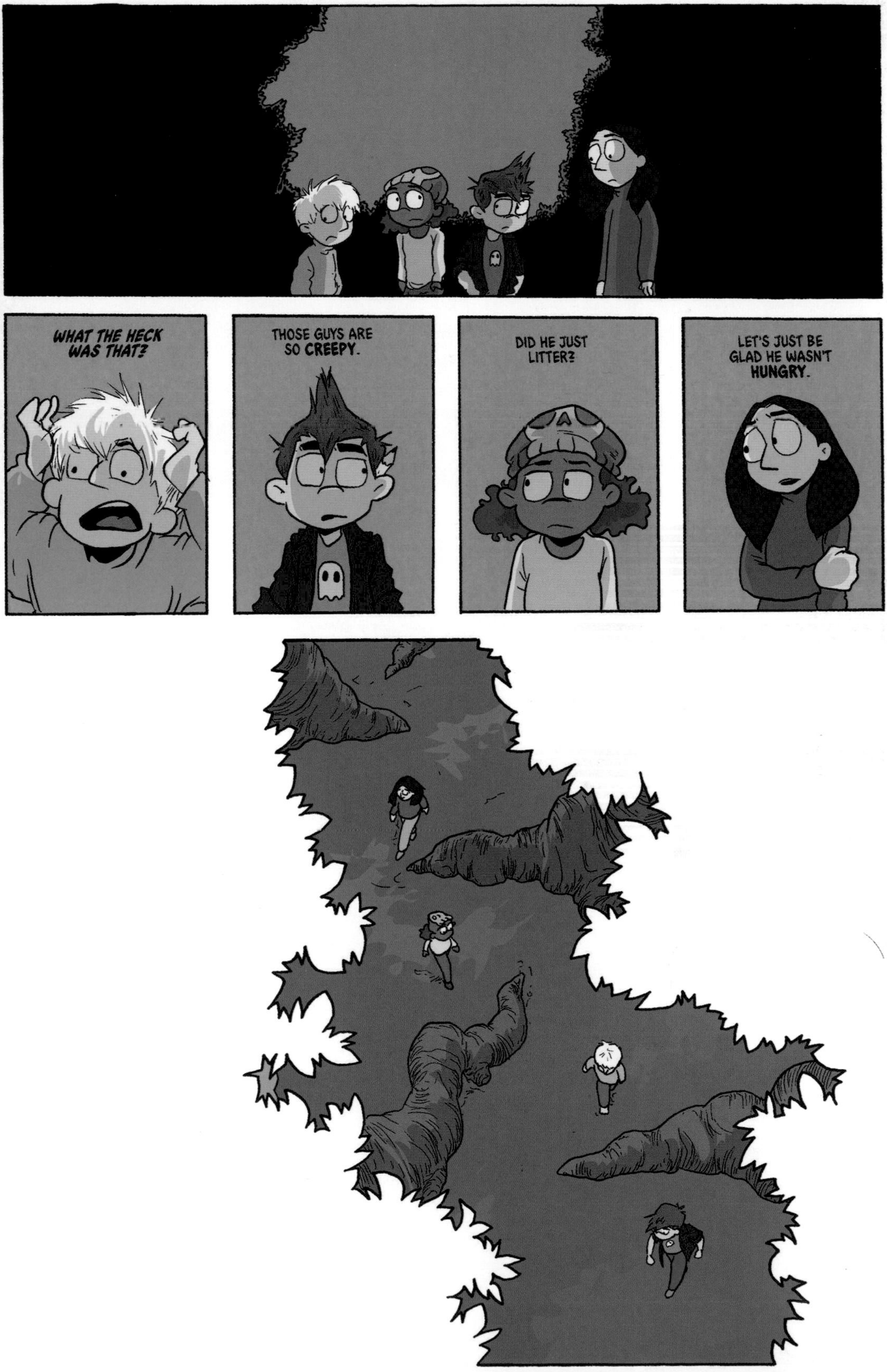

WHAT THE HECK WAS THAT?
THOSE GUYS ARE SO CREEPY.
DID HE JUST LITTER?
LET'S JUST BE GLAD HE WASN'T HUNGRY.

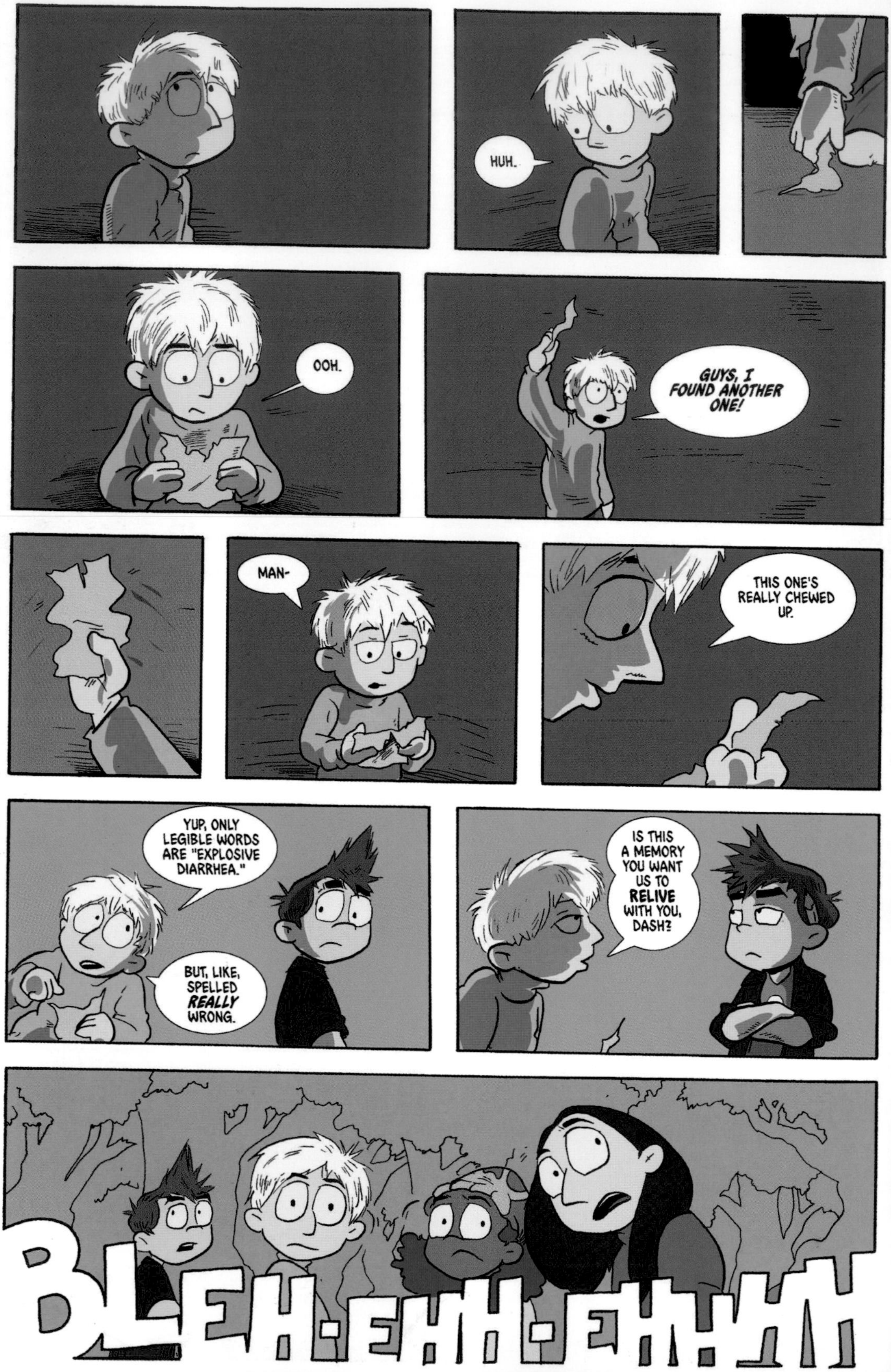

HUH.
OOH.
GUYS, I FOUND ANOTHER ONE!
MAN-
THIS ONE'S REALLY CHEWED UP.
YUP, ONLY LEGIBLE WORDS ARE "EXPLOSIVE DIARRHEA."
BUT, LIKE, SPELLED REALLY WRONG.
IS THIS A MEMORY YOU WANT US TO RELIVE WITH YOU, DASH?
BLEH-EHH-EHHM

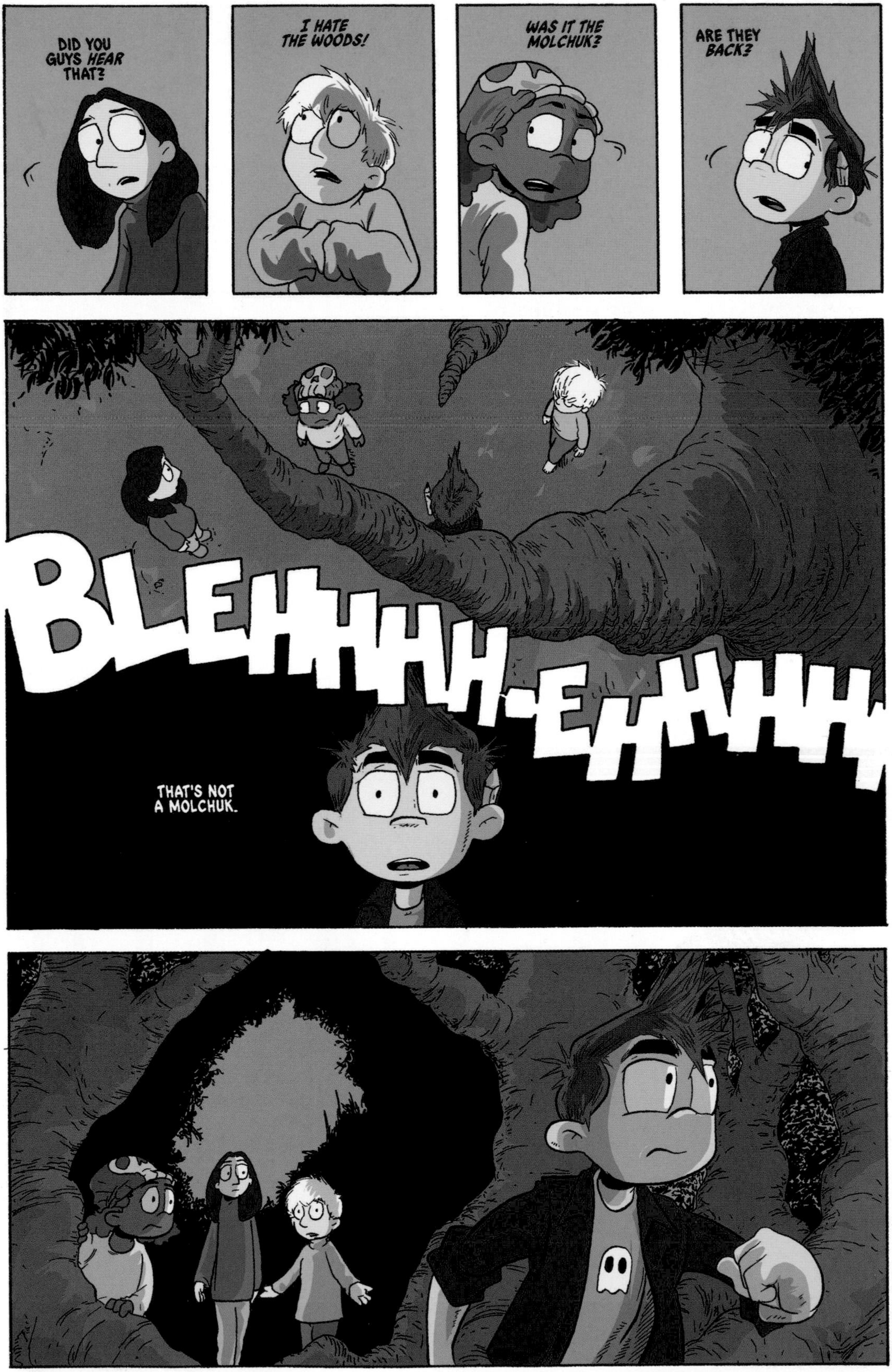
DID YOU GUYS *HEAR* THAT?
I HATE THE WOODS!
WAS IT THE MOLCHUK?
ARE THEY *BACK*?
BLEHHHHH-EHHHHHH
THAT'S NOT A MOLCHUK.

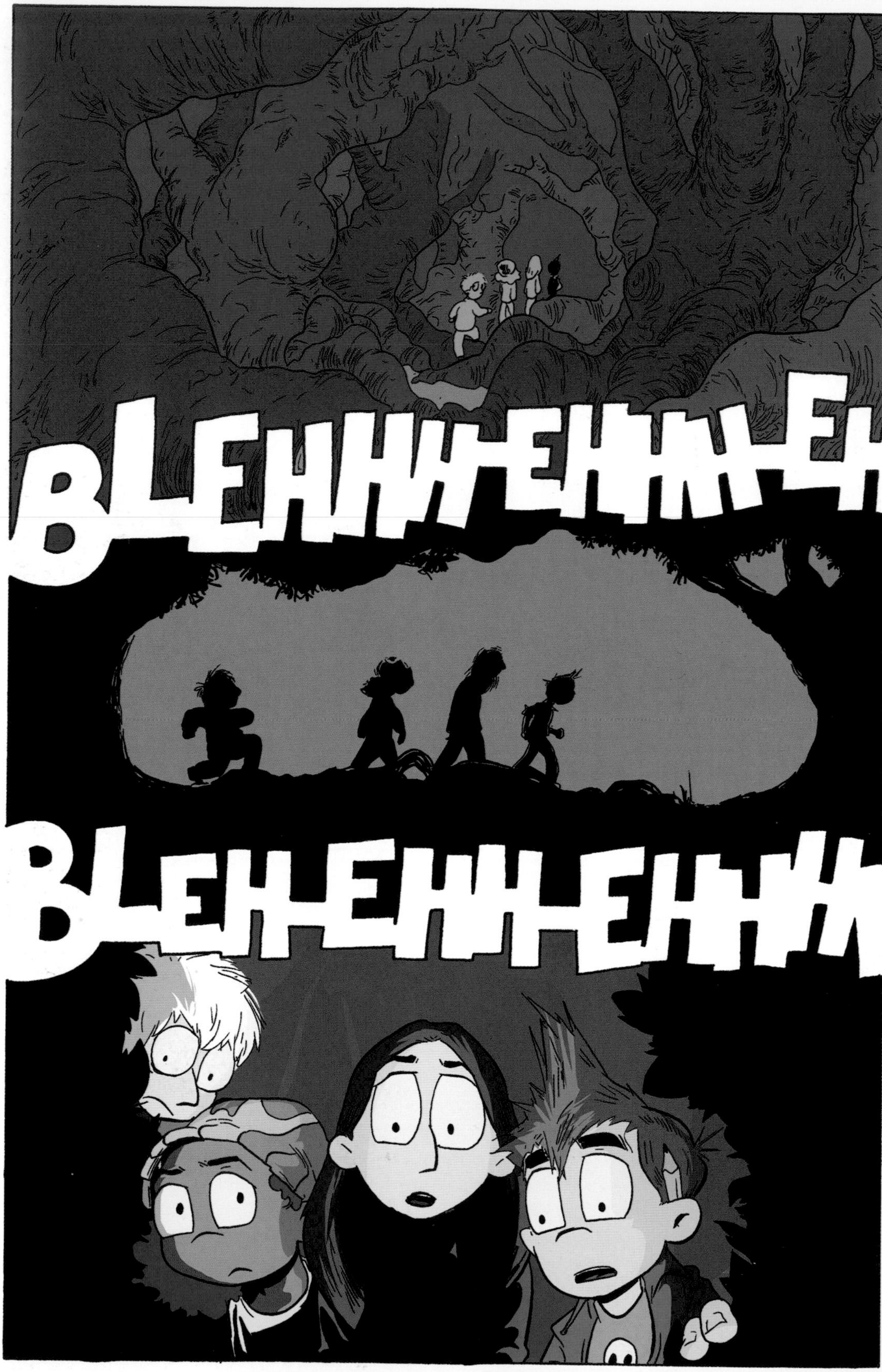
BLEHHHEHHHEH
BLEHEHHHEHHH

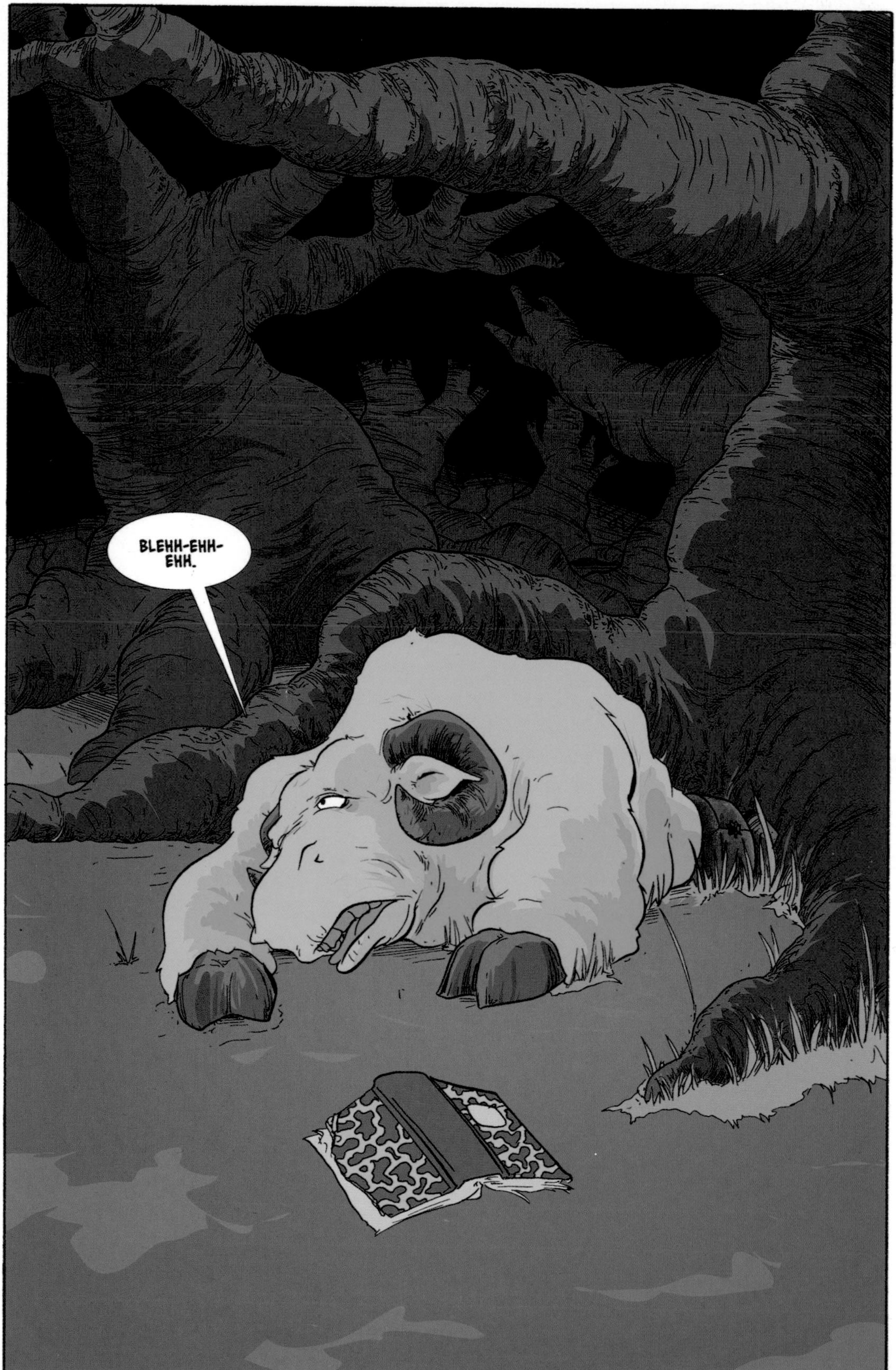
BLEHH-EHH-EHH.

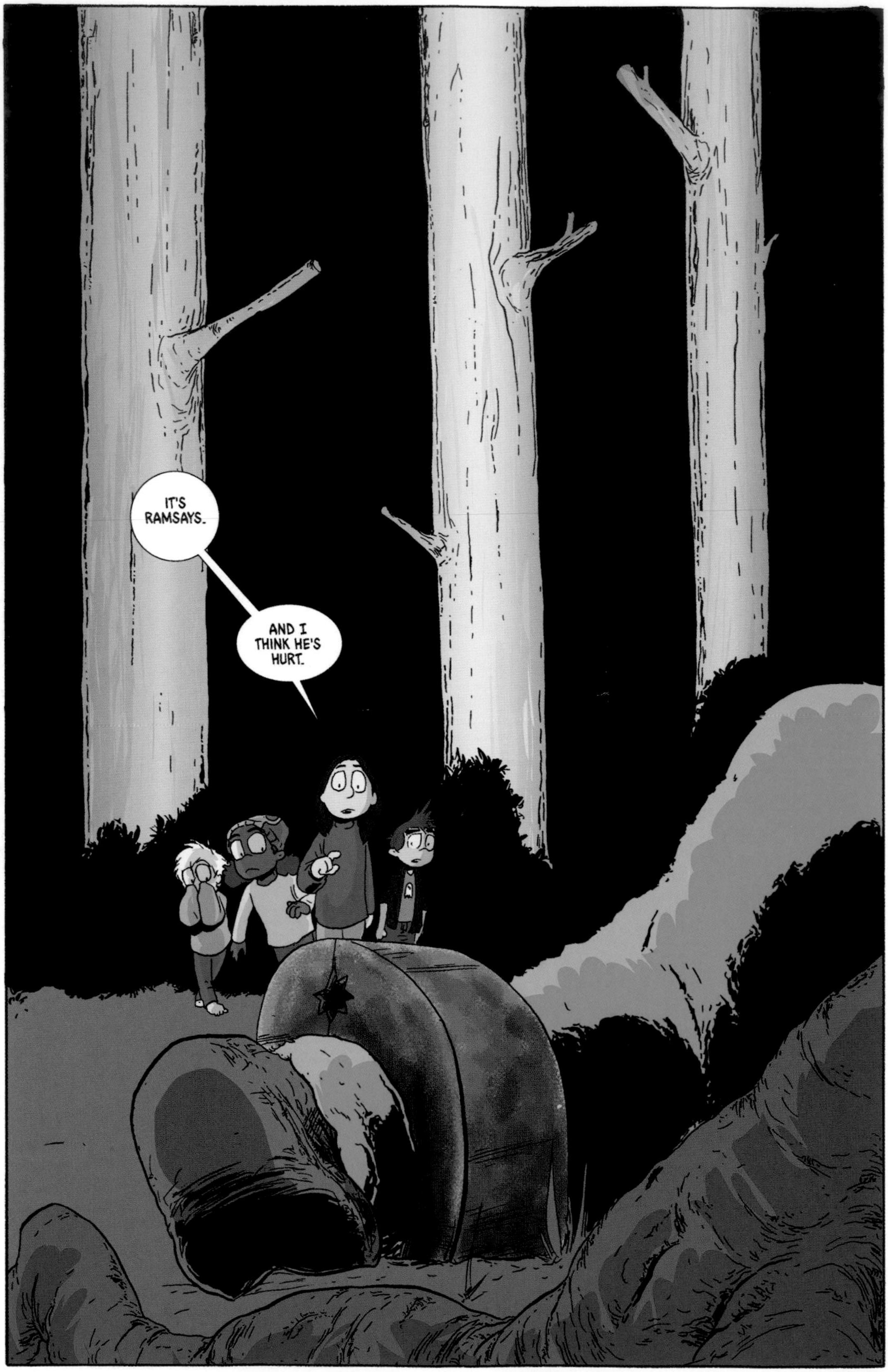
IT'S RAMSAYS.
AND I THINK HE'S HURT.

TO BE CONTINUED.

MAKE PRETEND

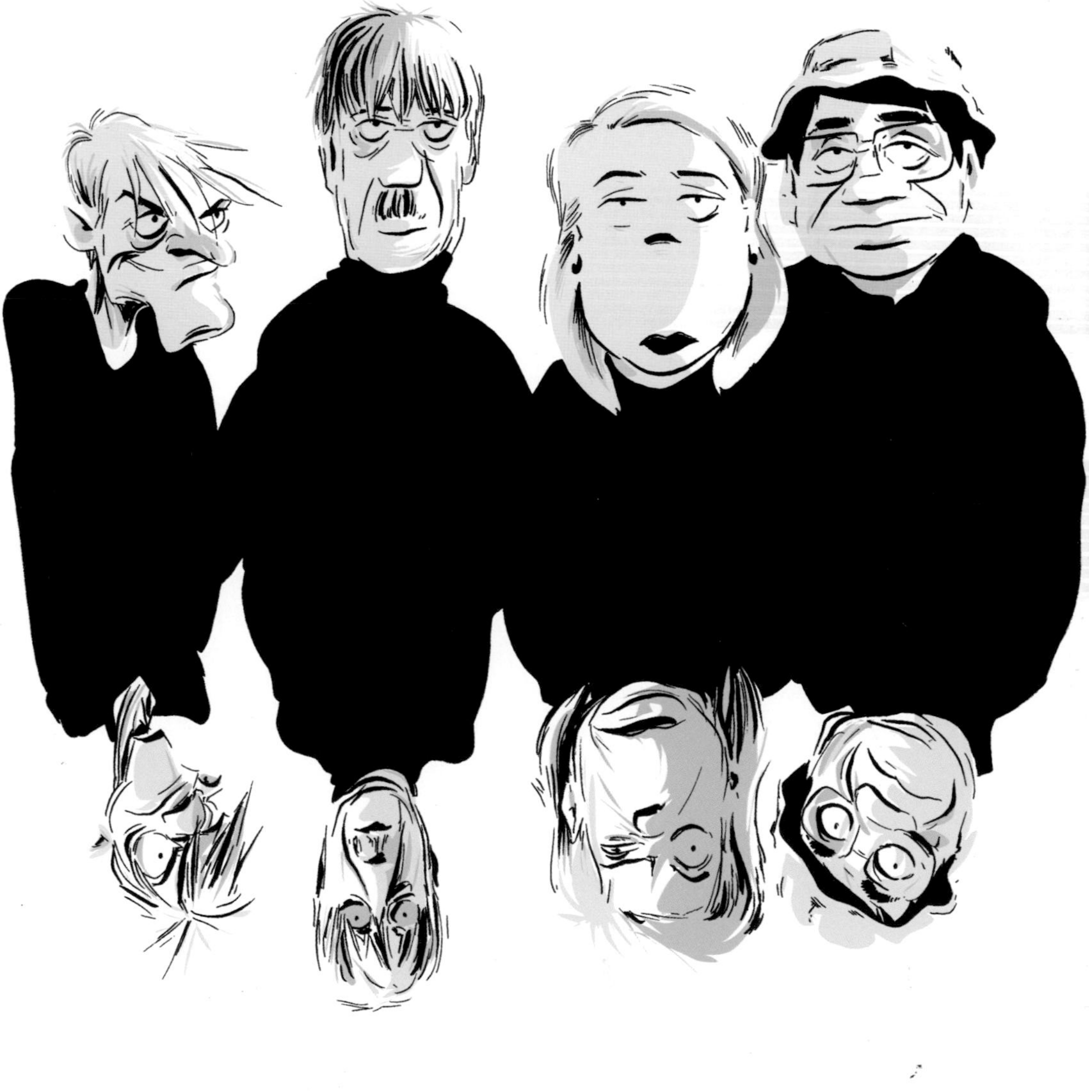

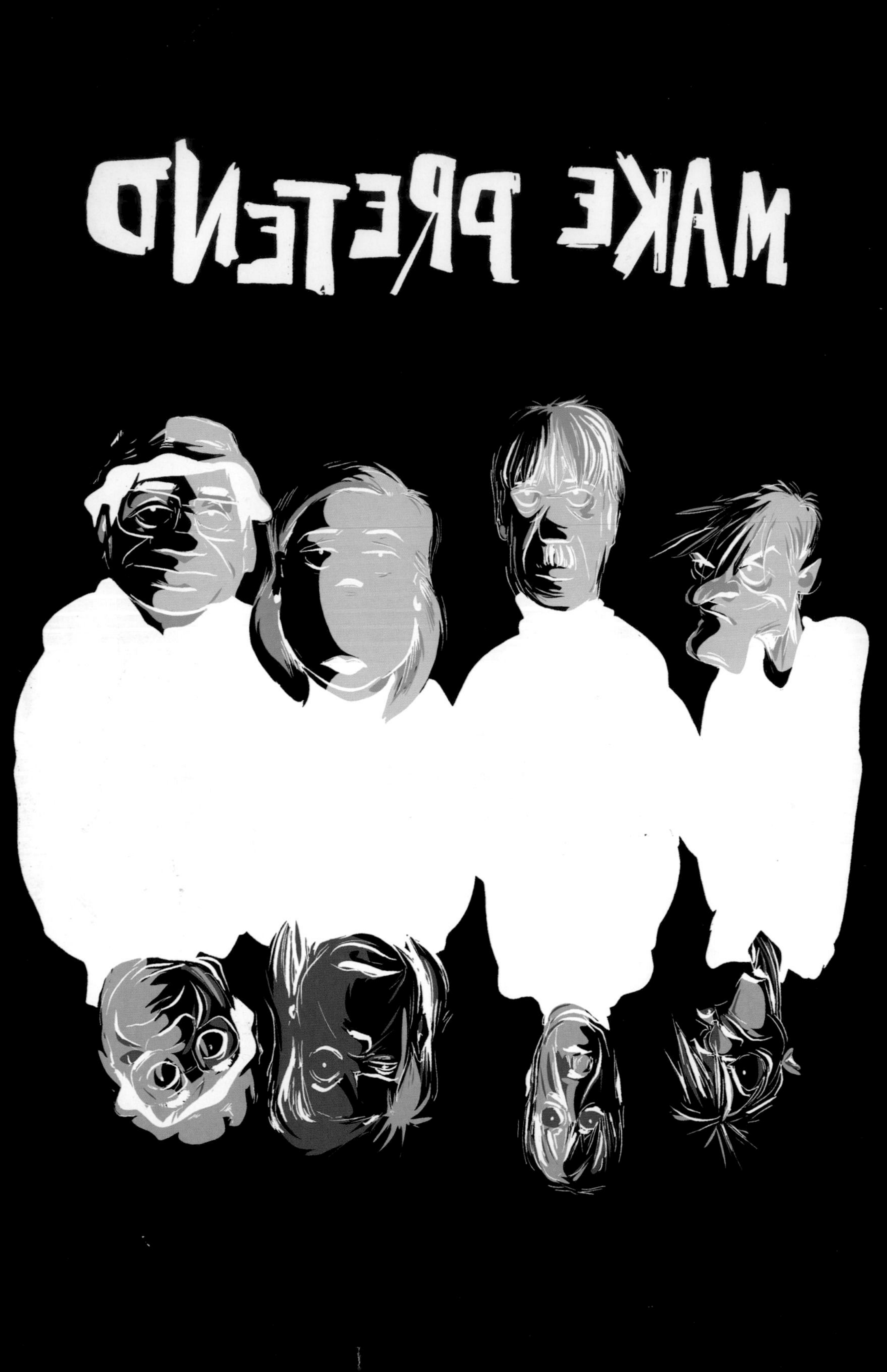
MAKE PRETEND

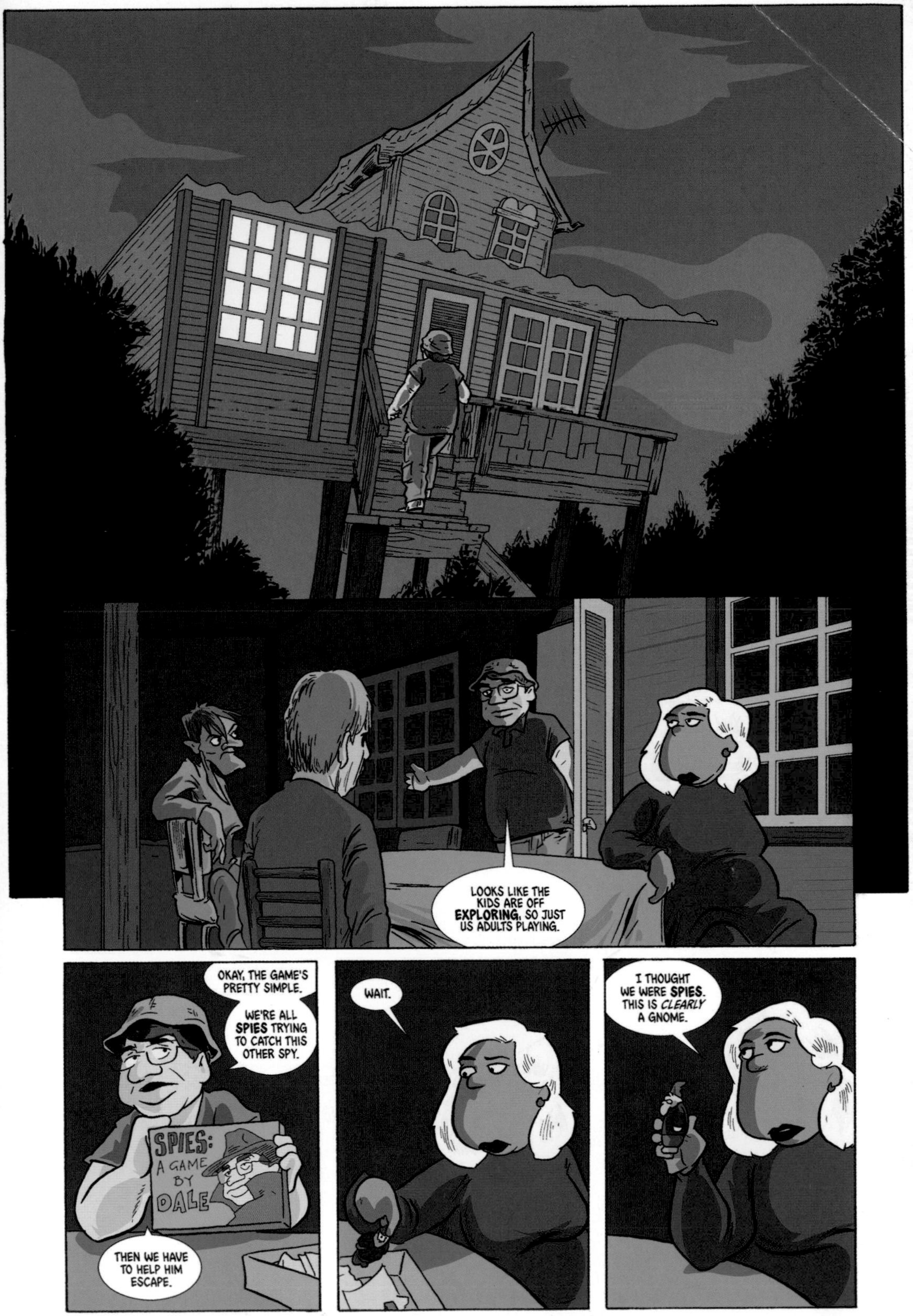
LOOKS LIKE THE KIDS ARE OFF **EXPLORING**, SO JUST US ADULTS PLAYING.
OKAY, THE GAME'S PRETTY SIMPLE.
WE'RE ALL **SPIES** TRYING TO CATCH THIS OTHER SPY.
SPIES: A GAME BY DALE
THEN WE HAVE TO HELP HIM ESCAPE.
WAIT.
I THOUGHT WE WERE **SPIES**. THIS IS *CLEARLY* A GNOME.

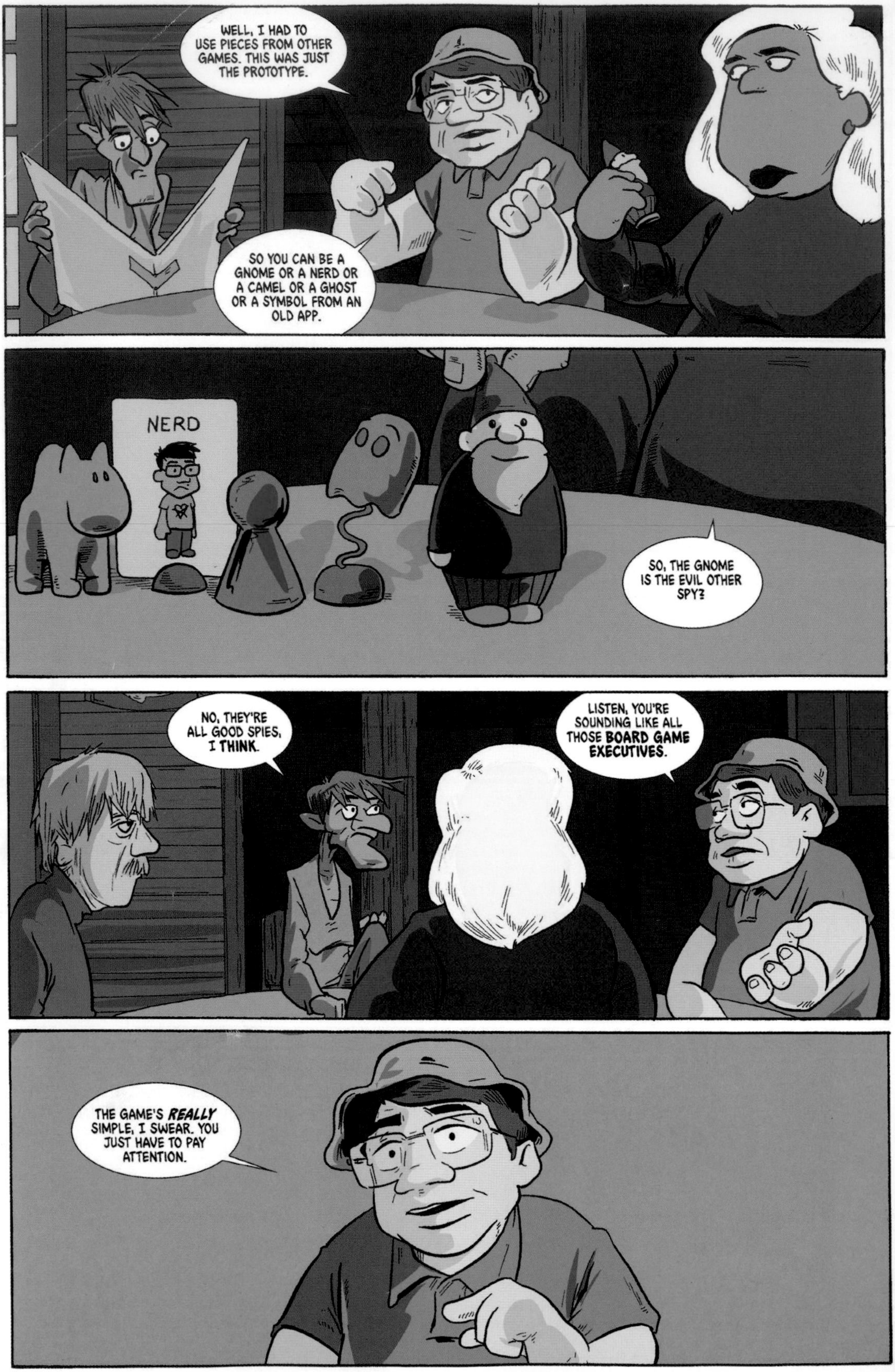
WELL, I HAD TO USE PIECES FROM OTHER GAMES. THIS WAS JUST THE PROTOTYPE.
SO YOU CAN BE A GNOME OR A NERD OR A CAMEL OR A GHOST OR A SYMBOL FROM AN OLD APP.
NERD
SO, THE GNOME IS THE EVIL OTHER SPY?
NO, THEY'RE ALL GOOD SPIES, I **THINK**.
LISTEN, YOU'RE SOUNDING LIKE ALL THOSE **BOARD GAME EXECUTIVES**.
THE GAME'S ***REALLY*** SIMPLE, I SWEAR. YOU JUST HAVE TO PAY ATTENTION.

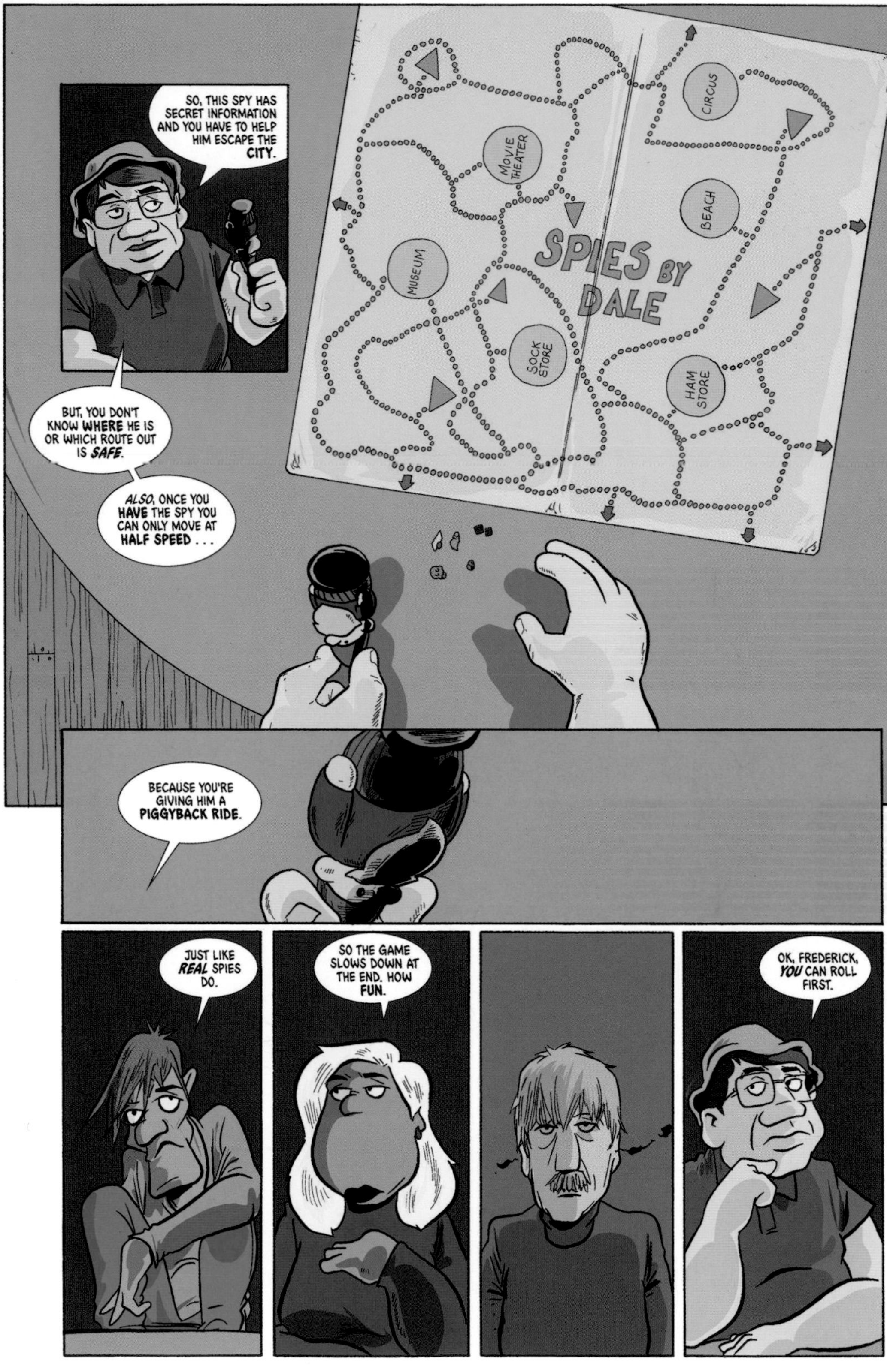
SO, THIS SPY HAS SECRET INFORMATION AND YOU HAVE TO HELP HIM ESCAPE THE **CITY**.
BUT, YOU DON'T KNOW **WHERE** HE IS OR WHICH ROUTE OUT IS ***SAFE***.
ALSO, ONCE YOU **HAVE** THE SPY YOU CAN ONLY MOVE AT **HALF SPEED** . . .
SPIES BY DALE
MOVIE THEATER
CIRCUS
BEACH
MUSEUM
SOCK STORE
HAM STORE
BECAUSE YOU'RE GIVING HIM A **PIGGYBACK RIDE**.
JUST LIKE ***REAL*** SPIES DO.
SO THE GAME SLOWS DOWN AT THE END. HOW **FUN**.
OK, FREDERICK, ***YOU*** CAN ROLL FIRST.

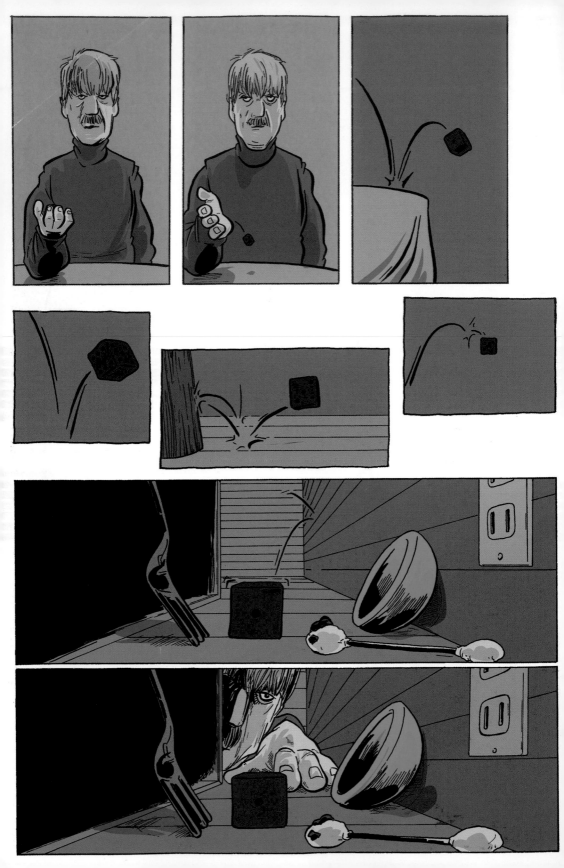

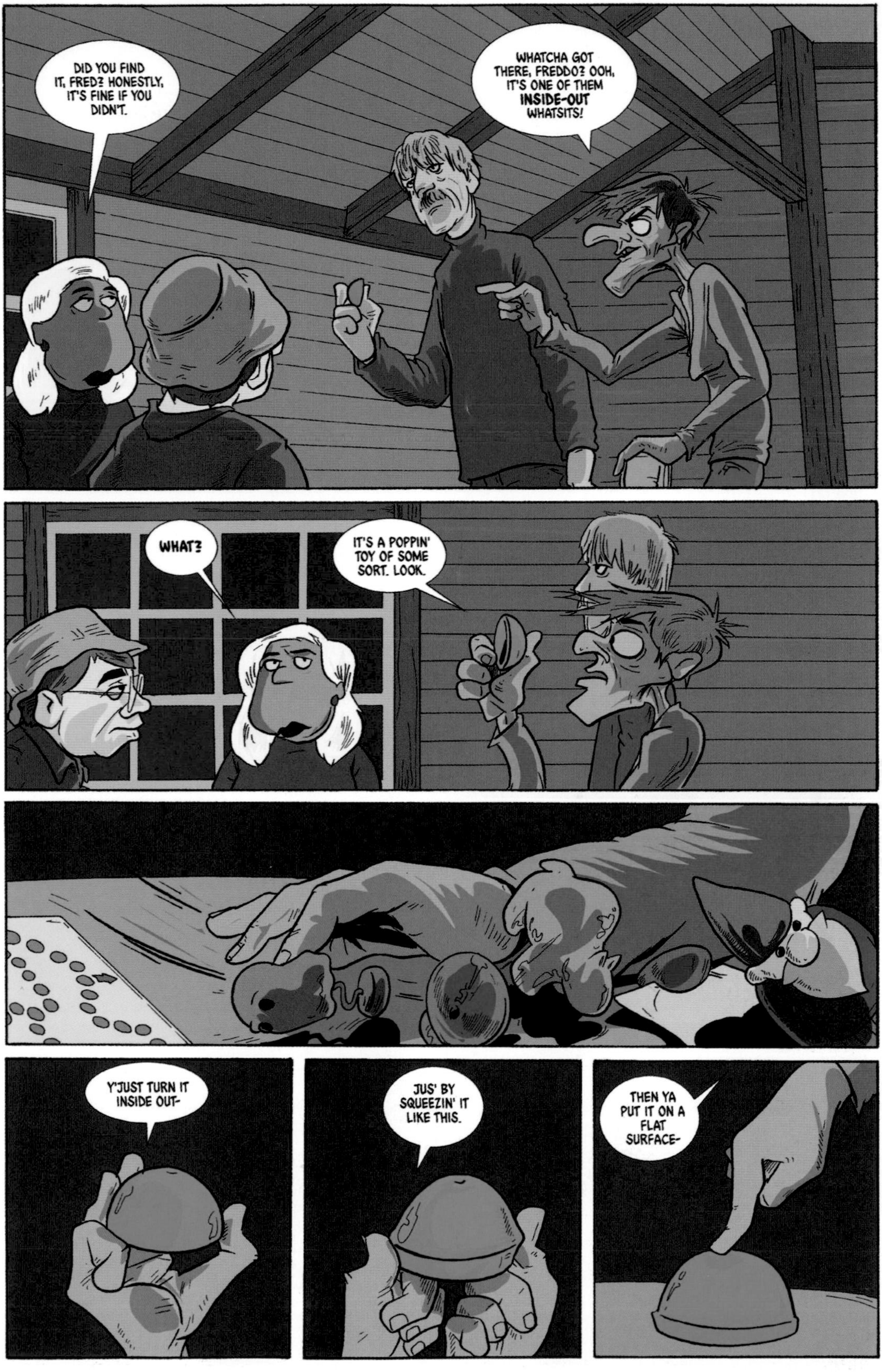

DID YOU FIND IT, FRED? HONESTLY, IT'S FINE IF YOU DIDN'T.
WHATCHA GOT THERE, FREDDO? OOH, IT'S ONE OF THEM **INSIDE-OUT** WHATSITS!
WHAT?
IT'S A POPPIN' TOY OF SOME SORT. LOOK.
Y'JUST TURN IT INSIDE OUT-
JUS' BY SQUEEZIN' IT LIKE THIS.
THEN YA PUT IT ON A FLAT SURFACE-

AN' YA WAIT FOR IT TO *POP*!
SO, WE JUST SIT AND WAIT? FUN.
MORE INTERESTING THAN YOUR BORING GAME.
YOU KNOW WHAT, SHARON? YOU CAN JUST **SHUT IT**.
SHUT YOUR ***STUPID*** MOUTH.
OOH, SHARON WAS **RIGHT** FOR ONCE!
THIS IS ***MUCH*** BETTER THAN THE GAME!

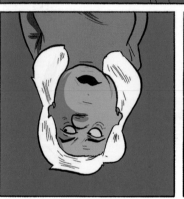

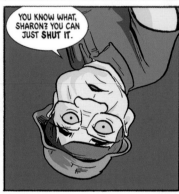

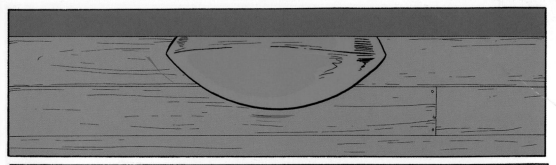

WELL, I DON'T SEE YOU INVENTING ANY FUN GAMES FOR PLAYERS AGED EIGHT TO EIGHTY, LYNNE, SO YOU CAN SHUT UP, TOO!

YOU REALLY WANNA TALK TO ME LIKE THAT, LITTLE BROTHER?

YOU KNOW *WHAT*, LYNNE?

I REALLY DO!

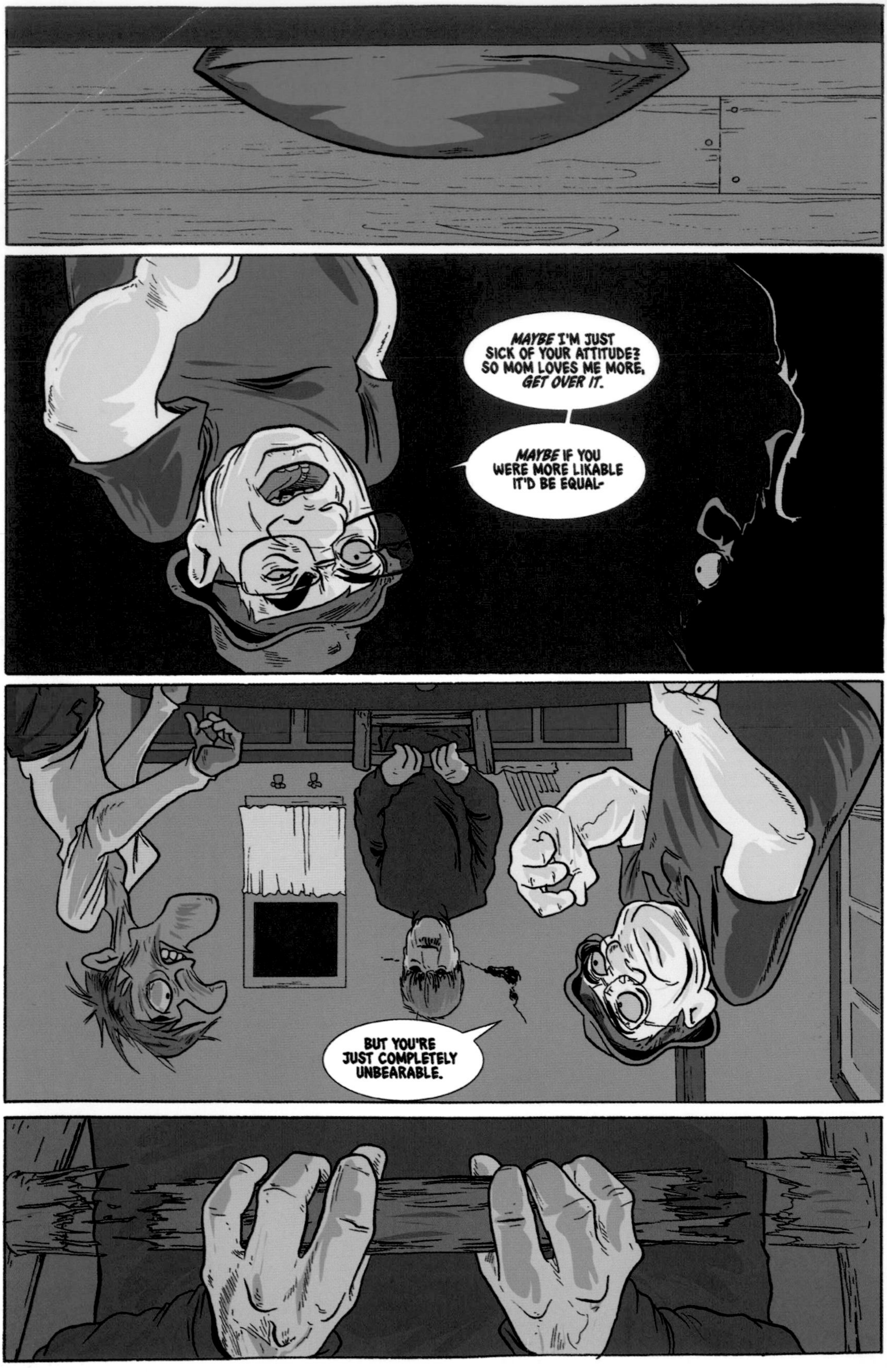
MAYBE I'M JUST SICK OF YOUR ATTITUDE? SO MOM LOVES ME MORE, GET OVER IT.
MAYBE IF YOU WERE MORE LIKABLE IT'D BE EQUAL-
BUT YOU'RE JUST COMPLETELY UNBEARABLE.

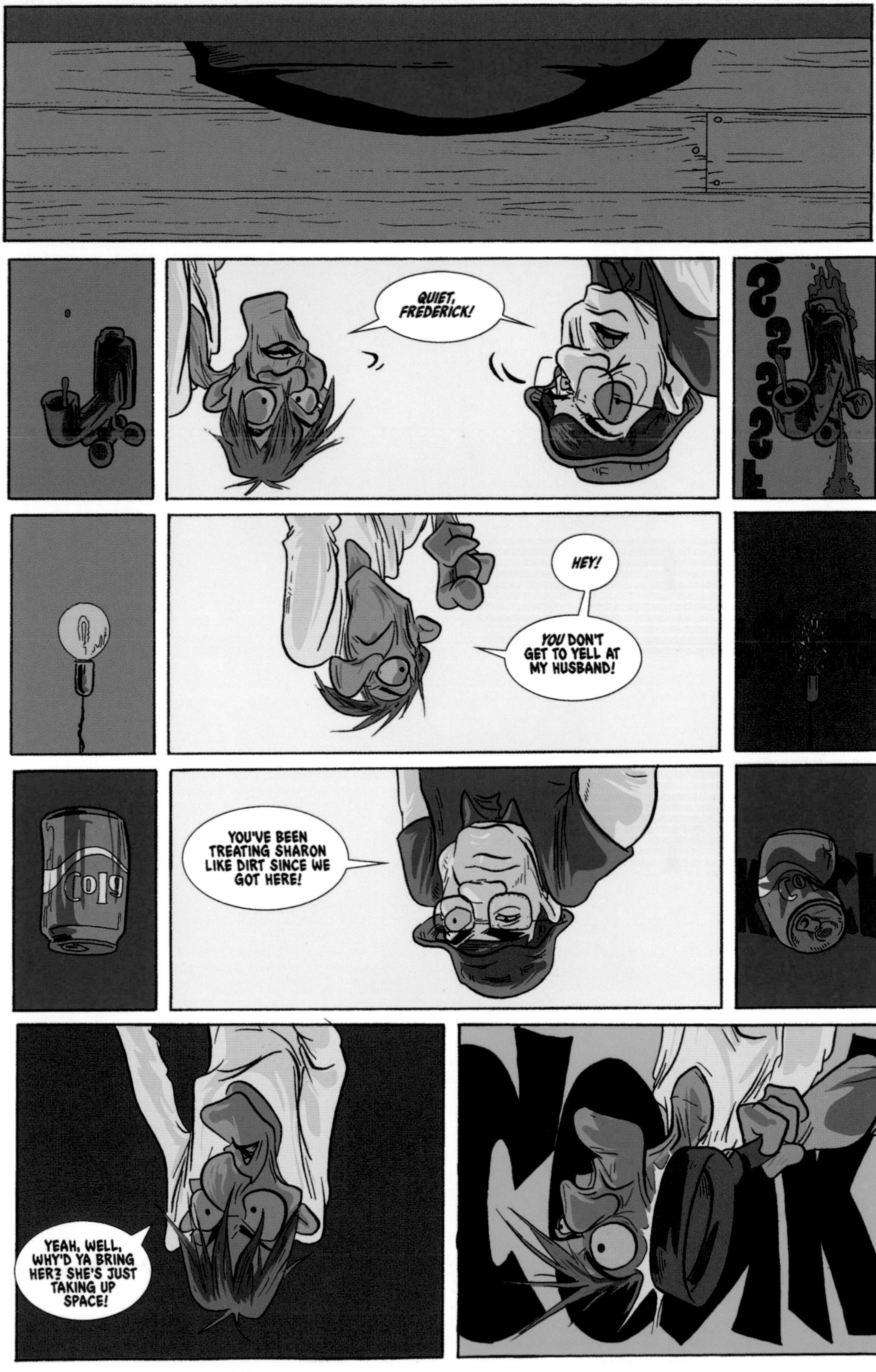
QUIET, FREDERICK!
HEY!
YOU DON'T GET TO YELL AT MY HUSBAND!
YOU'VE BEEN TREATING SHARON LIKE DIRT SINCE WE GOT HERE!
YEAH, WELL, WHY'D YA BRING HER? SHE'S JUST TAKING UP SPACE!

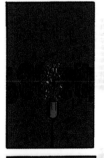

SHARON!

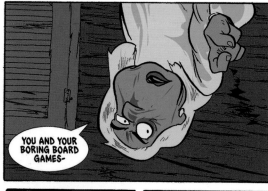

YOU AND YOUR BORING BOARD GAMES—

AND YOUR HORRIBLE SISTER—

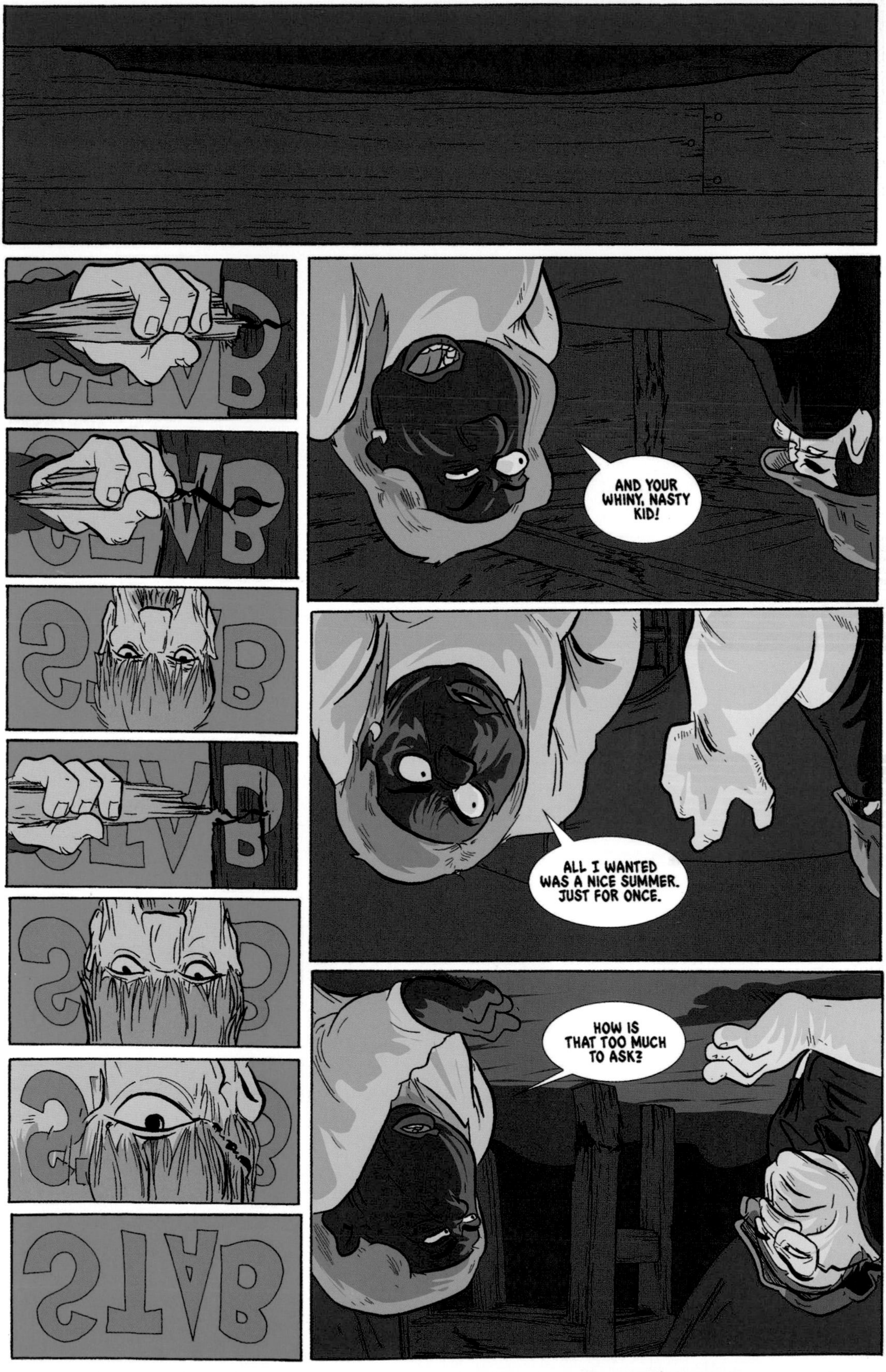
STAB
AND YOUR WHINY, NASTY KID!
ALL I WANTED WAS A NICE SUMMER. JUST FOR ONCE.
HOW IS THAT TOO MUCH TO ASK?

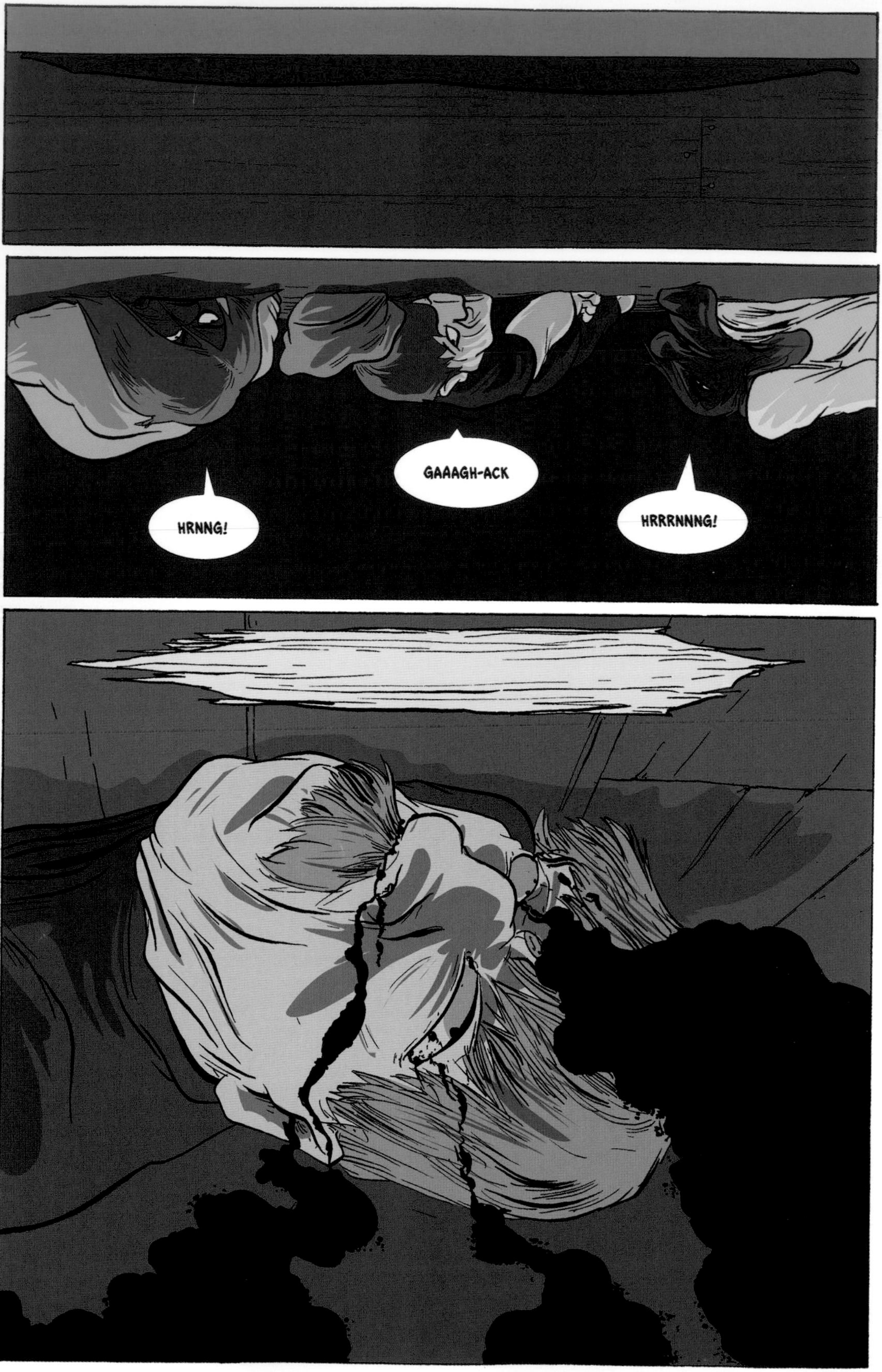
HRNNG!
GAAAGH-ACK
HRRRNNNG!

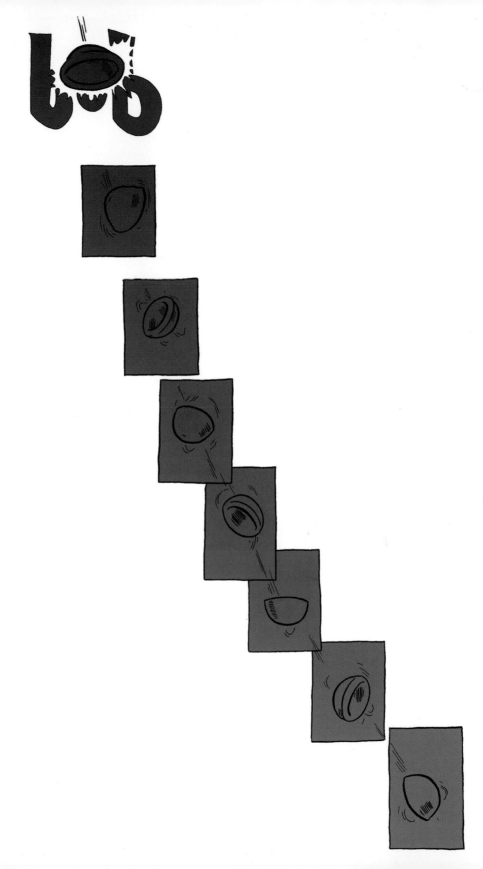

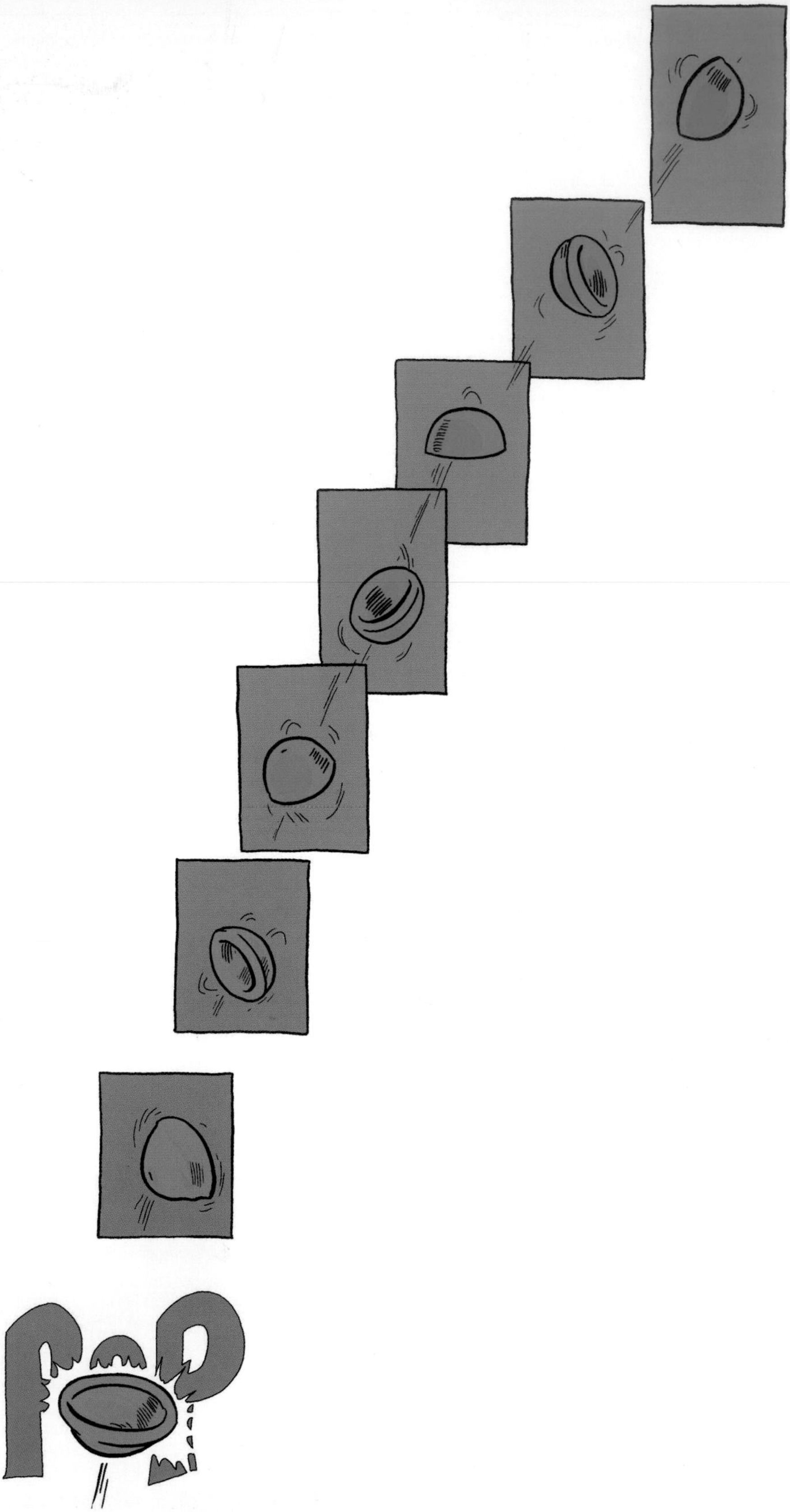
POP

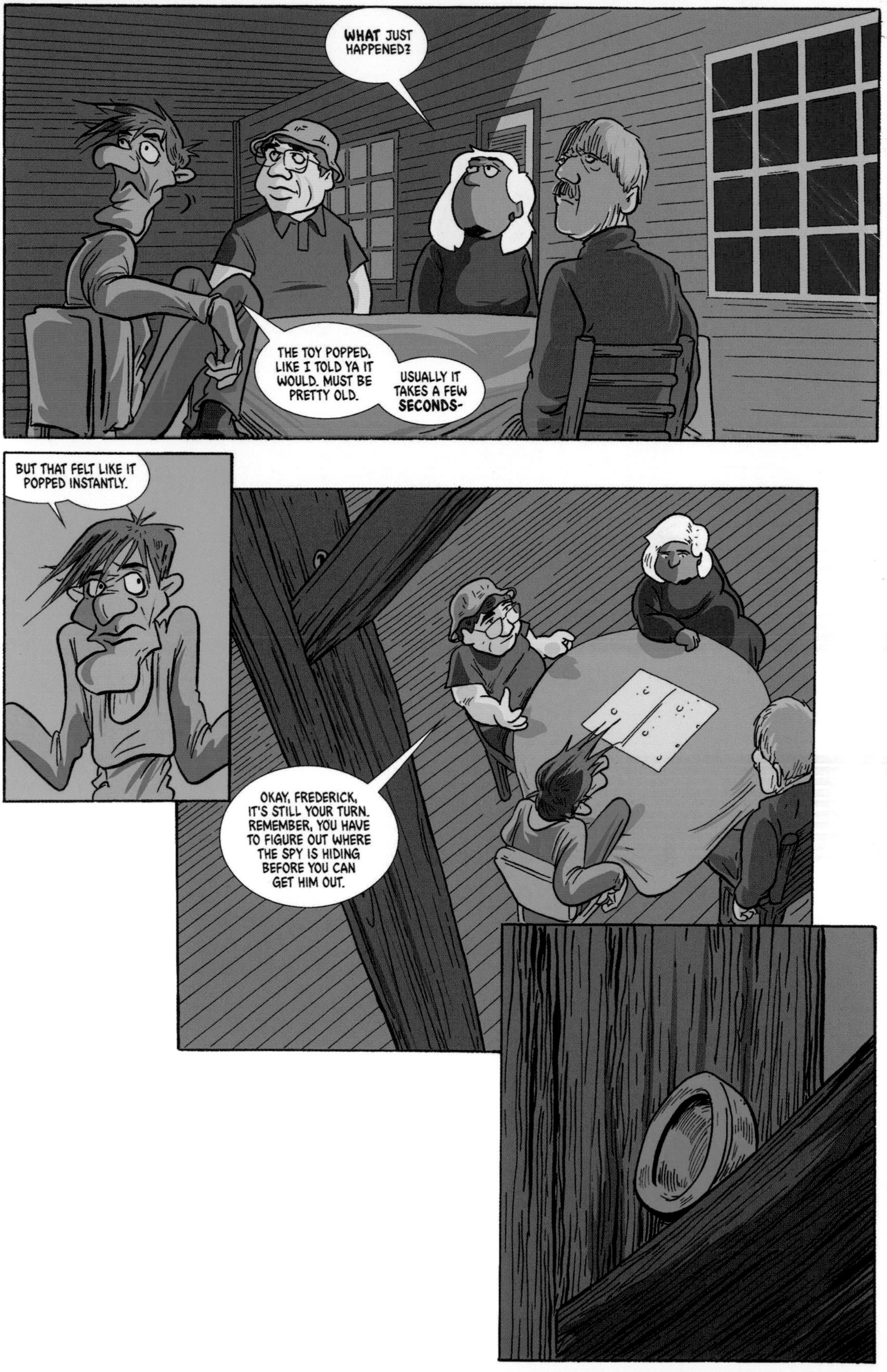
WHAT JUST HAPPENED?
THE TOY POPPED, LIKE I TOLD YA IT WOULD. MUST BE PRETTY OLD.
USUALLY IT TAKES A FEW SECONDS-
BUT THAT FELT LIKE IT POPPED INSTANTLY.
OKAY, FREDERICK, IT'S STILL YOUR TURN. REMEMBER, YOU HAVE TO FIGURE OUT WHERE THE SPY IS HIDING BEFORE YOU CAN GET HIM OUT.

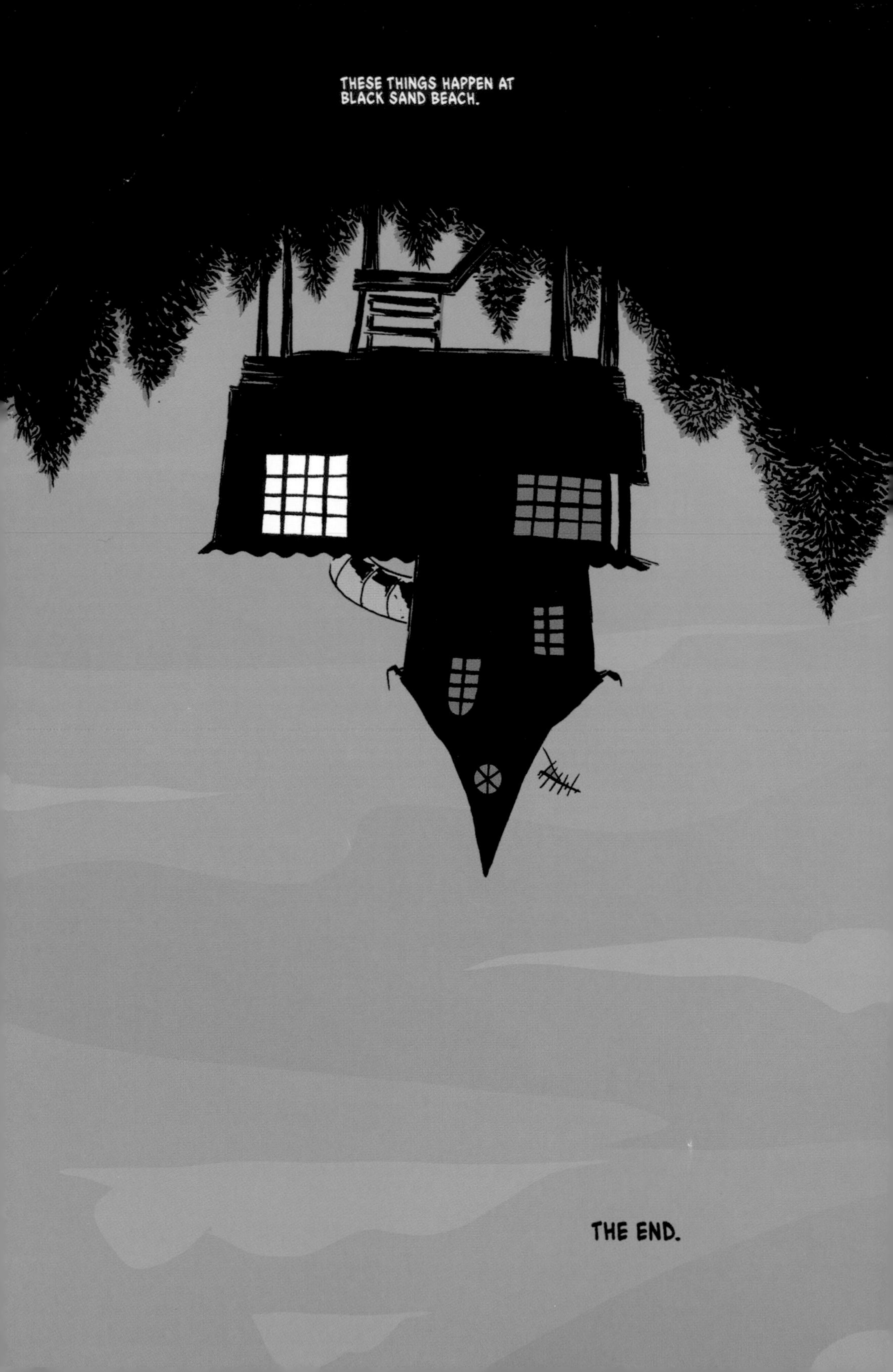
THESE THINGS HAPPEN AT
BLACK SAND BEACH.
THE END.

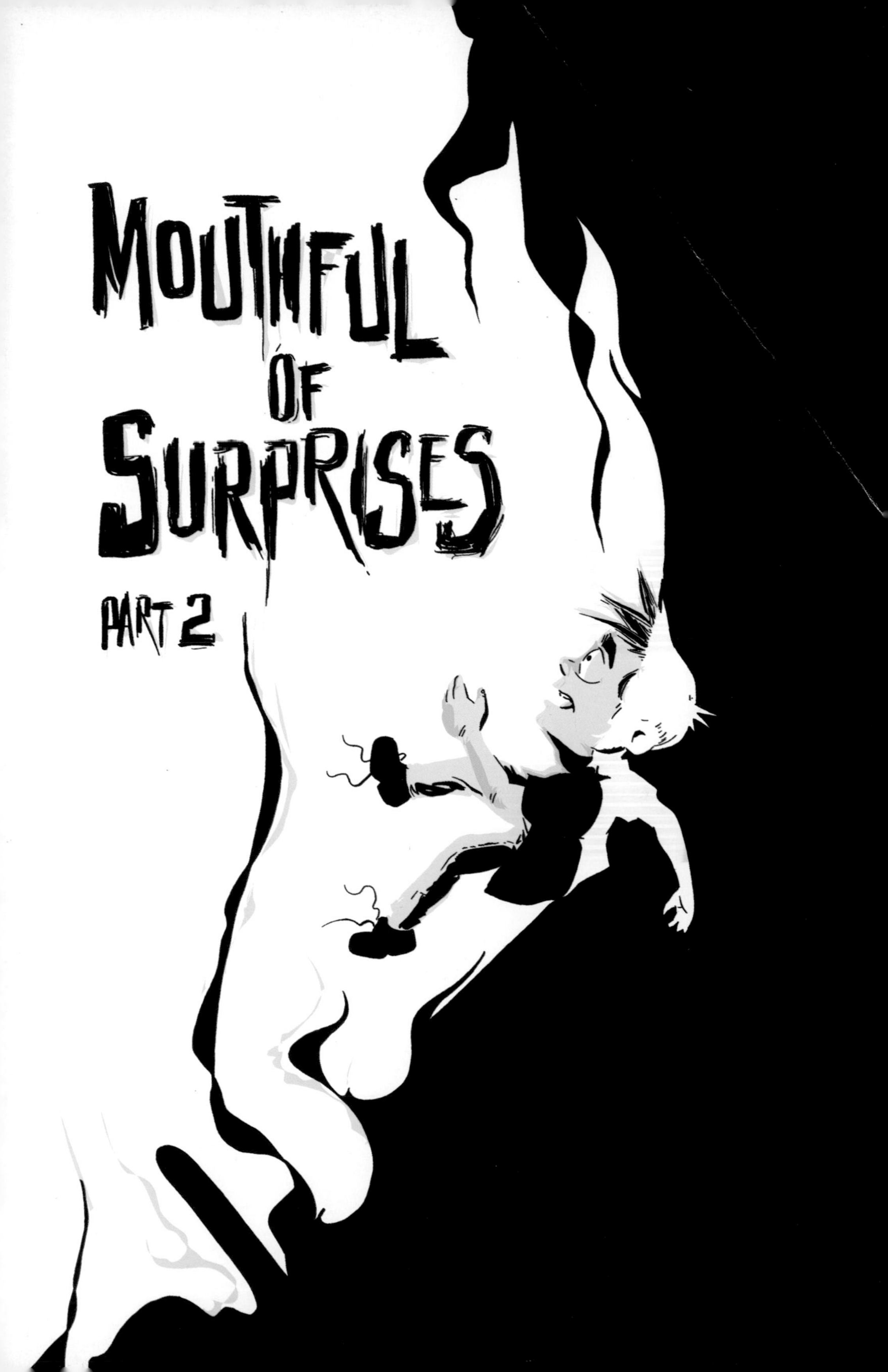
MOUTHFUL OF SURPRISES
PART 2

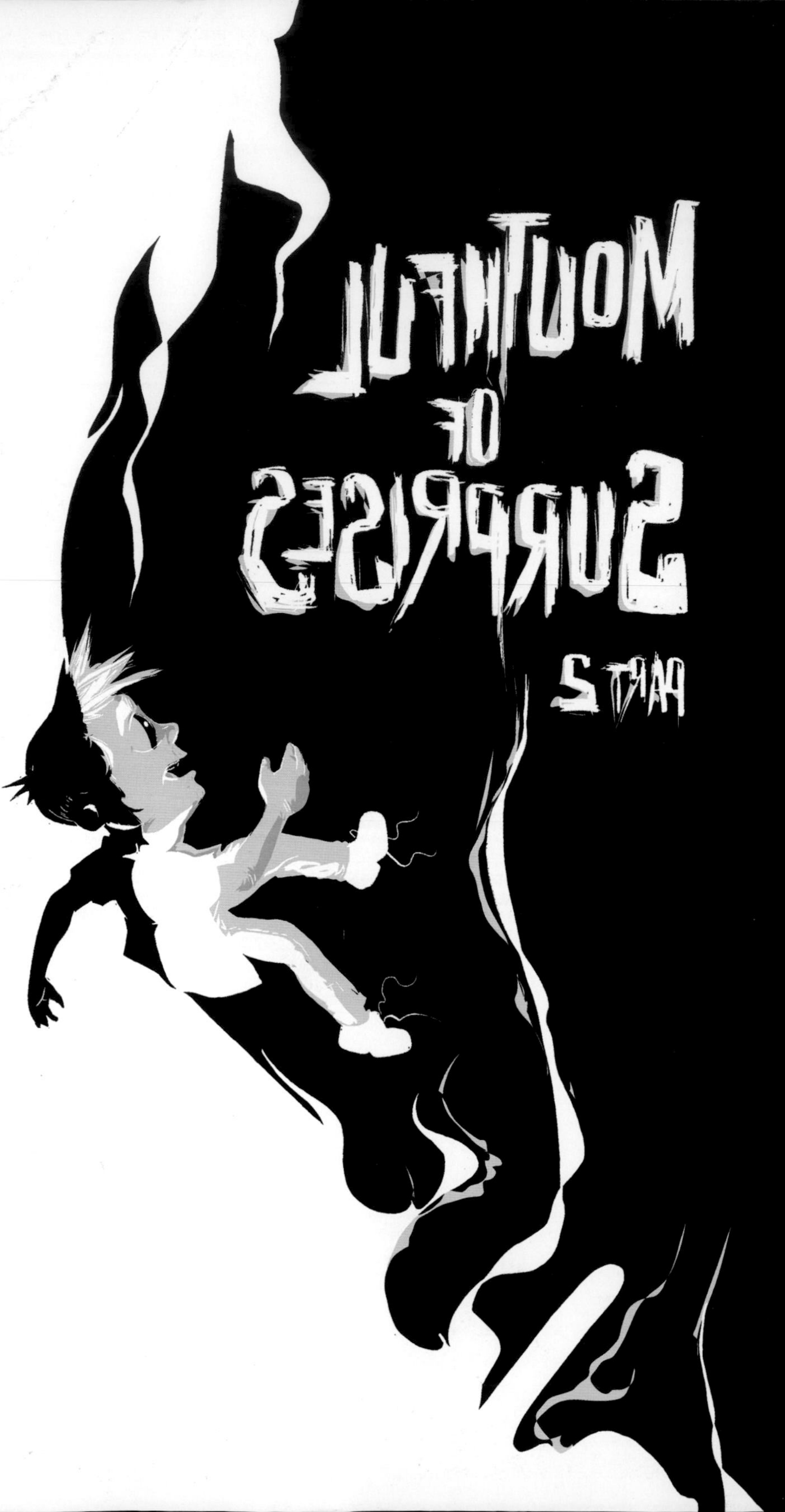
MOUTHFUL
OF
SURPRISES
PART 2

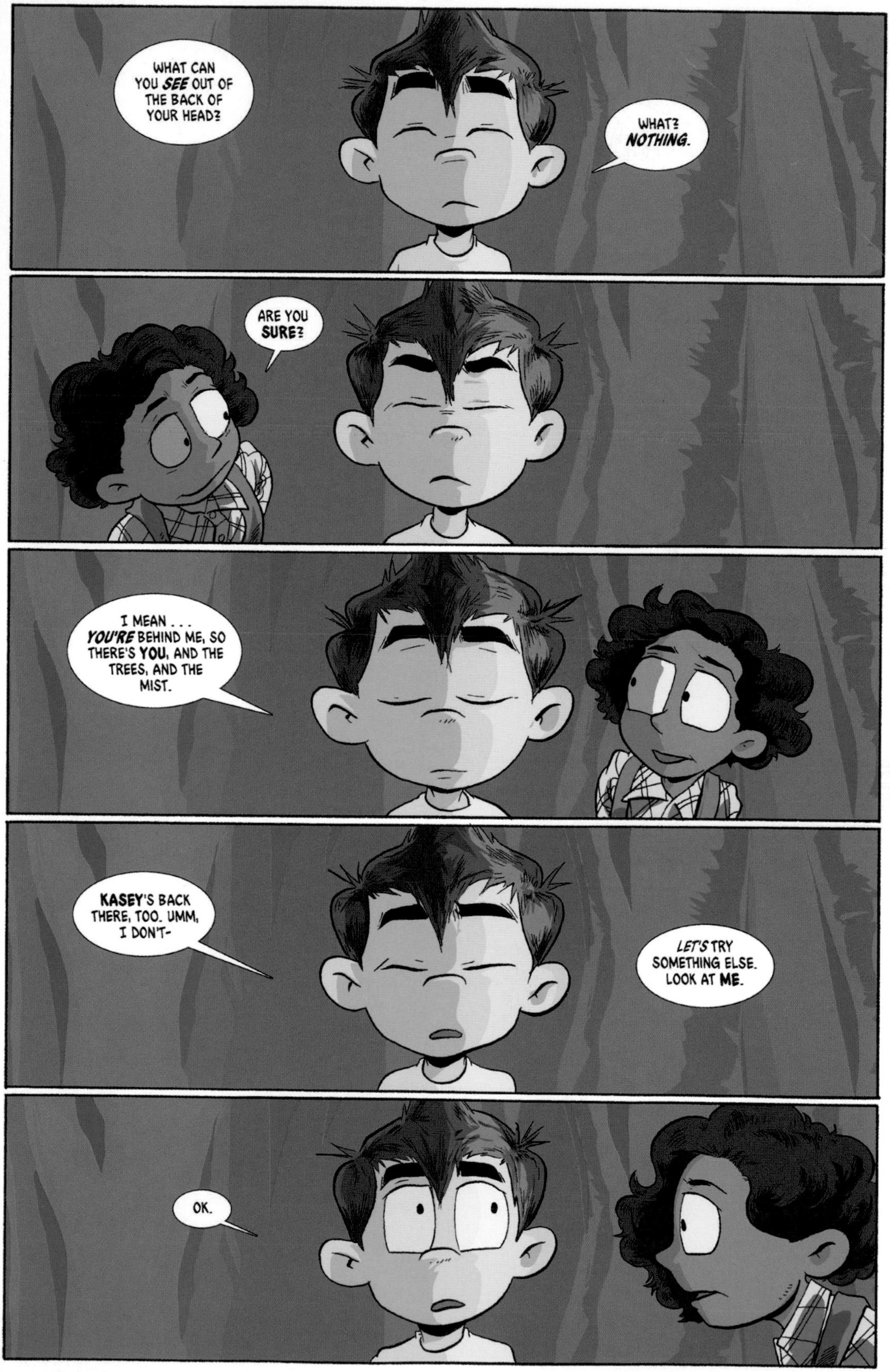
WHAT CAN YOU *SEE* OUT OF THE BACK OF YOUR HEAD?
WHAT? *NOTHING.*
ARE YOU **SURE?**
I MEAN . . . *YOU'RE* BEHIND ME, SO THERE'S **YOU**, AND THE TREES, AND THE MIST.
KASEY'S BACK THERE, TOO. UMM, I DON'T-
LET'S TRY SOMETHING ELSE. LOOK AT **ME**.
OK.

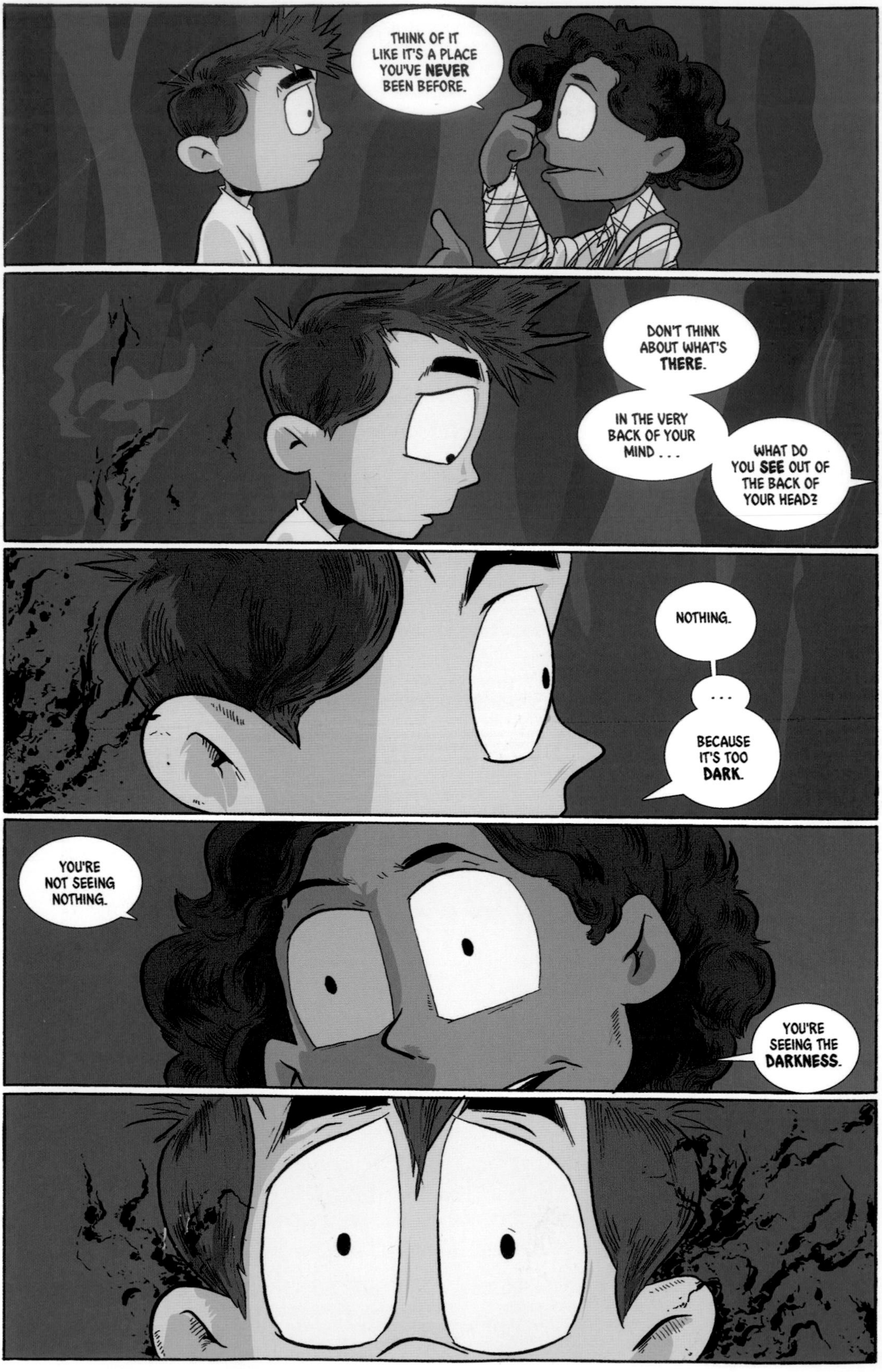
THINK OF IT LIKE IT'S A PLACE YOU'VE **NEVER** BEEN BEFORE.
DON'T THINK ABOUT WHAT'S **THERE**.
IN THE VERY BACK OF YOUR MIND . . .
WHAT DO YOU **SEE** OUT OF THE BACK OF YOUR HEAD?
NOTHING.
. . .
BECAUSE IT'S TOO **DARK**.
YOU'RE NOT SEEING NOTHING.
YOU'RE SEEING THE **DARKNESS**.

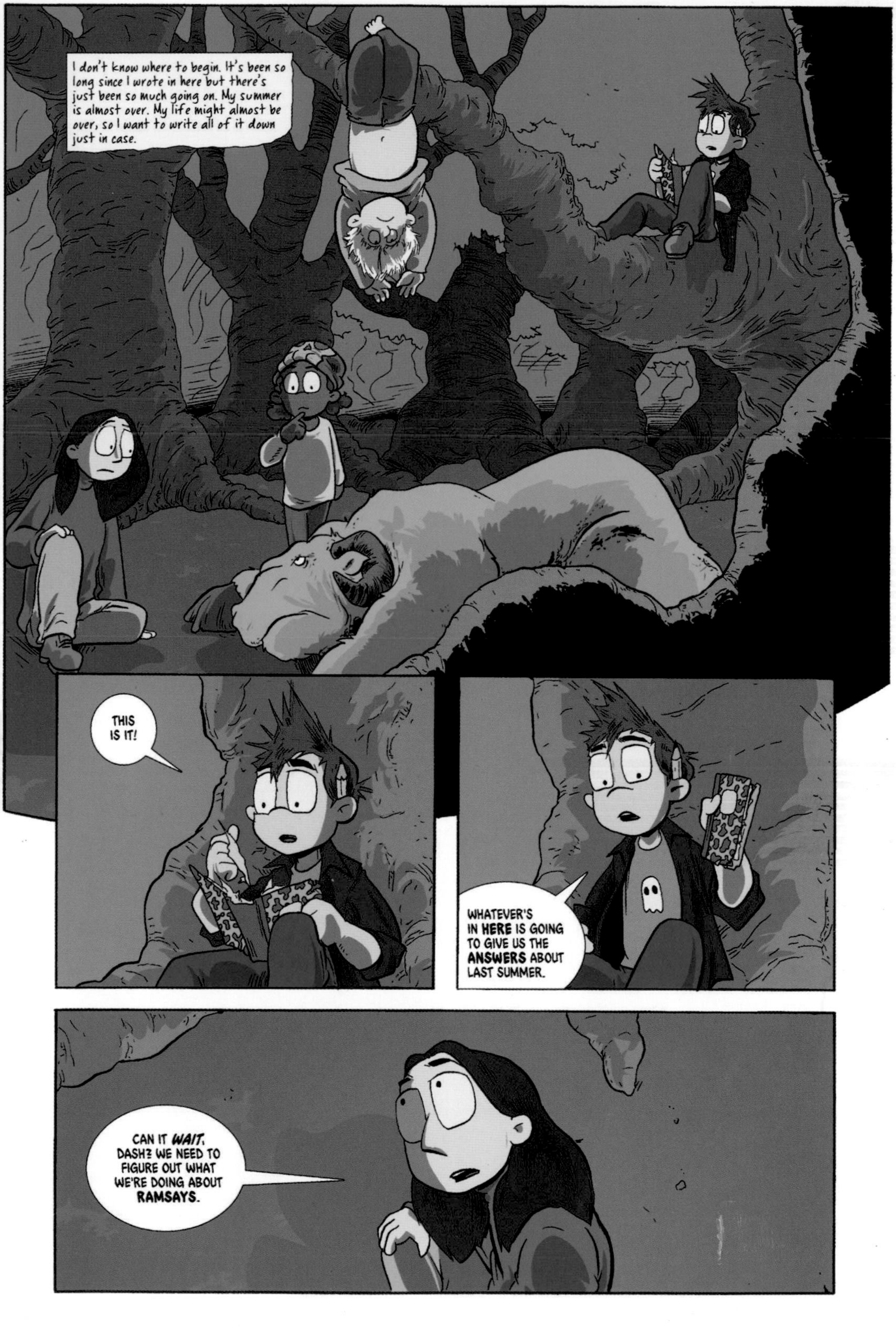
I don't know where to begin. It's been so long since I wrote in here but there's just been so much going on. My summer is almost over. My life might almost be over, so I want to write all of it down just in case.
THIS IS IT!
WHATEVER'S IN HERE IS GOING TO GIVE US THE ANSWERS ABOUT LAST SUMMER.
CAN IT WAIT, DASH? WE NEED TO FIGURE OUT WHAT WE'RE DOING ABOUT RAMSAYS.

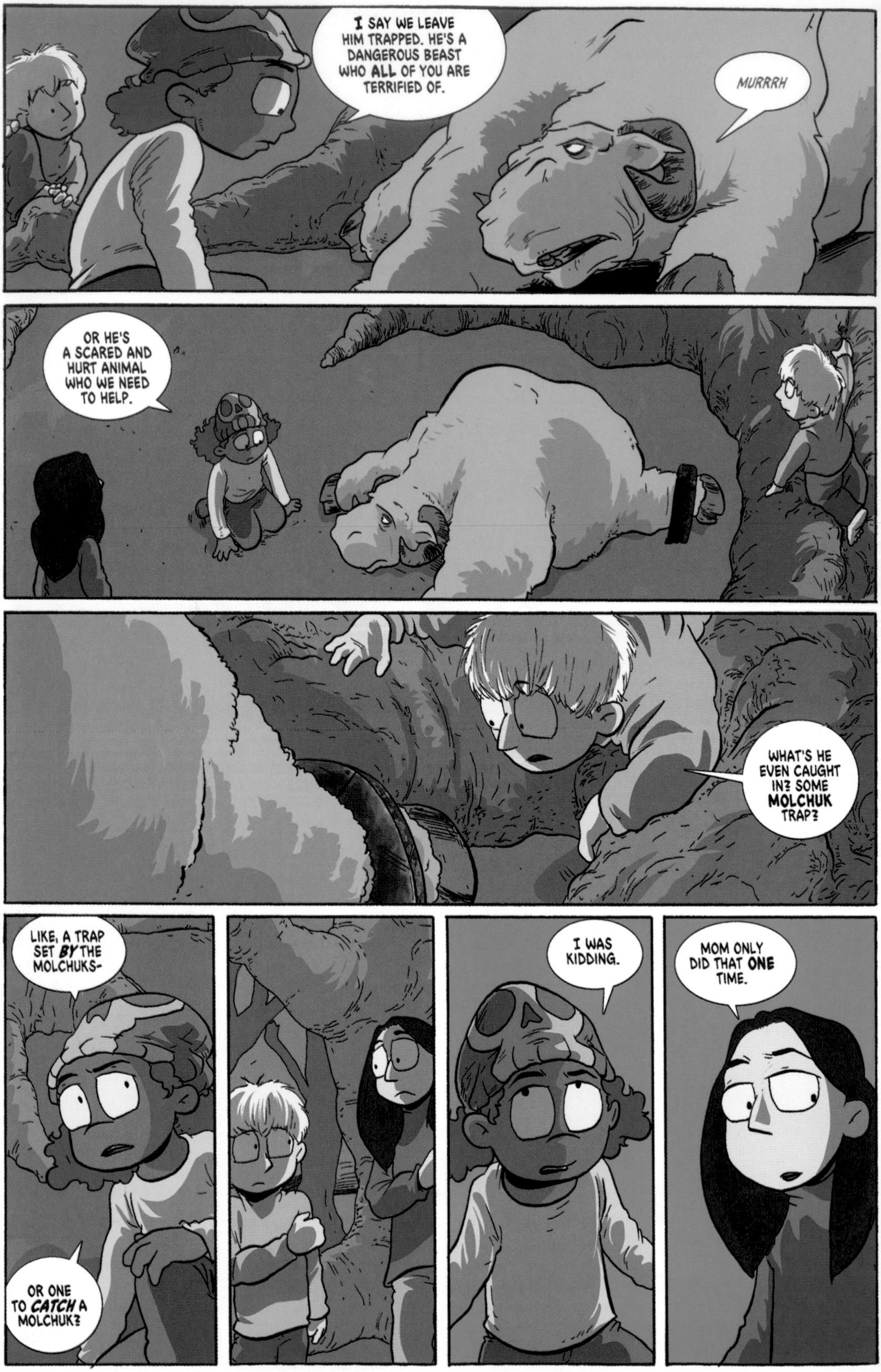
I SAY WE LEAVE HIM TRAPPED. HE'S A DANGEROUS BEAST WHO ALL OF YOU ARE TERRIFIED OF.
MURRRH
OR HE'S A SCARED AND HURT ANIMAL WHO WE NEED TO HELP.
WHAT'S HE EVEN CAUGHT IN? SOME MOLCHUK TRAP?
LIKE, A TRAP SET BY THE MOLCHUKS-
OR ONE TO CATCH A MOLCHUK?
I WAS KIDDING.
MOM ONLY DID THAT ONE TIME.

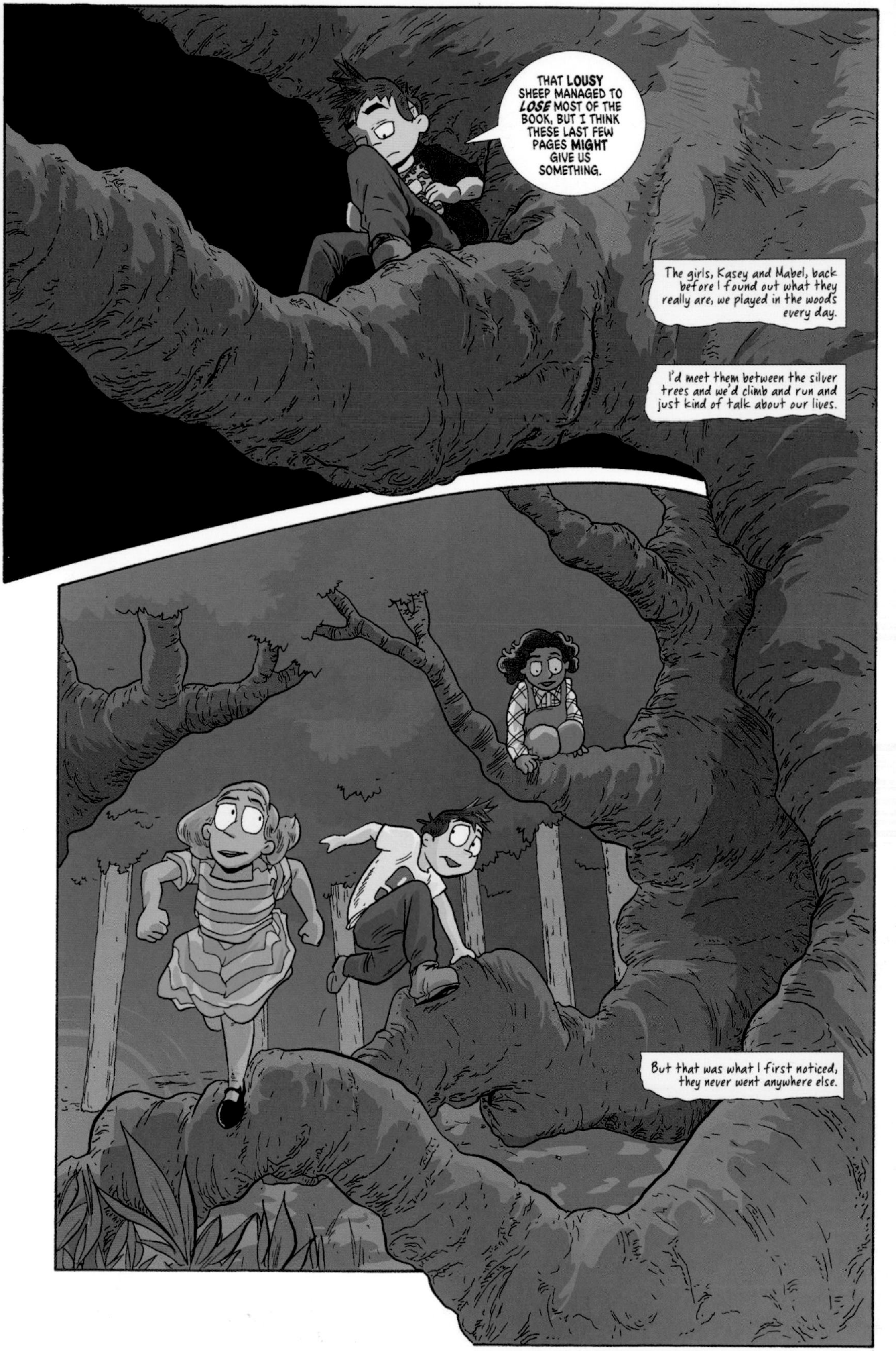
THAT **LOUSY** SHEEP MANAGED TO ***LOSE*** MOST OF THE BOOK, BUT I THINK THESE LAST FEW PAGES **MIGHT** GIVE US SOMETHING.
The girls, Kasey and Mabel, back before I found out what they really are, we played in the woods every day.
I'd meet them between the silver trees and we'd climb and run and just kind of talk about our lives.
But that was what I first noticed, they never went anywhere else.

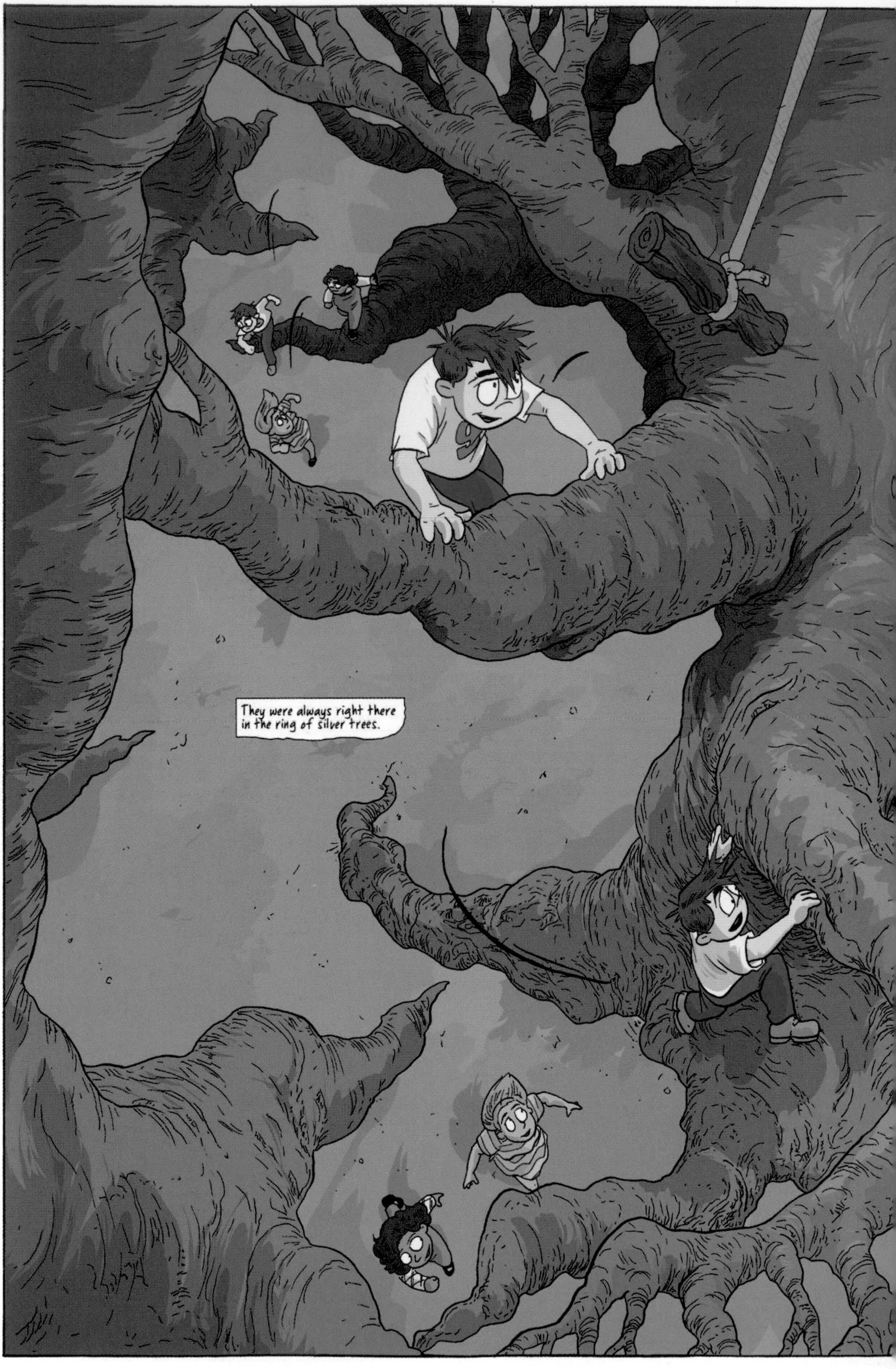
They were always right there
in the ring of silver trees.

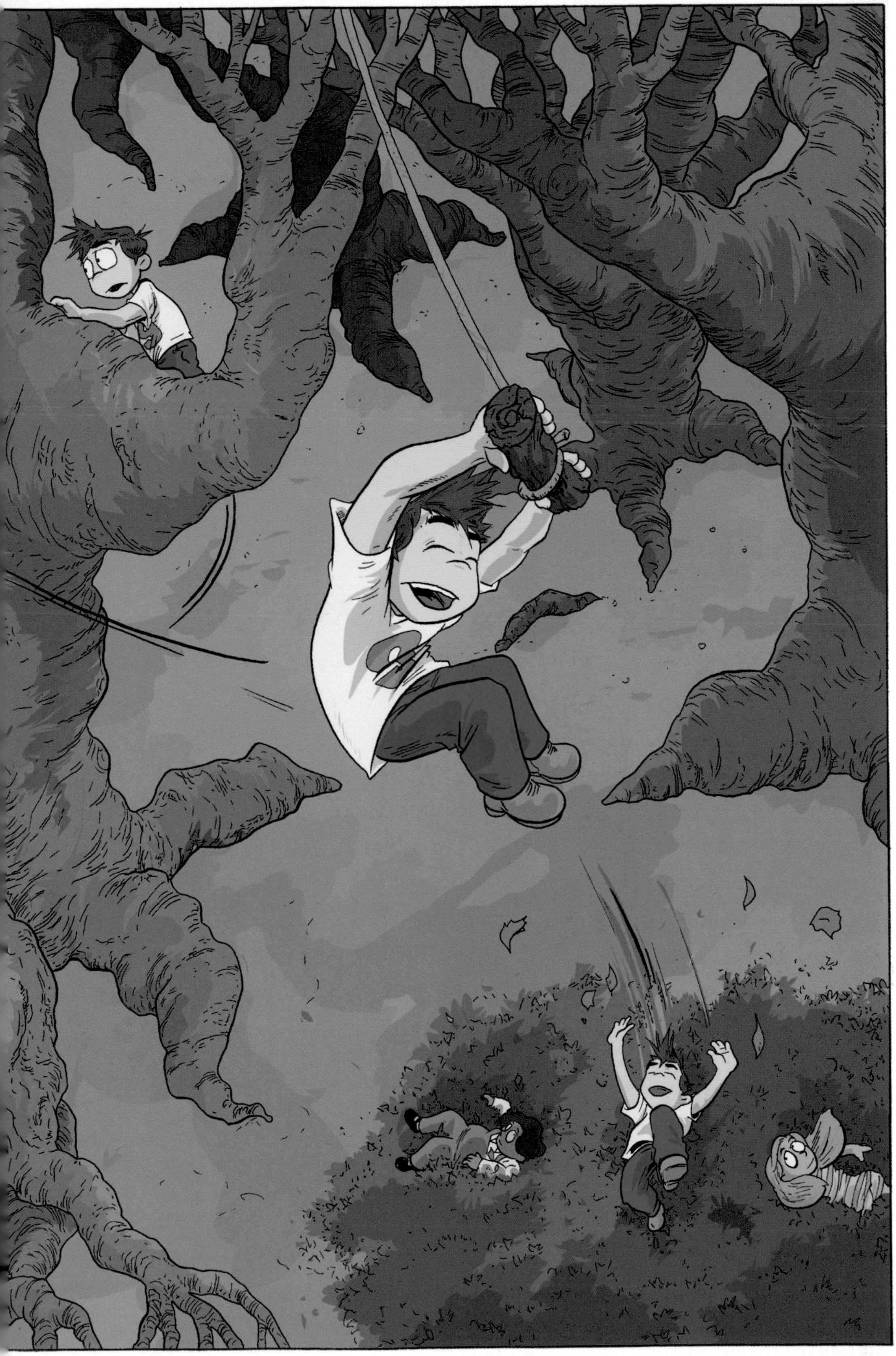

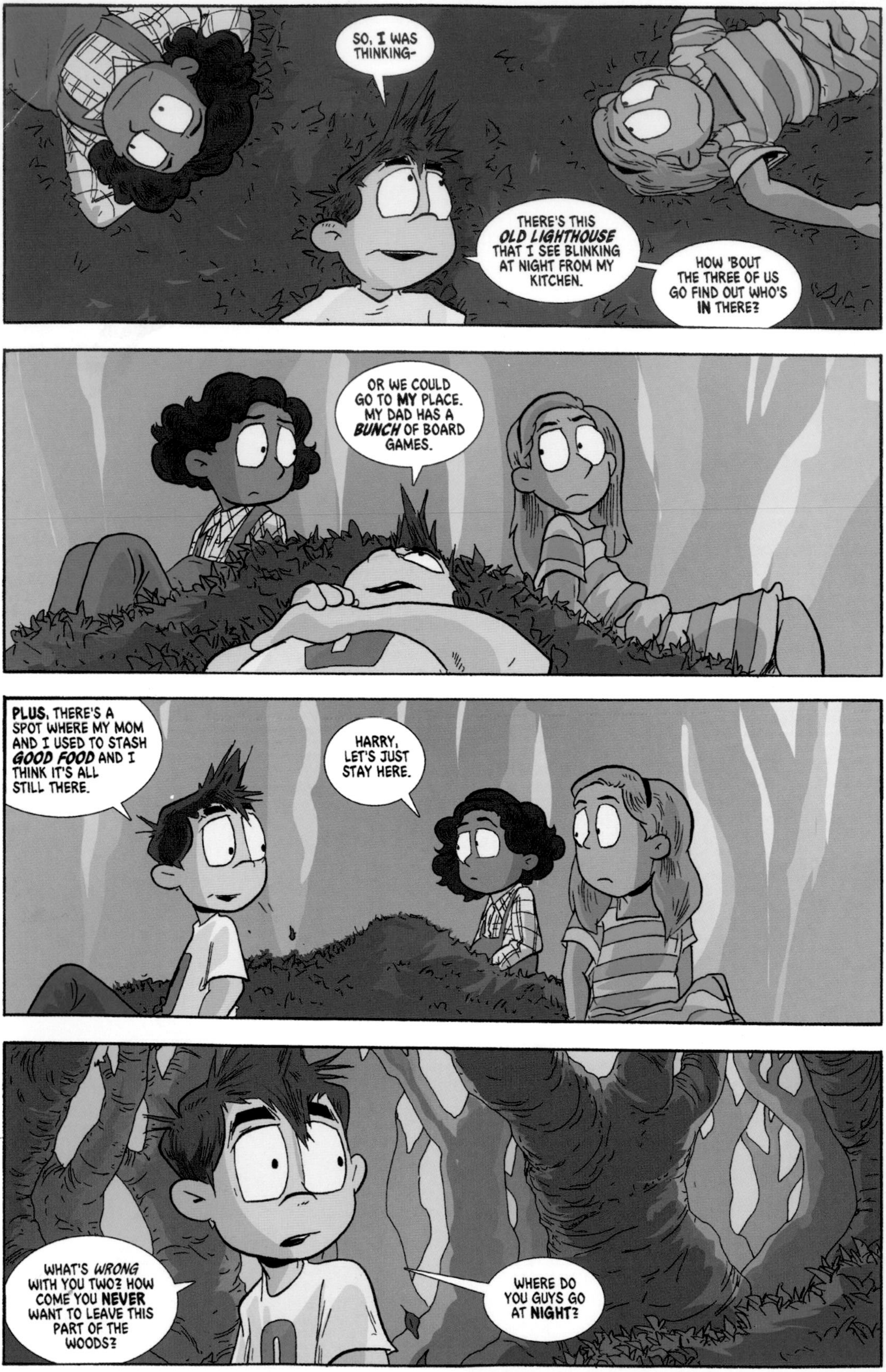
SO, I WAS THINKING-
THERE'S THIS OLD LIGHTHOUSE THAT I SEE BLINKING AT NIGHT FROM MY KITCHEN.
HOW 'BOUT THE THREE OF US GO FIND OUT WHO'S IN THERE?
OR WE COULD GO TO MY PLACE. MY DAD HAS A BUNCH OF BOARD GAMES.
PLUS, THERE'S A SPOT WHERE MY MOM AND I USED TO STASH GOOD FOOD AND I THINK IT'S ALL STILL THERE.
HARRY, LET'S JUST STAY HERE.
WHAT'S WRONG WITH YOU TWO? HOW COME YOU NEVER WANT TO LEAVE THIS PART OF THE WOODS?
WHERE DO YOU GUYS GO AT NIGHT?

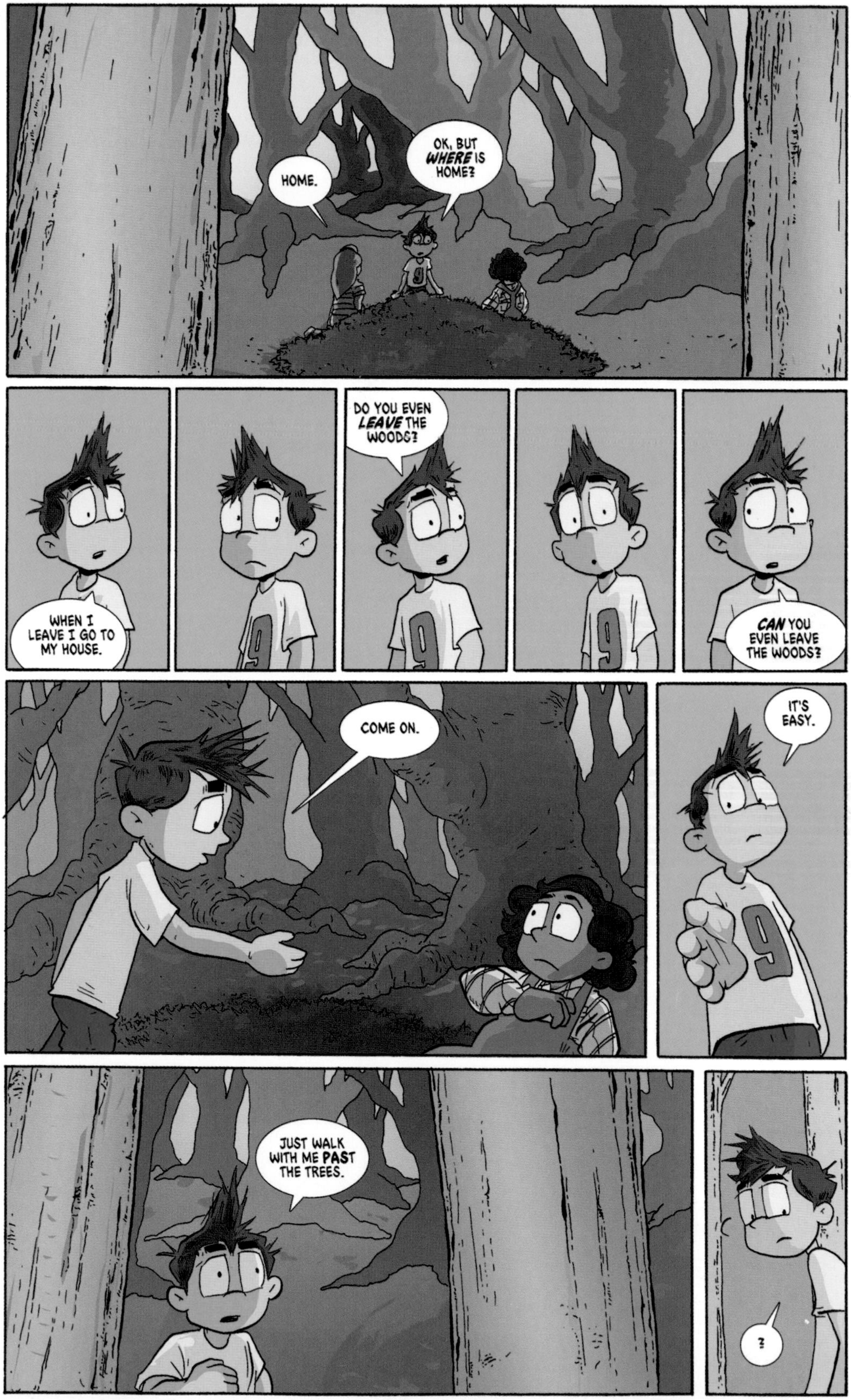
HOME.
OK, BUT WHERE IS HOME?
WHEN I LEAVE I GO TO MY HOUSE.
DO YOU EVEN LEAVE THE WOODS?
CAN YOU EVEN LEAVE THE WOODS?
COME ON.
IT'S EASY.
JUST WALK WITH ME PAST THE TREES.
?

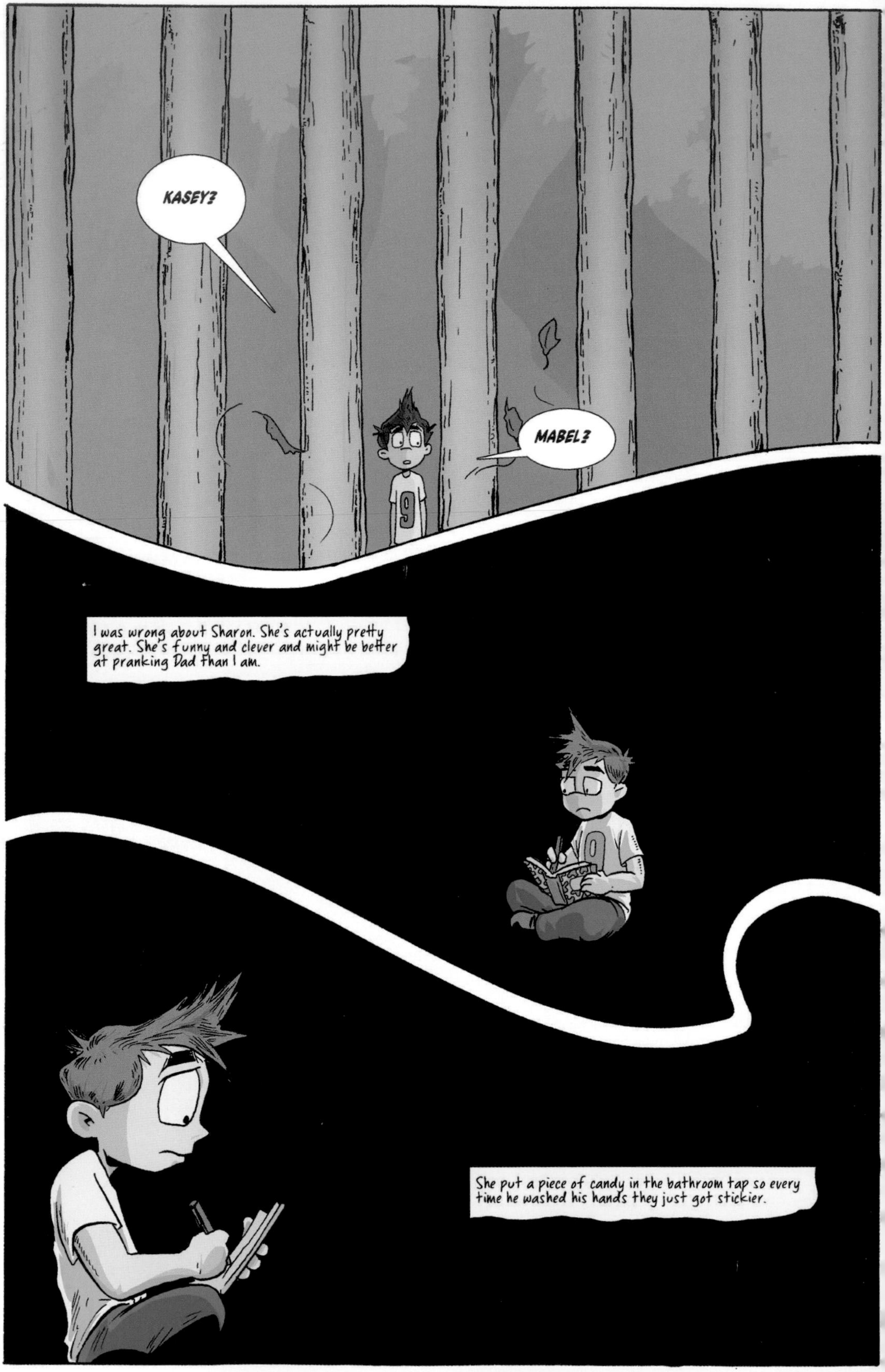
KASEY?
MABEL?
I was wrong about Sharon. She's actually pretty great. She's funny and clever and might be better at pranking Dad than I am.
She put a piece of candy in the bathroom tap so every time he washed his hands they just got stickier.

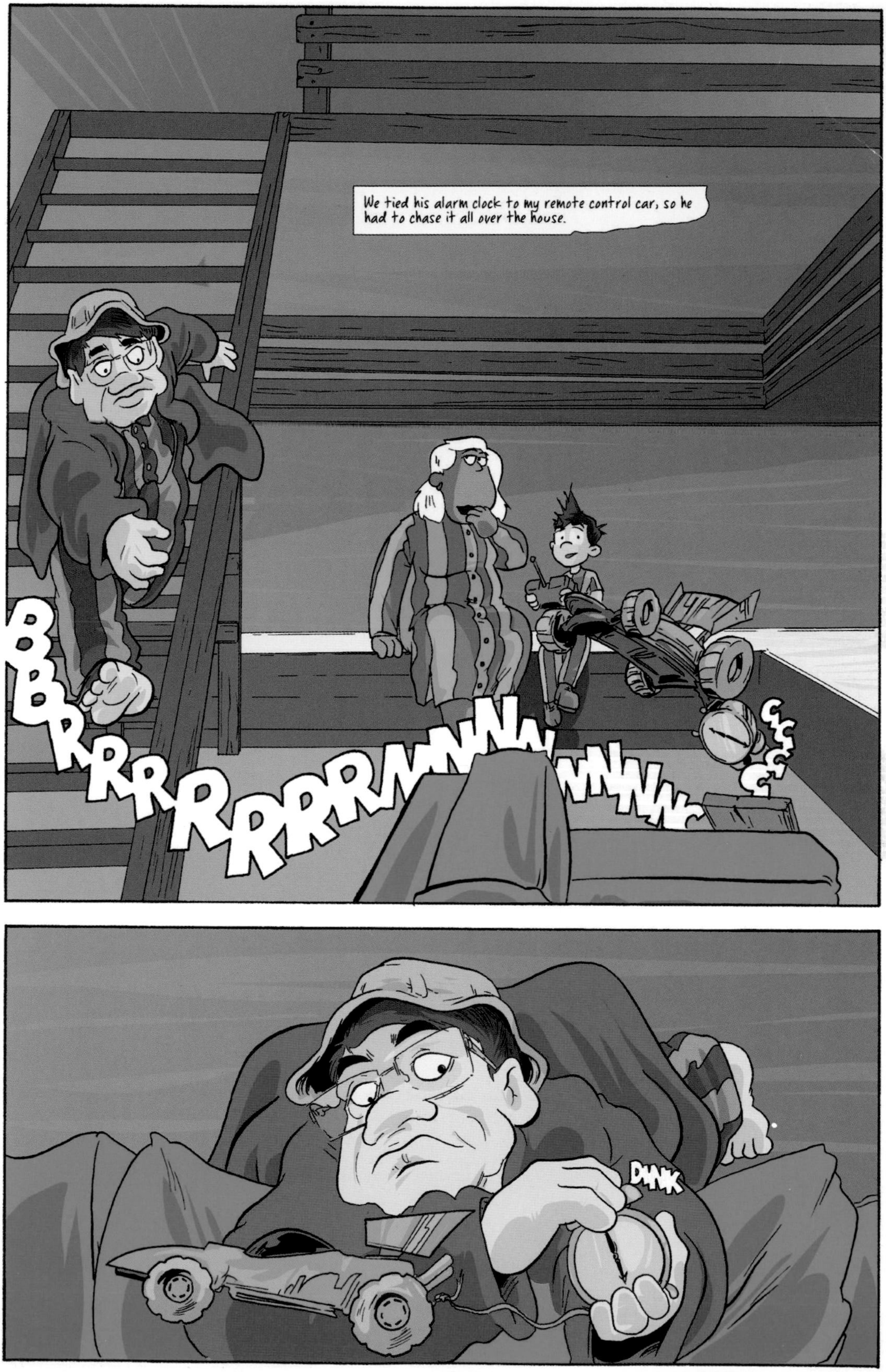
We tied his alarm clock to my remote control car, so he had to chase it all over the house.
BBRRRRRRRNNNNNNNNNNNC
CCCC
DINK

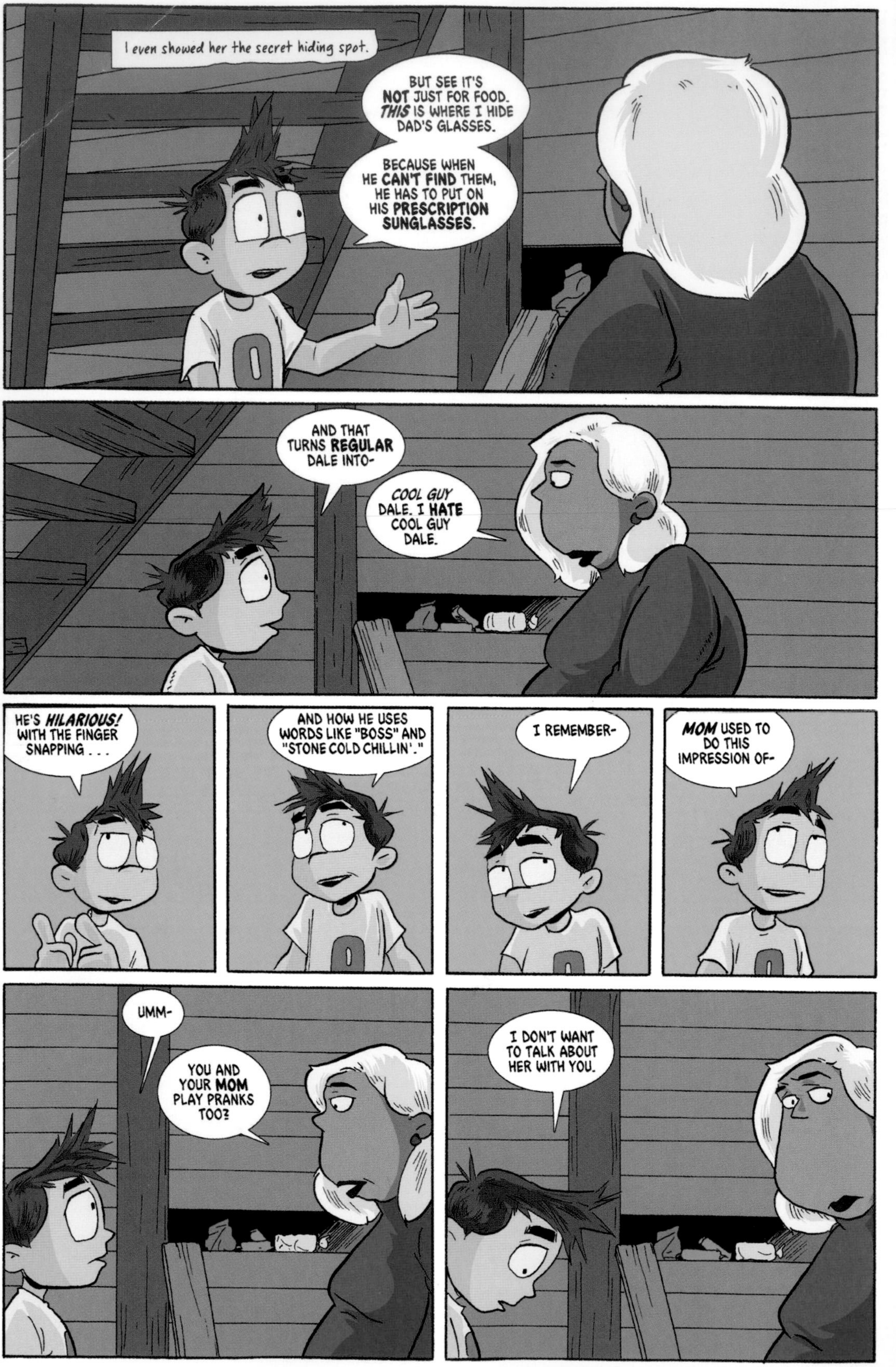

I even showed her the secret hiding spot.
BUT SEE IT'S NOT JUST FOR FOOD. THIS IS WHERE I HIDE DAD'S GLASSES.
BECAUSE WHEN HE CAN'T FIND THEM, HE HAS TO PUT ON HIS PRESCRIPTION SUNGLASSES.
AND THAT TURNS REGULAR DALE INTO-
COOL GUY DALE. I HATE COOL GUY DALE.
HE'S HILARIOUS! WITH THE FINGER SNAPPING . . .
AND HOW HE USES WORDS LIKE "BOSS" AND "STONE COLD CHILLIN'."
I REMEMBER-
MOM USED TO DO THIS IMPRESSION OF-
UMM-
YOU AND YOUR MOM PLAY PRANKS TOO?
I DON'T WANT TO TALK ABOUT HER WITH YOU.

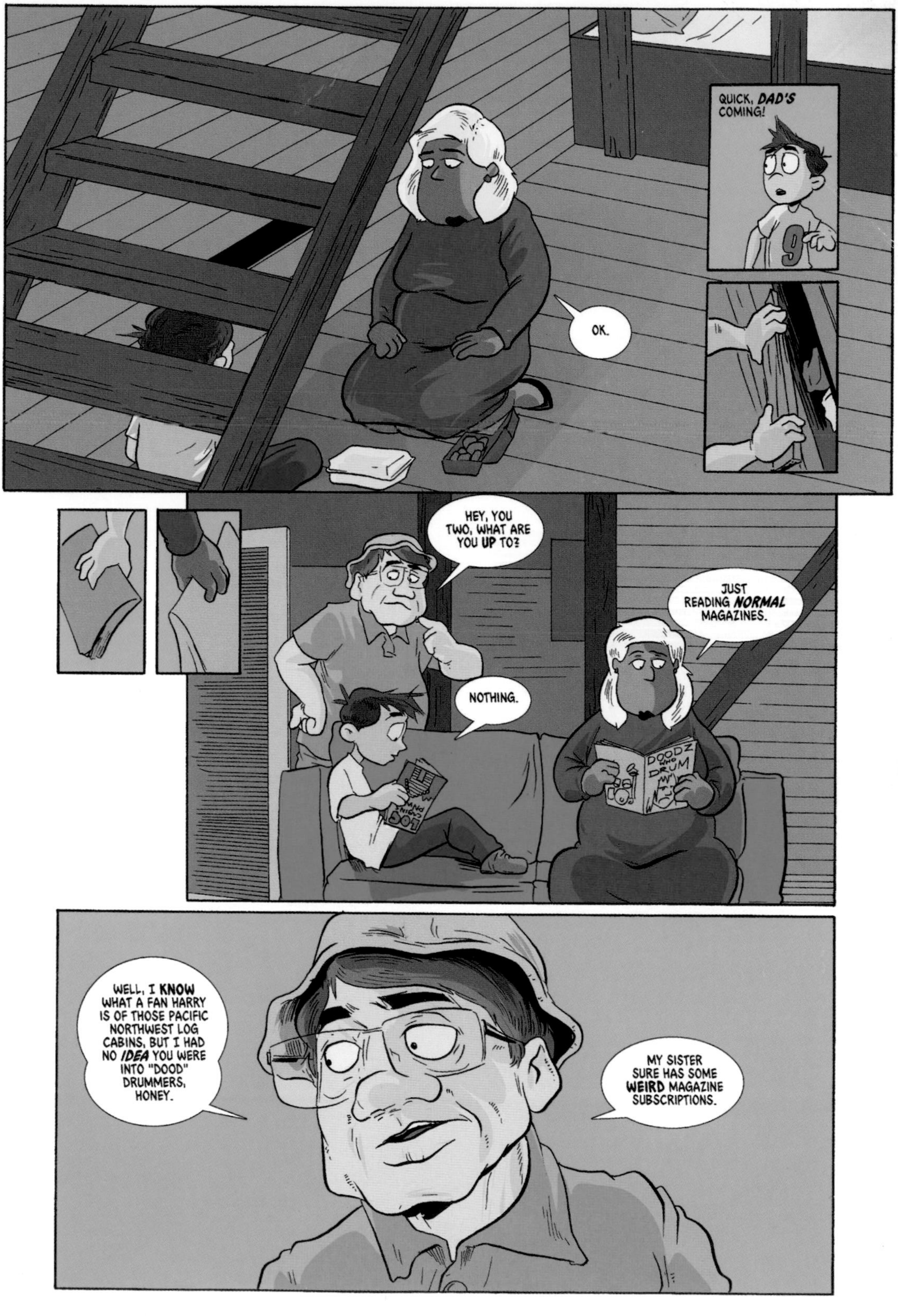
QUICK, DAD'S COMING!
OK.
HEY, YOU TWO, WHAT ARE YOU UP TO?
NOTHING.
JUST READING NORMAL MAGAZINES.
DOODZ WHO DRUM
WELL, I KNOW WHAT A FAN HARRY IS OF THOSE PACIFIC NORTHWEST LOG CABINS, BUT I HAD NO IDEA YOU WERE INTO "DOOD" DRUMMERS, HONEY.
MY SISTER SURE HAS SOME WEIRD MAGAZINE SUBSCRIPTIONS.

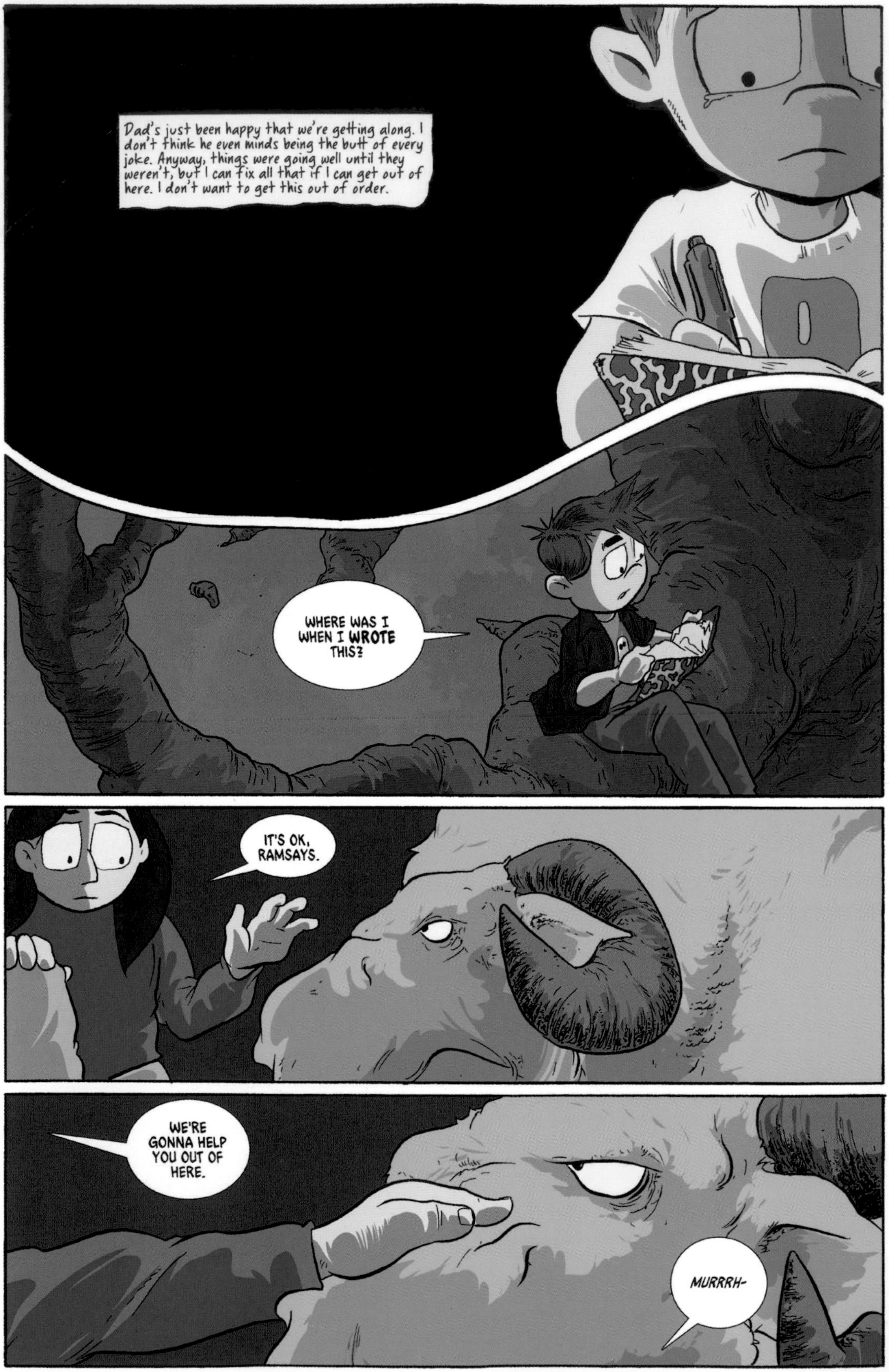
Dad's just been happy that we're getting along. I don't think he even minds being the butt of every joke. Anyway, things were going well until they weren't, but I can fix all that if I can get out of here. I don't want to get this out of order.
WHERE WAS I WHEN I WROTE THIS?
IT'S OK, RAMSAYS.
WE'RE GONNA HELP YOU OUT OF HERE.
MURRRH-

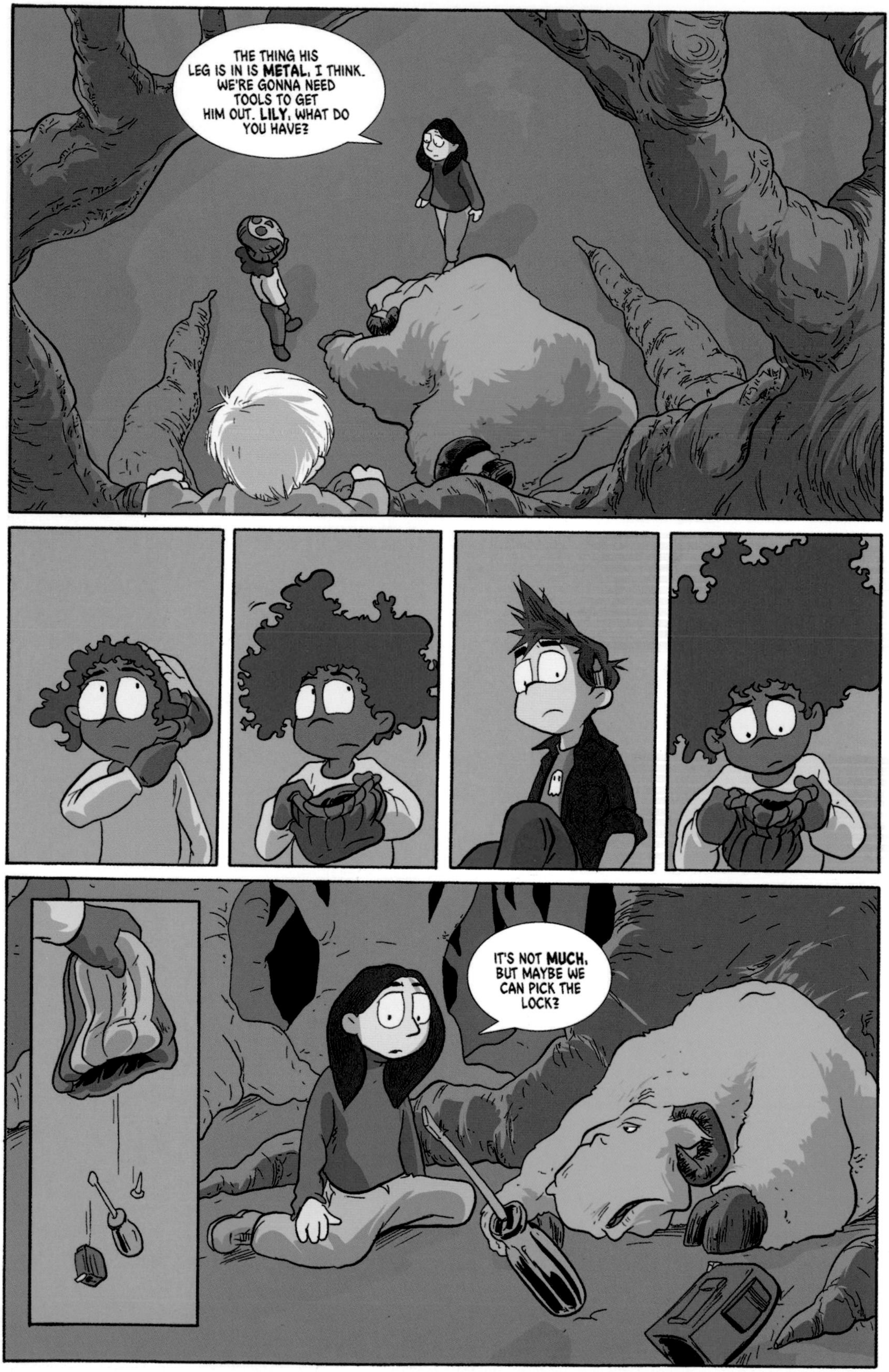
THE THING HIS LEG IS IN IS METAL, I THINK. WE'RE GONNA NEED TOOLS TO GET HIM OUT. LILY, WHAT DO YOU HAVE?
IT'S NOT MUCH, BUT MAYBE WE CAN PICK THE LOCK?

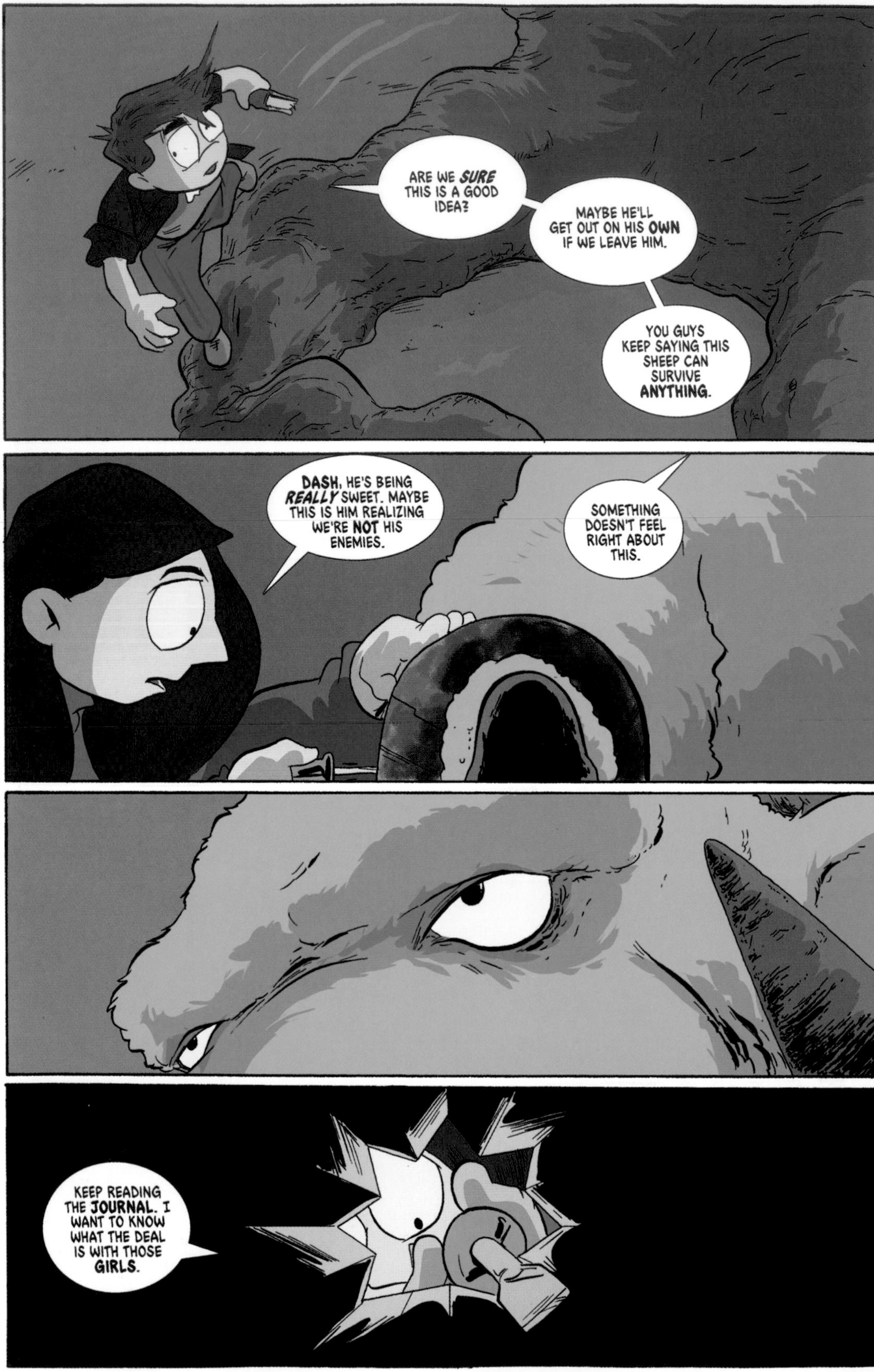
ARE WE SURE THIS IS A GOOD IDEA?
MAYBE HE'LL GET OUT ON HIS OWN IF WE LEAVE HIM.
YOU GUYS KEEP SAYING THIS SHEEP CAN SURVIVE ANYTHING.
DASH, HE'S BEING REALLY SWEET. MAYBE THIS IS HIM REALIZING WE'RE NOT HIS ENEMIES.
SOMETHING DOESN'T FEEL RIGHT ABOUT THIS.
KEEP READING THE JOURNAL. I WANT TO KNOW WHAT THE DEAL IS WITH THOSE GIRLS.

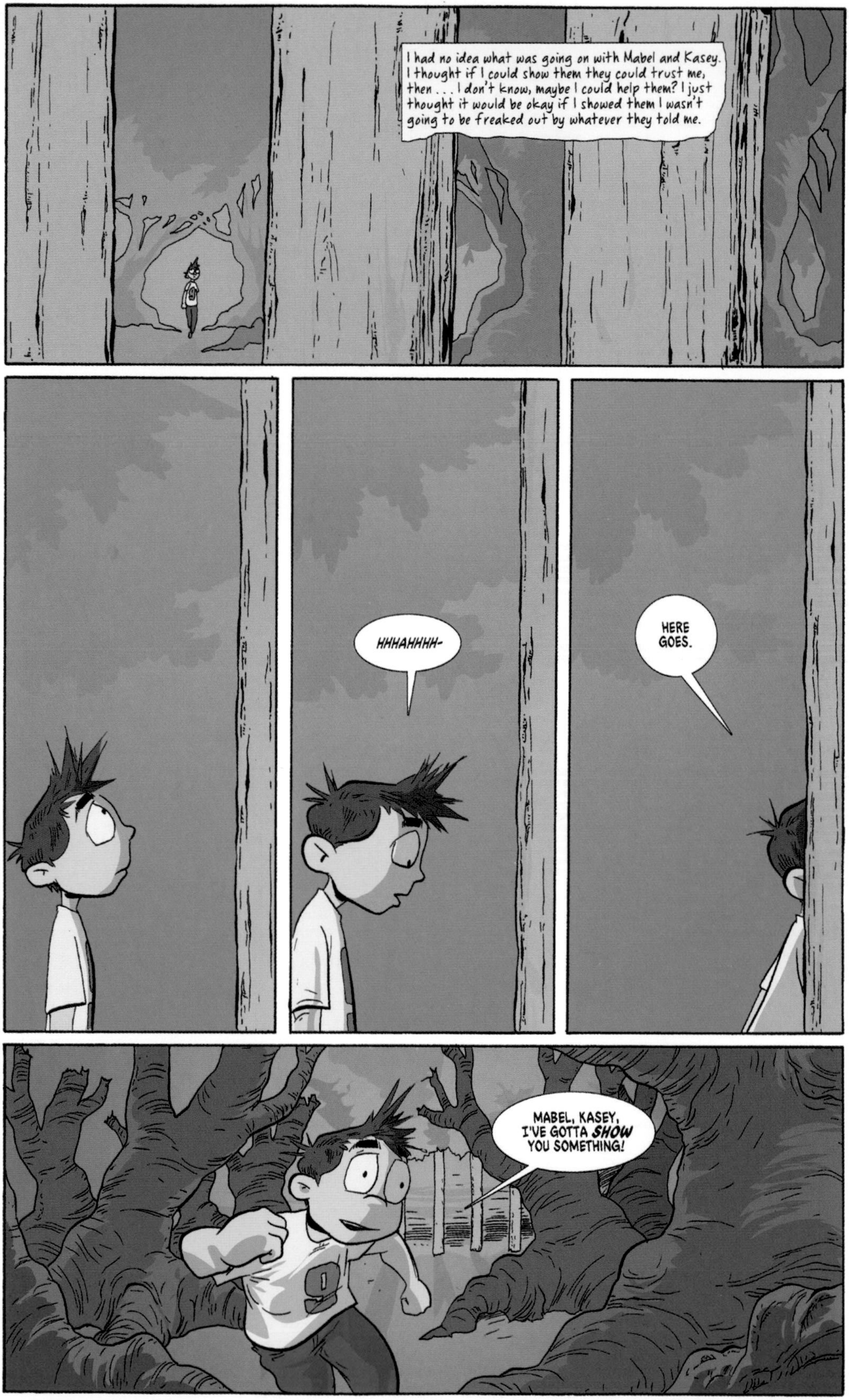
I had no idea what was going on with Mabel and Kasey. I thought if I could show them they could trust me, then . . . I don't know, maybe I could help them? I just thought it would be okay if I showed them I wasn't going to be freaked out by whatever they told me.
HHHAHHHH-
HERE GOES.
MABEL, KASEY, I'VE GOTTA *SHOW* YOU SOMETHING!

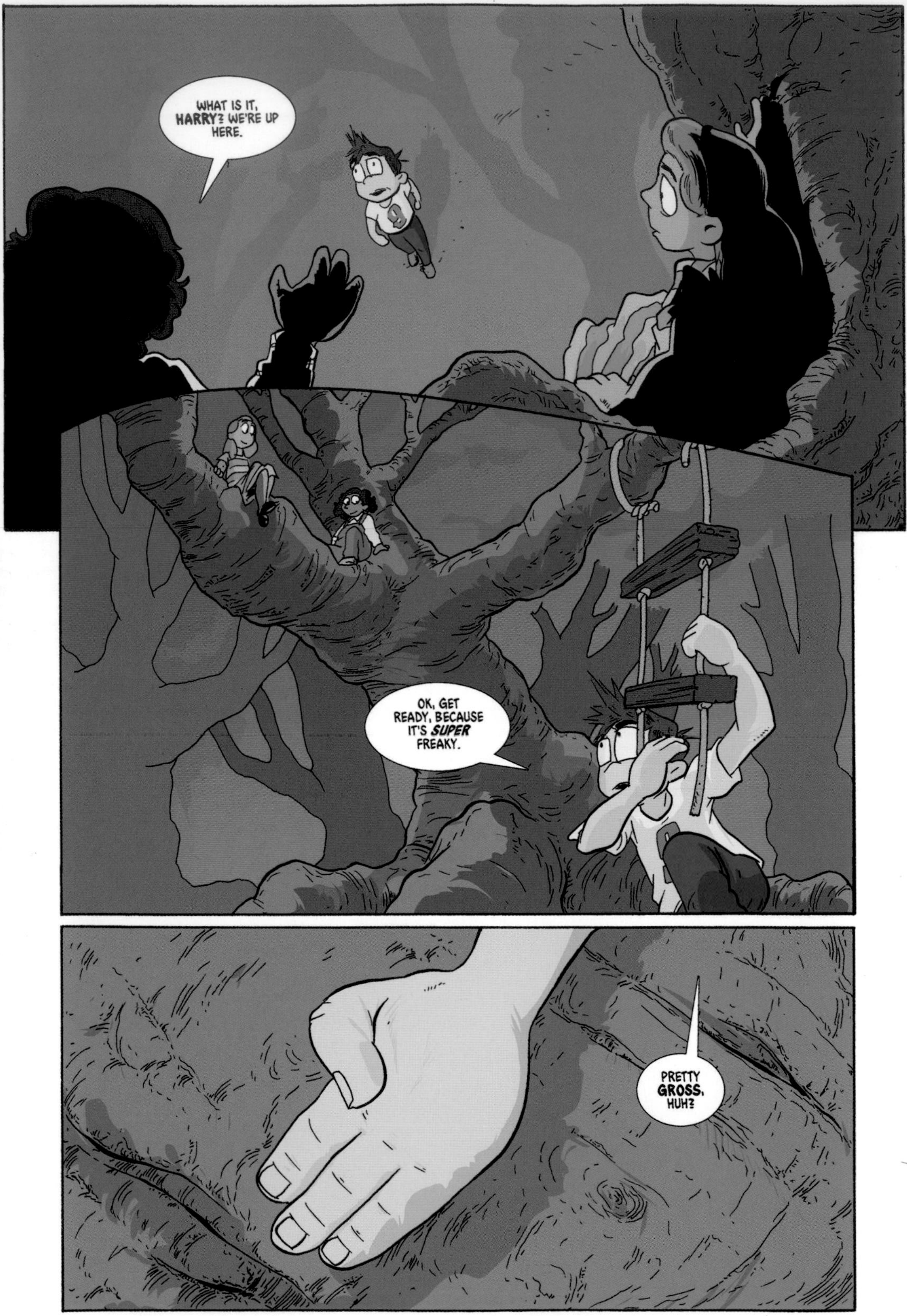
WHAT IS IT, HARRY? WE'RE UP HERE.
OK, GET READY, BECAUSE IT'S SUPER FREAKY.
PRETTY GROSS, HUH?

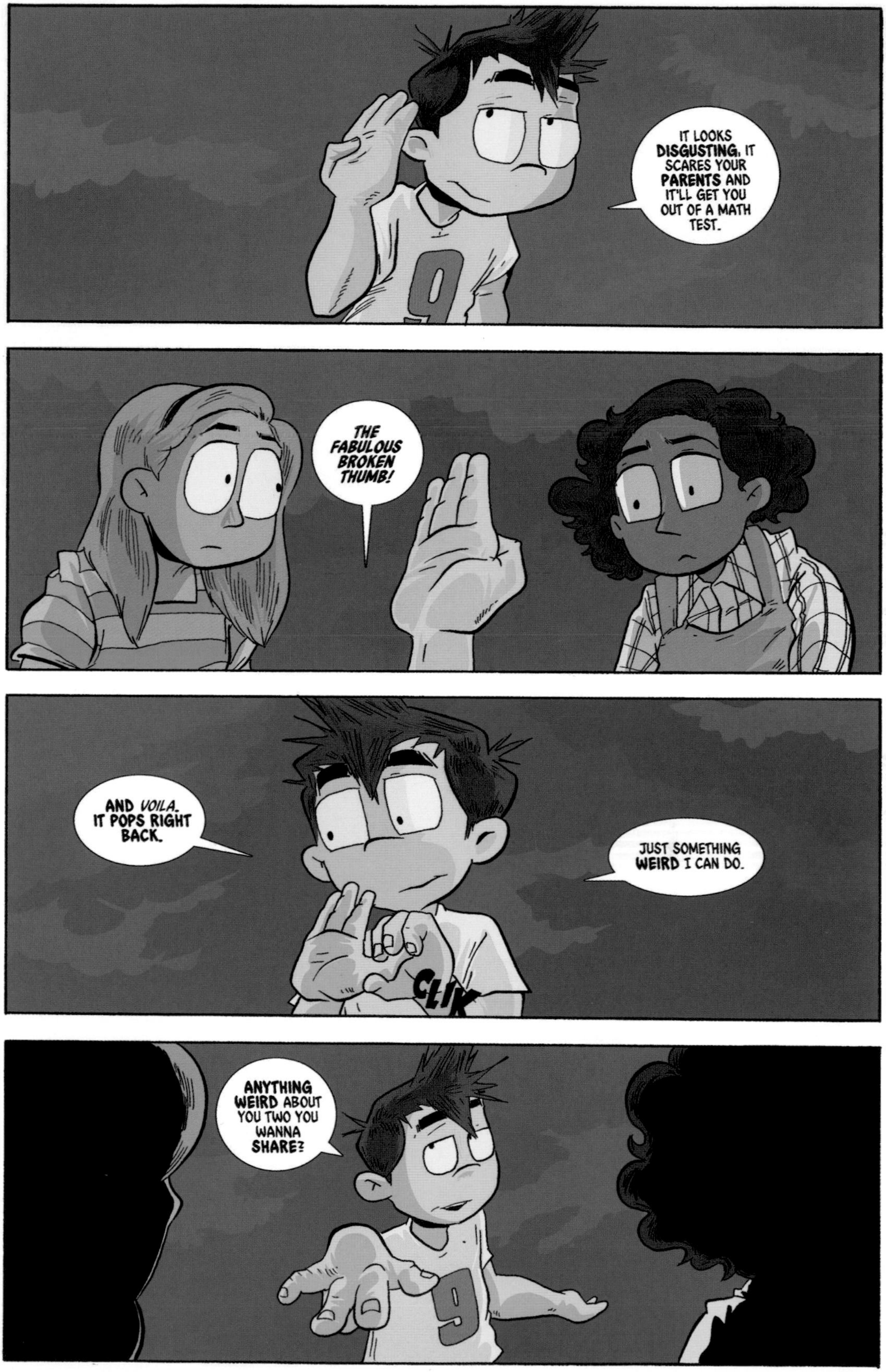
IT LOOKS DISGUSTING, IT SCARES YOUR PARENTS AND IT'LL GET YOU OUT OF A MATH TEST.
THE FABULOUS BROKEN THUMB!
AND VOILA. IT POPS RIGHT BACK.
JUST SOMETHING WEIRD I CAN DO.
CLIK
ANYTHING WEIRD ABOUT YOU TWO YOU WANNA SHARE?

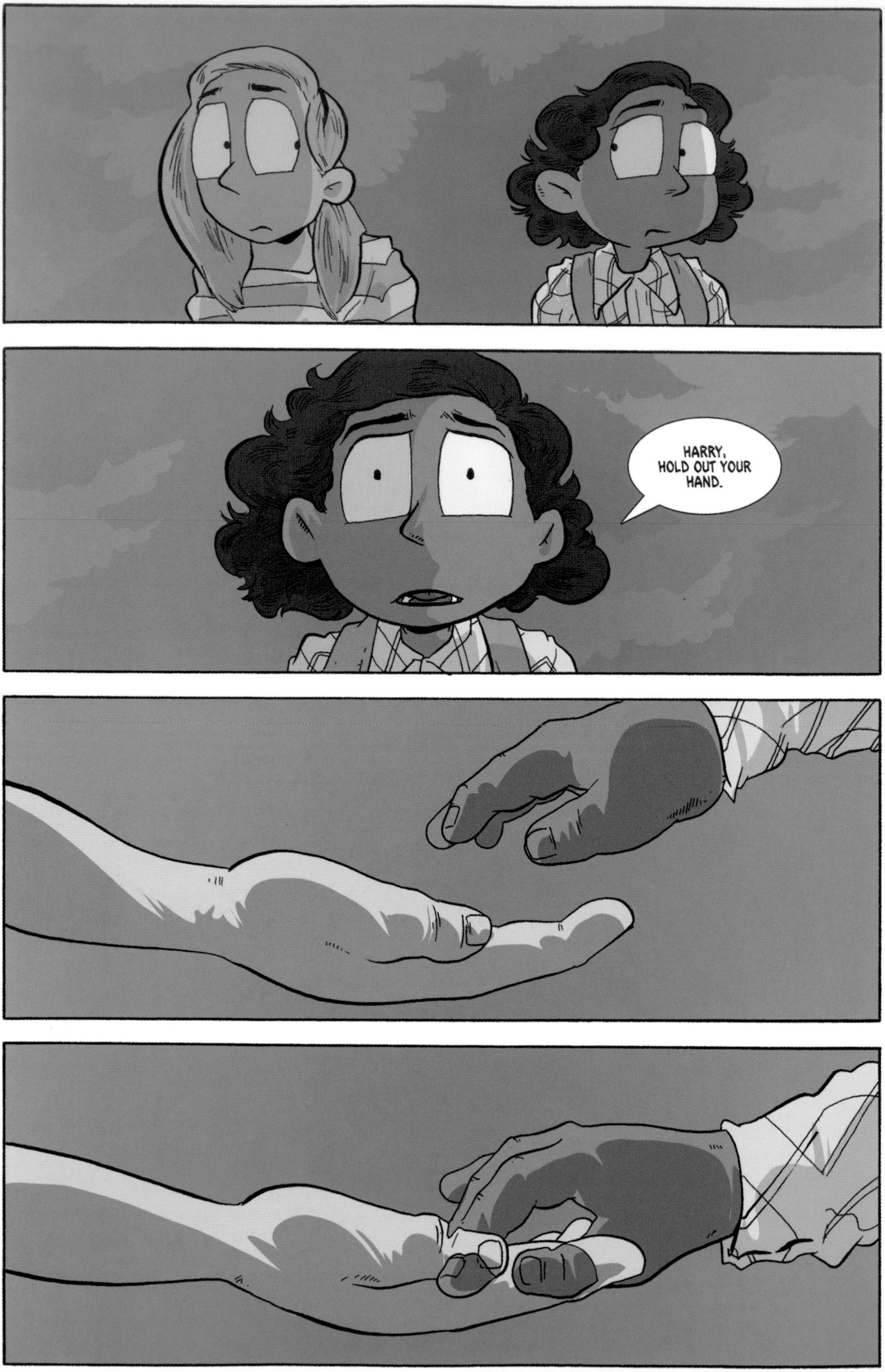
HARRY, HOLD OUT YOUR HAND.

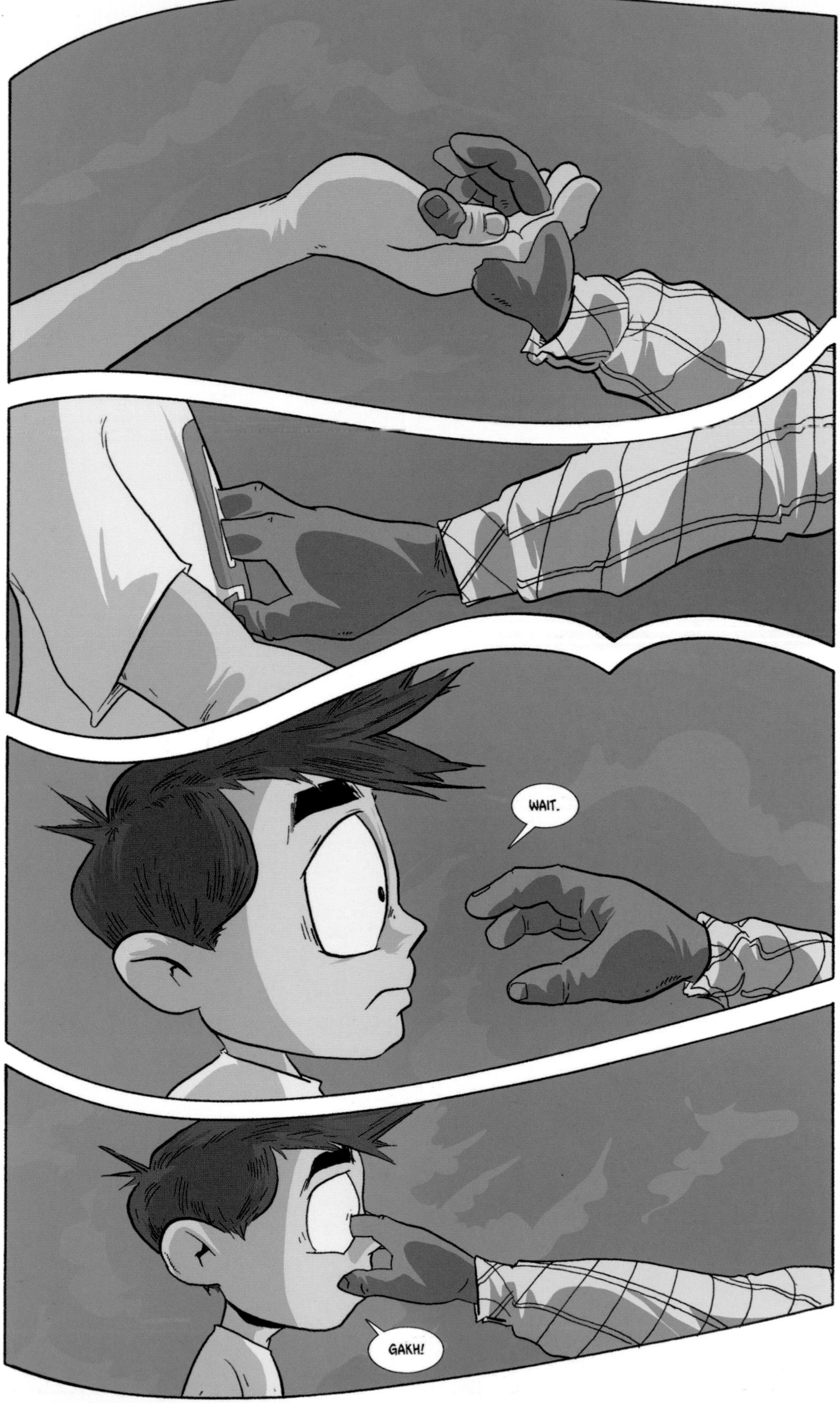
WAIT.
GAKH!

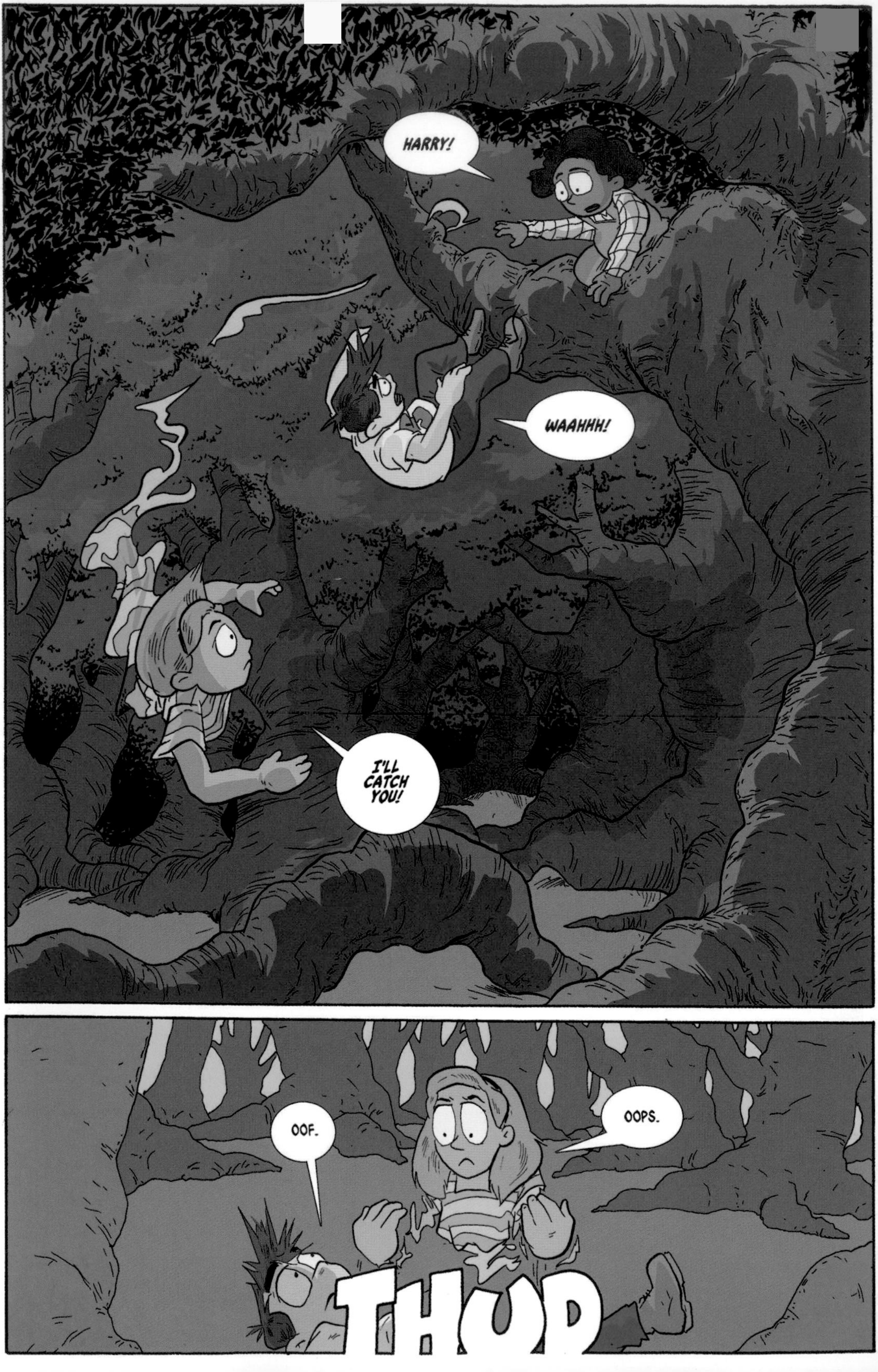
HARRY!
WAAHHH!
I'LL CATCH YOU!
OOF.
OOPS.
THUD

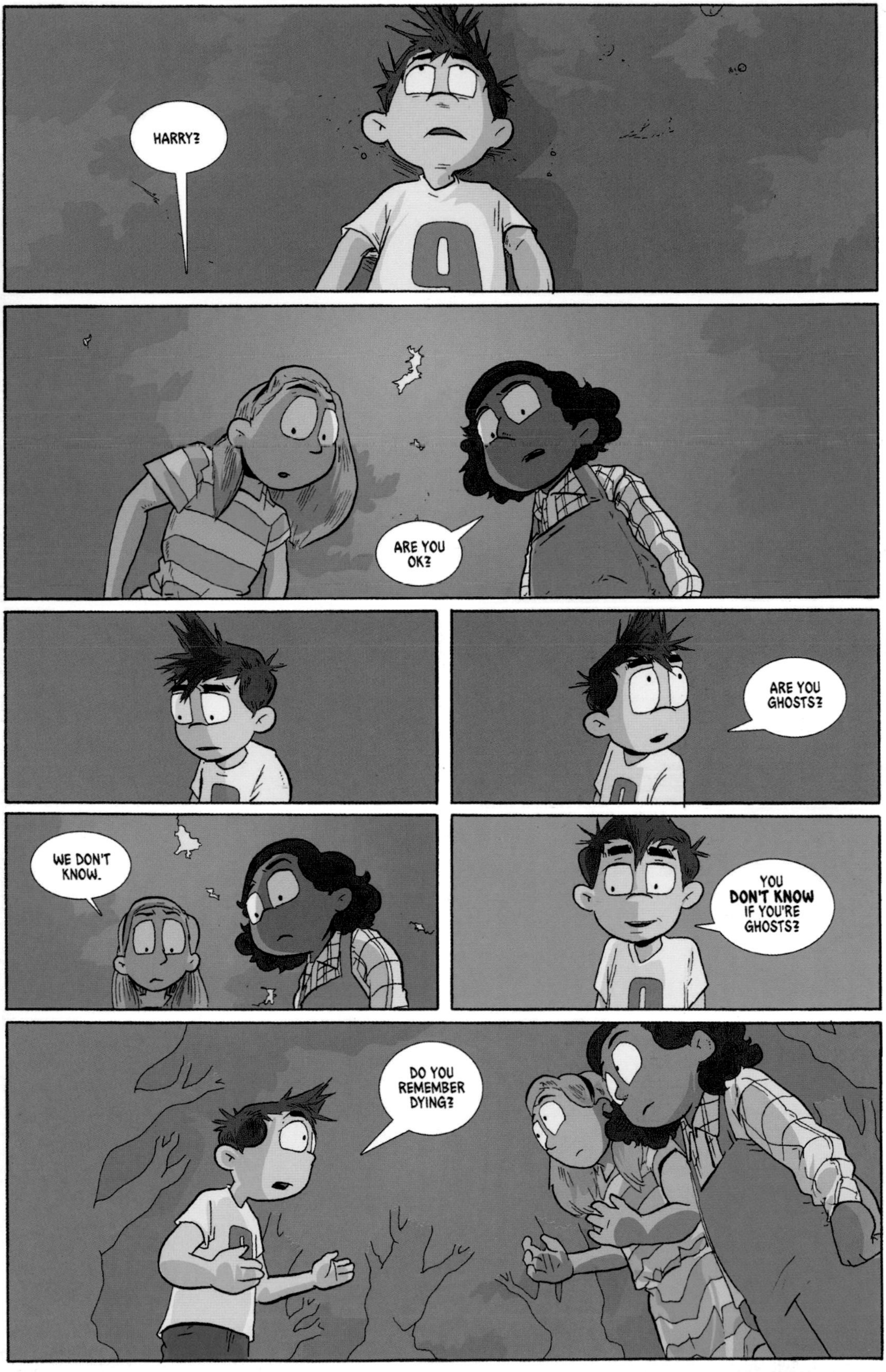

HARRY?
ARE YOU OK?
ARE YOU GHOSTS?
WE DON'T KNOW.
YOU **DON'T KNOW** IF YOU'RE GHOSTS?
DO YOU REMEMBER DYING?

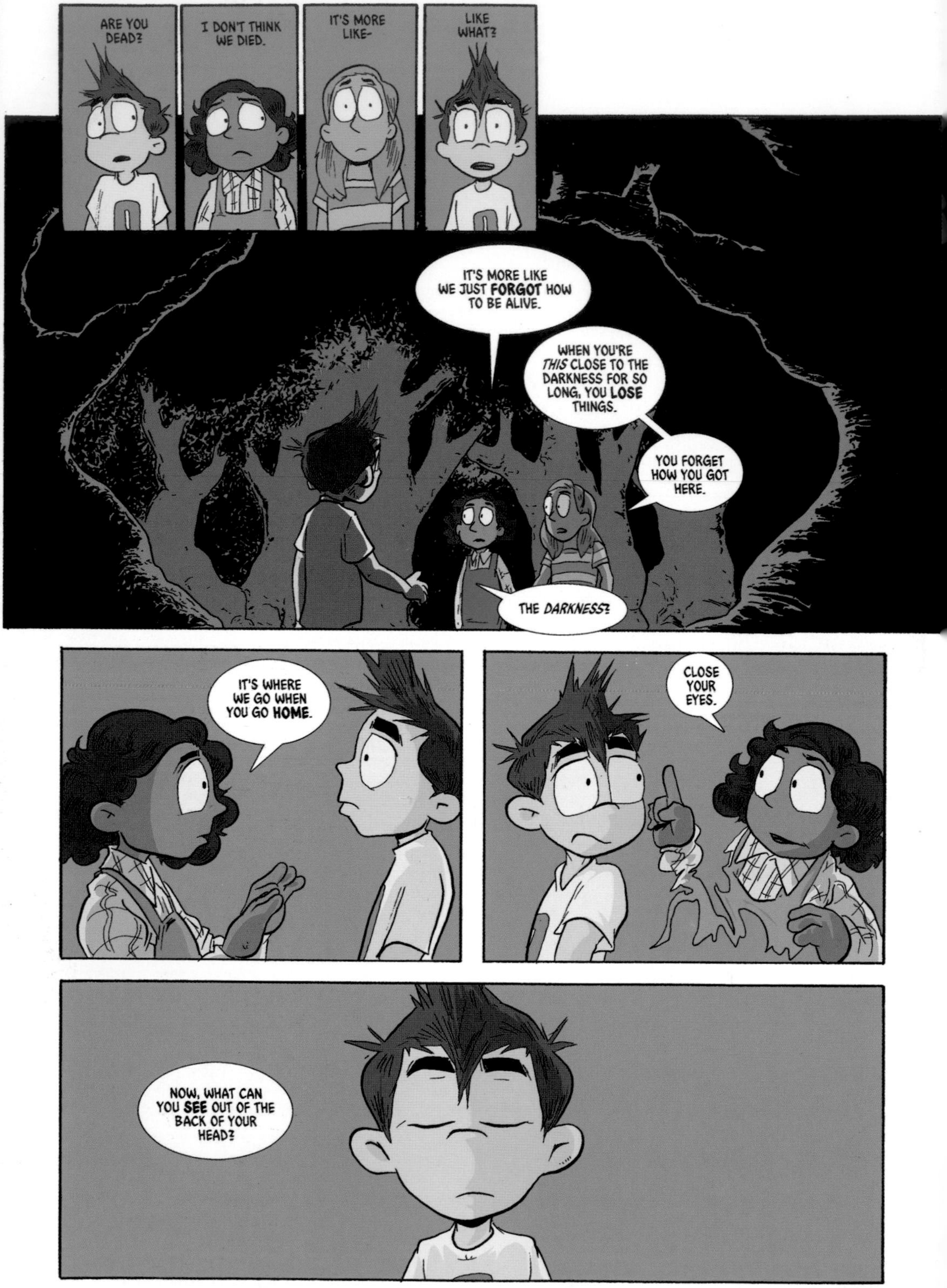
ARE YOU DEAD?
I DON'T THINK WE DIED.
IT'S MORE LIKE-
LIKE WHAT?
IT'S MORE LIKE WE JUST **FORGOT** HOW TO BE ALIVE.
WHEN YOU'RE *THIS* CLOSE TO THE DARKNESS FOR SO LONG, YOU **LOSE** THINGS.
YOU FORGET HOW YOU GOT HERE.
THE *DARKNESS*?
IT'S WHERE WE GO WHEN YOU GO **HOME**.
CLOSE YOUR EYES.
NOW, WHAT CAN YOU **SEE** OUT OF THE BACK OF YOUR HEAD?

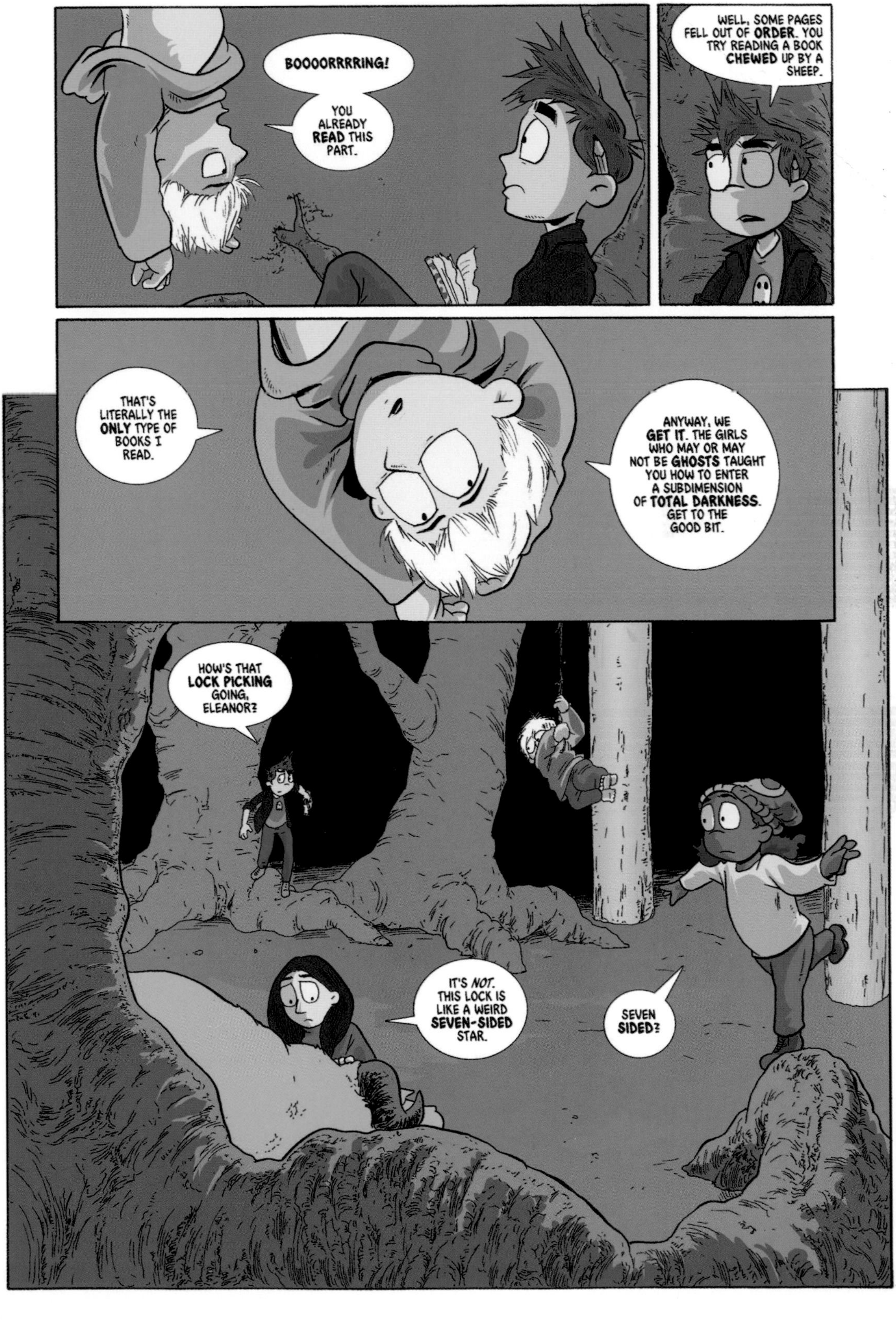
BOOOORRRRING!
YOU ALREADY READ THIS PART.
WELL, SOME PAGES FELL OUT OF ORDER. YOU TRY READING A BOOK CHEWED UP BY A SHEEP.
THAT'S LITERALLY THE ONLY TYPE OF BOOKS I READ.
ANYWAY, WE GET IT. THE GIRLS WHO MAY OR MAY NOT BE GHOSTS TAUGHT YOU HOW TO ENTER A SUBDIMENSION OF TOTAL DARKNESS. GET TO THE GOOD BIT.
HOW'S THAT LOCK PICKING GOING, ELEANOR?
IT'S NOT. THIS LOCK IS LIKE A WEIRD SEVEN-SIDED STAR.
SEVEN SIDED?

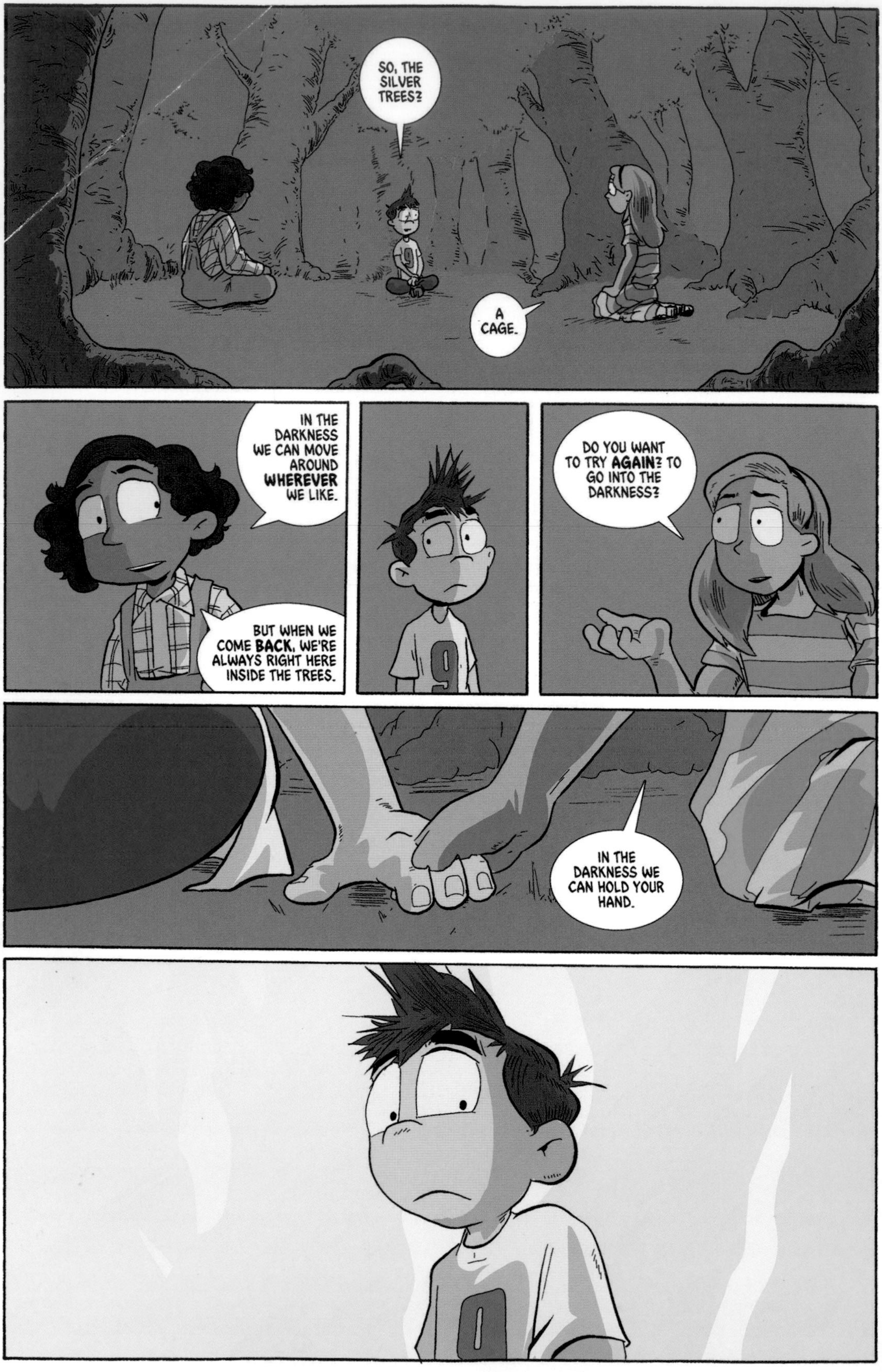
SO, THE SILVER TREES?
A CAGE.
IN THE DARKNESS WE CAN MOVE AROUND WHEREVER WE LIKE.
BUT WHEN WE COME BACK, WE'RE ALWAYS RIGHT HERE INSIDE THE TREES.
DO YOU WANT TO TRY AGAIN? TO GO INTO THE DARKNESS?
IN THE DARKNESS WE CAN HOLD YOUR HAND.

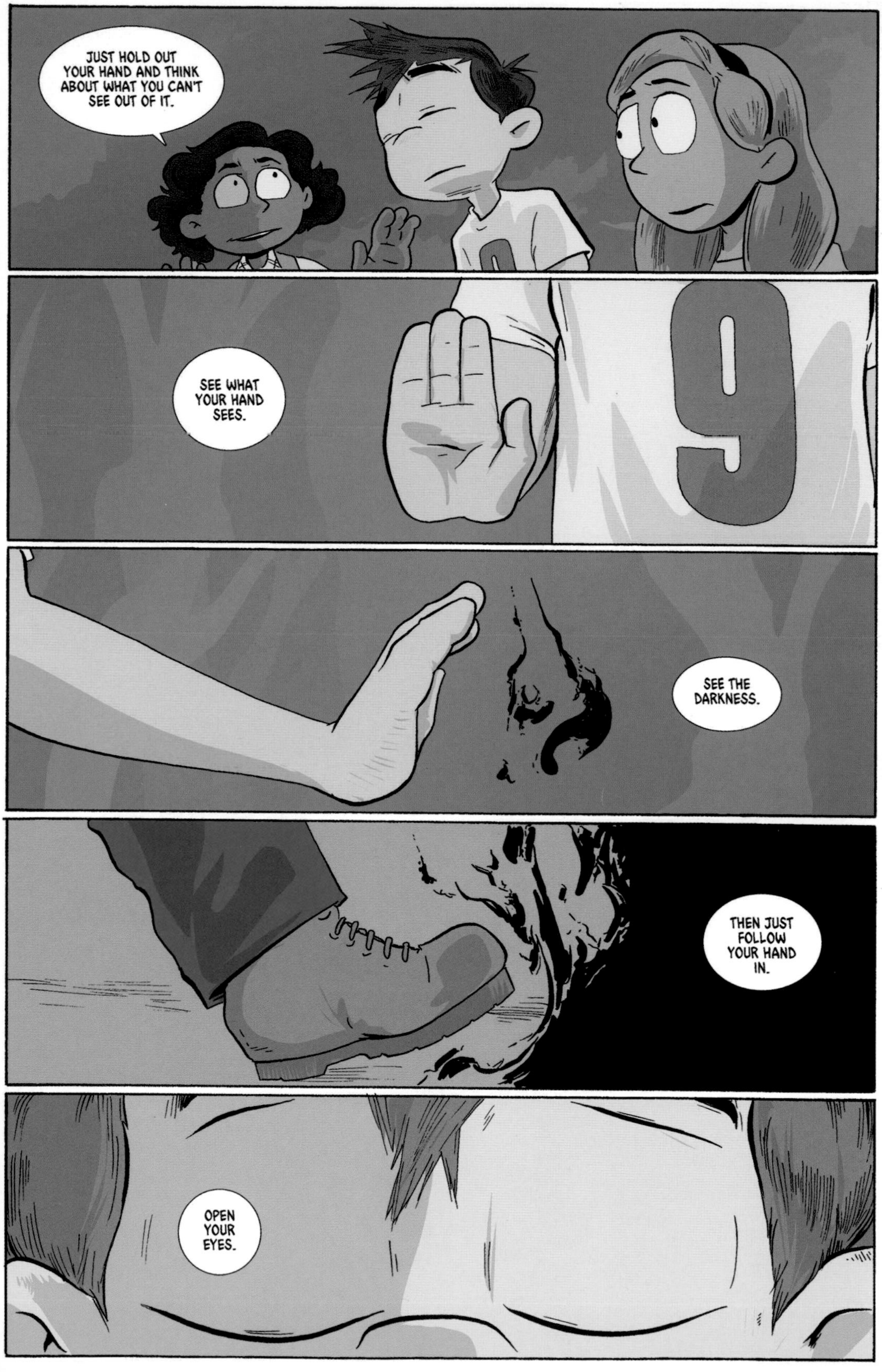
JUST HOLD OUT YOUR HAND AND THINK ABOUT WHAT YOU CAN'T SEE OUT OF IT.
9
SEE WHAT YOUR HAND SEES.
SEE THE DARKNESS.
THEN JUST FOLLOW YOUR HAND IN.
OPEN YOUR EYES.

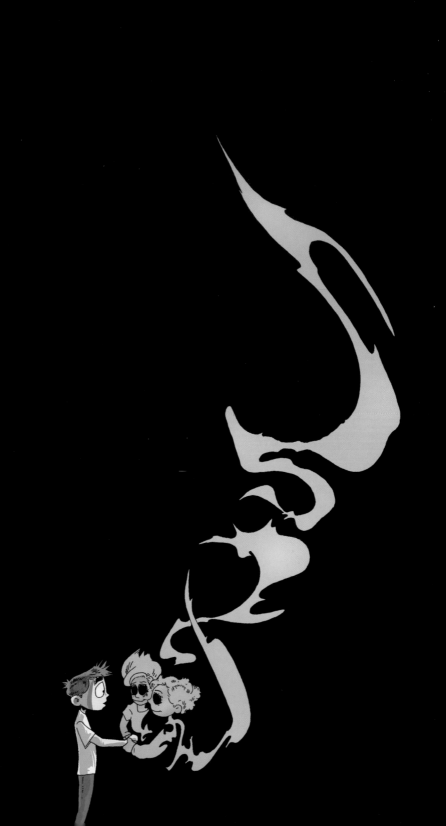

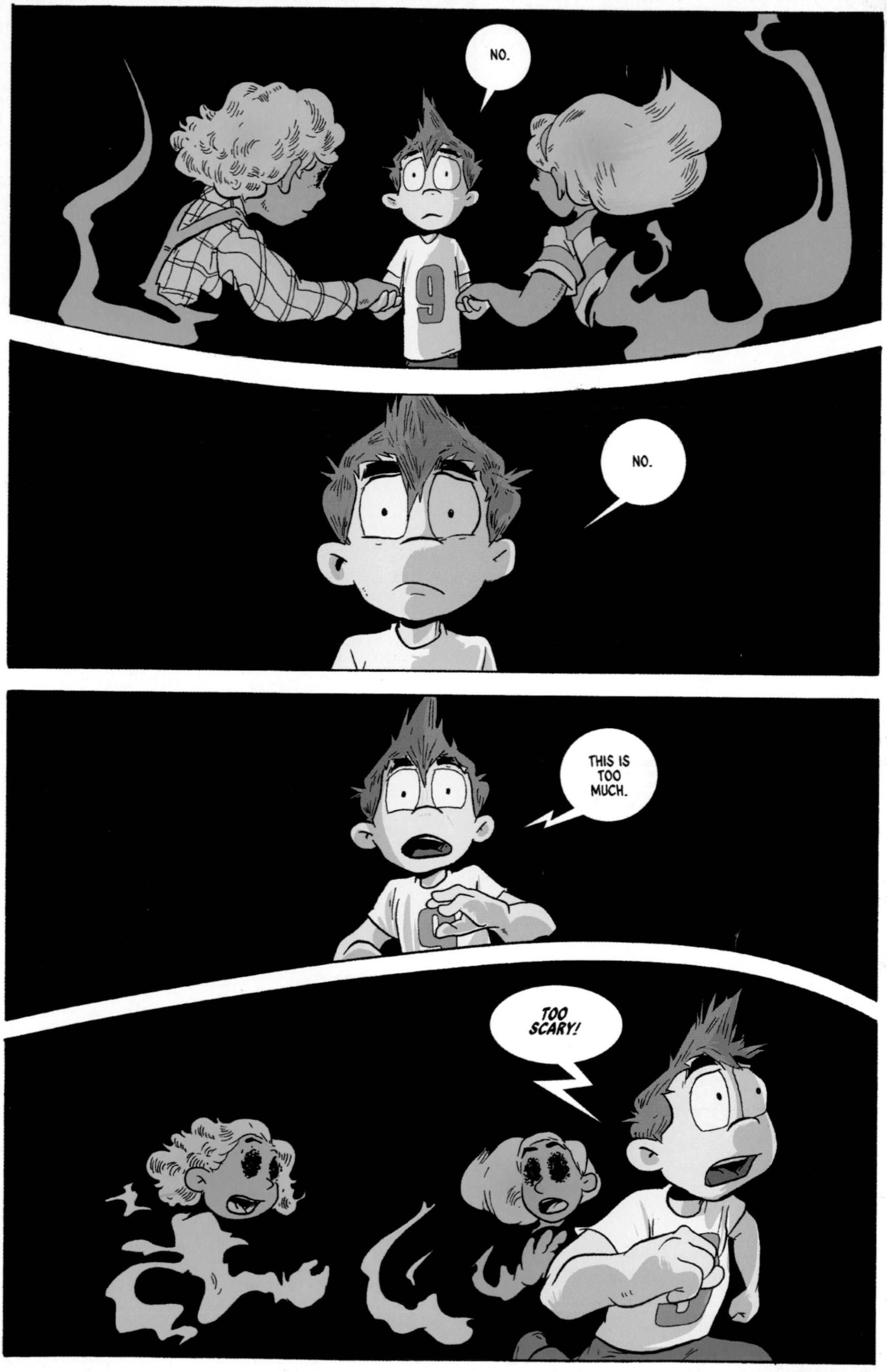
NO.
NO.
THIS IS TOO MUCH.
TOO SCARY!

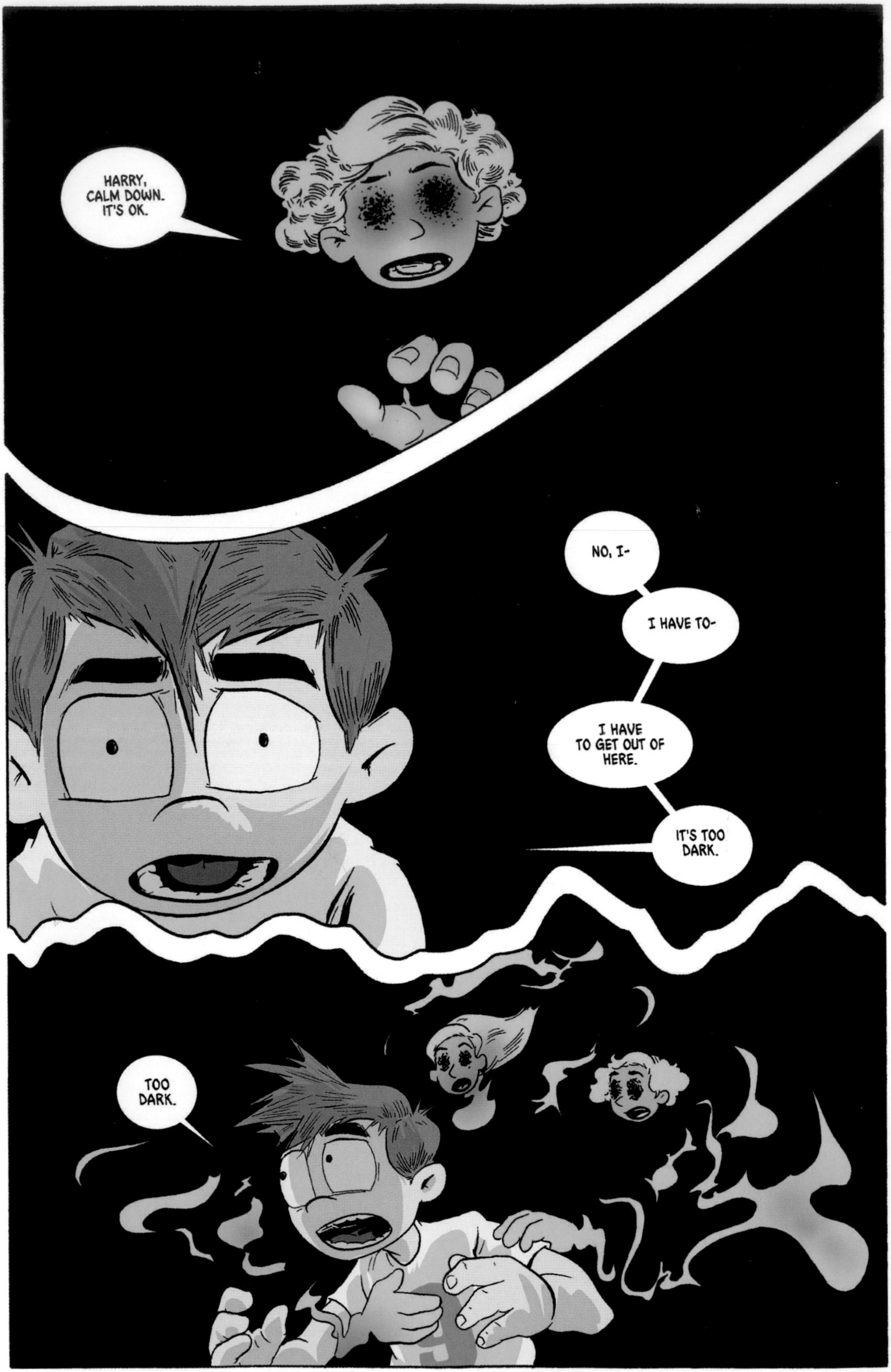
HARRY, CALM DOWN. IT'S OK.
NO, I-
I HAVE TO-
I HAVE TO GET OUT OF HERE.
IT'S TOO DARK.
TOO DARK.

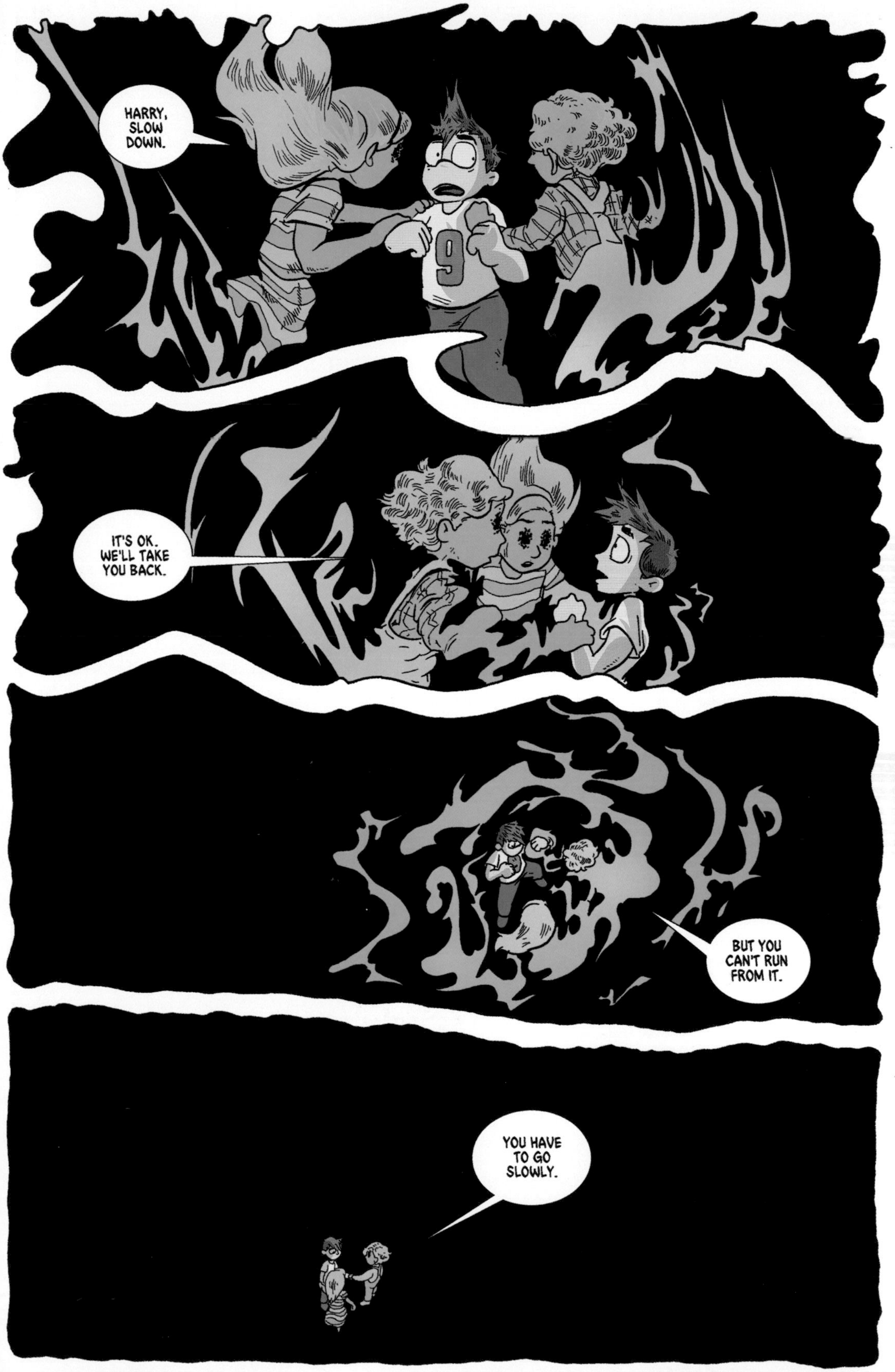
HARRY, SLOW DOWN.
IT'S OK. WE'LL TAKE YOU BACK.
BUT YOU CAN'T RUN FROM IT.
YOU HAVE TO GO SLOWLY.

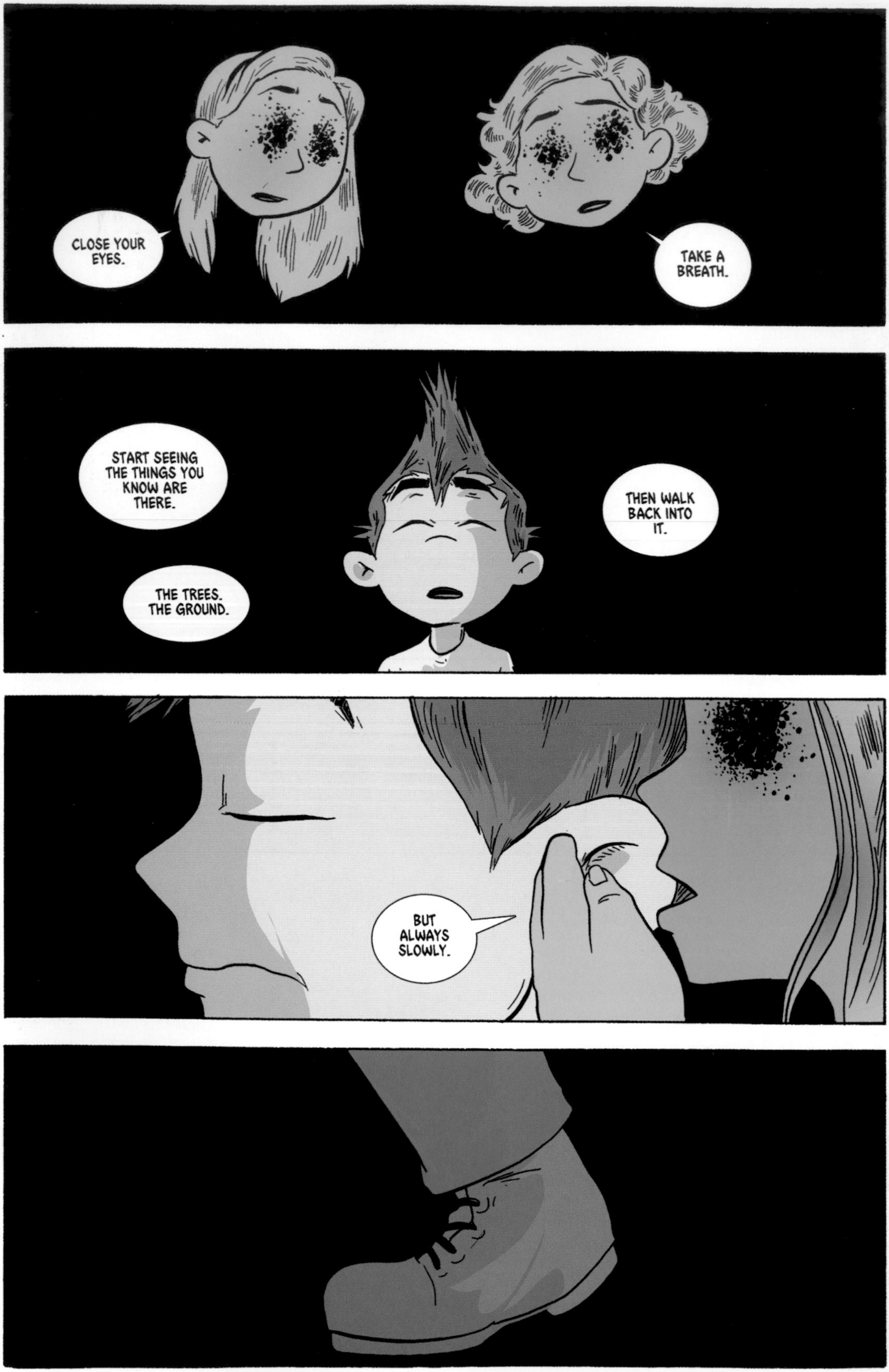
CLOSE YOUR EYES.
TAKE A BREATH.
START SEEING THE THINGS YOU KNOW ARE THERE.
THE TREES. THE GROUND.
THEN WALK BACK INTO IT.
BUT ALWAYS SLOWLY.

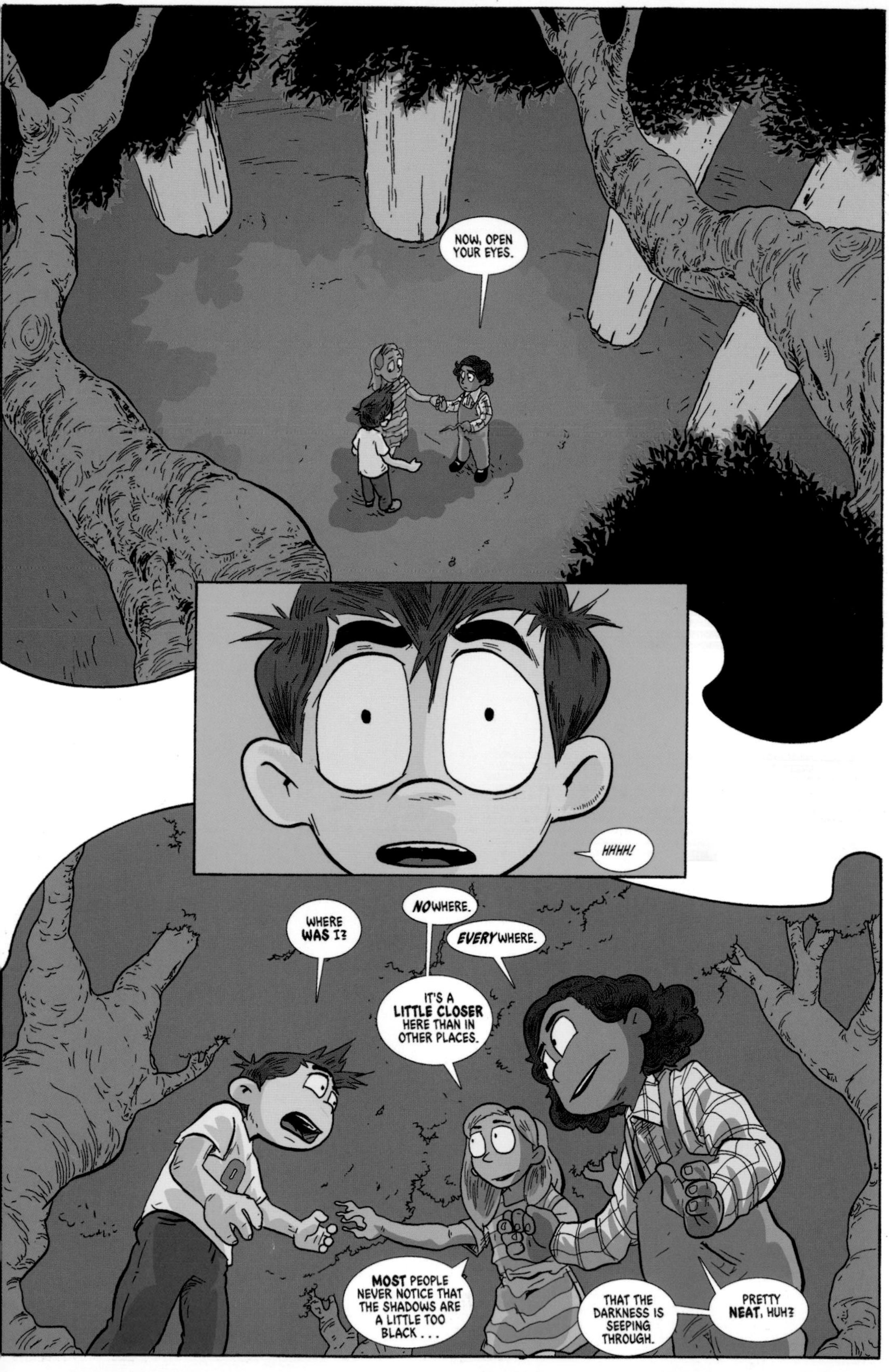
NOW, OPEN YOUR EYES.
HHHH!
WHERE WAS I?
NOWHERE.
EVERYWHERE.
IT'S A LITTLE CLOSER HERE THAN IN OTHER PLACES.
MOST PEOPLE NEVER NOTICE THAT THE SHADOWS ARE A LITTLE TOO BLACK . . .
THAT THE DARKNESS IS SEEPING THROUGH.
PRETTY NEAT, HUH?

HHAH
HURH
HHHEURHH
HAHHH
HARRY, IT'S OK .
NO.
HHHH
TOO MUCH.
HARRY, IT'S NOT SCARY.
JUST GO SLOWLY AND NEVER STAY TOO LONG.
HHHRRHH
HHAHH
HHKKHH
HARRY-
WHAT ARE YOU DOING?
HHHH
HHHH
HARRY?
I JUST-HHHH
HHHH
NEED TO CATCH-
HHHHH
HHHHH
MY BREATH.
WHAT'S BREATH?

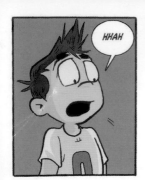

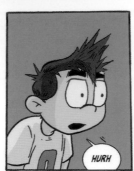

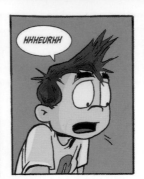

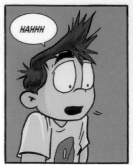

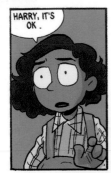

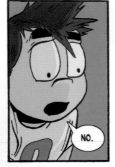

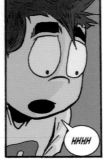

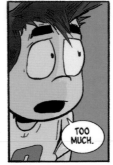

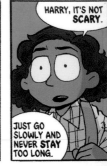

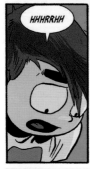

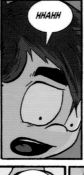

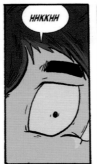

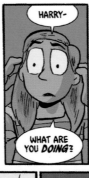

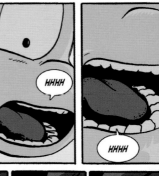

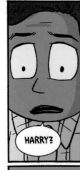

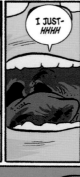

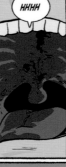

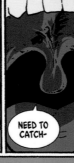

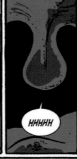

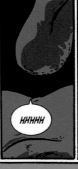

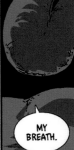

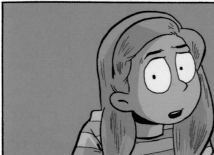

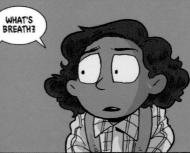

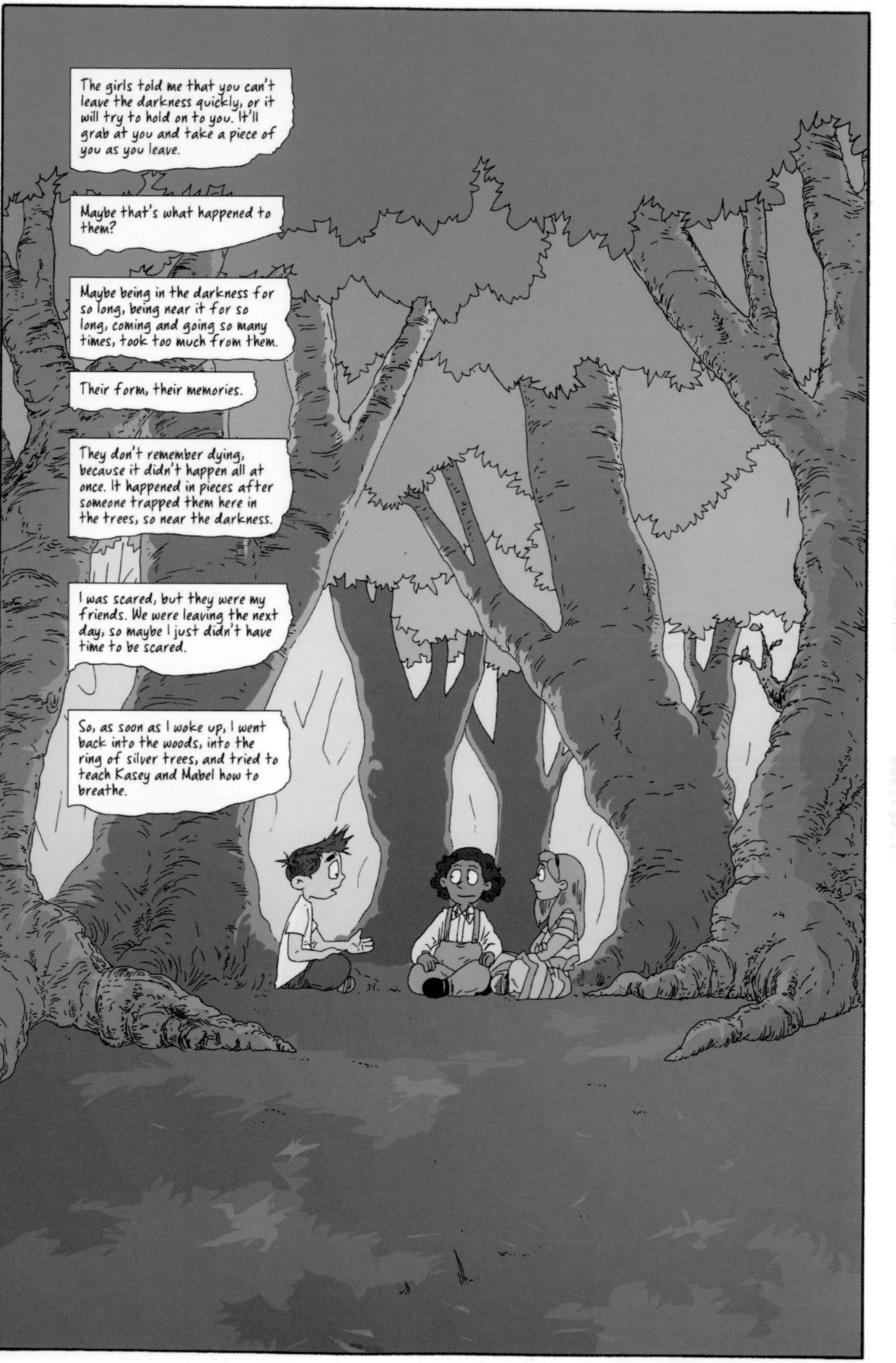

The girls told me that you can't leave the darkness quickly, or it will try to hold on to you. It'll grab at you and take a piece of you as you leave.
Maybe that's what happened to them?
Maybe being in the darkness for so long, being near it for so long, coming and going so many times, took too much from them.
Their form, their memories.
They don't remember dying, because it didn't happen all at once. It happened in pieces after someone trapped them here in the trees, so near the darkness.
I was scared, but they were my friends. We were leaving the next day, so maybe I just didn't have time to be scared.
So, as soon as I woke up, I went back into the woods, into the ring of silver trees, and tried to teach Kasey and Mabel how to breathe.

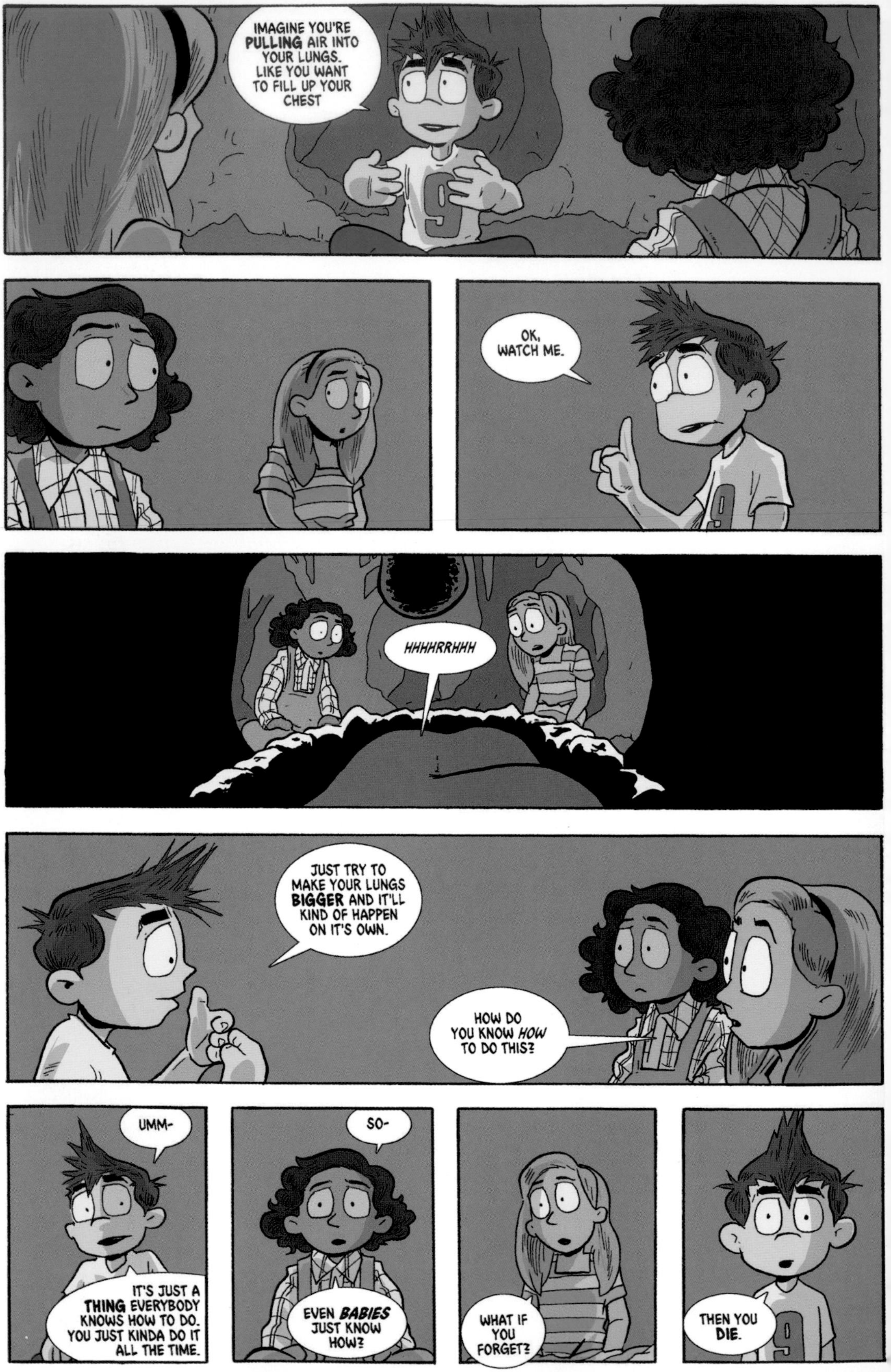
IMAGINE YOU'RE PULLING AIR INTO YOUR LUNGS. LIKE YOU WANT TO FILL UP YOUR CHEST
OK, WATCH ME.
HHHHRRHHH
JUST TRY TO MAKE YOUR LUNGS BIGGER AND IT'LL KIND OF HAPPEN ON IT'S OWN.
HOW DO YOU KNOW HOW TO DO THIS?
UMM-
IT'S JUST A THING EVERYBODY KNOWS HOW TO DO. YOU JUST KINDA DO IT ALL THE TIME.
SO-
EVEN BABIES JUST KNOW HOW?
WHAT IF YOU FORGET?
THEN YOU DIE.

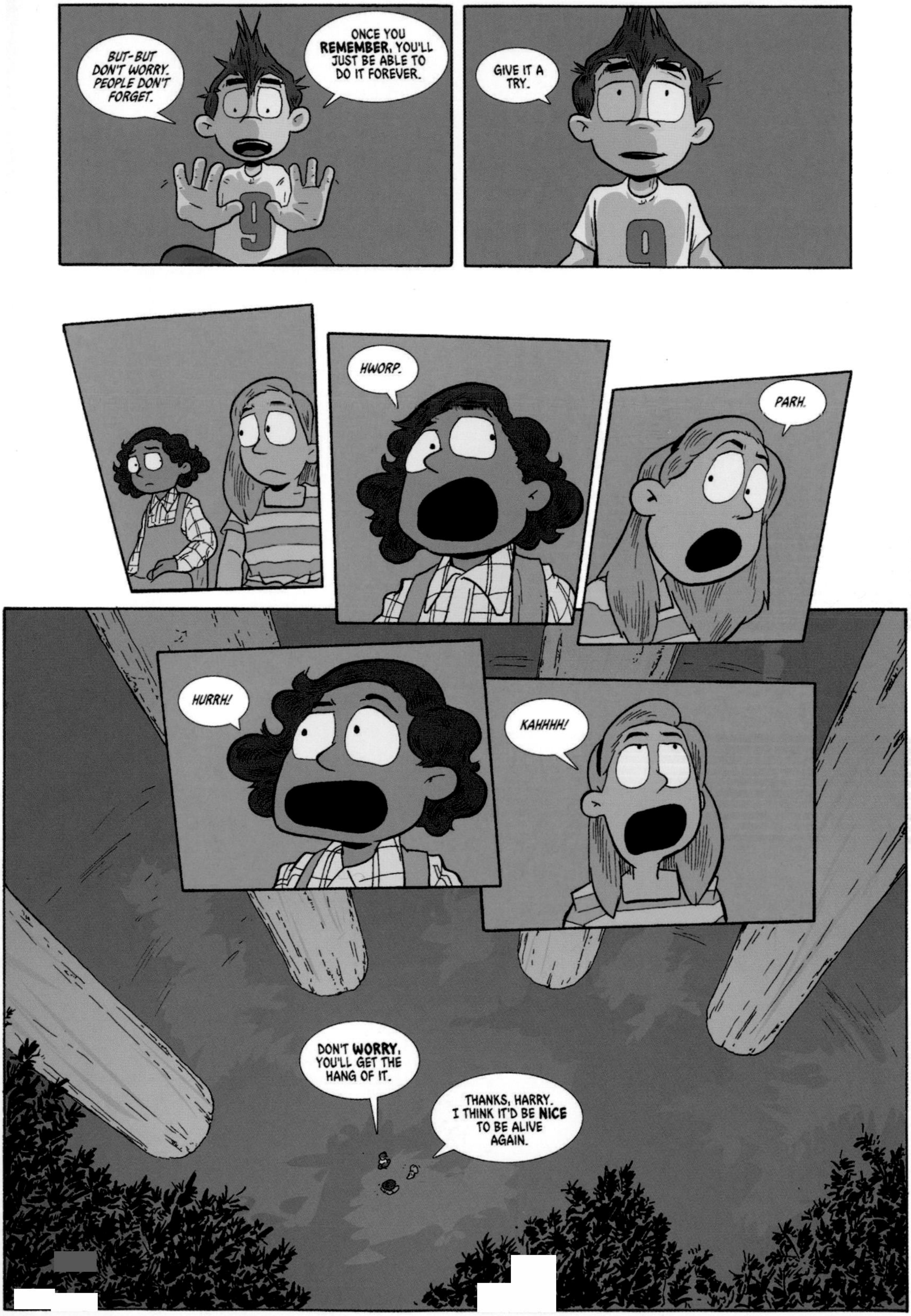
BUT-BUT DON'T WORRY. PEOPLE DON'T FORGET.
ONCE YOU REMEMBER, YOU'LL JUST BE ABLE TO DO IT FOREVER.
GIVE IT A TRY.
HWORP.
PARH.
HURRH!
KAHHHH!
DON'T WORRY, YOU'LL GET THE HANG OF IT.
THANKS, HARRY. I THINK IT'D BE NICE TO BE ALIVE AGAIN.

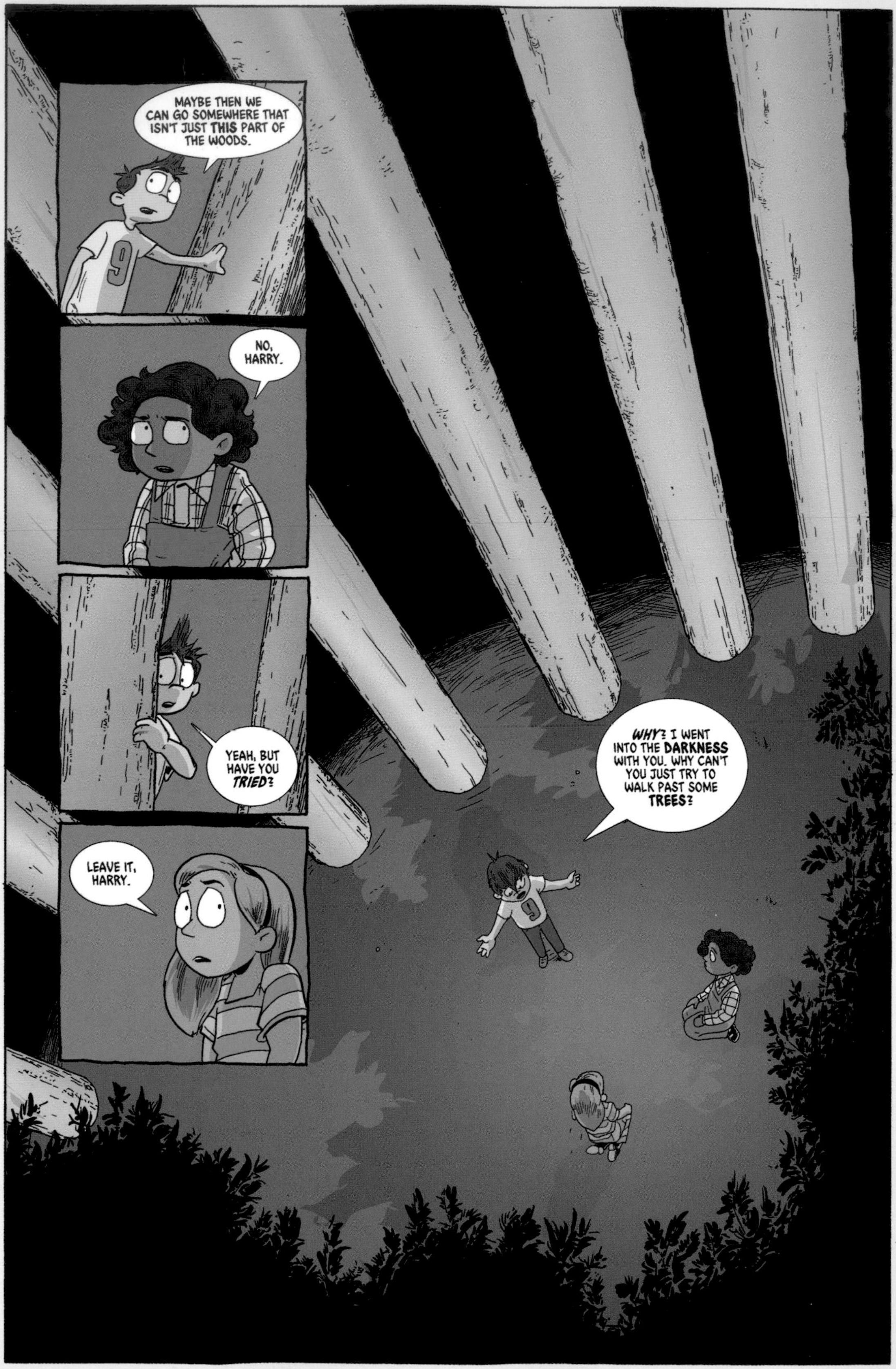
MAYBE THEN WE CAN GO SOMEWHERE THAT ISN'T JUST THIS PART OF THE WOODS.
NO, HARRY.
YEAH, BUT HAVE YOU TRIED?
LEAVE IT, HARRY.
WHY? I WENT INTO THE DARKNESS WITH YOU. WHY CAN'T YOU JUST TRY TO WALK PAST SOME TREES?

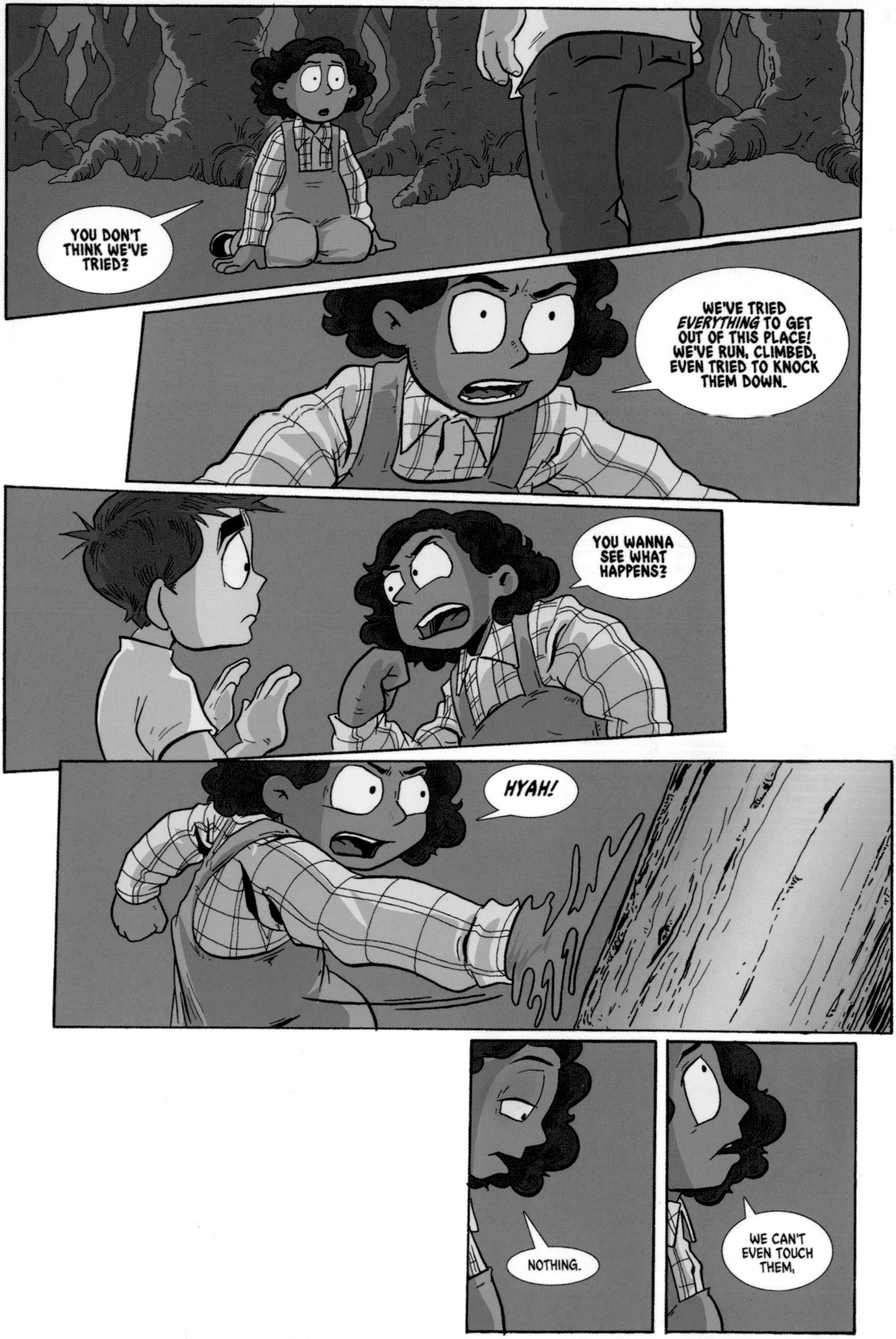
YOU DON'T THINK WE'VE TRIED?
WE'VE TRIED *EVERYTHING* TO GET OUT OF THIS PLACE! WE'VE RUN, CLIMBED, EVEN TRIED TO KNOCK THEM DOWN.
YOU WANNA SEE WHAT HAPPENS?
HYAH!
NOTHING.
WE CAN'T EVEN TOUCH THEM,

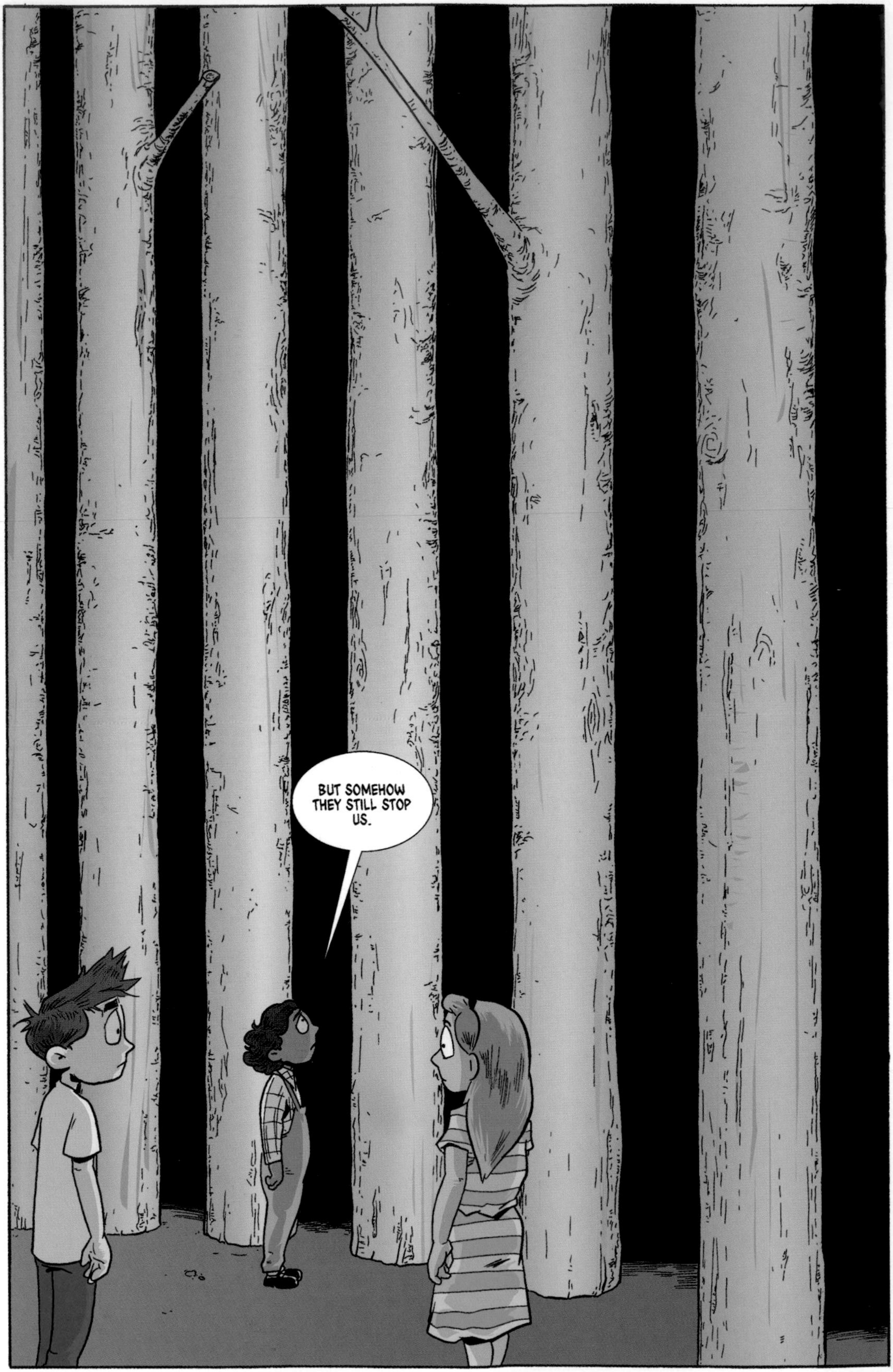
BUT SOMEHOW THEY STILL STOP US.

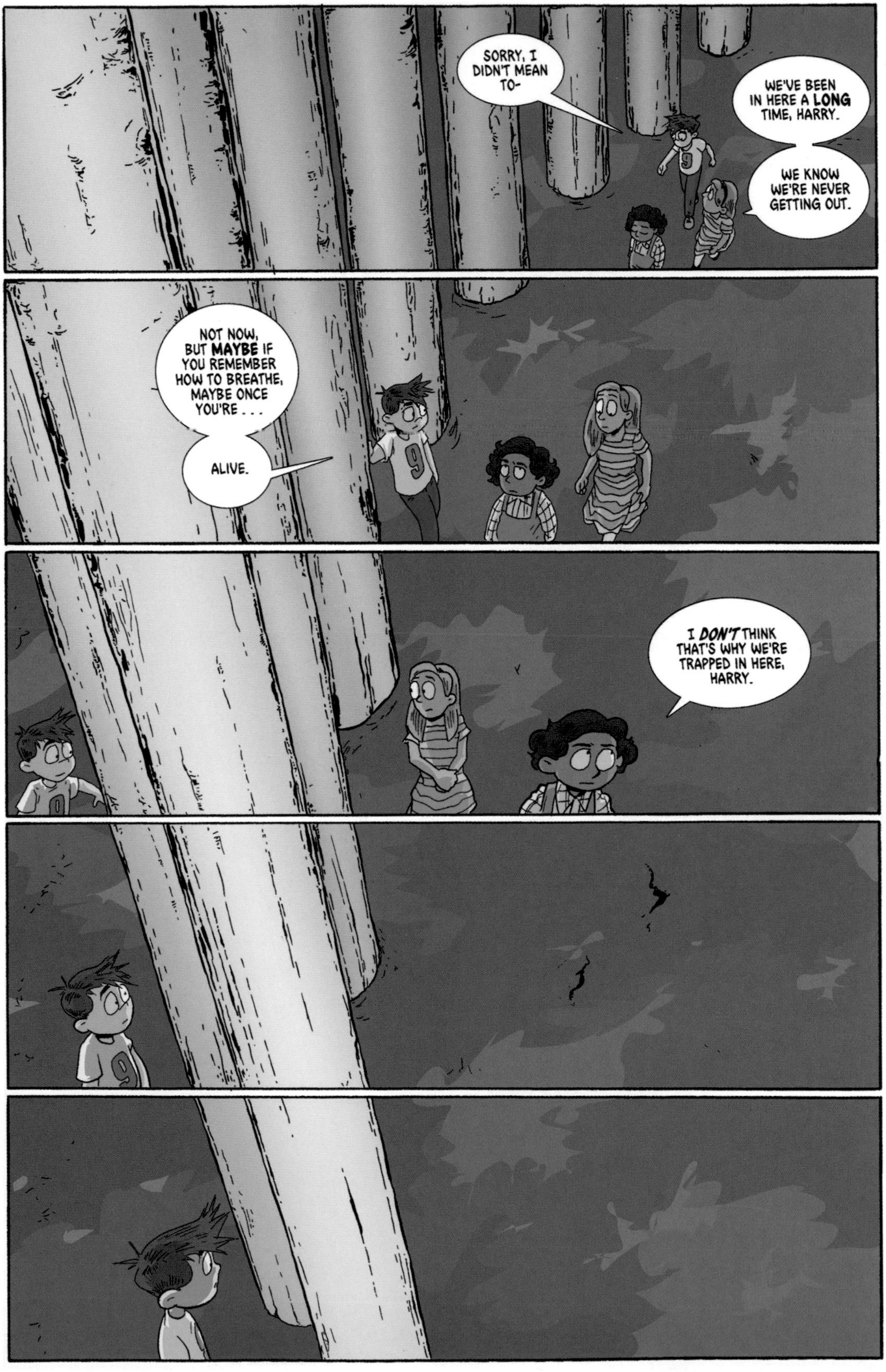
SORRY, I DIDN'T MEAN TO-
WE'VE BEEN IN HERE A LONG TIME, HARRY.
WE KNOW WE'RE NEVER GETTING OUT.
NOT NOW, BUT MAYBE IF YOU REMEMBER HOW TO BREATHE, MAYBE ONCE YOU'RE . . .
ALIVE.
I DON'T THINK THAT'S WHY WE'RE TRAPPED IN HERE, HARRY.

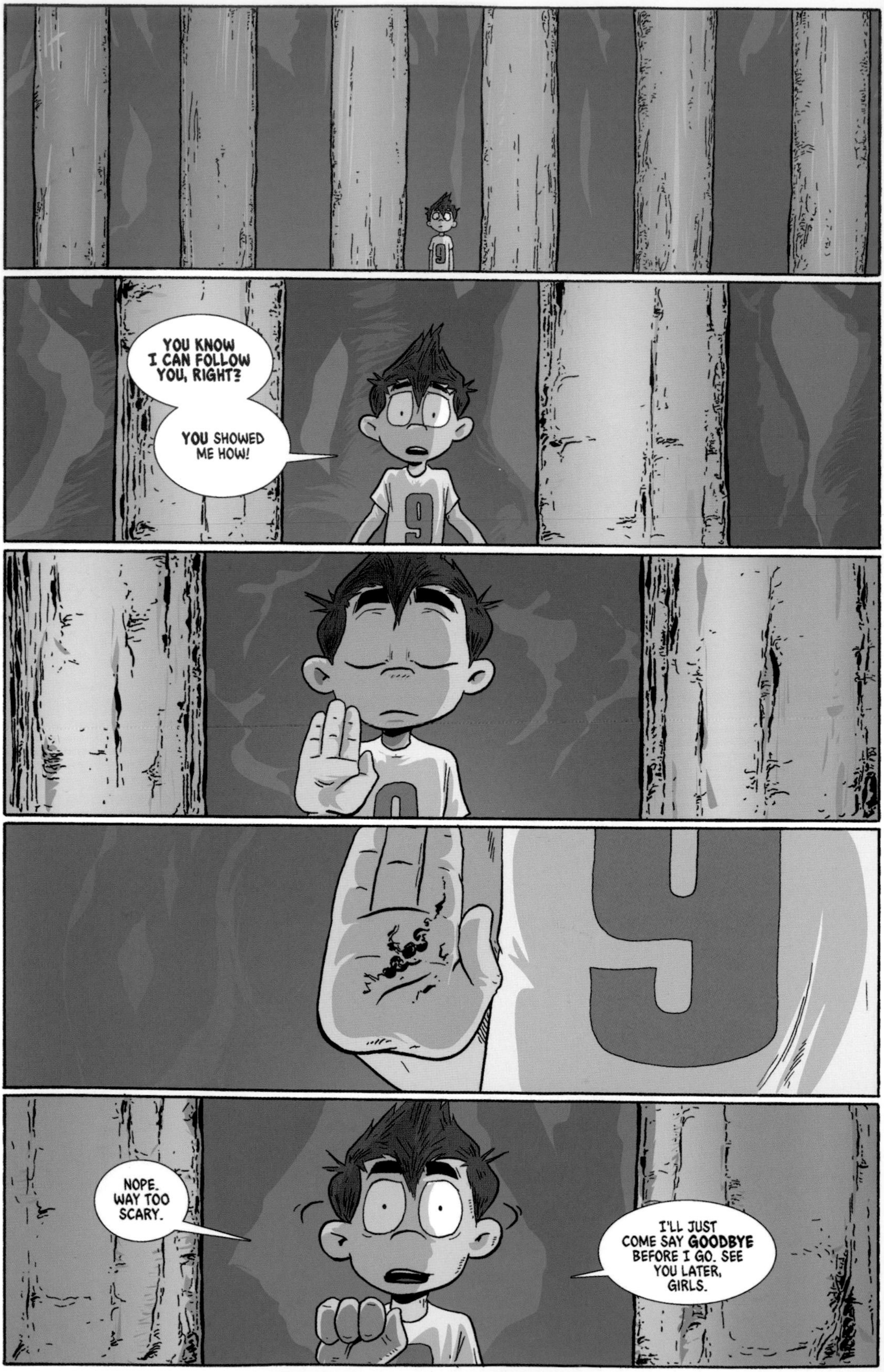
YOU KNOW I CAN FOLLOW YOU, RIGHT?
YOU SHOWED ME HOW!
NOPE. WAY TOO SCARY.
I'LL JUST COME SAY GOODBYE BEFORE I GO. SEE YOU LATER, GIRLS.

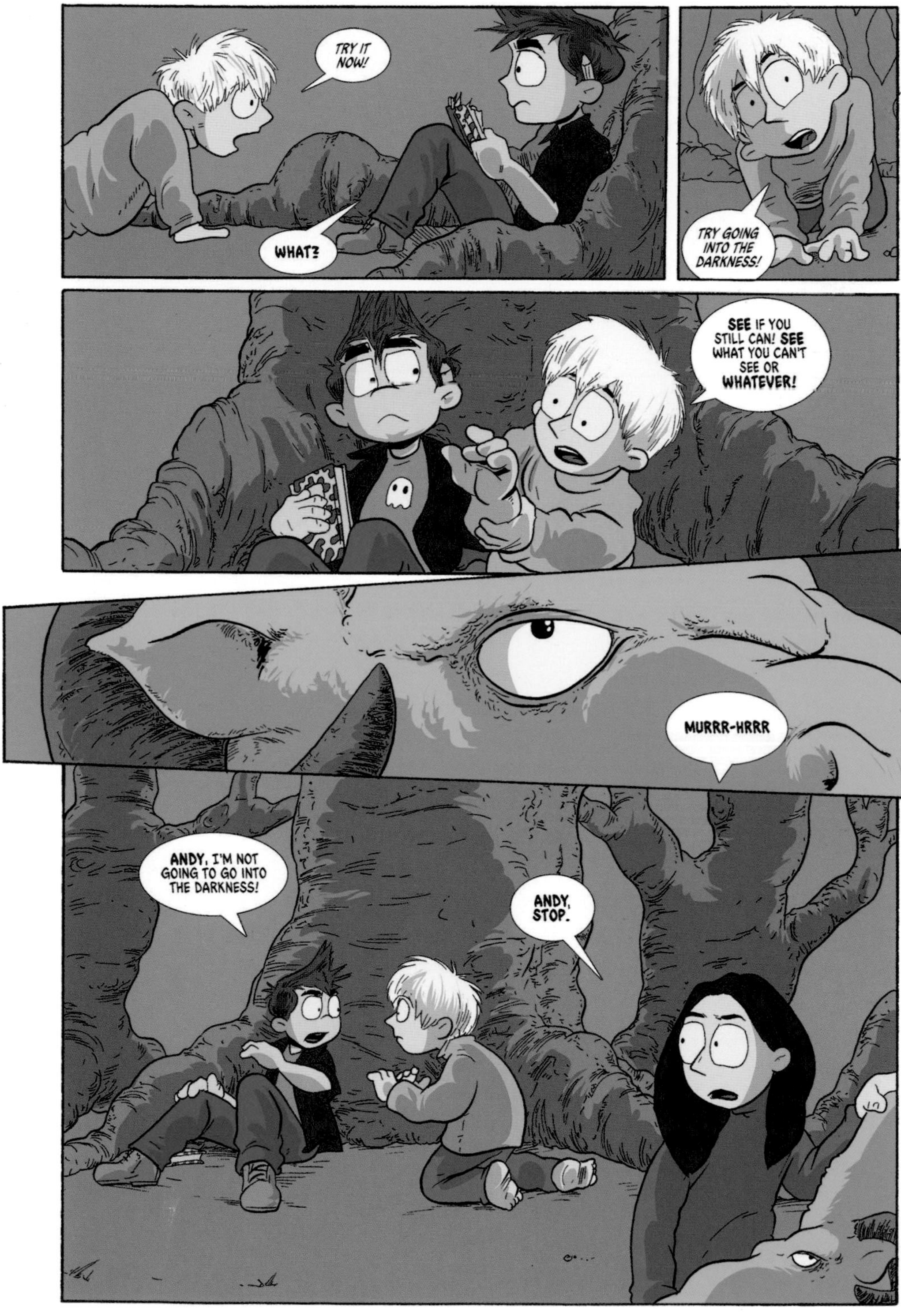
TRY IT NOW!
WHAT?
TRY GOING INTO THE DARKNESS!
SEE IF YOU STILL CAN! SEE WHAT YOU CAN'T SEE OR WHATEVER!
MURRR-HRRR
ANDY, I'M NOT GOING TO GO INTO THE DARKNESS!
ANDY, STOP.

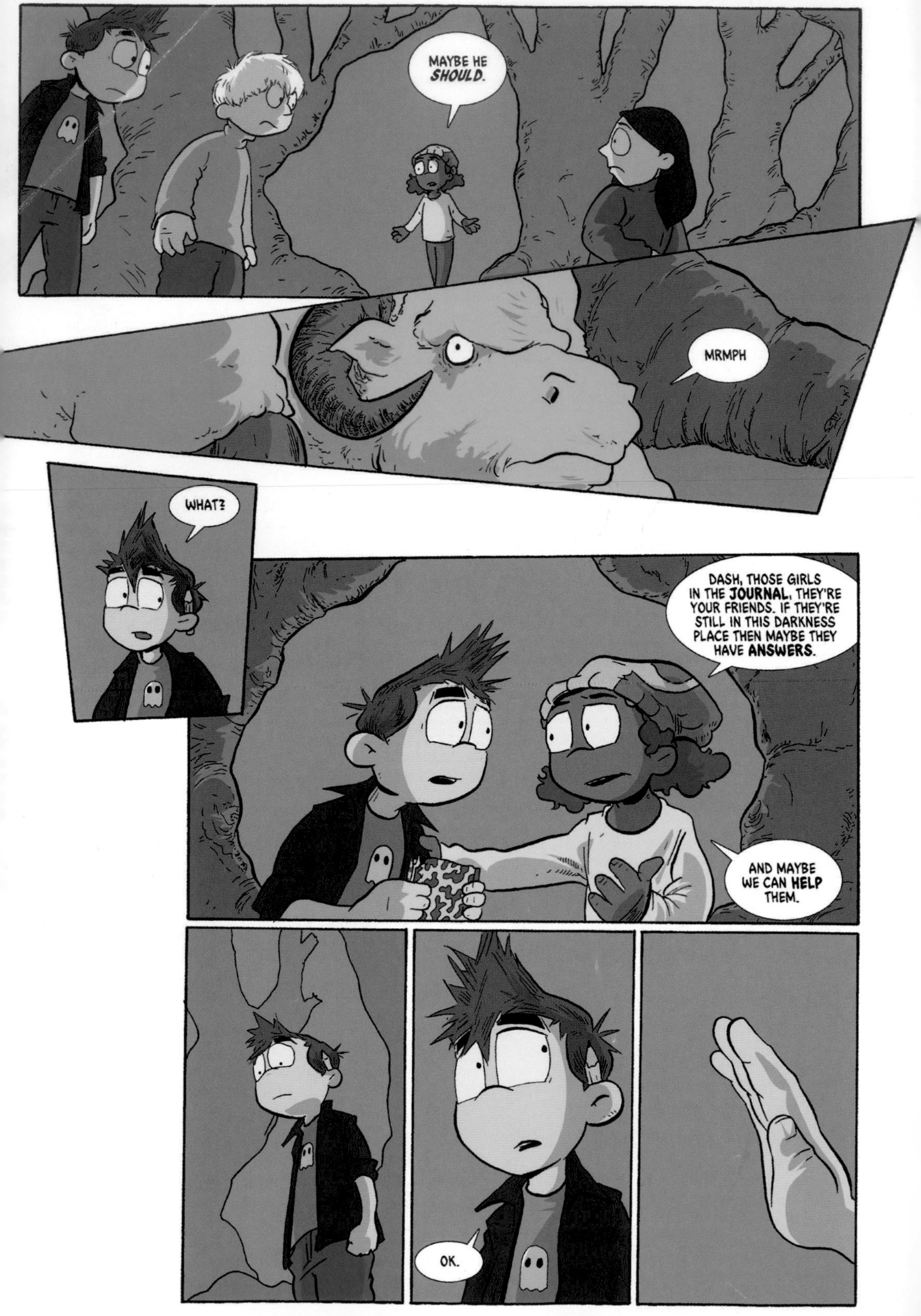
MAYBE HE SHOULD.
MRMPH
WHAT?
DASH, THOSE GIRLS IN THE JOURNAL, THEY'RE YOUR FRIENDS. IF THEY'RE STILL IN THIS DARKNESS PLACE THEN MAYBE THEY HAVE ANSWERS.
AND MAYBE WE CAN HELP THEM.
OK.

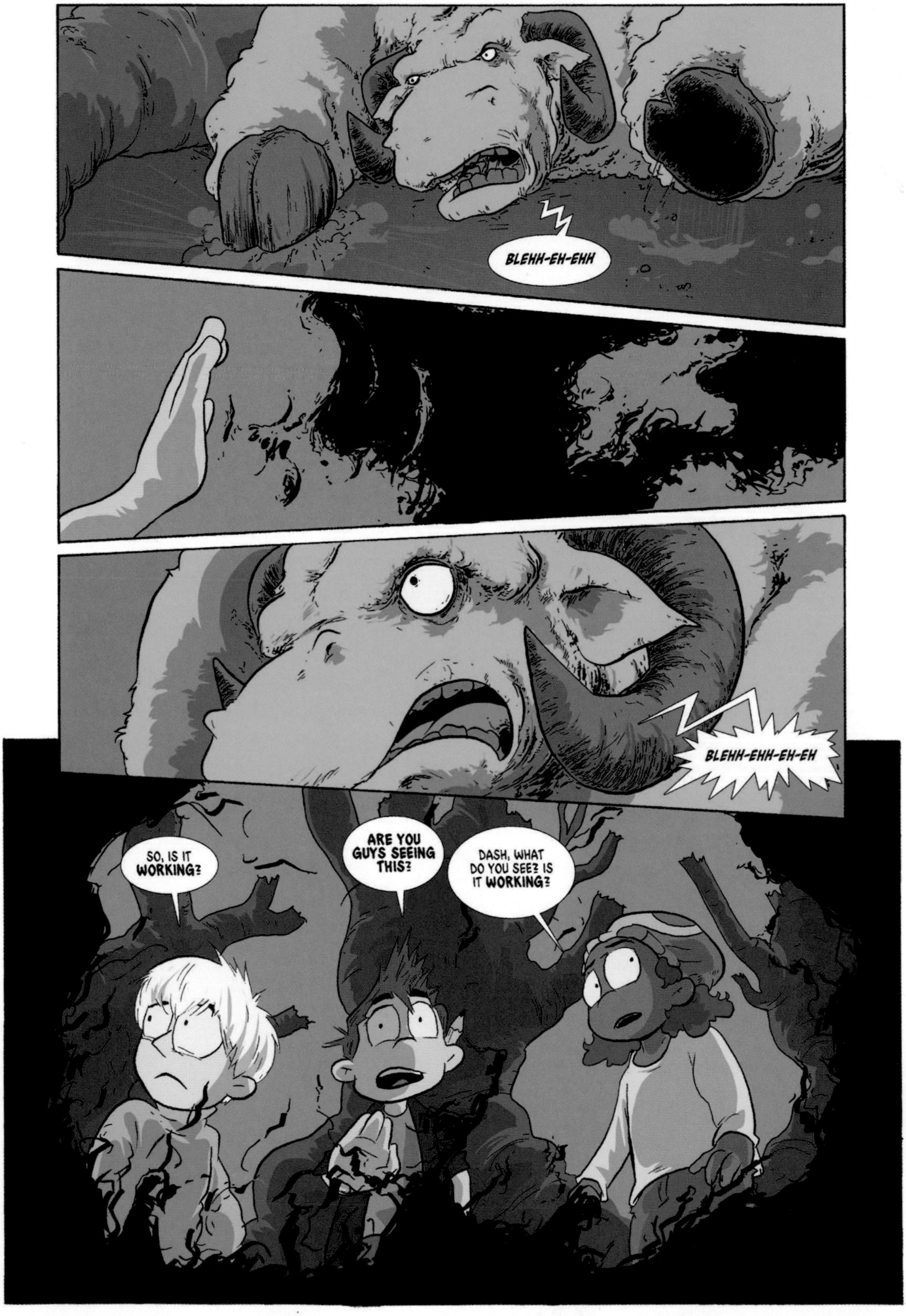
BLEHH-EH-EHH
BLEHH-EHH-EH-EH
SO, IS IT WORKING?
ARE YOU GUYS SEEING THIS?
DASH, WHAT DO YOU SEE? IS IT WORKING?

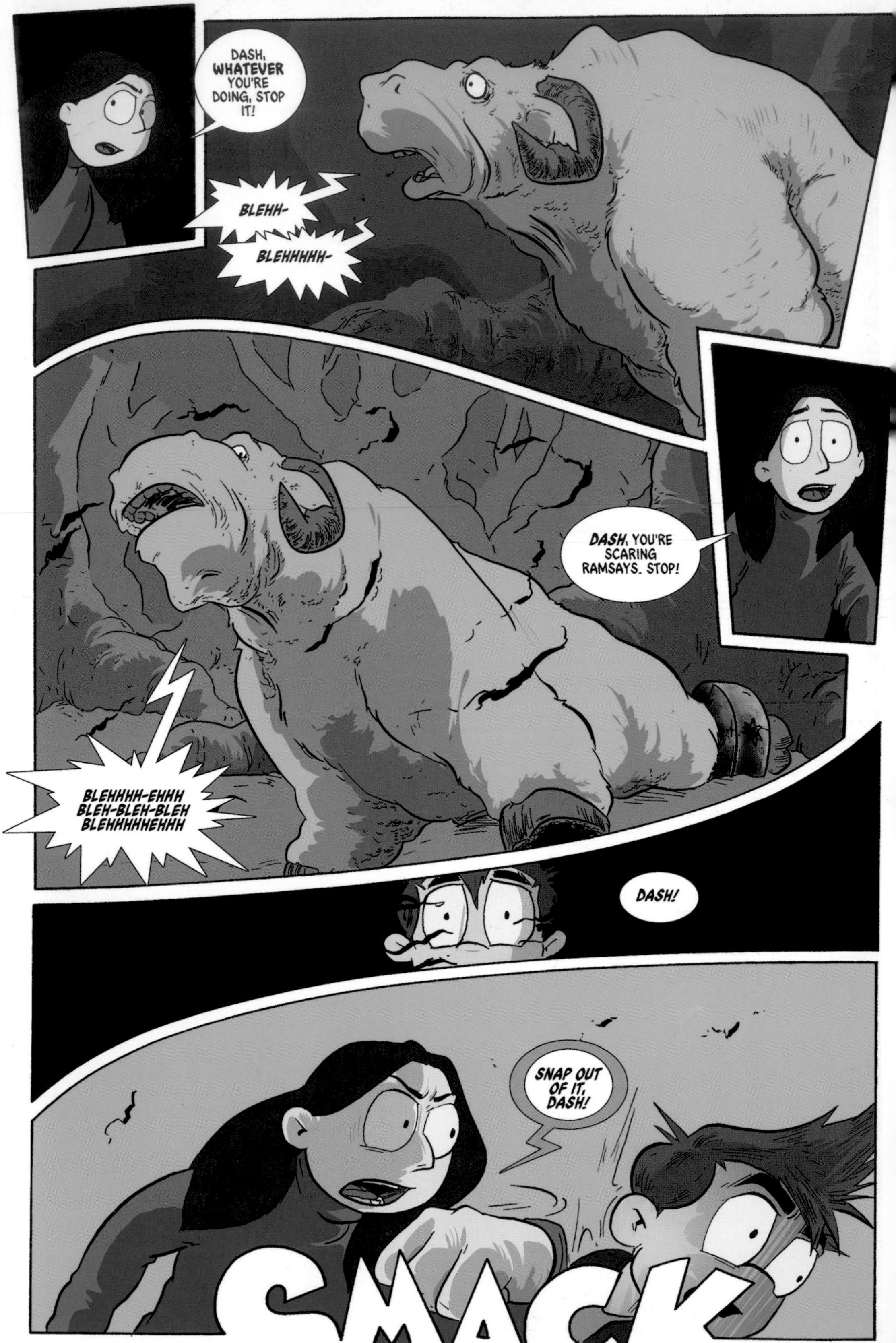
DASH, WHATEVER YOU'RE DOING, STOP IT!
BLEHH-
BLEHHHHH-
DASH, YOU'RE SCARING RAMSAYS. STOP!
BLEHHHH-EHHH
BLEH-BLEH-BLEH
BLEHHHHHEHHH
DASH!
SNAP OUT OF IT, DASH!
SMACK

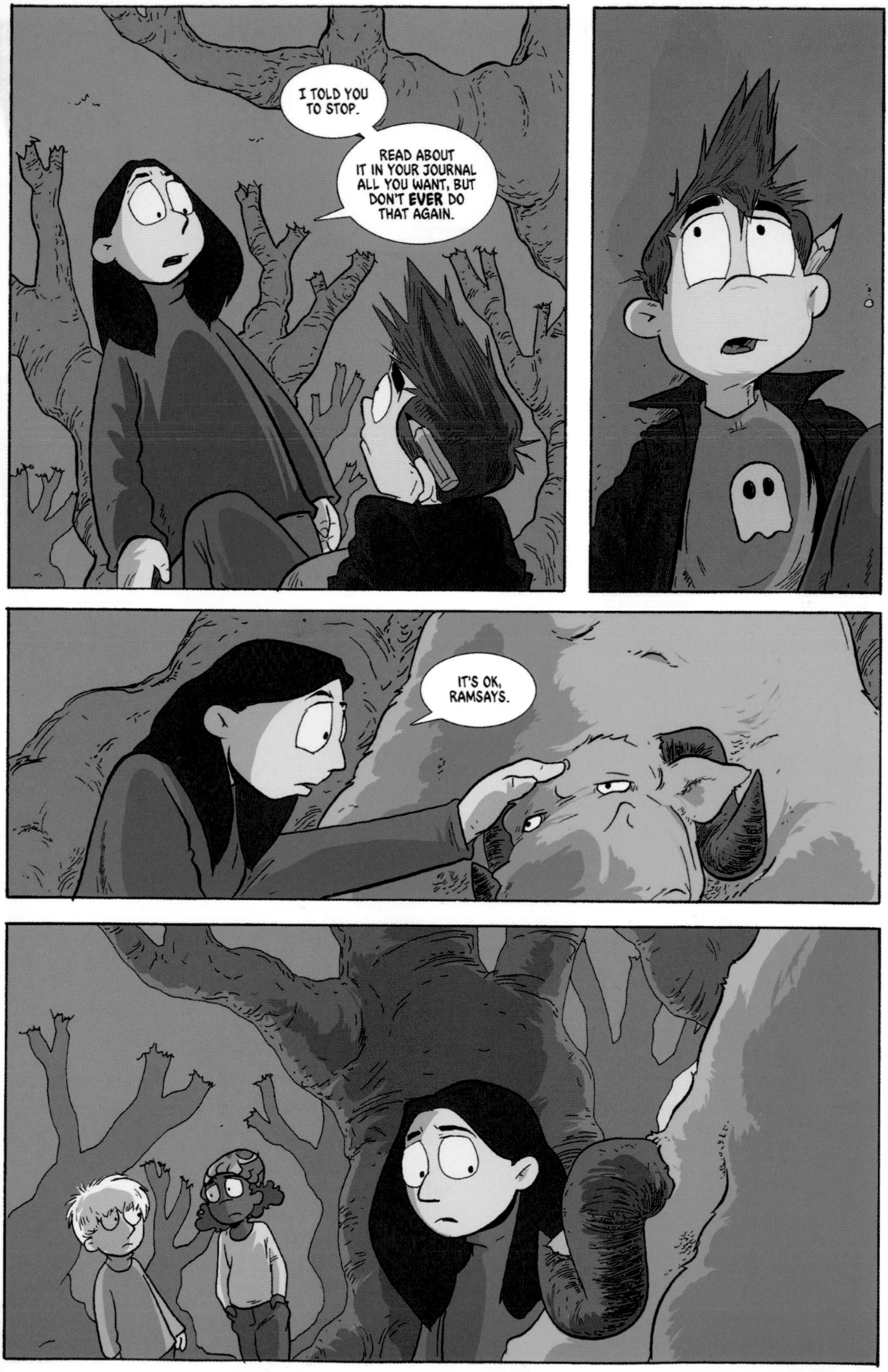
I TOLD YOU TO STOP.
READ ABOUT IT IN YOUR JOURNAL ALL YOU WANT, BUT DON'T EVER DO THAT AGAIN.
IT'S OK, RAMSAYS.

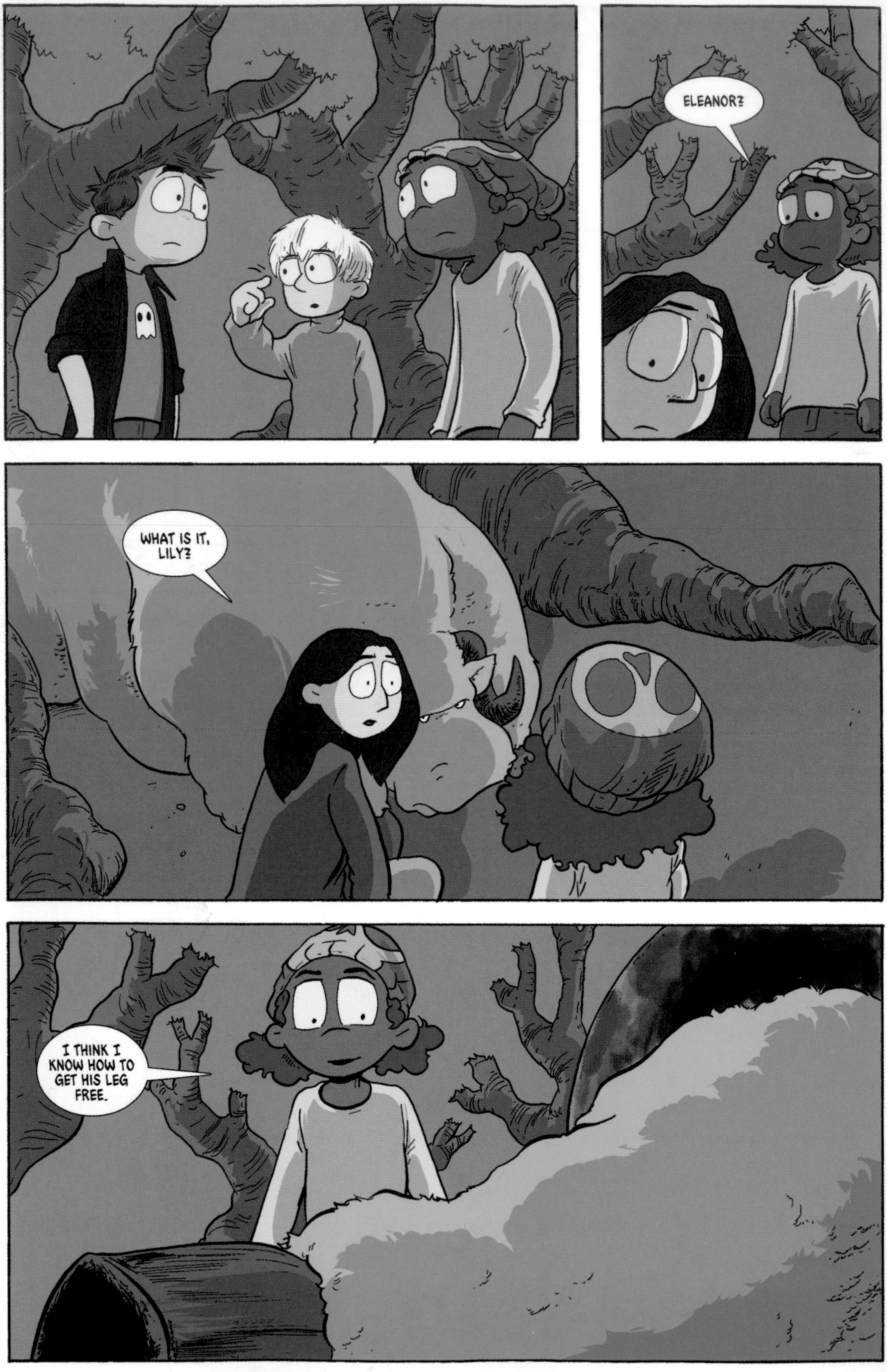
ELEANOR?
WHAT IS IT, LILY?
I THINK I KNOW HOW TO GET HIS LEG FREE.

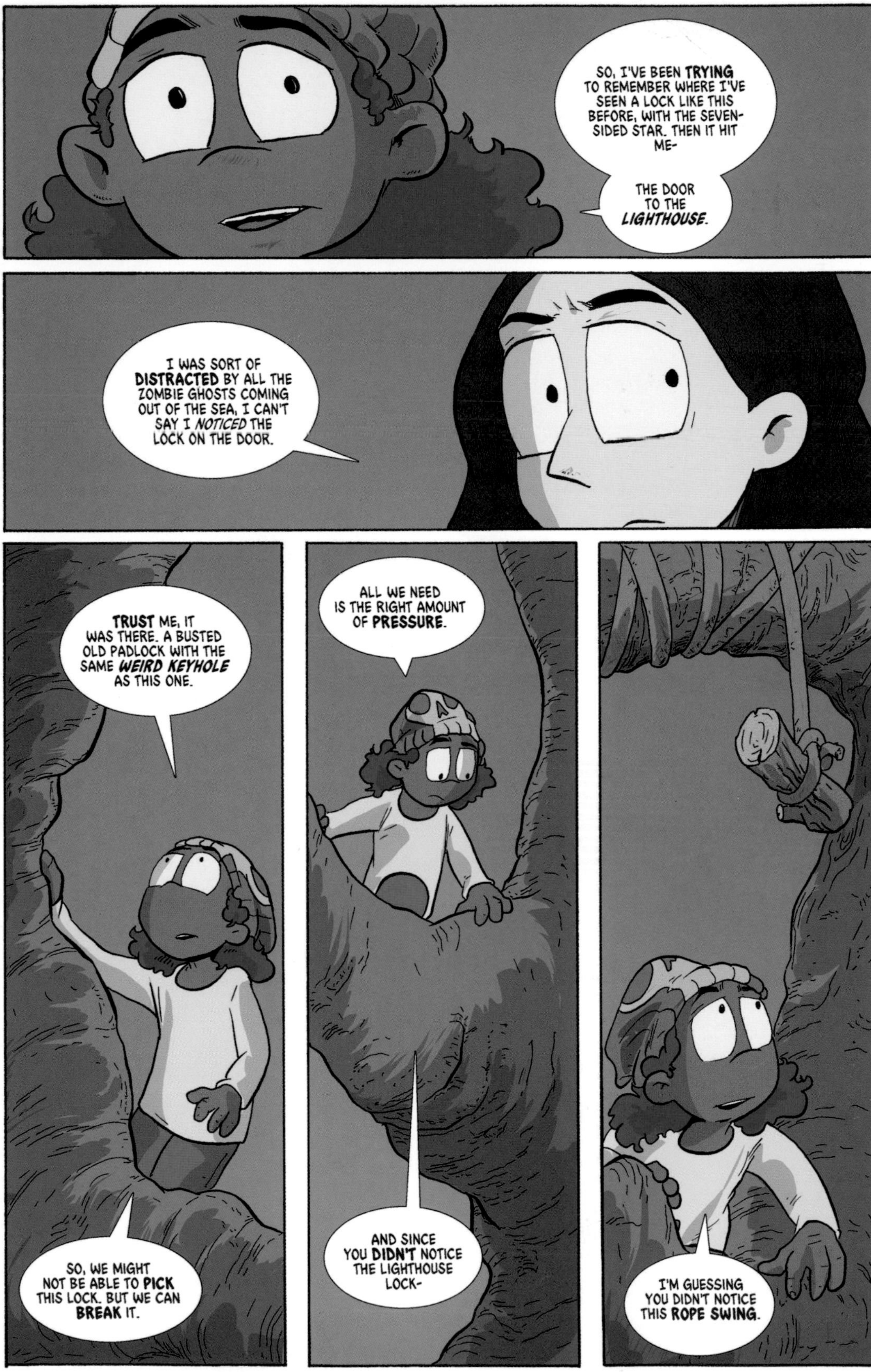
SO, I'VE BEEN **TRYING** TO REMEMBER WHERE I'VE SEEN A LOCK LIKE THIS BEFORE, WITH THE SEVEN-SIDED STAR. THEN IT HIT ME-
THE DOOR TO THE ***LIGHTHOUSE***.
I WAS SORT OF **DISTRACTED** BY ALL THE ZOMBIE GHOSTS COMING OUT OF THE SEA, I CAN'T SAY I *NOTICED* THE LOCK ON THE DOOR.
TRUST ME, IT WAS THERE. A BUSTED OLD PADLOCK WITH THE SAME ***WEIRD KEYHOLE*** AS THIS ONE.
SO, WE MIGHT NOT BE ABLE TO **PICK** THIS LOCK. BUT WE CAN **BREAK** IT.
ALL WE NEED IS THE RIGHT AMOUNT OF **PRESSURE**.
AND SINCE YOU **DIDN'T** NOTICE THE LIGHTHOUSE LOCK-
I'M GUESSING YOU DIDN'T NOTICE THIS **ROPE SWING**.

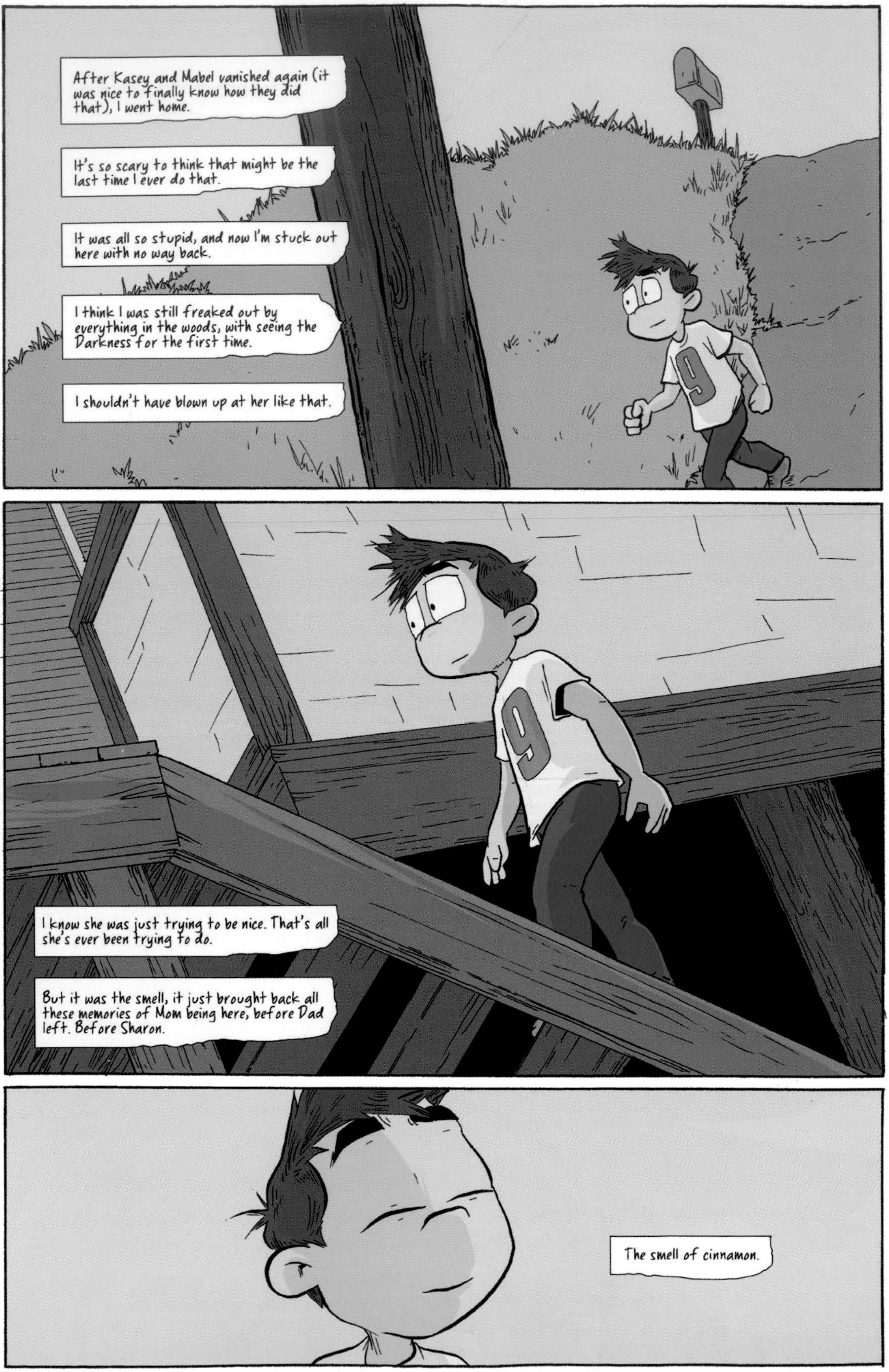
After Kasey and Mabel vanished again (it was nice to finally know how they did that), I went home.
It's so scary to think that might be the last time I ever do that.
It was all so stupid, and now I'm stuck out here with no way back.
I think I was still freaked out by everything in the woods, with seeing the Darkness for the first time.
I shouldn't have blown up at her like that.
I know she was just trying to be nice. That's all she's ever been trying to do.
But it was the smell, it just brought back all these memories of Mom being here, before Dad left. Before Sharon.
The smell of cinnamon.

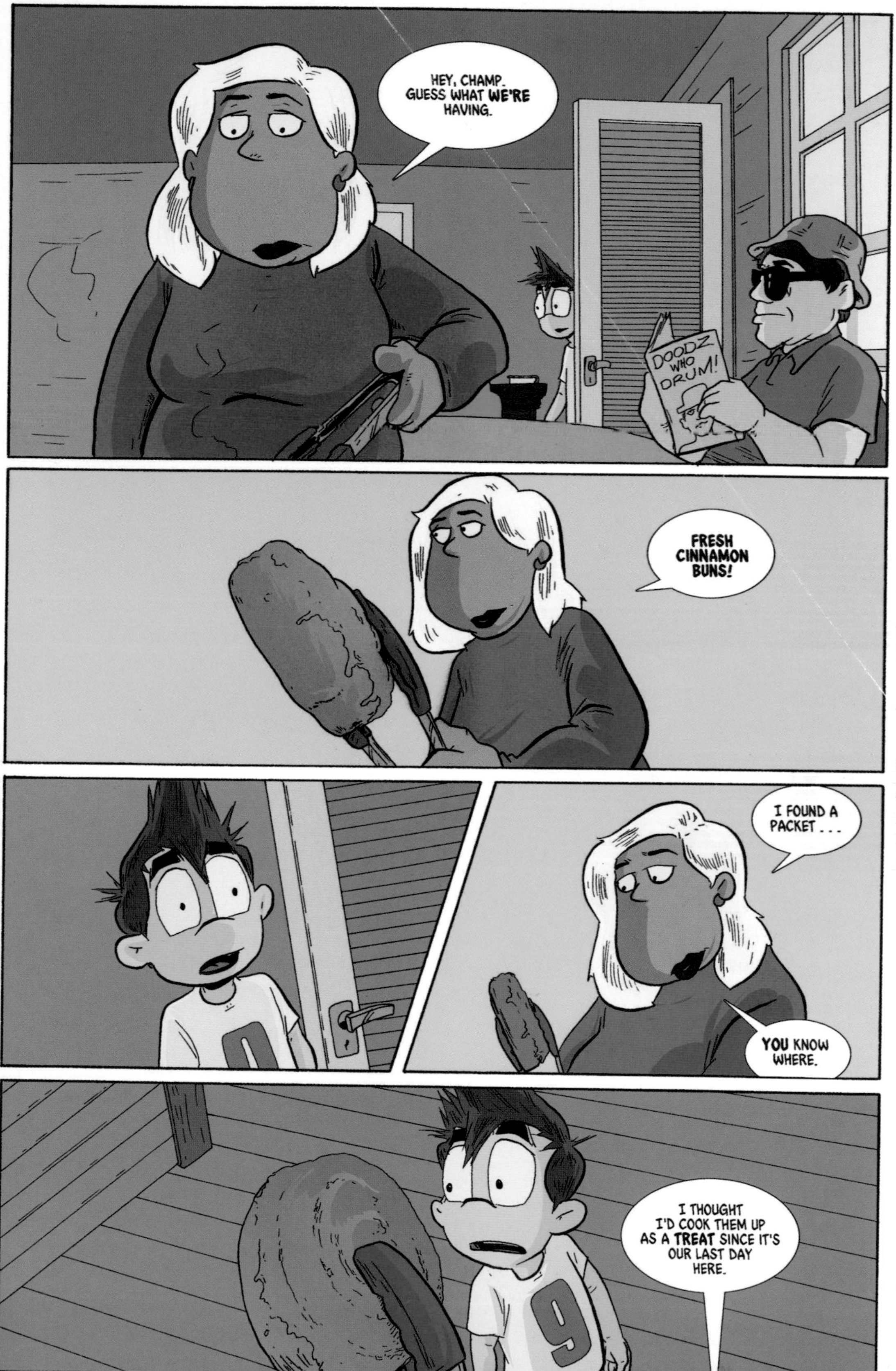
HEY, CHAMP. GUESS WHAT WE'RE HAVING.
DOODZ WHO DRUM!
FRESH CINNAMON BUNS!
I FOUND A PACKET . . .
YOU KNOW WHERE.
I THOUGHT I'D COOK THEM UP AS A TREAT SINCE IT'S OUR LAST DAY HERE.

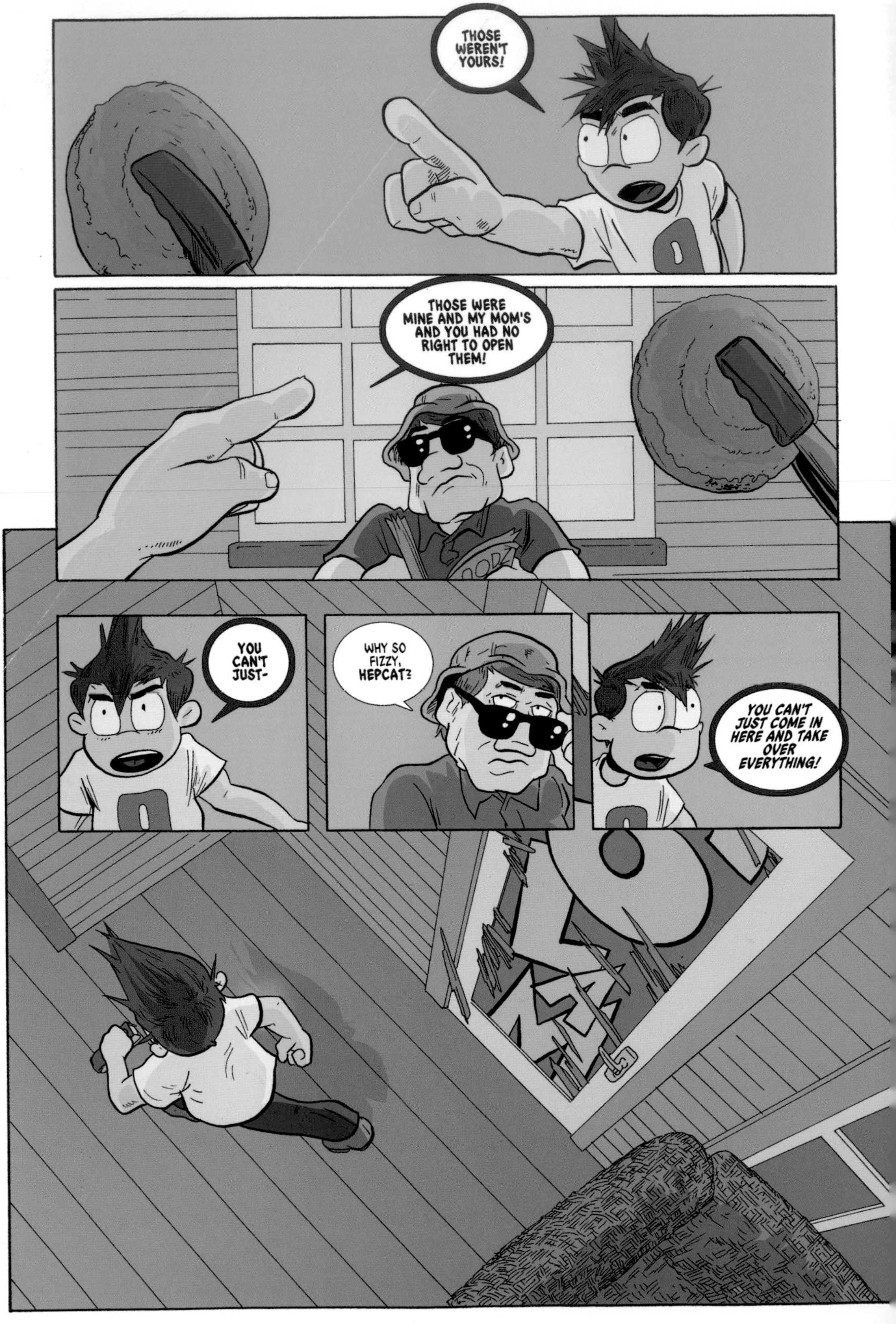
THOSE WEREN'T YOURS!
THOSE WERE MINE AND MY MOM'S AND YOU HAD NO RIGHT TO OPEN THEM!
YOU CAN'T JUST-
WHY SO FIZZY, HEPCAT?
YOU CAN'T JUST COME IN HERE AND TAKE OVER EVERYTHING!

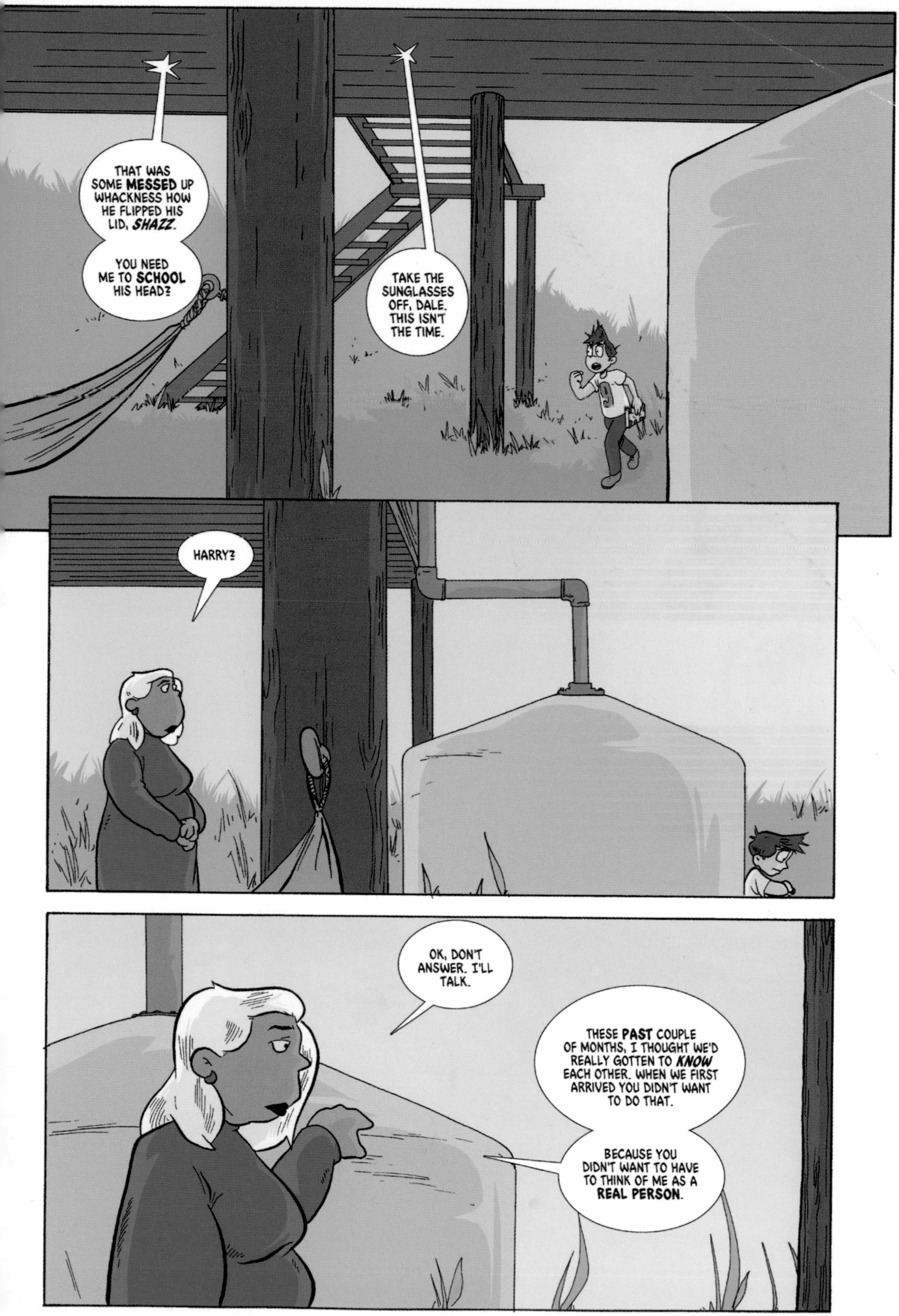
THAT WAS SOME MESSED UP WHACKNESS HOW HE FLIPPED HIS LID, SHAZZ.
YOU NEED ME TO SCHOOL HIS HEAD?
TAKE THE SUNGLASSES OFF, DALE. THIS ISN'T THE TIME.
HARRY?
OK, DON'T ANSWER. I'LL TALK.
THESE PAST COUPLE OF MONTHS, I THOUGHT WE'D REALLY GOTTEN TO KNOW EACH OTHER. WHEN WE FIRST ARRIVED YOU DIDN'T WANT TO DO THAT.
BECAUSE YOU DIDN'T WANT TO HAVE TO THINK OF ME AS A REAL PERSON.

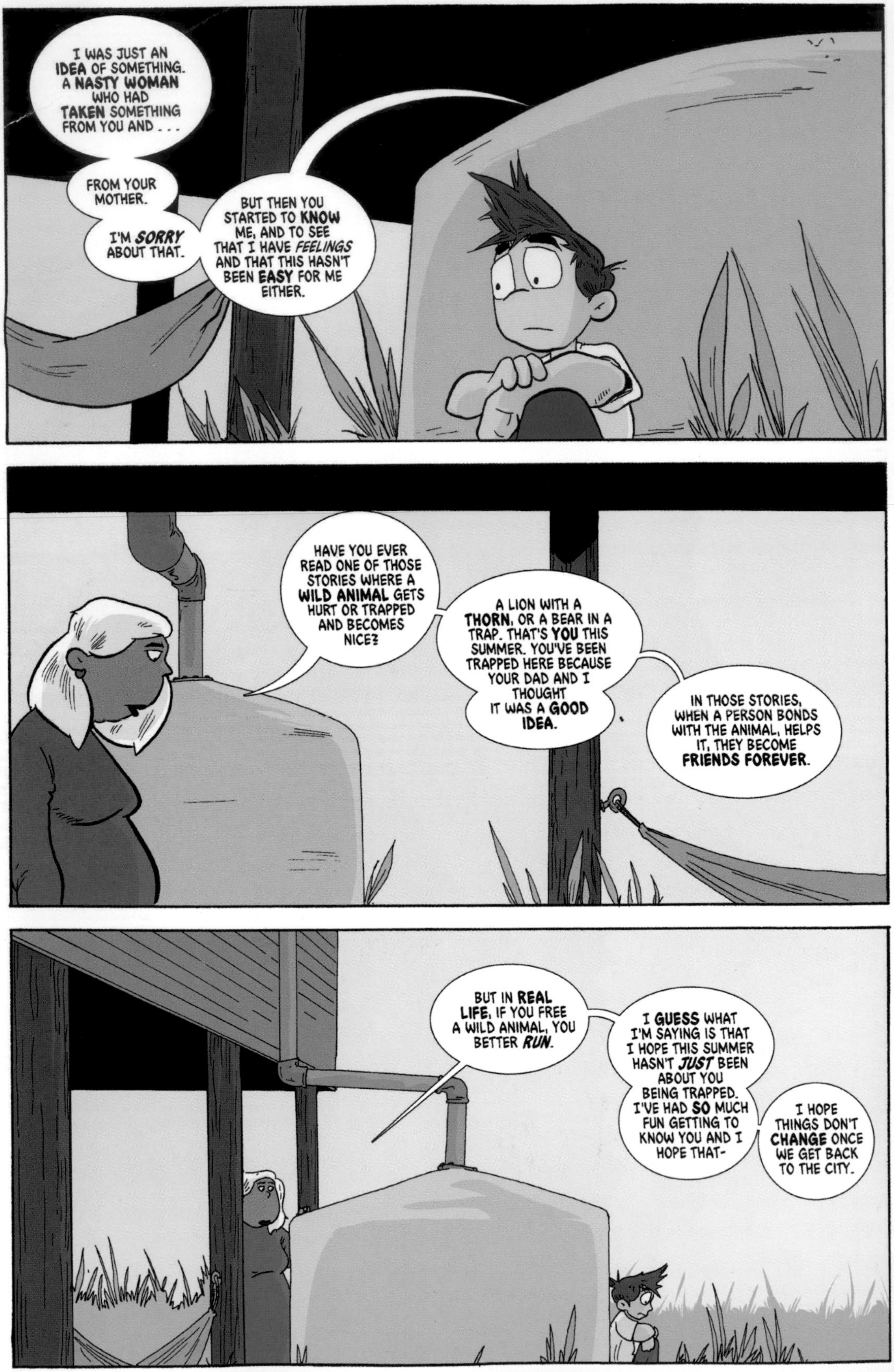
I WAS JUST AN IDEA OF SOMETHING. A NASTY WOMAN WHO HAD TAKEN SOMETHING FROM YOU AND . . .
FROM YOUR MOTHER.
I'M SORRY ABOUT THAT.
BUT THEN YOU STARTED TO KNOW ME, AND TO SEE THAT I HAVE FEELINGS AND THAT THIS HASN'T BEEN EASY FOR ME EITHER.
HAVE YOU EVER READ ONE OF THOSE STORIES WHERE A WILD ANIMAL GETS HURT OR TRAPPED AND BECOMES NICE?
A LION WITH A THORN, OR A BEAR IN A TRAP. THAT'S YOU THIS SUMMER. YOU'VE BEEN TRAPPED HERE BECAUSE YOUR DAD AND I THOUGHT IT WAS A GOOD IDEA.
IN THOSE STORIES, WHEN A PERSON BONDS WITH THE ANIMAL, HELPS IT, THEY BECOME FRIENDS FOREVER.
BUT IN REAL LIFE, IF YOU FREE A WILD ANIMAL, YOU BETTER RUN.
I GUESS WHAT I'M SAYING IS THAT I HOPE THIS SUMMER HASN'T JUST BEEN ABOUT YOU BEING TRAPPED. I'VE HAD SO MUCH FUN GETTING TO KNOW YOU AND I HOPE THAT-
I HOPE THINGS DON'T CHANGE ONCE WE GET BACK TO THE CITY.

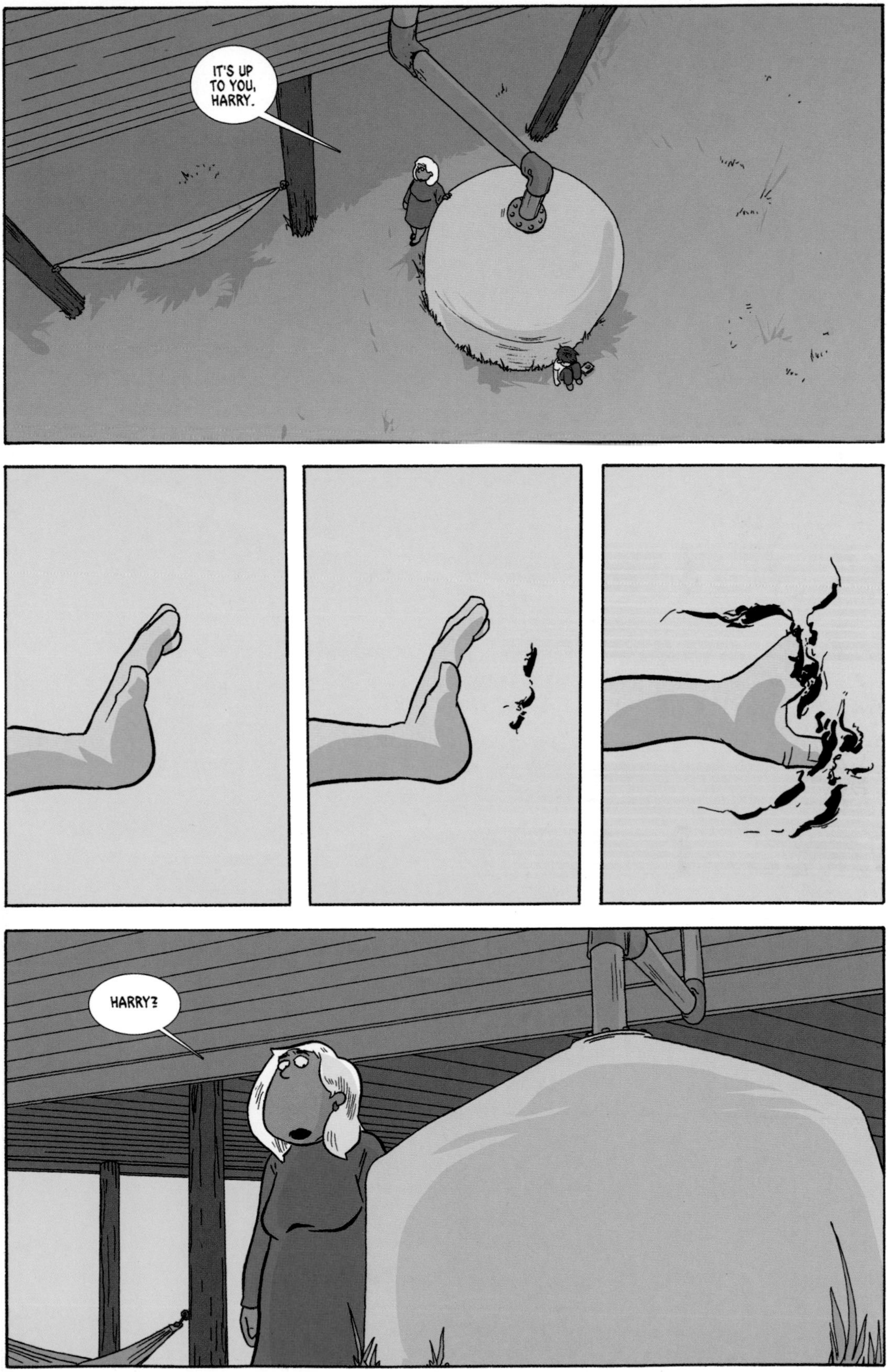
IT'S UP TO YOU, HARRY.
HARRY?

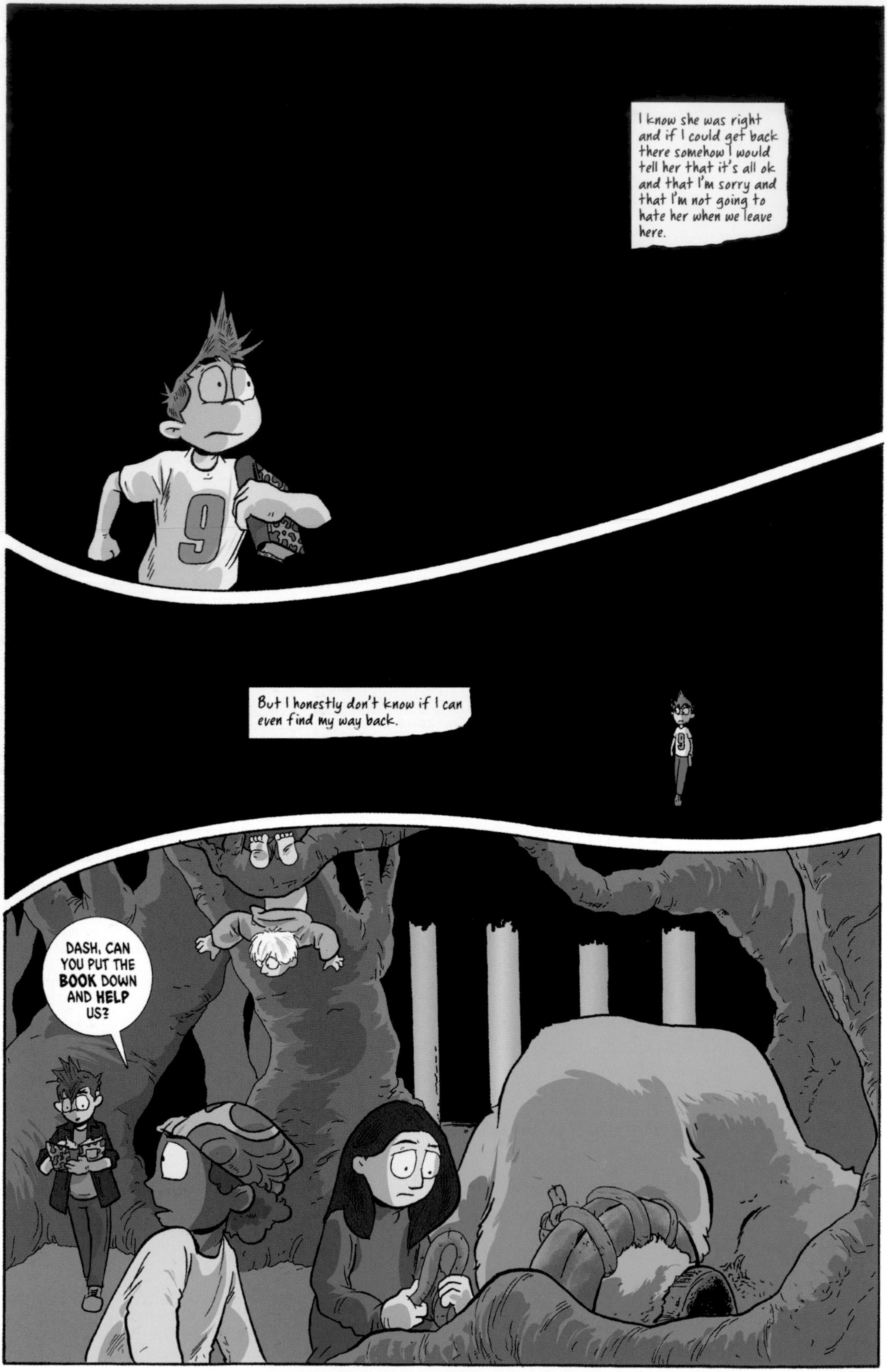
I know she was right and if I could get back there somehow I would tell her that it's all ok and that I'm sorry and that I'm not going to hate her when we leave here.
But I honestly don't know if I can even find my way back.
DASH, CAN YOU PUT THE **BOOK** DOWN AND **HELP** US?

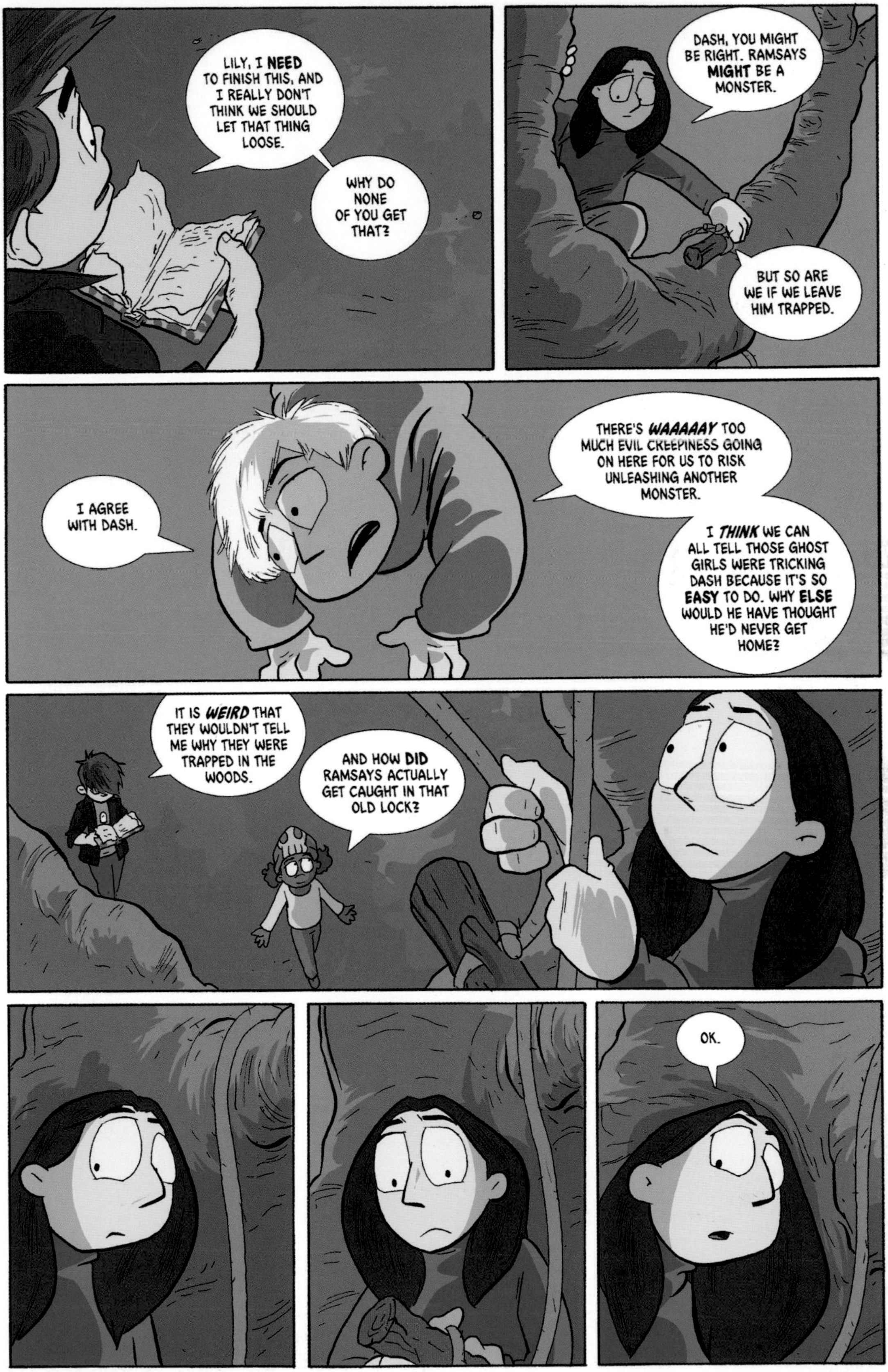
LILY, I **NEED** TO FINISH THIS, AND I REALLY DON'T THINK WE SHOULD LET THAT THING LOOSE.
WHY DO NONE OF YOU GET THAT?
DASH, YOU MIGHT BE RIGHT. RAMSAYS **MIGHT** BE A MONSTER.
BUT SO ARE WE IF WE LEAVE HIM TRAPPED.
I AGREE WITH DASH.
THERE'S ***WAAAAAY*** TOO MUCH EVIL CREEPINESS GOING ON HERE FOR US TO RISK UNLEASHING ANOTHER MONSTER.
I ***THINK*** WE CAN ALL TELL THOSE GHOST GIRLS WERE TRICKING DASH BECAUSE IT'S SO **EASY** TO DO. WHY **ELSE** WOULD HE HAVE THOUGHT HE'D NEVER GET HOME?
IT IS ***WEIRD*** THAT THEY WOULDN'T TELL ME WHY THEY WERE TRAPPED IN THE WOODS.
AND HOW **DID** RAMSAYS ACTUALLY GET CAUGHT IN THAT OLD LOCK?
OK.

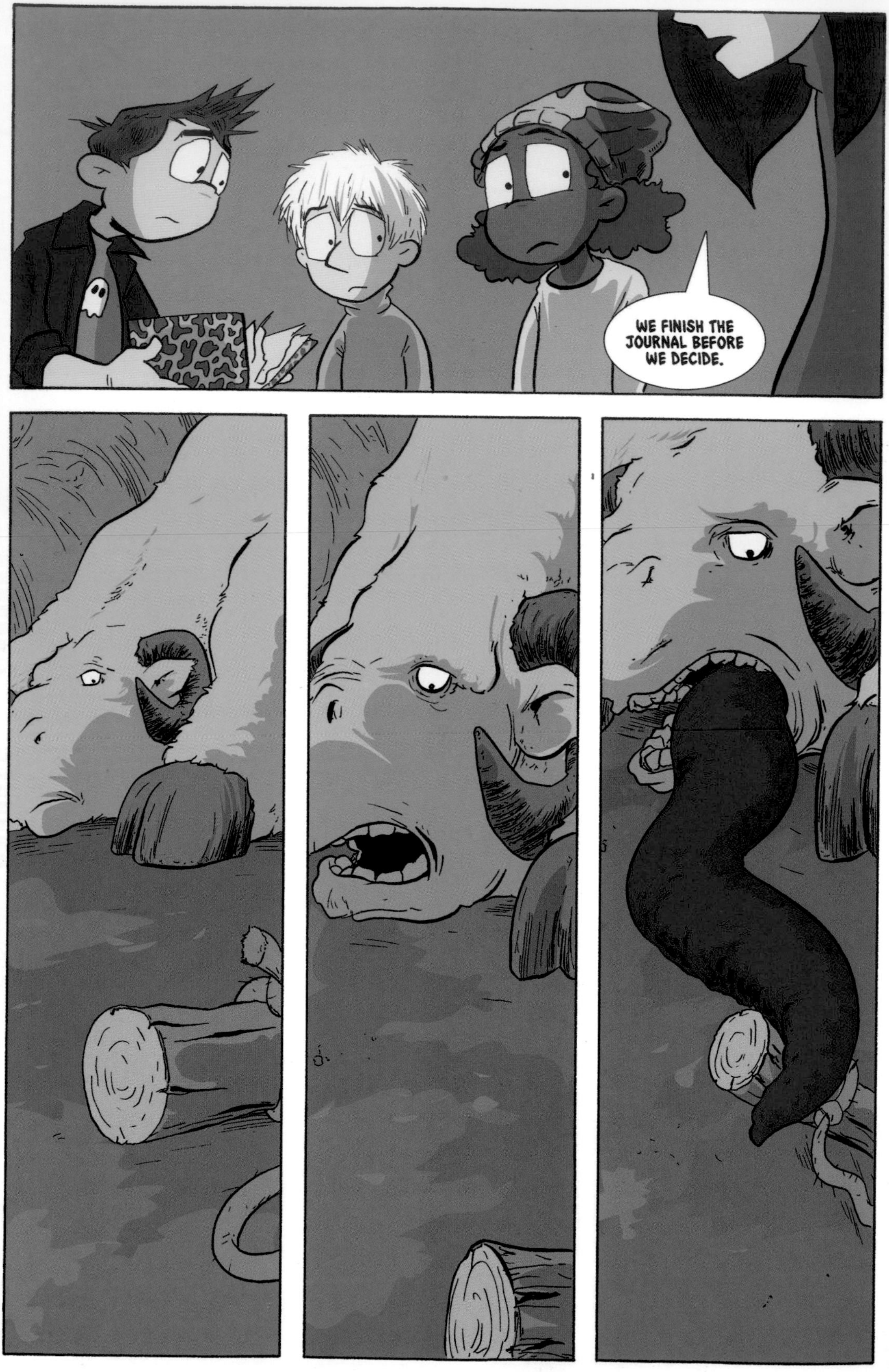
WE FINISH THE JOURNAL BEFORE WE DECIDE.

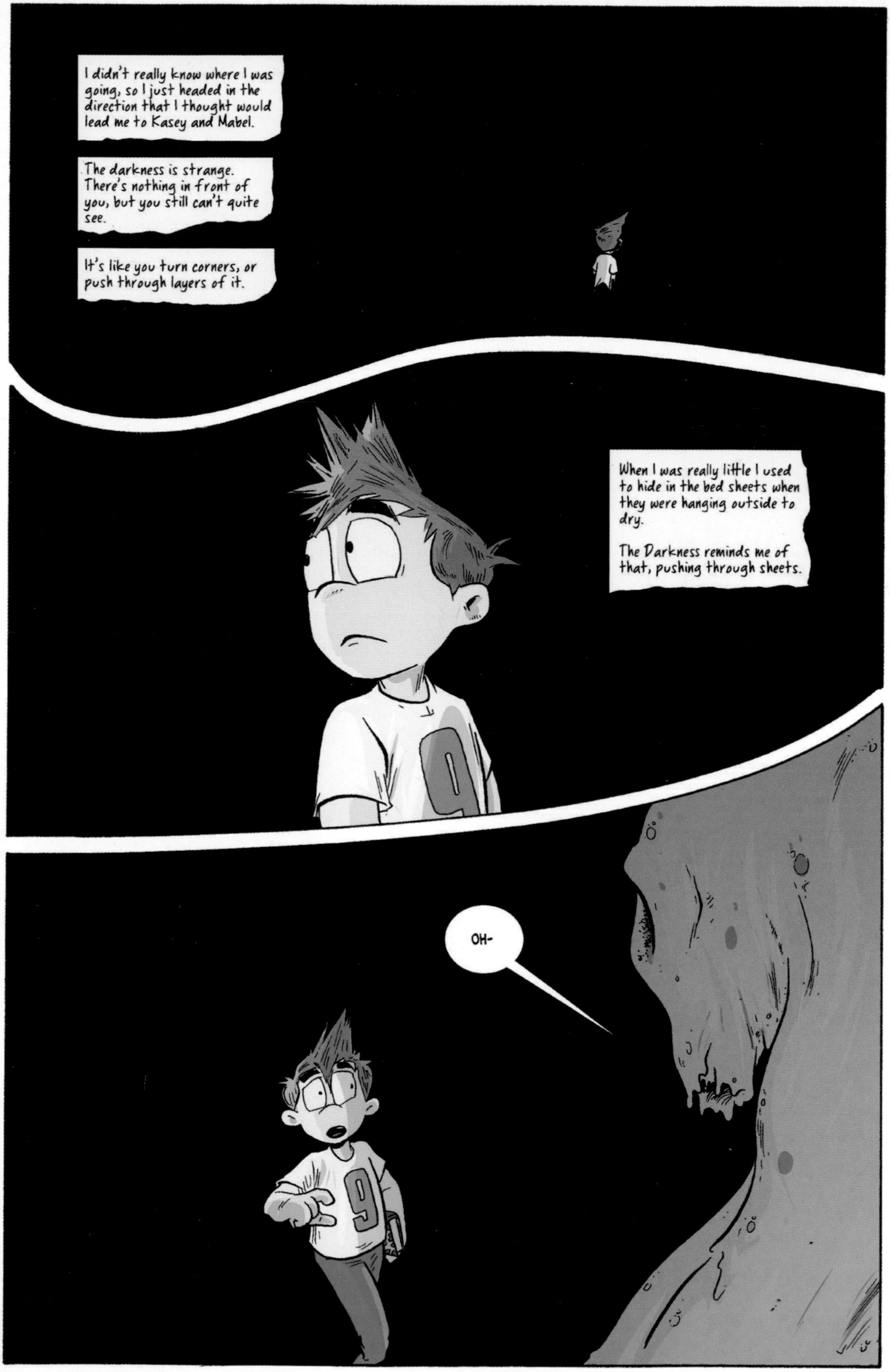
I didn't really know where I was going, so I just headed in the direction that I thought would lead me to Kasey and Mabel.
The darkness is strange. There's nothing in front of you, but you still can't quite see.
It's like you turn corners, or push through layers of it.
When I was really little I used to hide in the bed sheets when they were hanging outside to dry.
The Darkness reminds me of that, pushing through sheets.
OH-

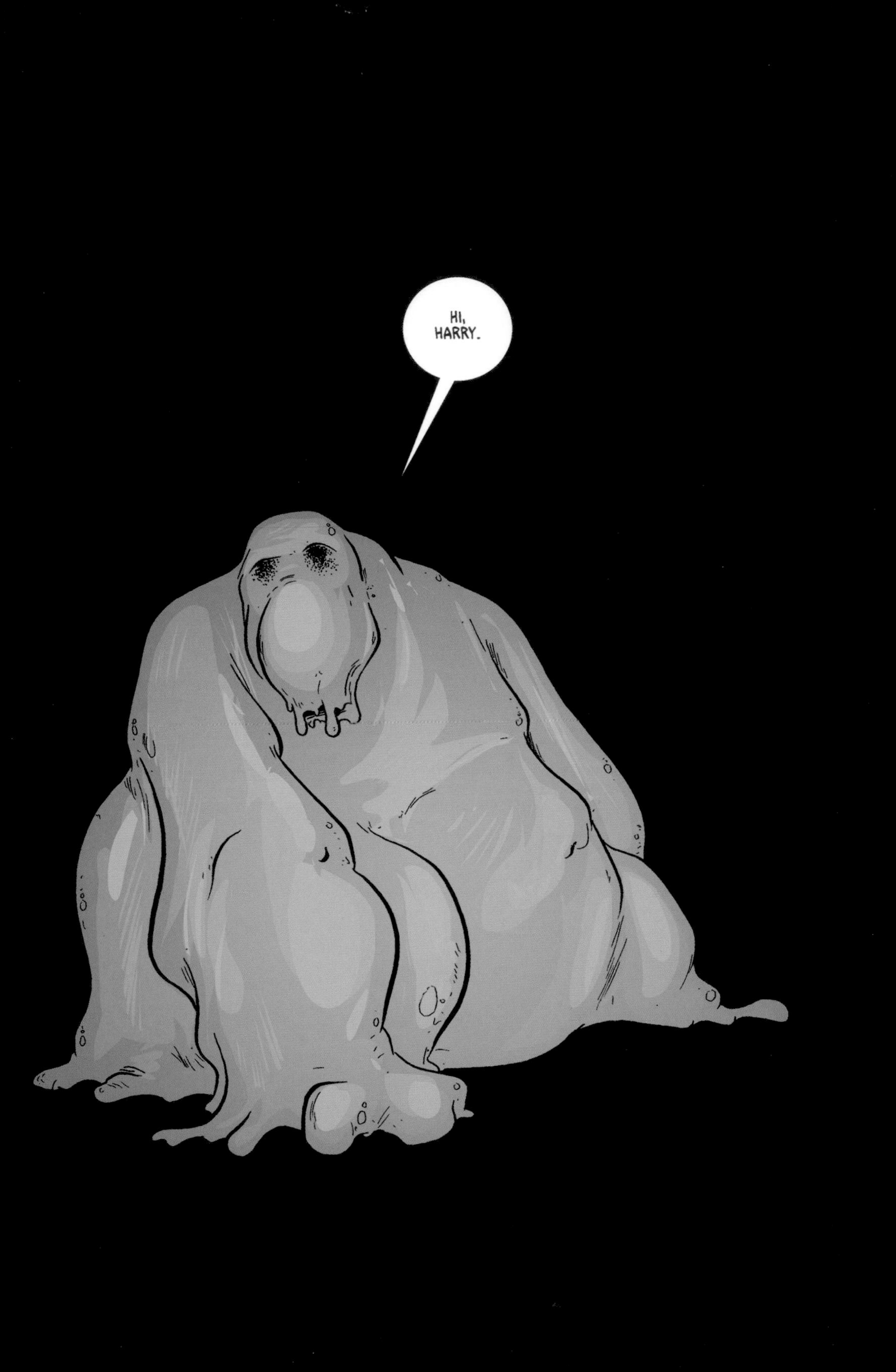
HI, HARRY.

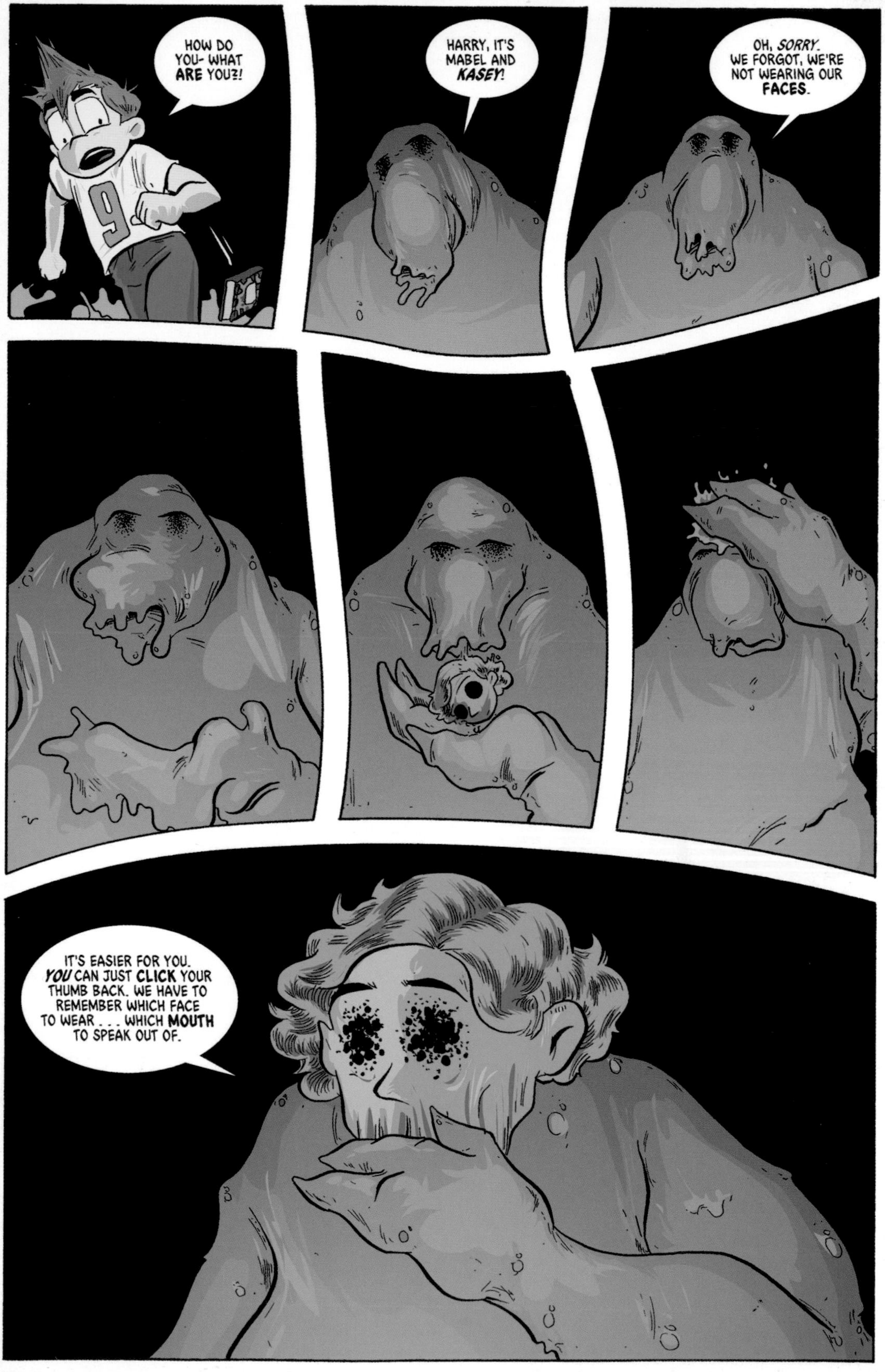
HOW DO YOU- WHAT ARE YOU?!
HARRY, IT'S MABEL AND KASEY!
OH, SORRY. WE FORGOT, WE'RE NOT WEARING OUR FACES.
IT'S EASIER FOR YOU. YOU CAN JUST CLICK YOUR THUMB BACK. WE HAVE TO REMEMBER WHICH FACE TO WEAR . . . WHICH MOUTH TO SPEAK OUT OF.

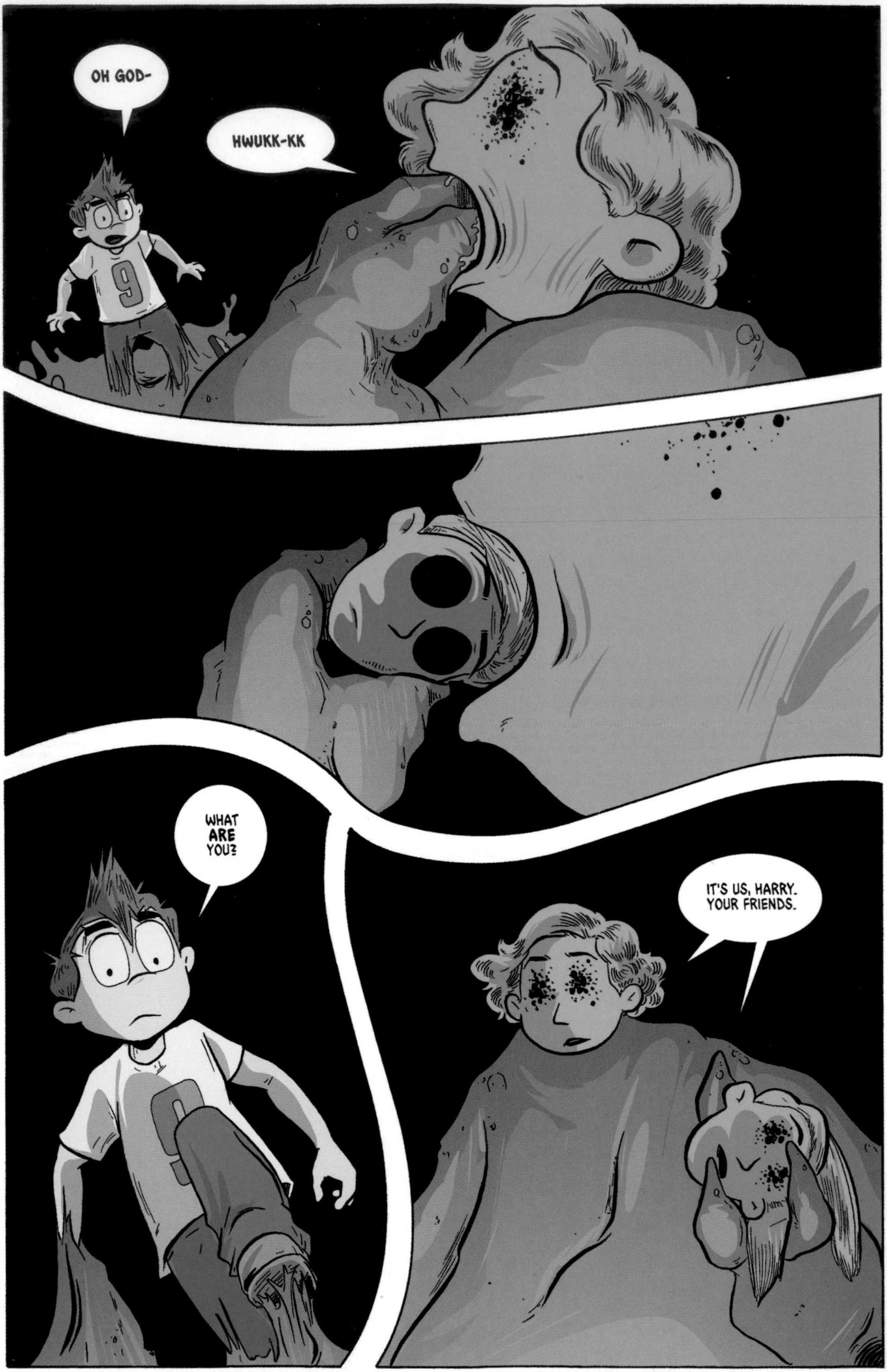
OH GOD-
HWUKK-KK
WHAT ARE YOU?
IT'S US, HARRY. YOUR FRIENDS.

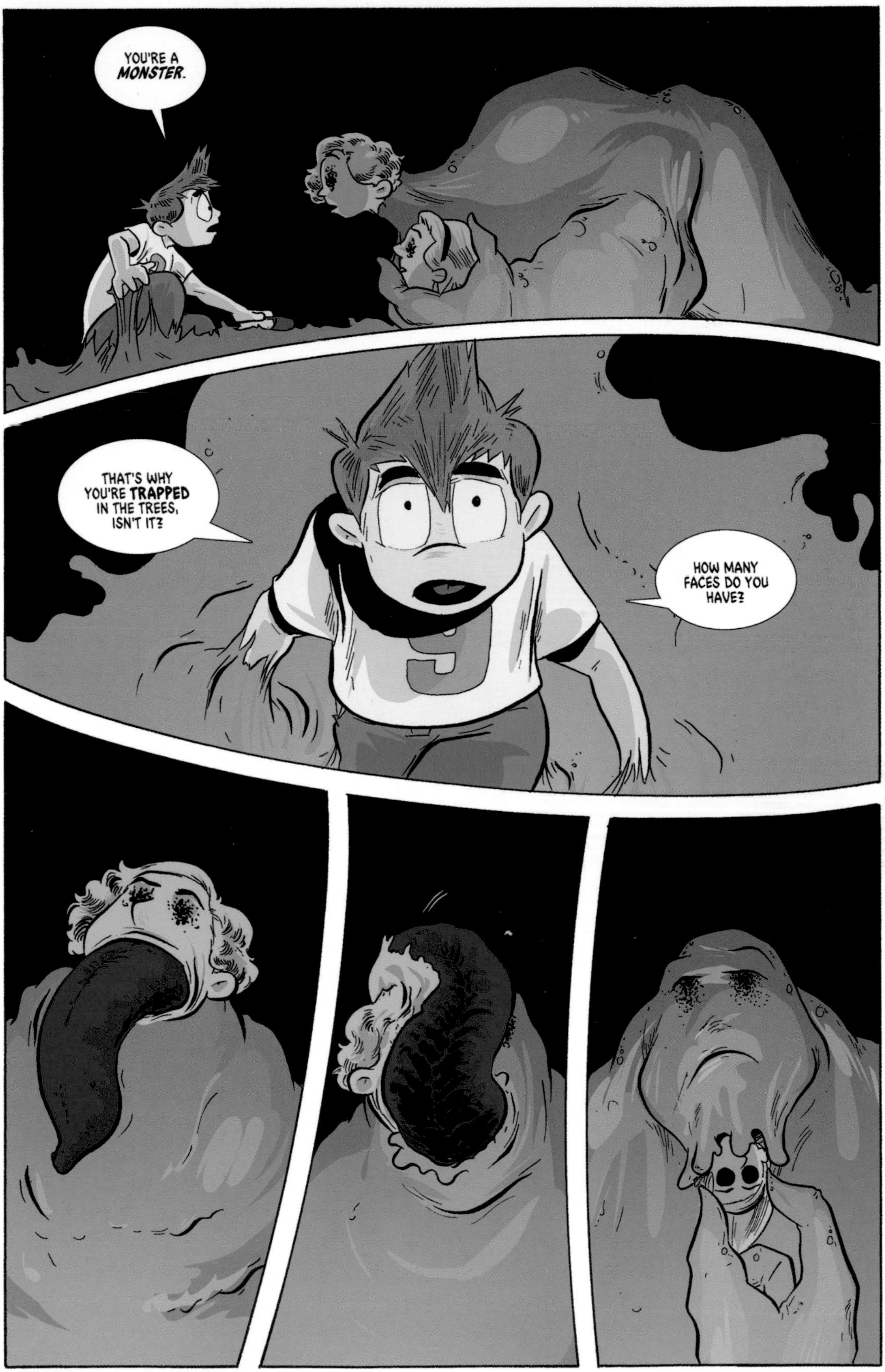
YOU'RE A MONSTER.
THAT'S WHY YOU'RE TRAPPED IN THE TREES, ISN'T IT?
HOW MANY FACES DO YOU HAVE?

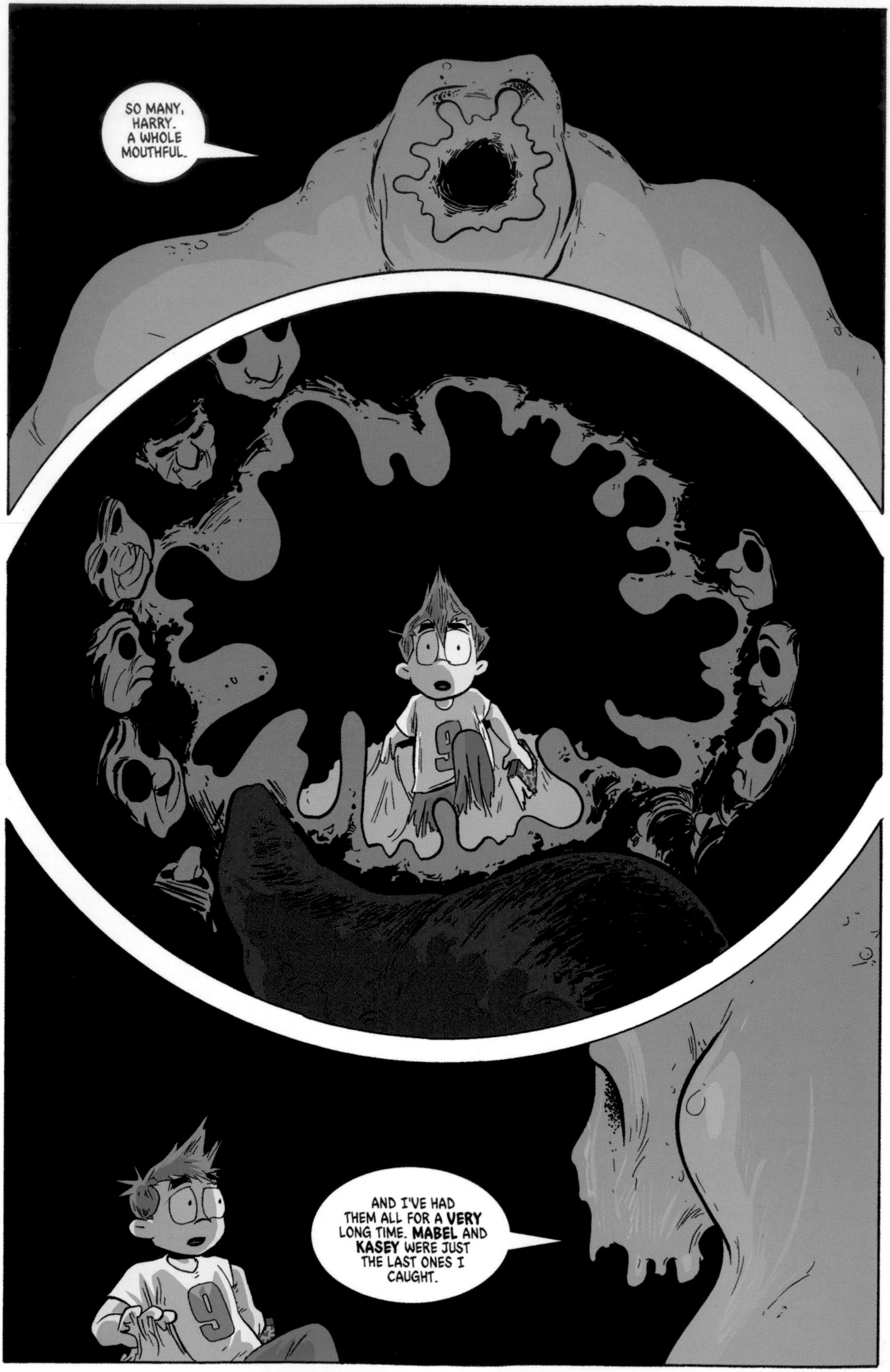
SO MANY, HARRY. A WHOLE MOUTHFUL.
AND I'VE HAD THEM ALL FOR A **VERY** LONG TIME. **MABEL** AND **KASEY** WERE JUST THE LAST ONES I CAUGHT.

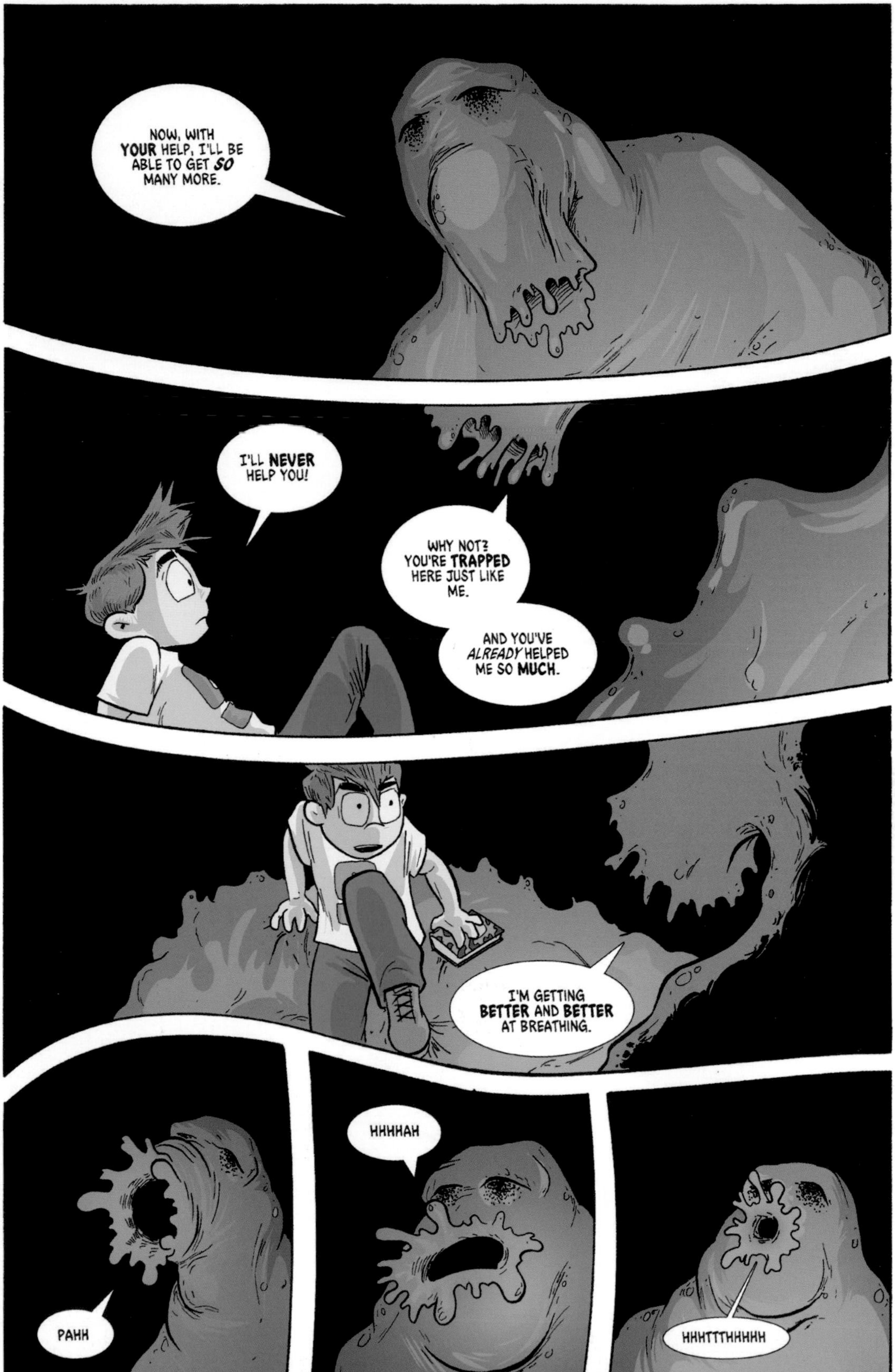
NOW, WITH YOUR HELP, I'LL BE ABLE TO GET SO MANY MORE.
I'LL NEVER HELP YOU!
WHY NOT? YOU'RE TRAPPED HERE JUST LIKE ME.
AND YOU'VE ALREADY HELPED ME SO MUCH.
I'M GETTING BETTER AND BETTER AT BREATHING.
PAHH
HHHHAH
HHHTTTHHHHH

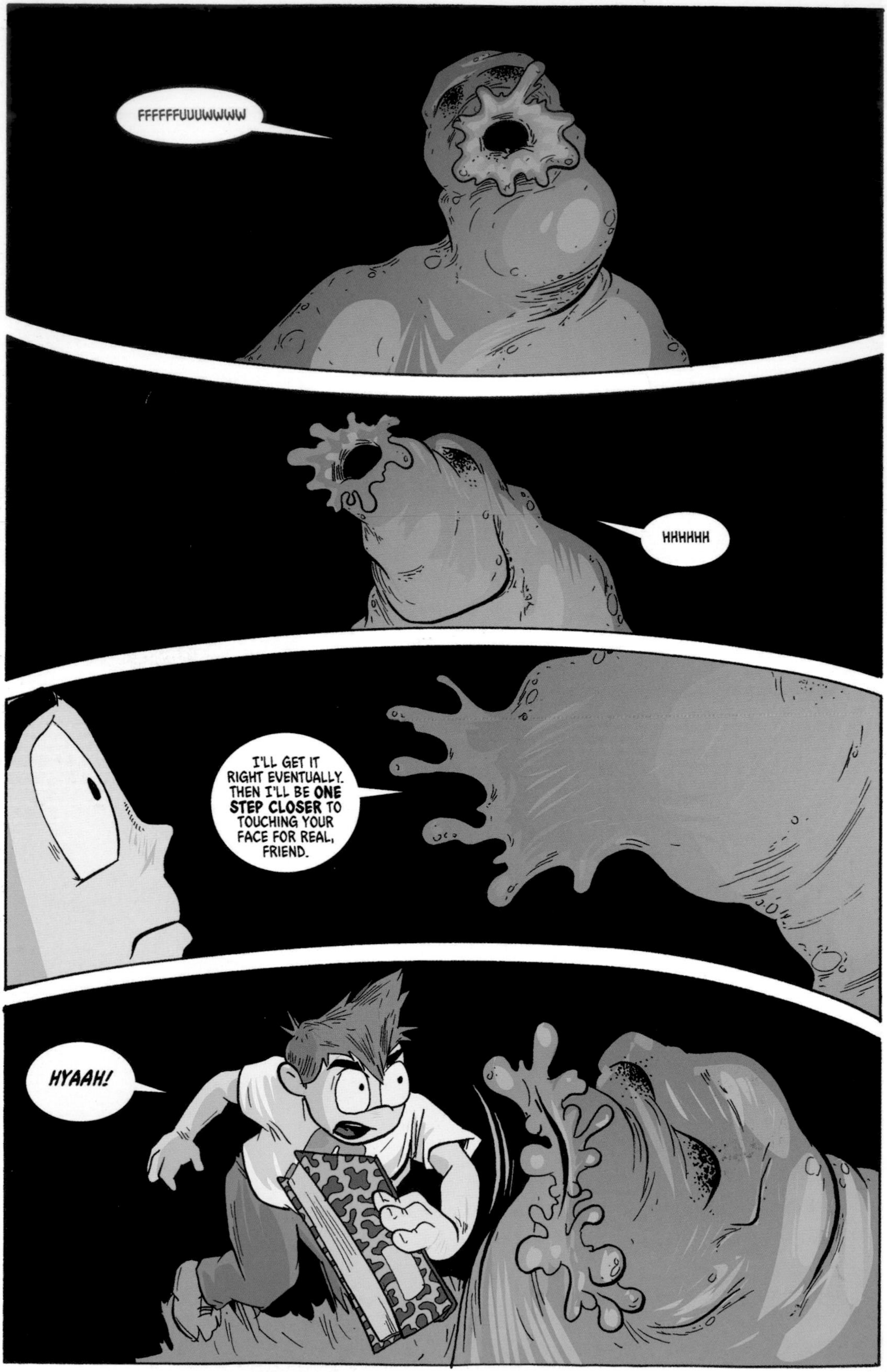
FFFFFFUUUWWWW
HHHHHH
I'LL GET IT RIGHT EVENTUALLY. THEN I'LL BE **ONE STEP CLOSER** TO TOUCHING YOUR FACE FOR REAL, FRIEND.
HYAAH!

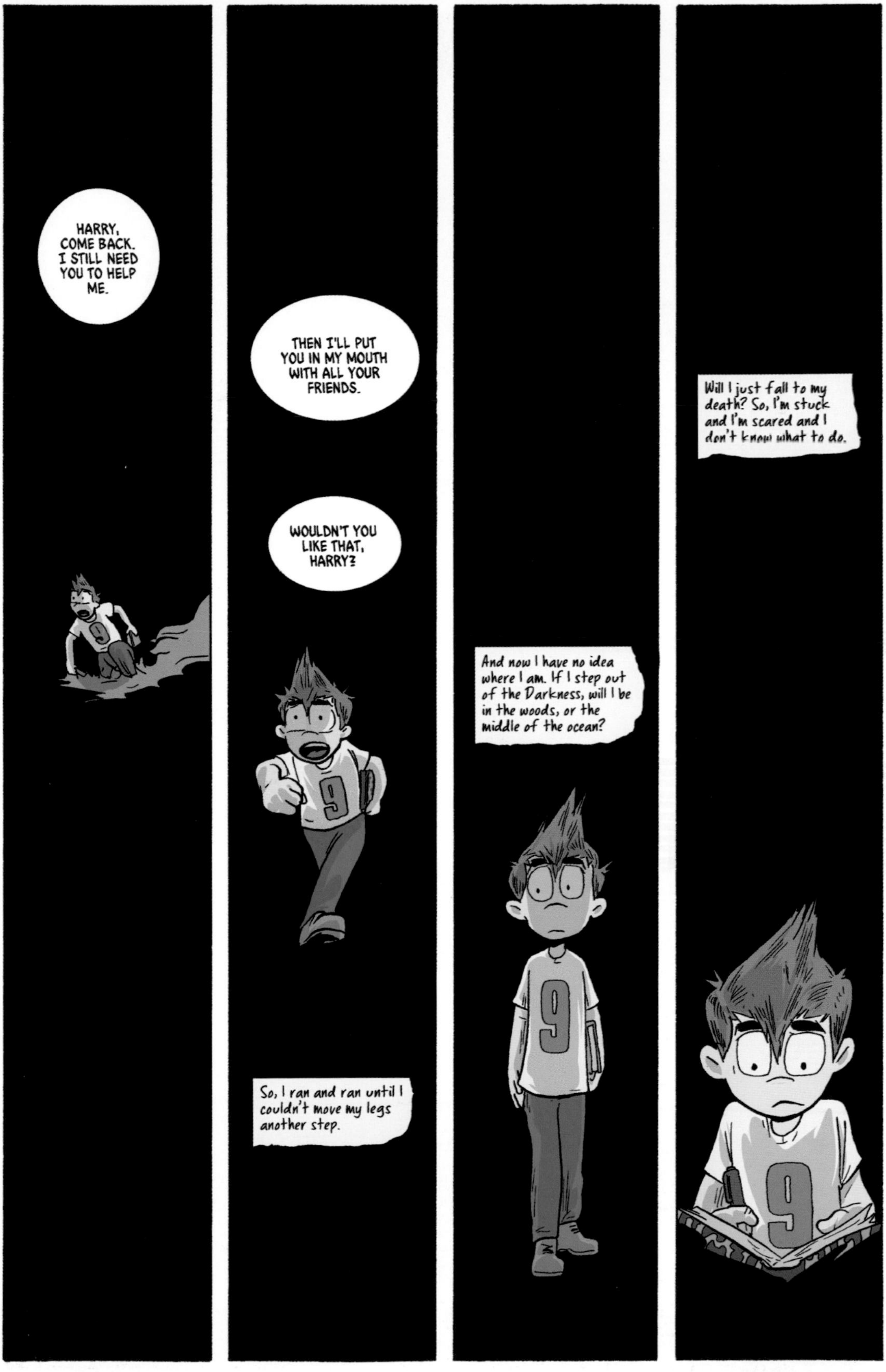
HARRY, COME BACK. I STILL NEED YOU TO HELP ME.
THEN I'LL PUT YOU IN MY MOUTH WITH ALL YOUR FRIENDS.
WOULDN'T YOU LIKE THAT, HARRY?
So, I ran and ran until I couldn't move my legs another step.
And now I have no idea where I am. If I step out of the Darkness, will I be in the woods, or the middle of the ocean?
Will I just fall to my death? So, I'm stuck and I'm scared and I don't know what to do.

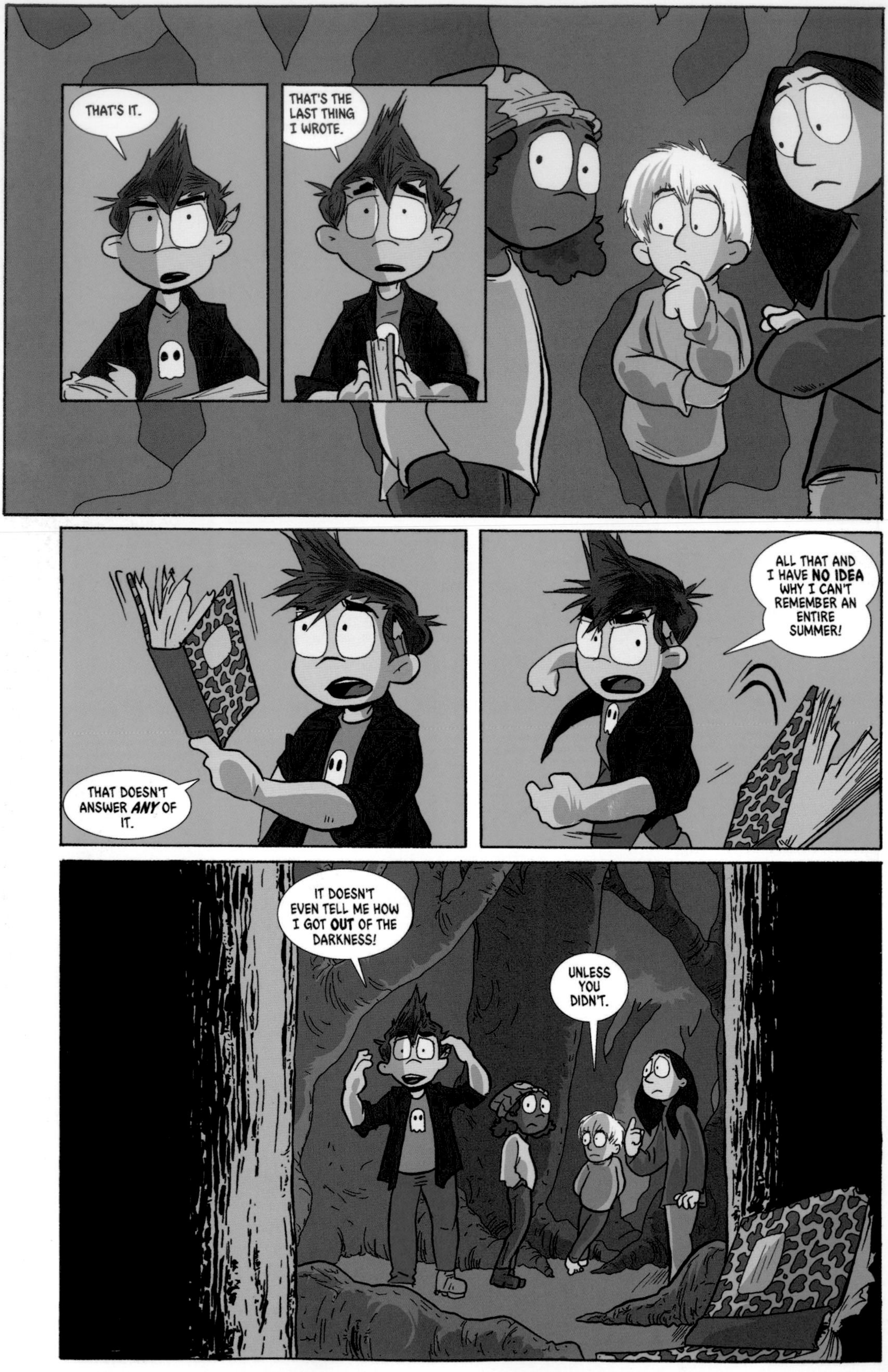

THAT'S IT.
THAT'S THE LAST THING I WROTE.
THAT DOESN'T ANSWER ANY OF IT.
ALL THAT AND I HAVE NO IDEA WHY I CAN'T REMEMBER AN ENTIRE SUMMER!
IT DOESN'T EVEN TELL ME HOW I GOT OUT OF THE DARKNESS!
UNLESS YOU DIDN'T.

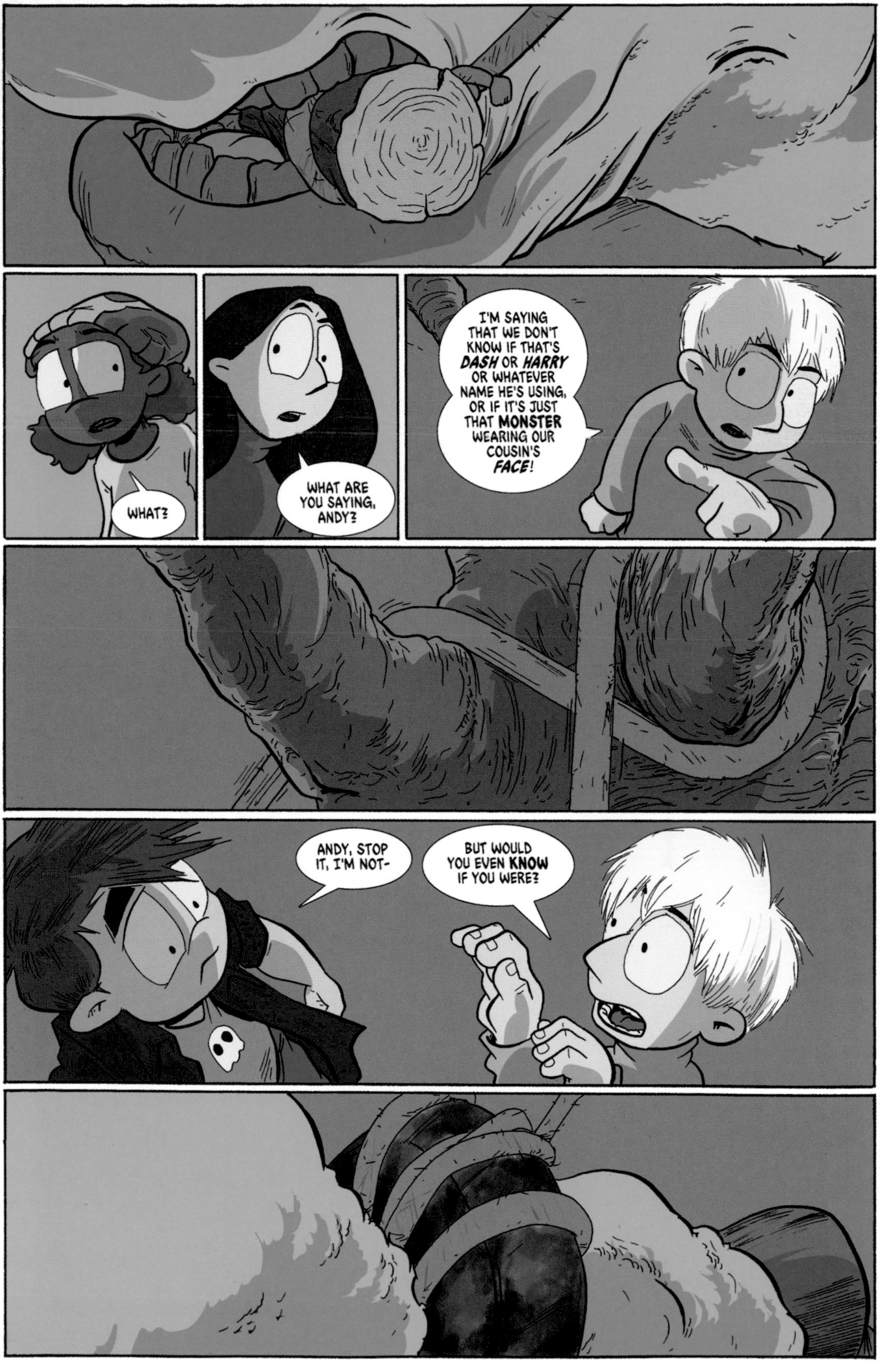
WHAT?
WHAT ARE YOU SAYING, ANDY?
I'M SAYING THAT WE DON'T KNOW IF THAT'S DASH OR HARRY OR WHATEVER NAME HE'S USING,
OR IF IT'S JUST THAT MONSTER WEARING OUR COUSIN'S FACE!
ANDY, STOP IT, I'M NOT-
BUT WOULD YOU EVEN KNOW IF YOU WERE?

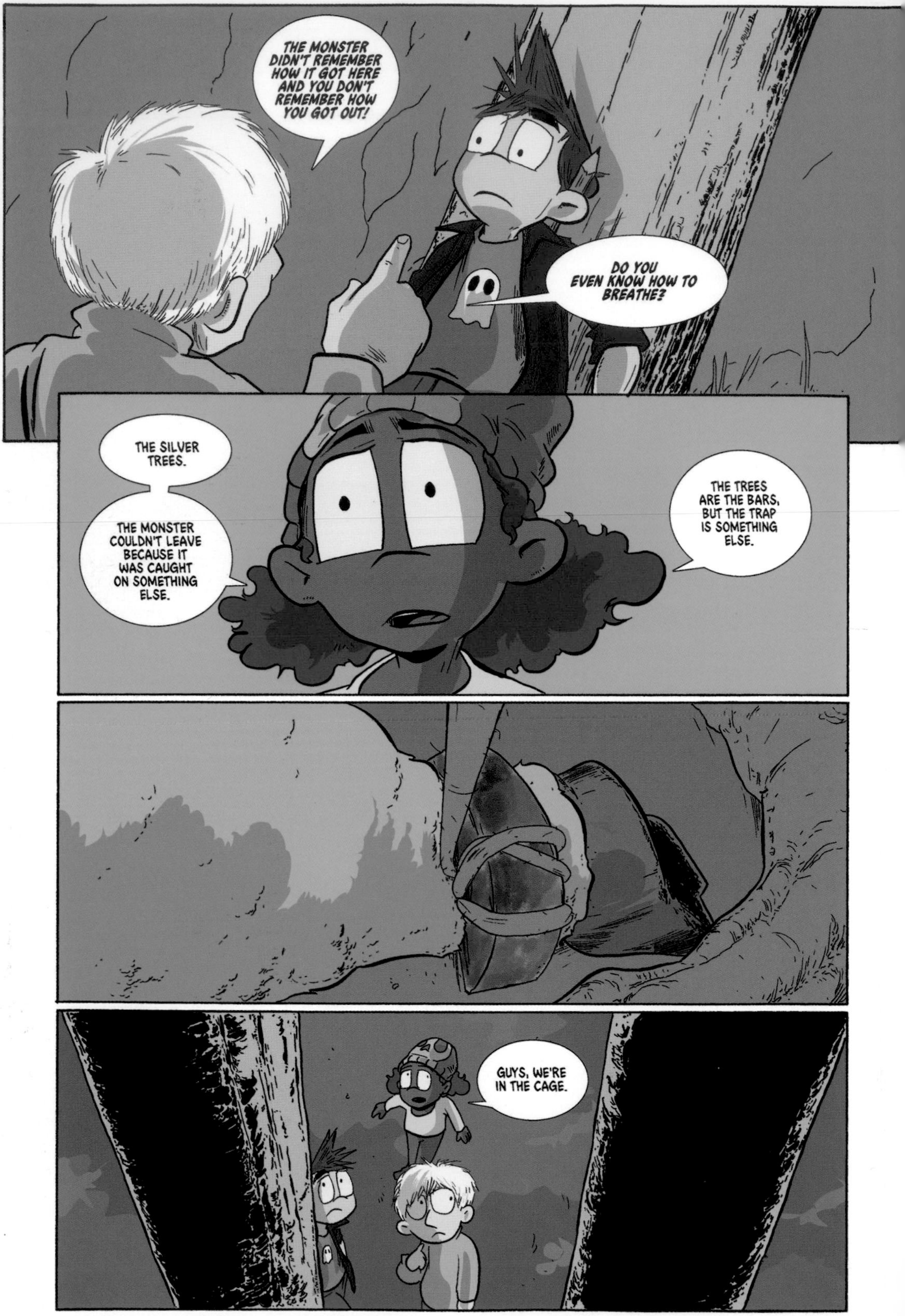
THE MONSTER DIDN'T REMEMBER HOW IT GOT HERE AND YOU DON'T REMEMBER HOW YOU GOT OUT!
DO YOU EVEN KNOW HOW TO BREATHE?
THE SILVER TREES.
THE MONSTER COULDN'T LEAVE BECAUSE IT WAS CAUGHT ON SOMETHING ELSE.
THE TREES ARE THE BARS, BUT THE TRAP IS SOMETHING ELSE.
GUYS, WE'RE IN THE CAGE.

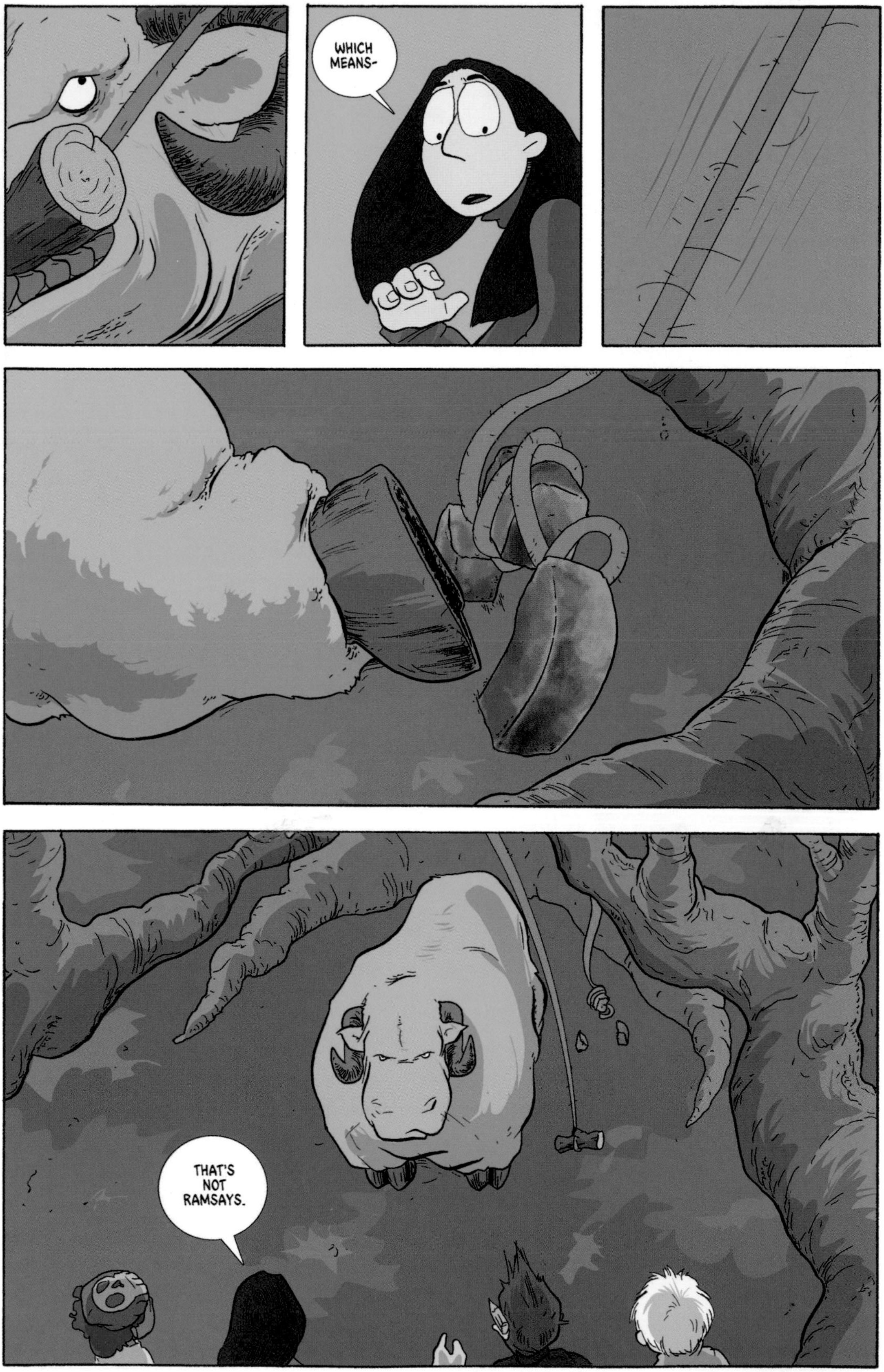
WHICH MEANS-
THAT'S NOT RAMSAYS.

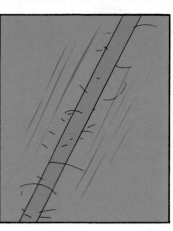

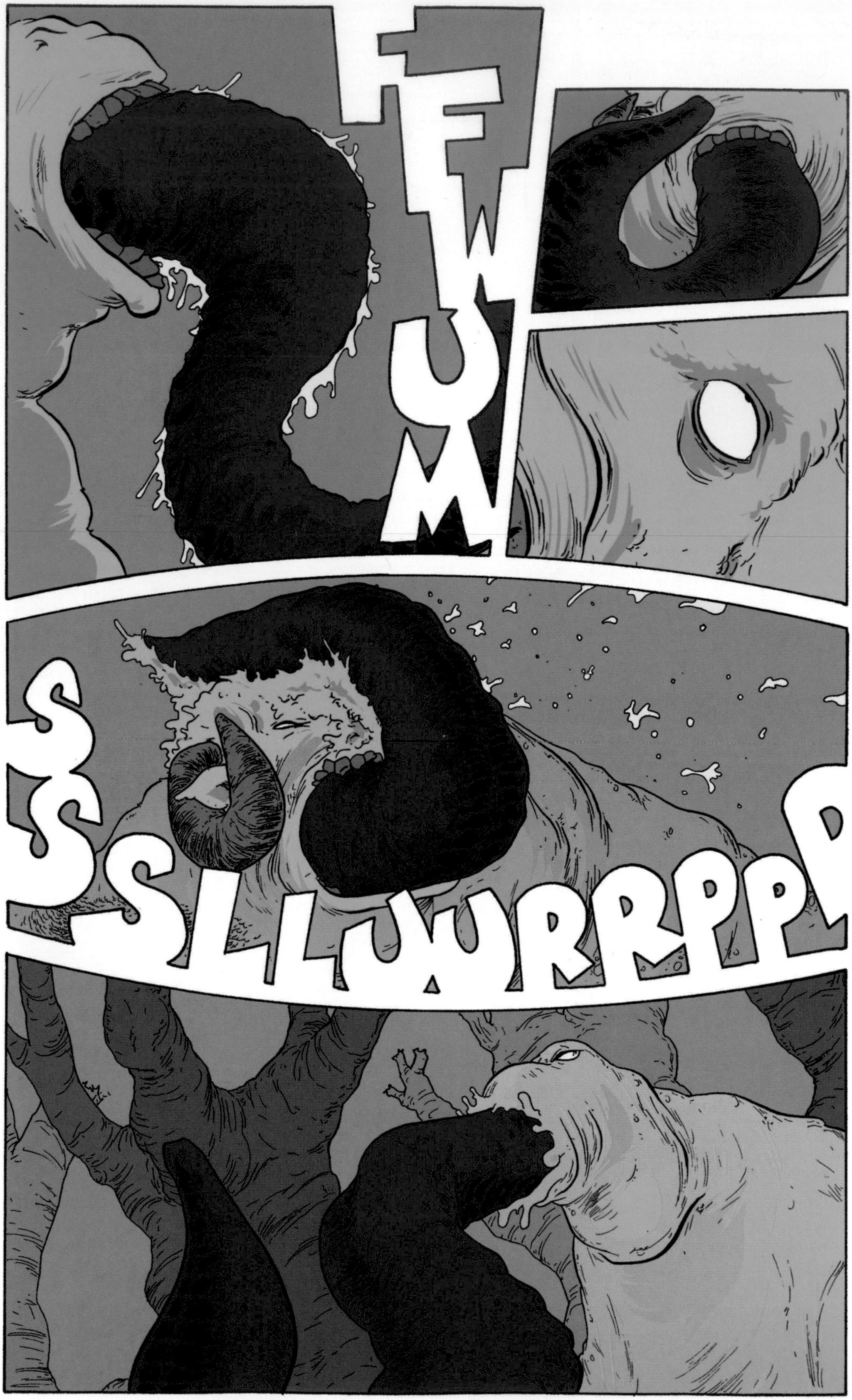
FWUM
SSSLLURRPPP

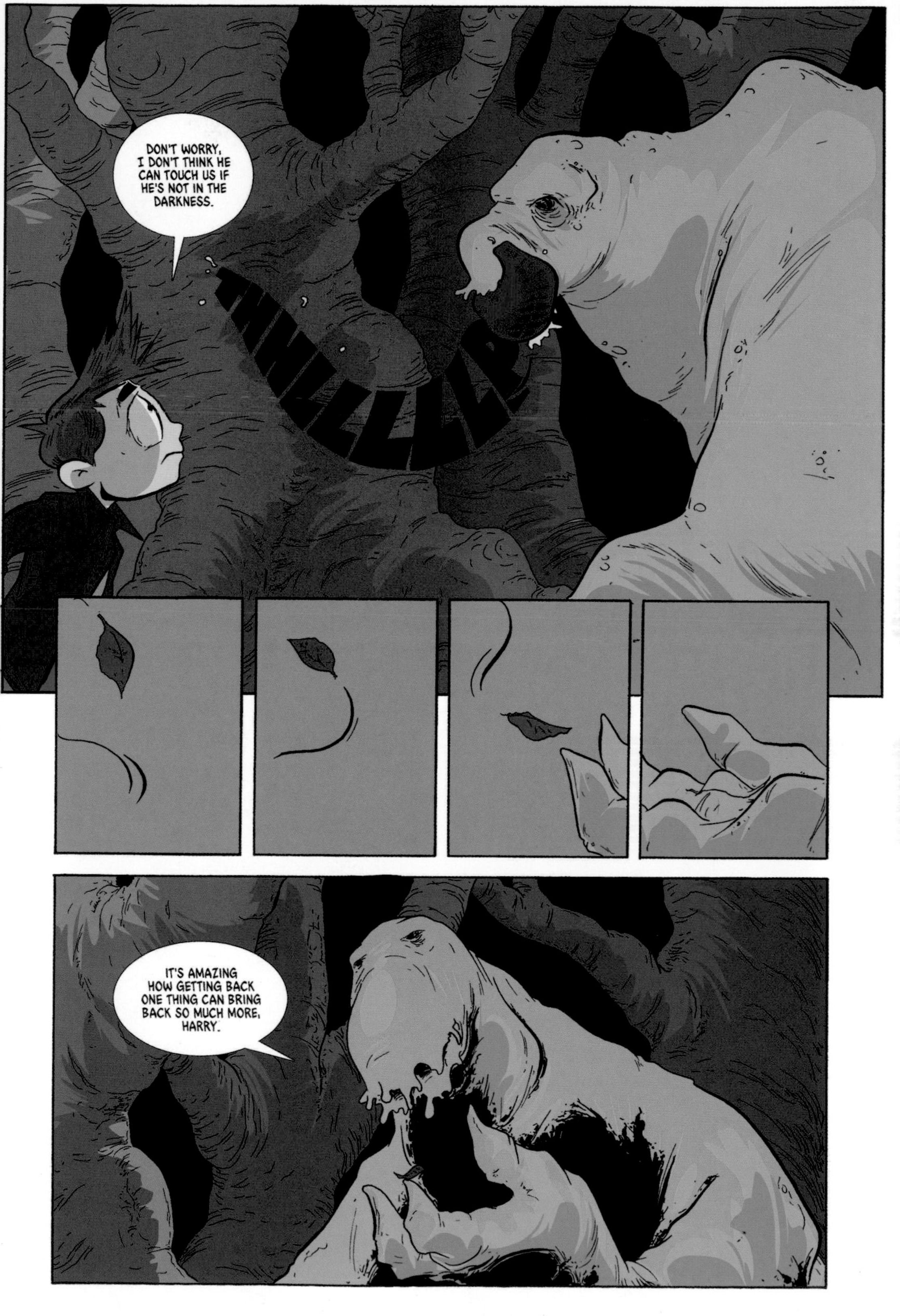
DON'T WORRY, I DON'T THINK HE CAN TOUCH US IF HE'S NOT IN THE DARKNESS.
THWLLZP
IT'S AMAZING HOW GETTING BACK ONE THING CAN BRING BACK SO MUCH MORE, HARRY.

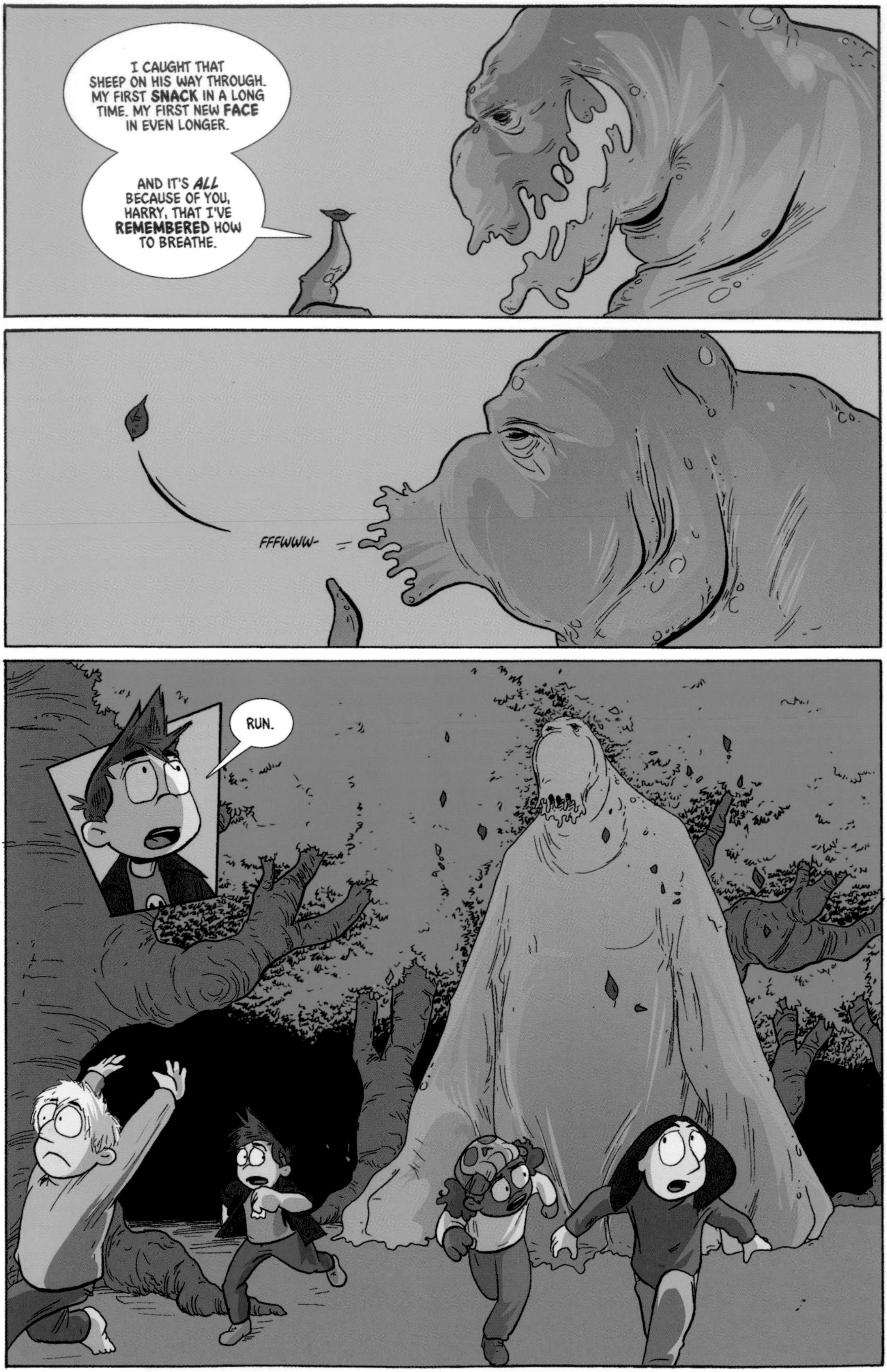
I CAUGHT THAT SHEEP ON HIS WAY THROUGH. MY FIRST SNACK IN A LONG TIME. MY FIRST NEW FACE IN EVEN LONGER.
AND IT'S ALL BECAUSE OF YOU, HARRY, THAT I'VE REMEMBERED HOW TO BREATHE.
FFFWWW-
RUN.

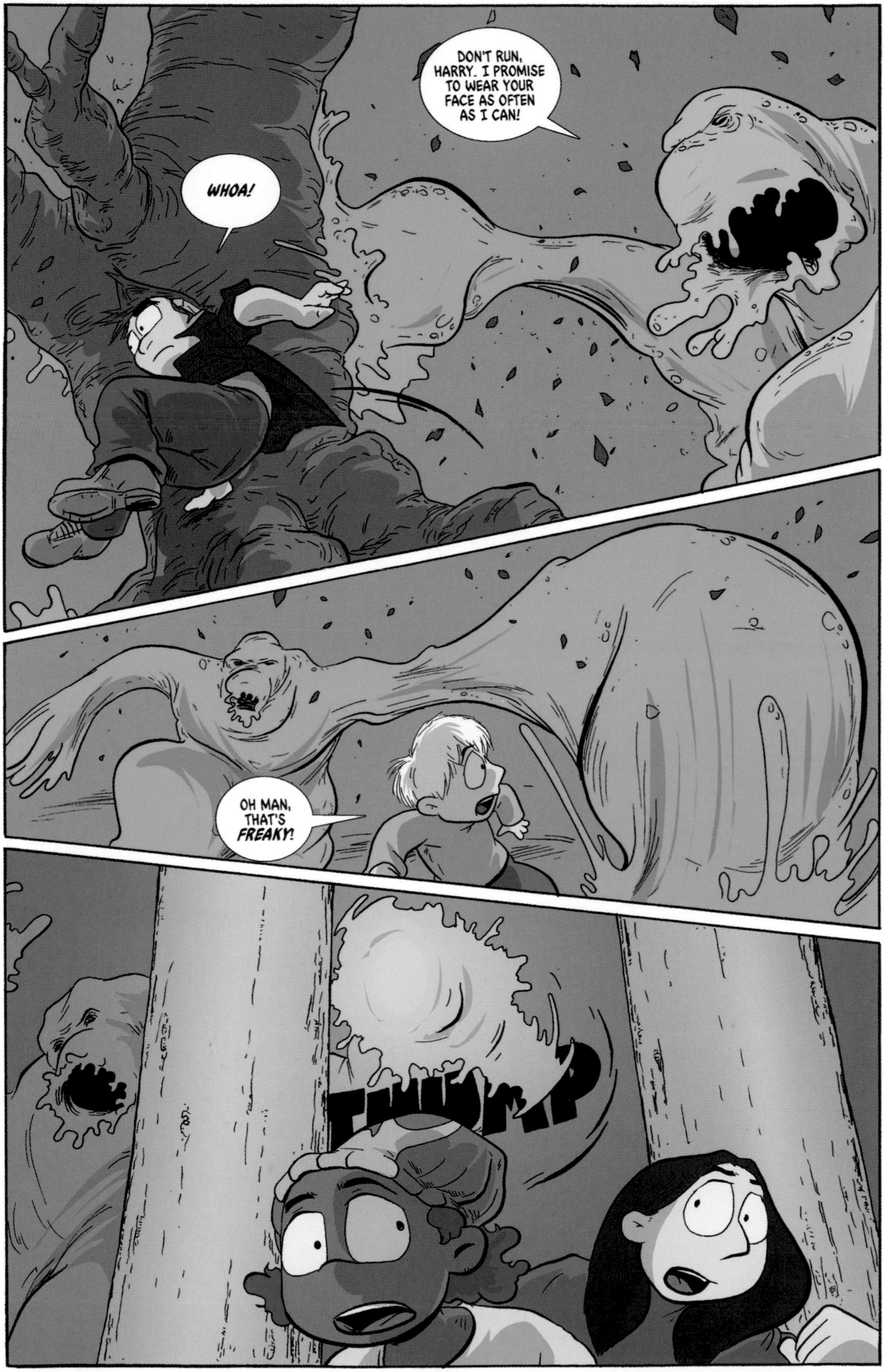
WHOA!
DON'T RUN, HARRY. I PROMISE TO WEAR YOUR FACE AS OFTEN AS I CAN!
OH MAN, THAT'S FREAKY!
THUMP

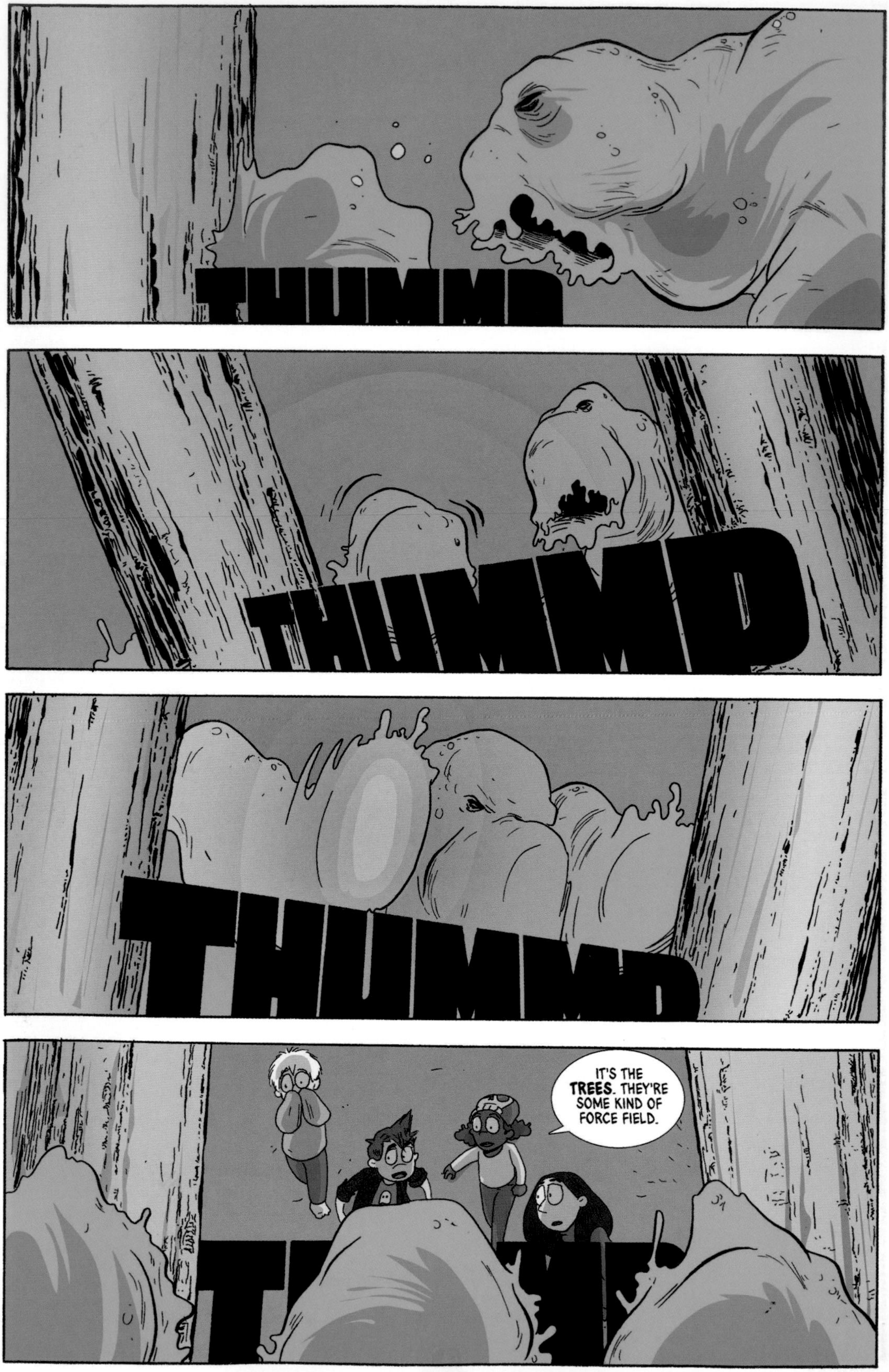
THUMMD
THUMMD
THUMMD
IT'S THE TREES. THEY'RE SOME KIND OF FORCE FIELD.

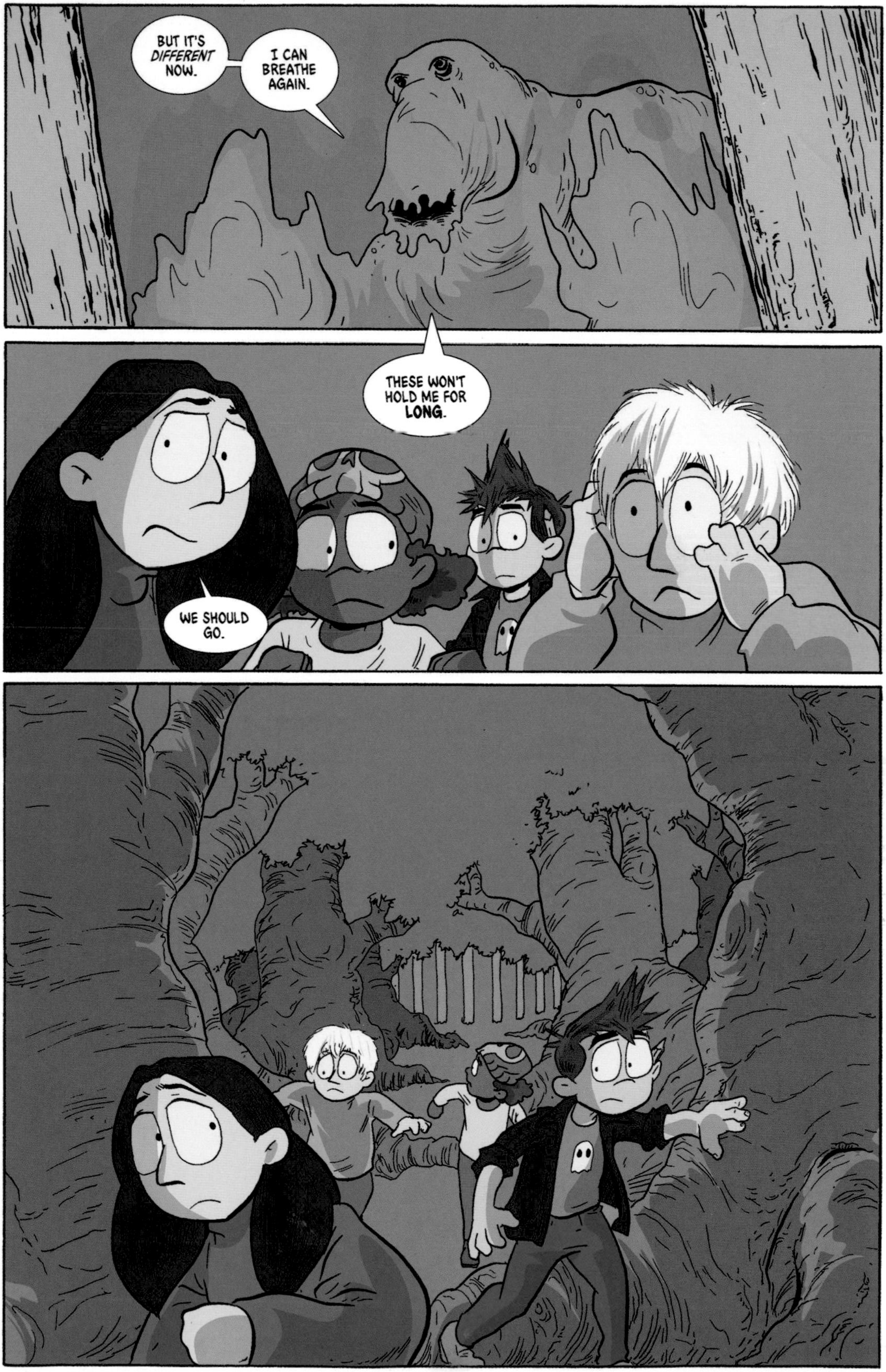
BUT IT'S *DIFFERENT* NOW.
I CAN BREATHE AGAIN.
THESE WON'T HOLD ME FOR **LONG**.
WE SHOULD GO.

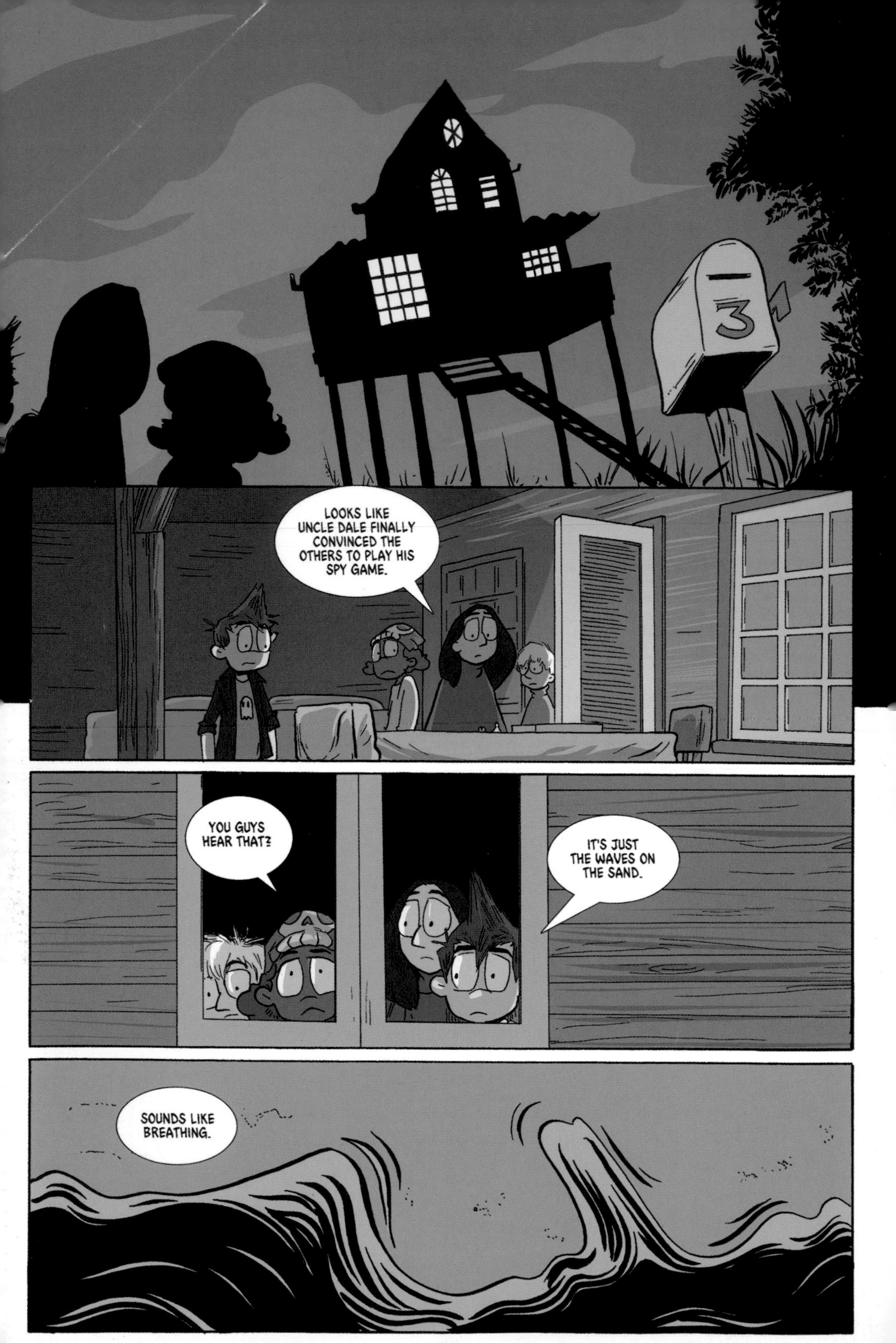
3
LOOKS LIKE UNCLE DALE FINALLY CONVINCED THE OTHERS TO PLAY HIS SPY GAME.
YOU GUYS HEAR THAT?
IT'S JUST THE WAVES ON THE SAND.
SOUNDS LIKE BREATHING.

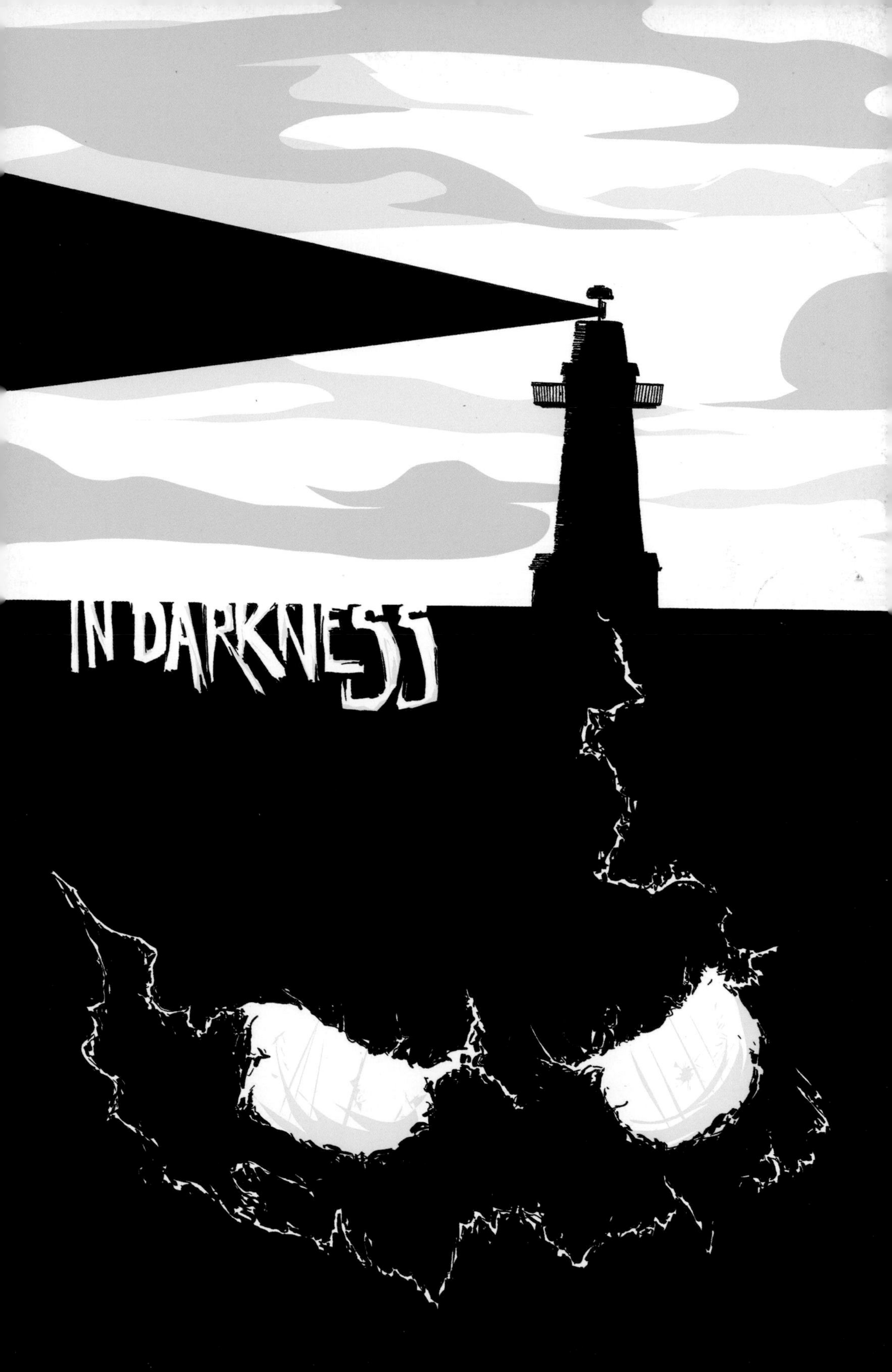
IN DARKNESS

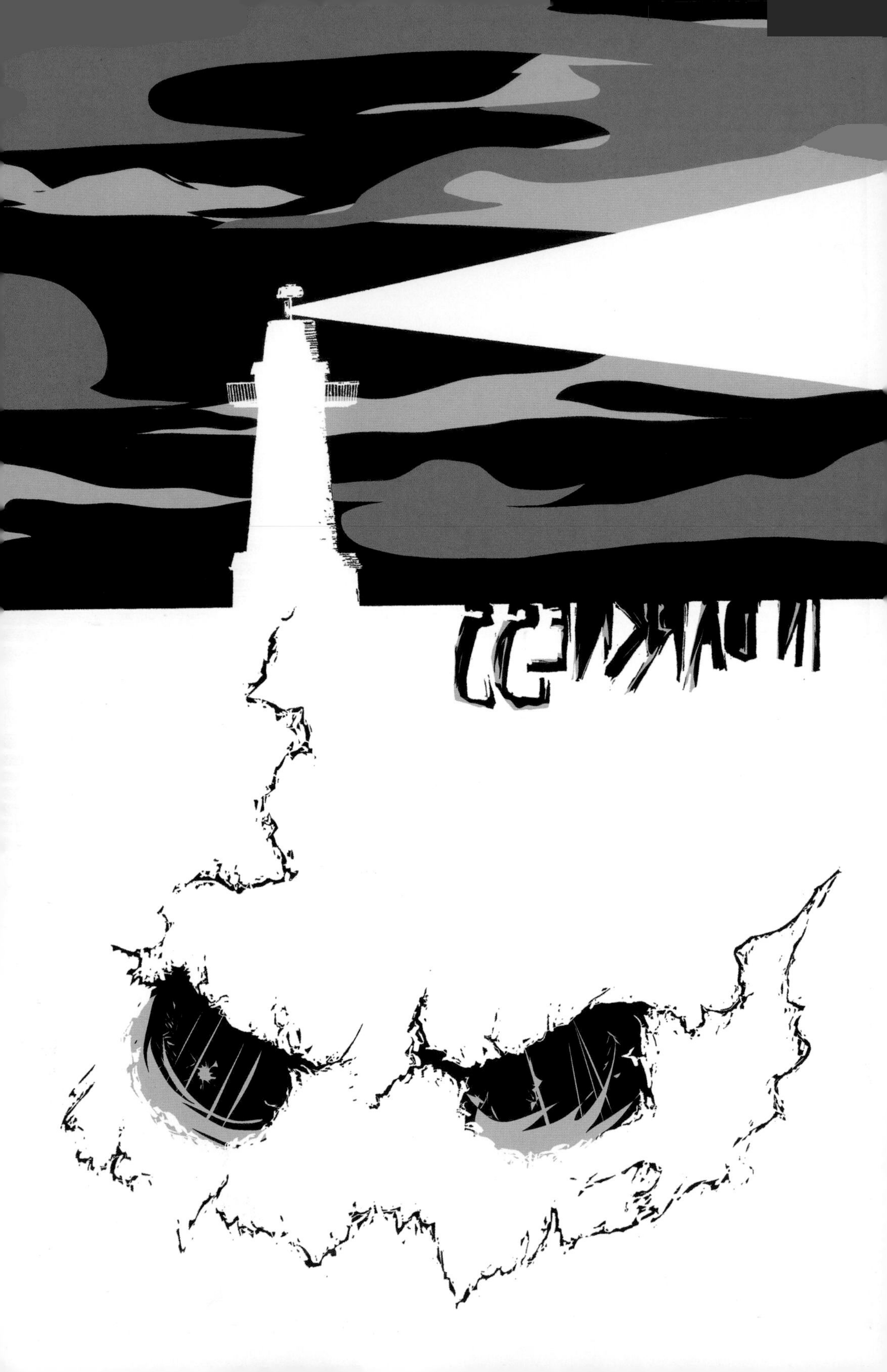

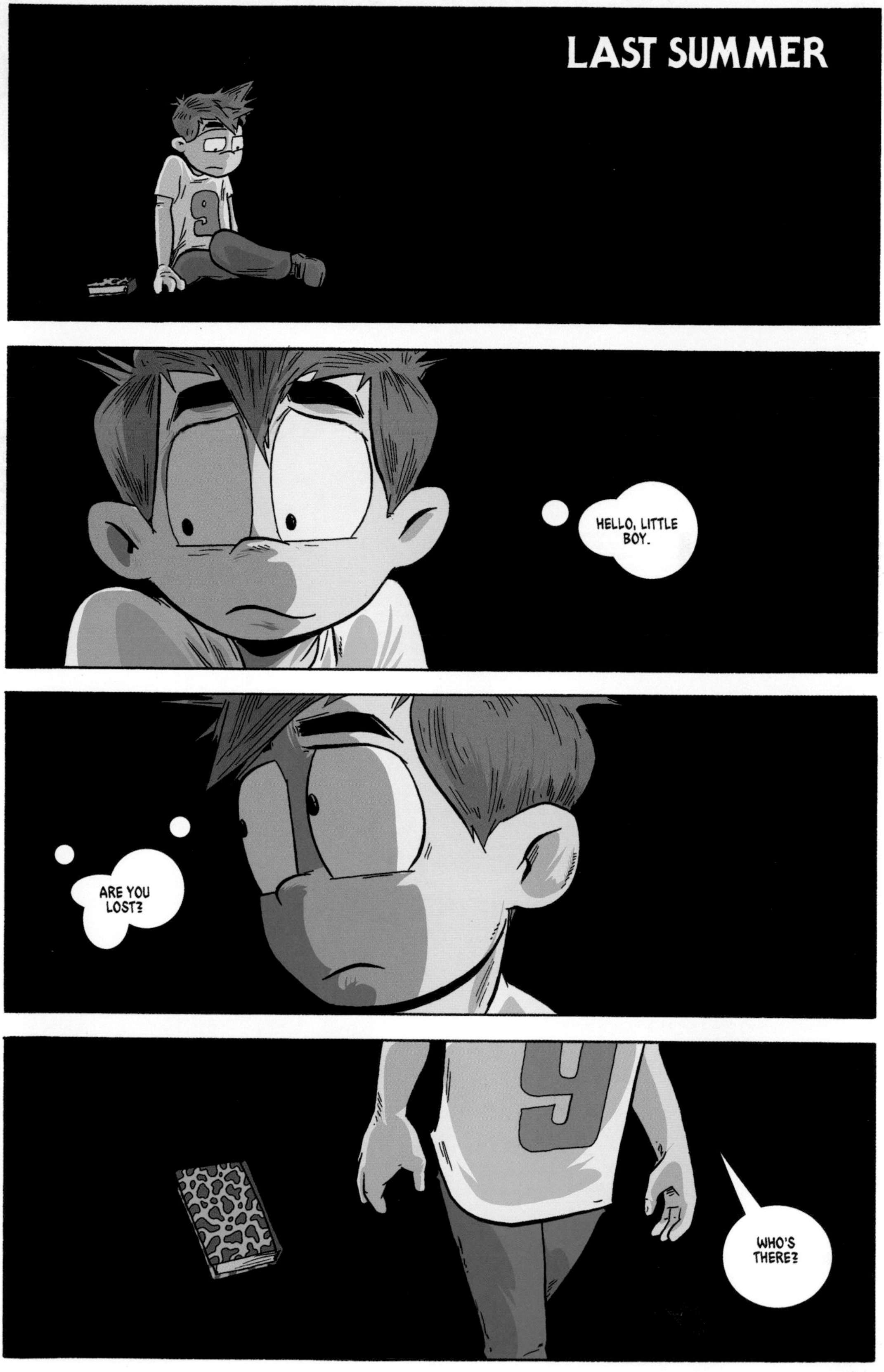
LAST SUMMER
HELLO, LITTLE BOY.
ARE YOU LOST?
WHO'S THERE?

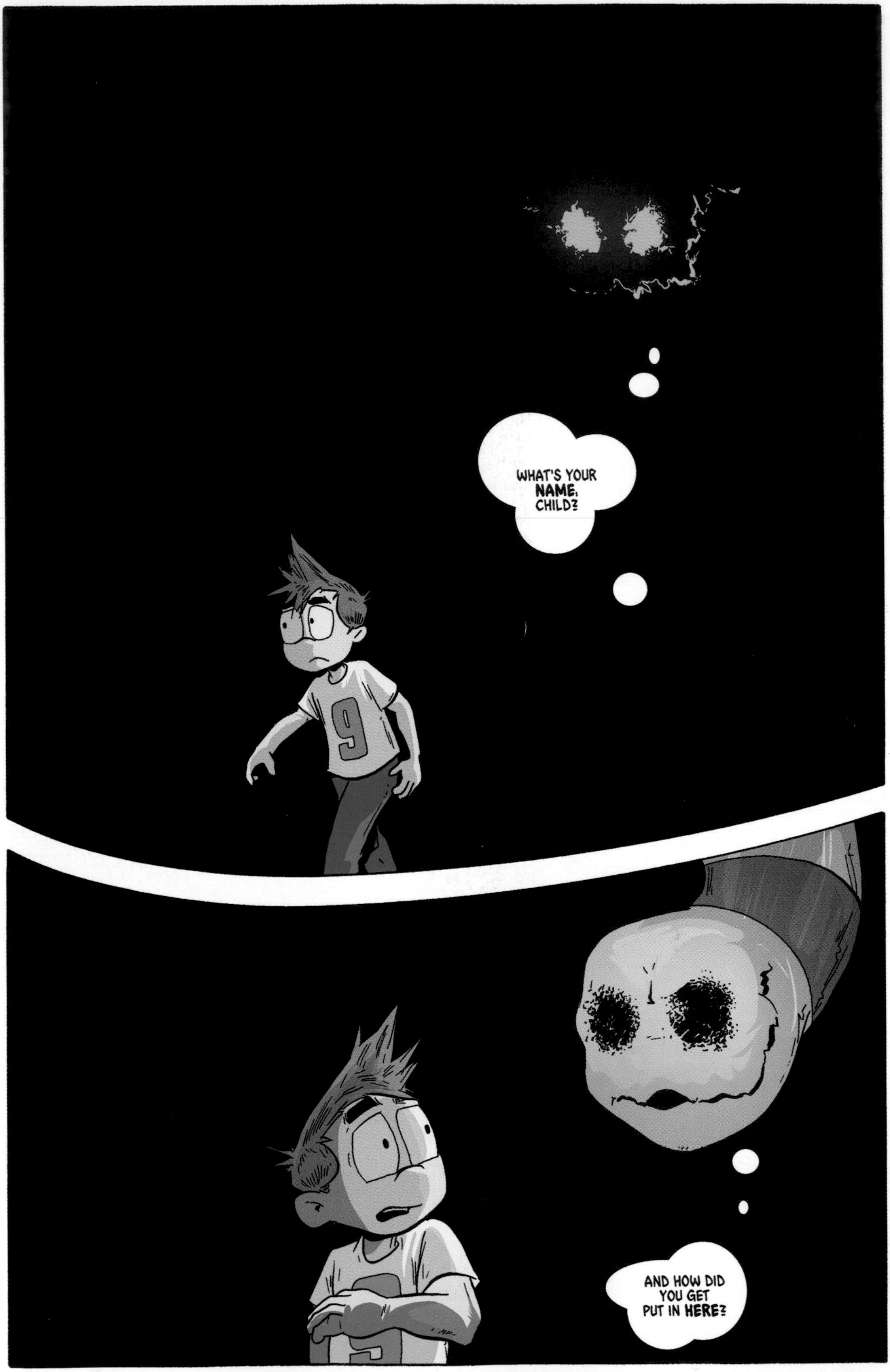
WHAT'S YOUR NAME, CHILD?
AND HOW DID YOU GET PUT IN HERE?

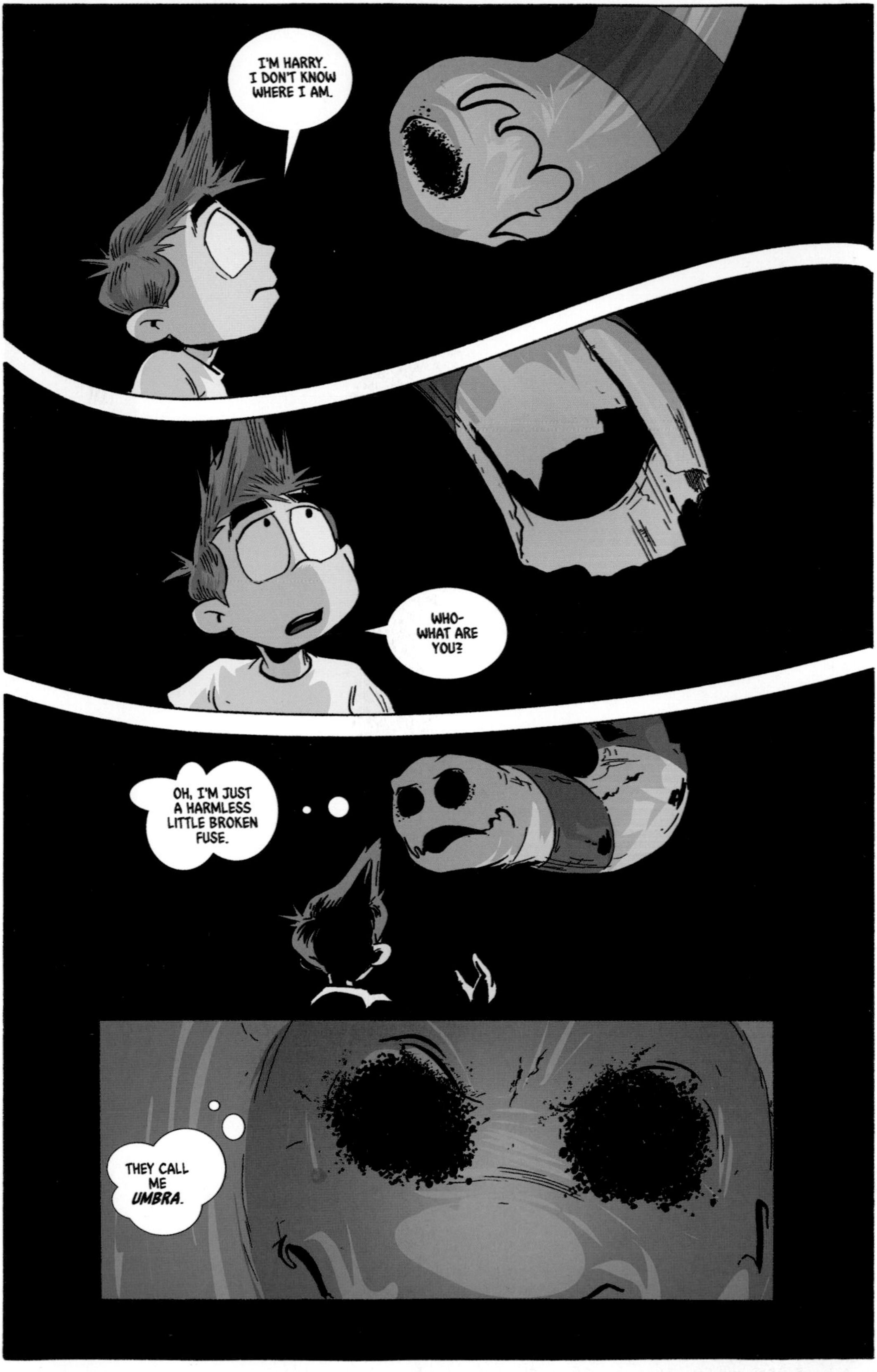
I'M HARRY. I DON'T KNOW WHERE I AM.
WHO- WHAT ARE YOU?
OH, I'M JUST A HARMLESS LITTLE BROKEN FUSE.
THEY CALL ME *UMBRA*.

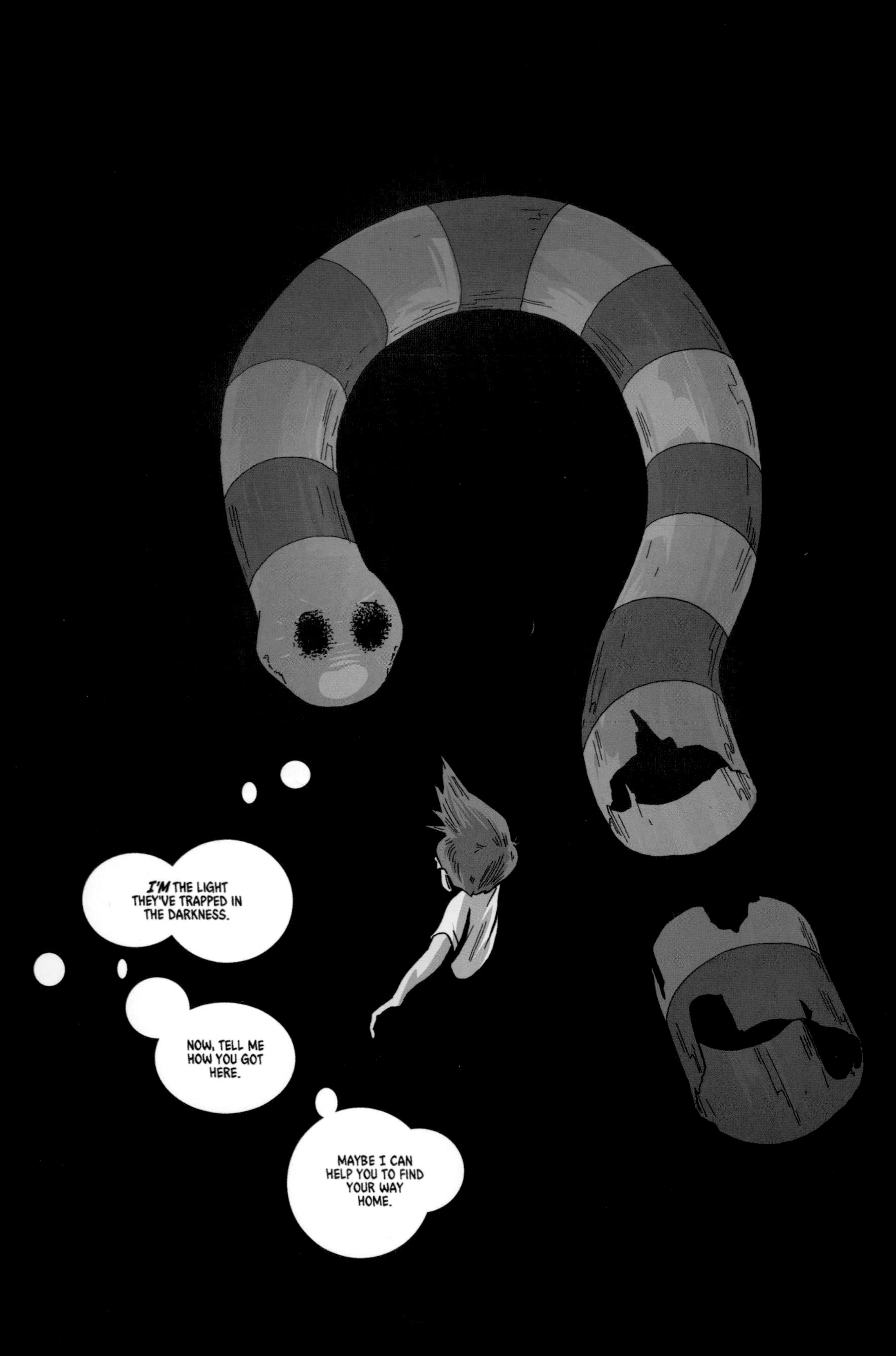
I'M THE LIGHT THEY'VE TRAPPED IN THE DARKNESS.
NOW, TELL ME HOW YOU GOT HERE.
MAYBE I CAN HELP YOU TO FIND YOUR WAY HOME.

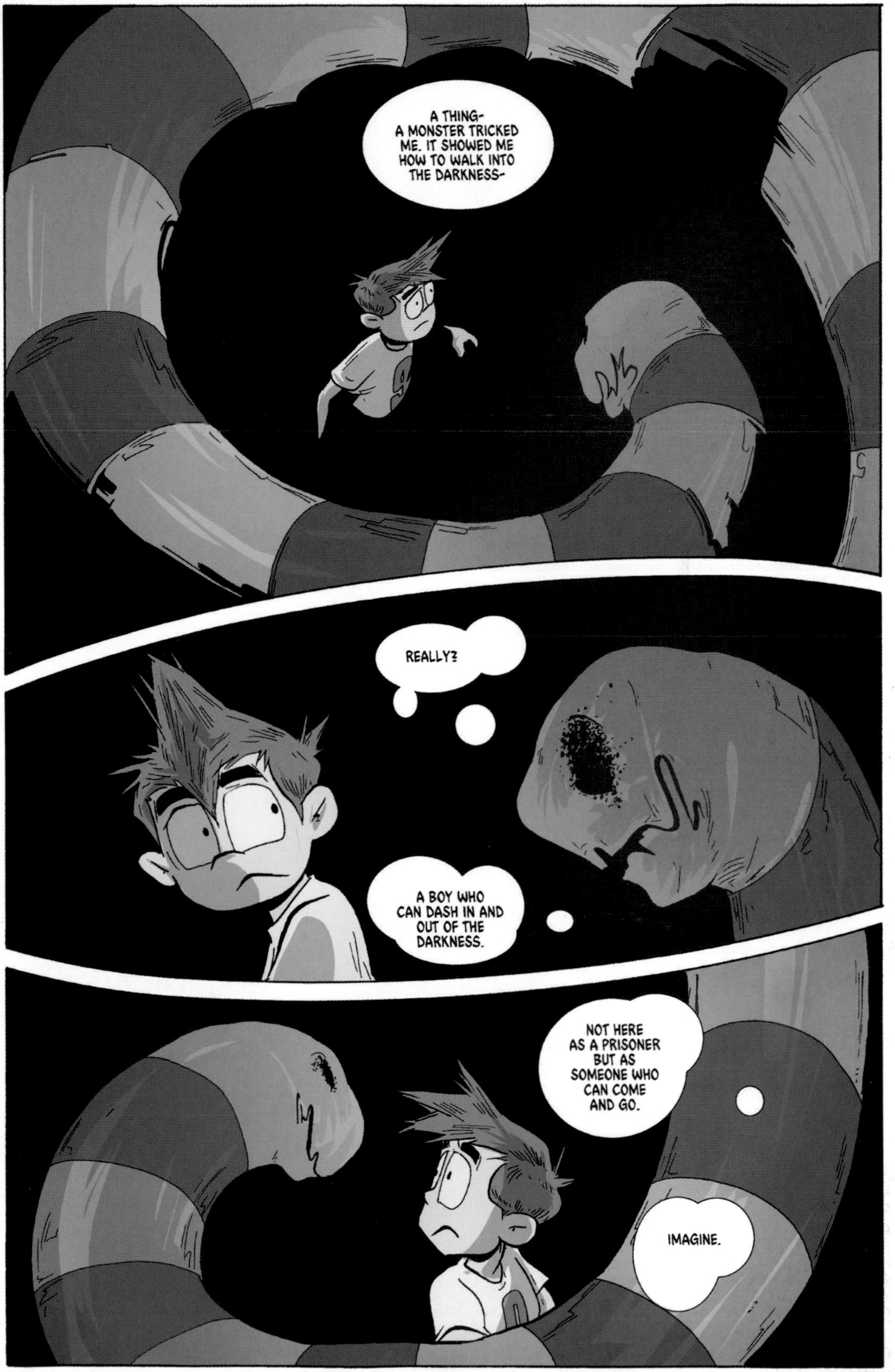
A THING-
A MONSTER TRICKED ME. IT SHOWED ME HOW TO WALK INTO THE DARKNESS-
REALLY?
A BOY WHO CAN DASH IN AND OUT OF THE DARKNESS.
NOT HERE AS A PRISONER BUT AS SOMEONE WHO CAN COME AND GO.
IMAGINE.

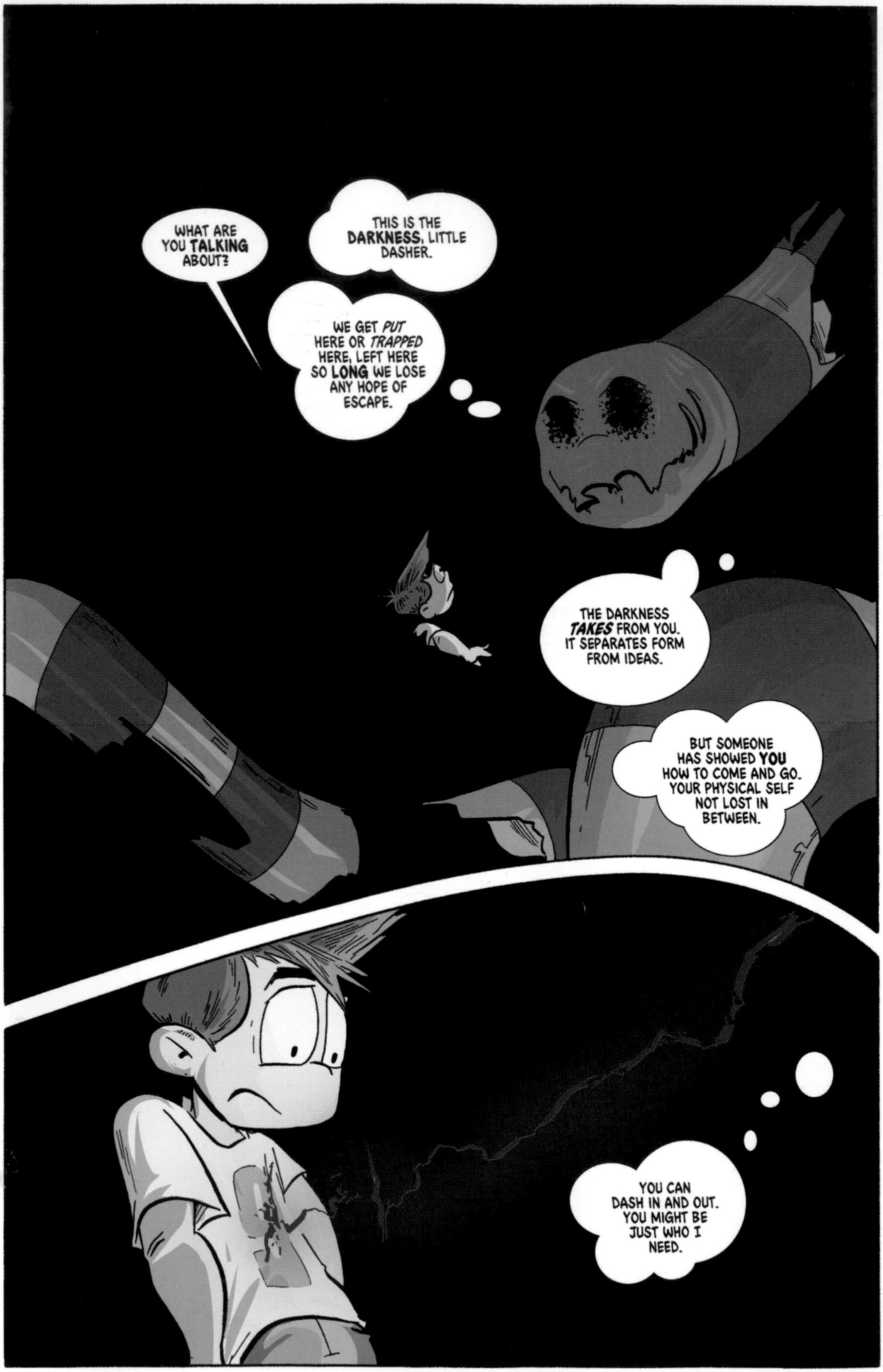
WHAT ARE YOU TALKING ABOUT?
THIS IS THE DARKNESS, LITTLE DASHER.
WE GET PUT HERE OR TRAPPED HERE, LEFT HERE SO LONG WE LOSE ANY HOPE OF ESCAPE.
THE DARKNESS TAKES FROM YOU. IT SEPARATES FORM FROM IDEAS.
BUT SOMEONE HAS SHOWED YOU HOW TO COME AND GO. YOUR PHYSICAL SELF NOT LOST IN BETWEEN.
YOU CAN DASH IN AND OUT. YOU MIGHT BE JUST WHO I NEED.

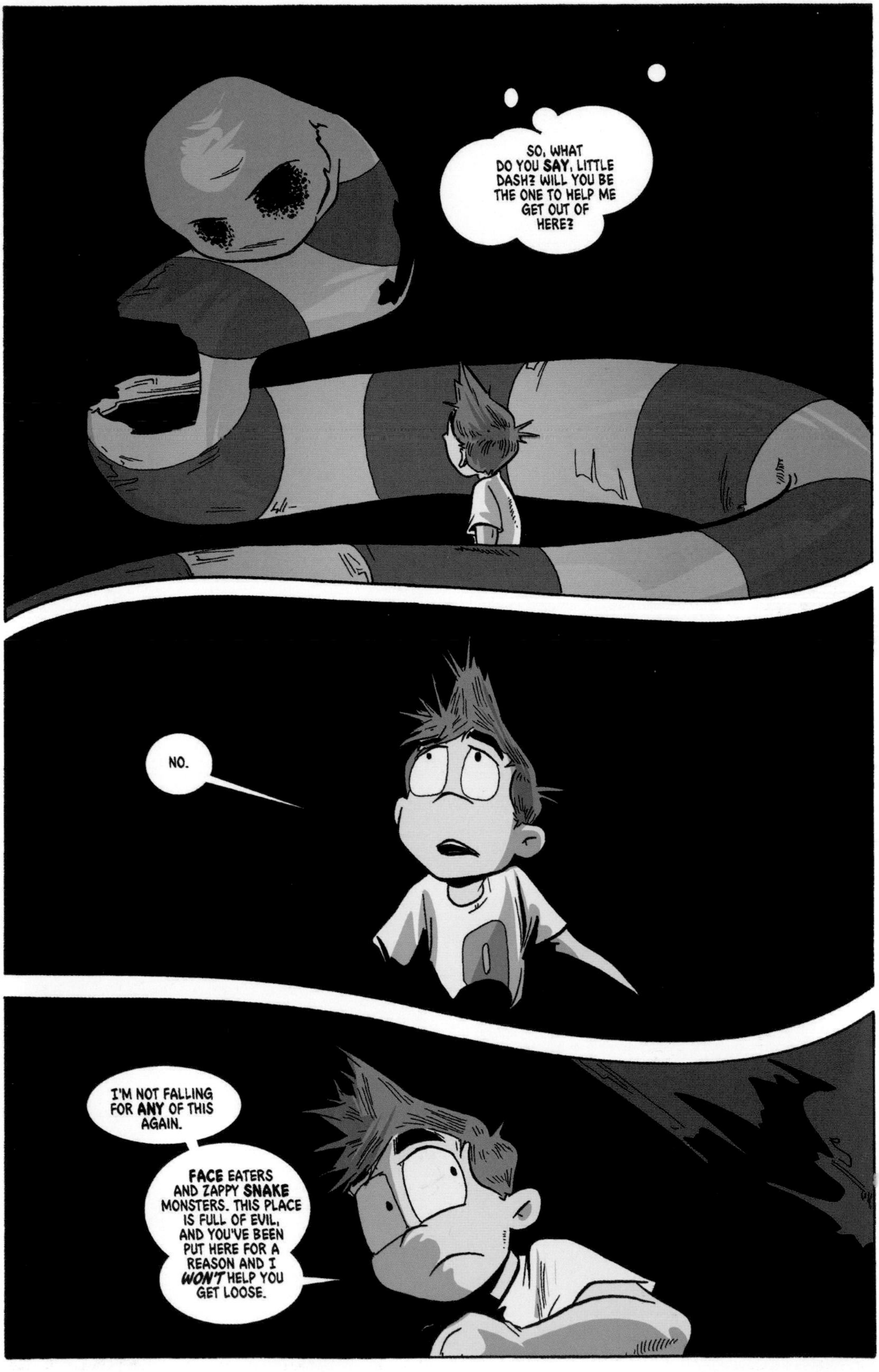
SO, WHAT DO YOU SAY, LITTLE DASH? WILL YOU BE THE ONE TO HELP ME GET OUT OF HERE?
NO.
I'M NOT FALLING FOR ANY OF THIS AGAIN.
FACE EATERS AND ZAPPY SNAKE MONSTERS. THIS PLACE IS FULL OF EVIL, AND YOU'VE BEEN PUT HERE FOR A REASON AND I WON'T HELP YOU GET LOOSE.

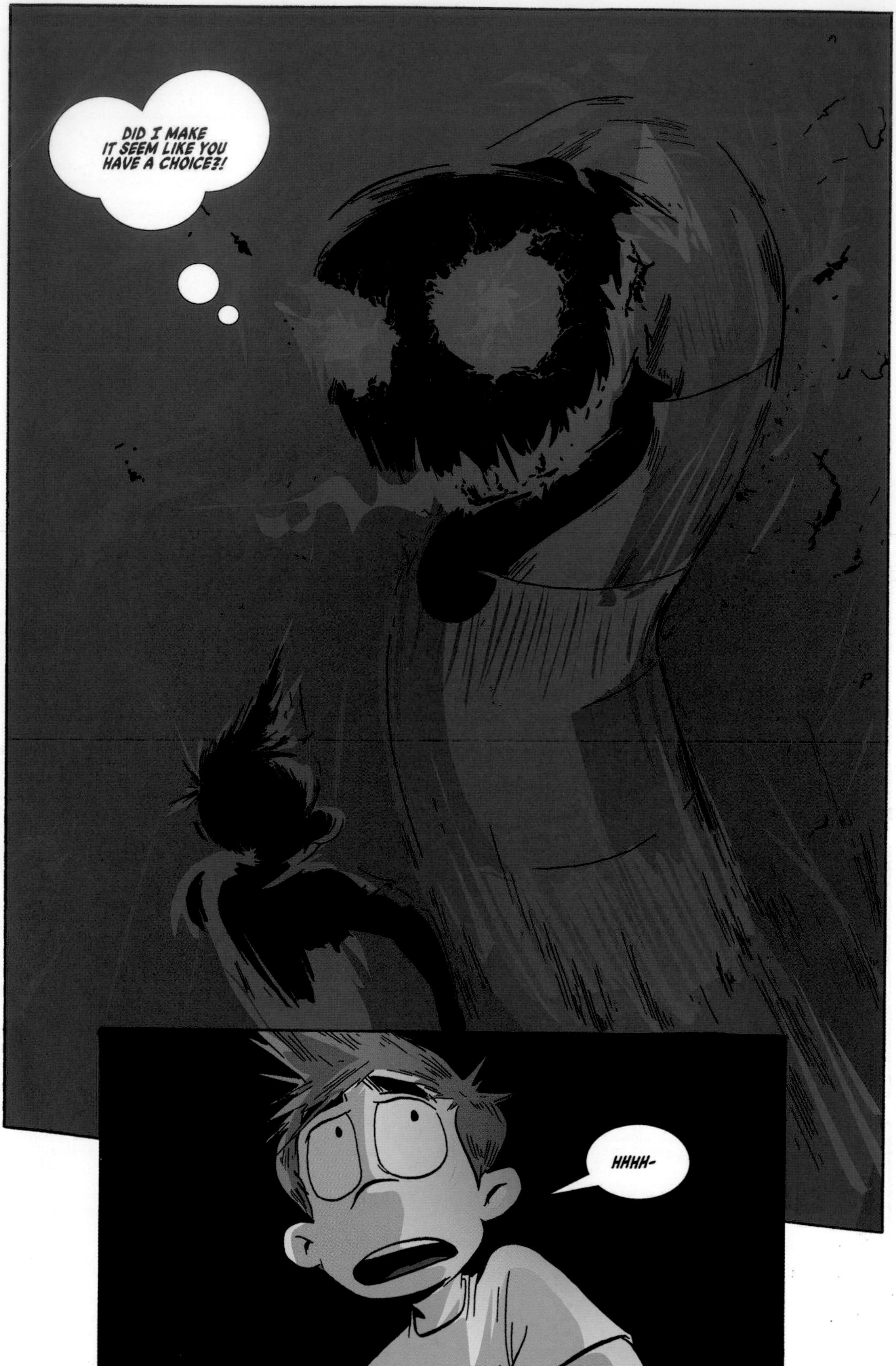
DID I MAKE IT SEEM LIKE YOU HAVE A CHOICE?!
HHHH-

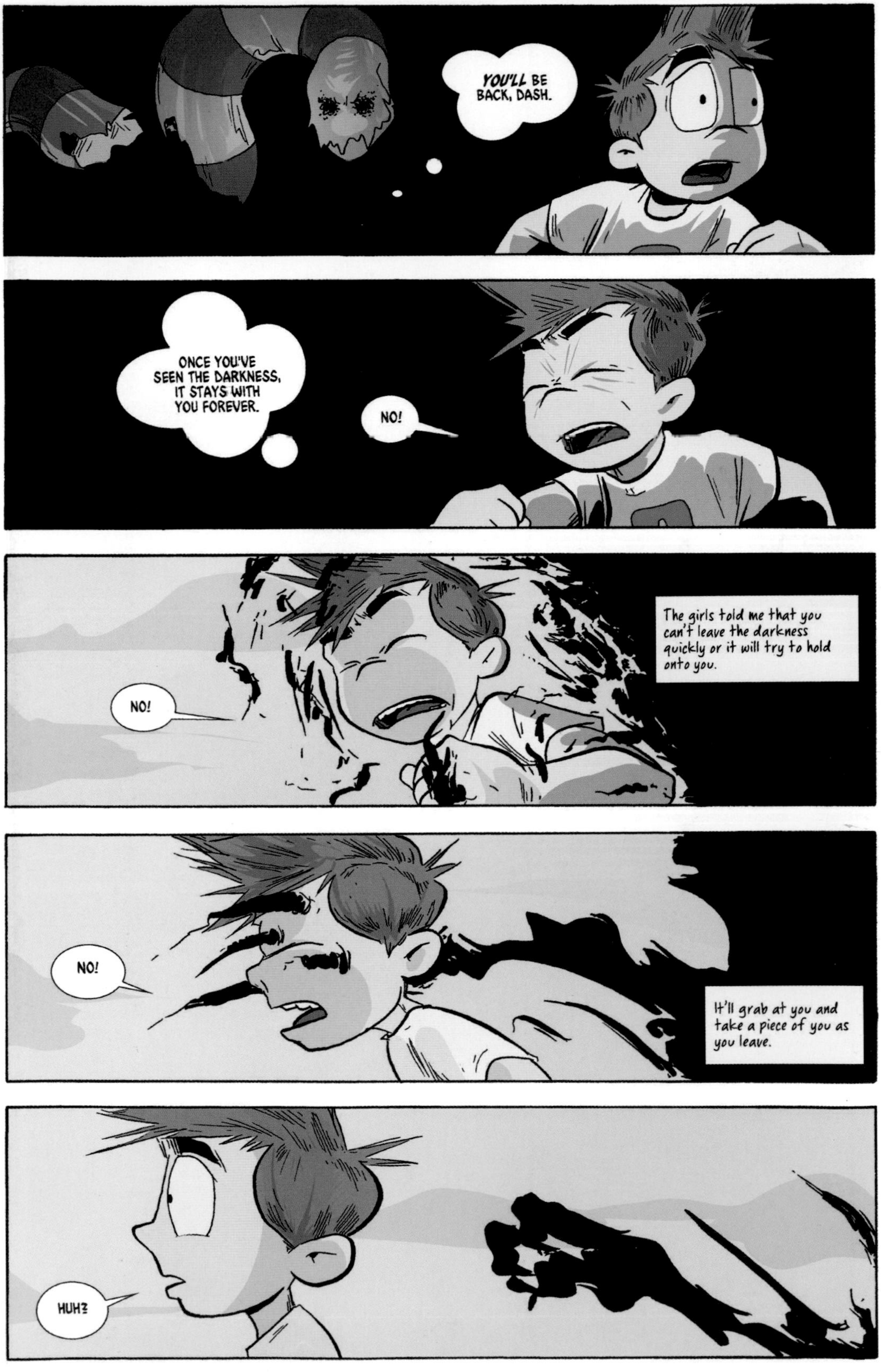
YOU'LL BE BACK, DASH.
ONCE YOU'VE SEEN THE DARKNESS, IT STAYS WITH YOU FOREVER.
NO!
The girls told me that you can't leave the darkness quickly or it will try to hold onto you.
NO!
NO!
It'll grab at you and take a piece of you as you leave.
HUH?

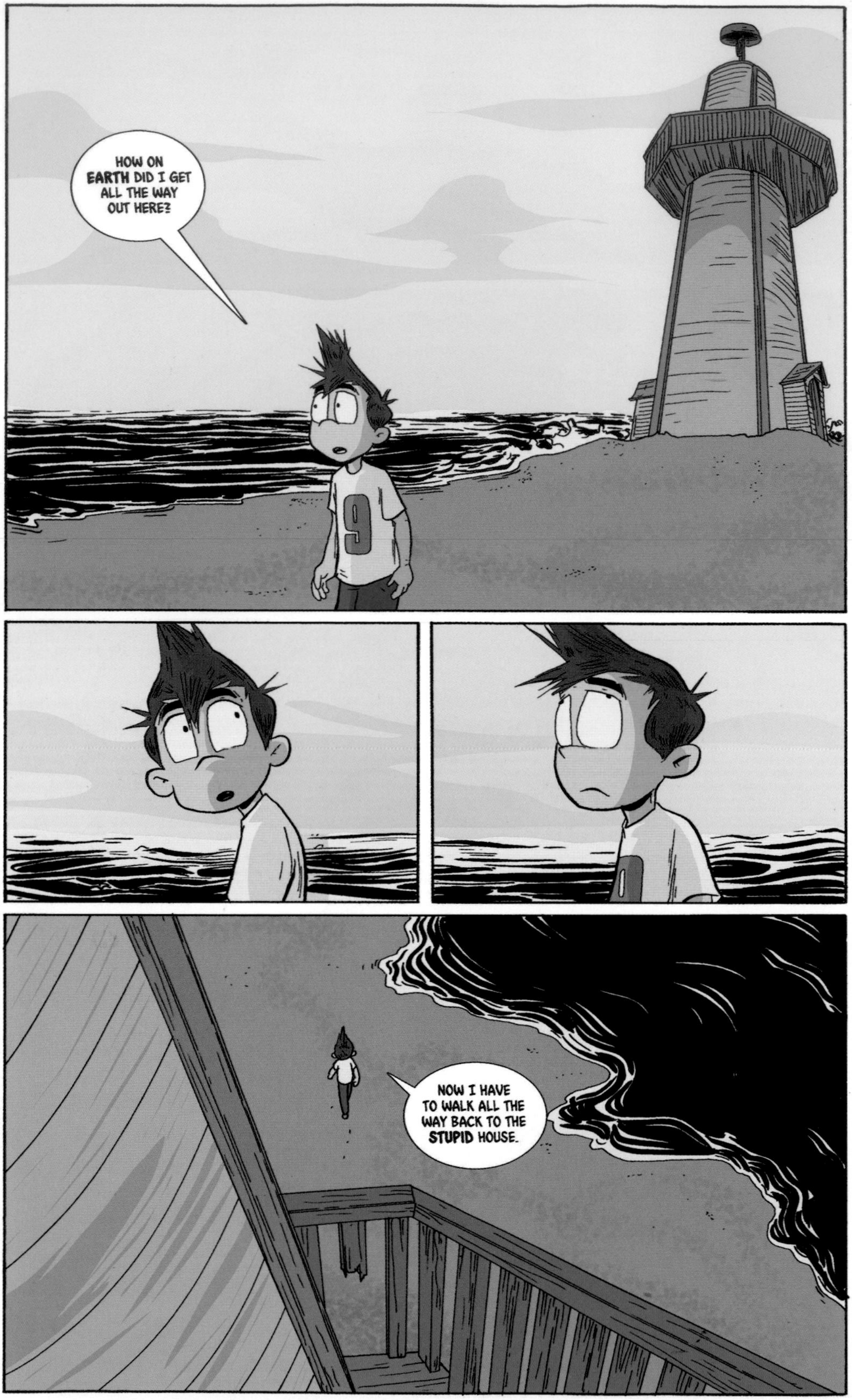
HOW ON EARTH DID I GET ALL THE WAY OUT HERE?
NOW I HAVE TO WALK ALL THE WAY BACK TO THE STUPID HOUSE.

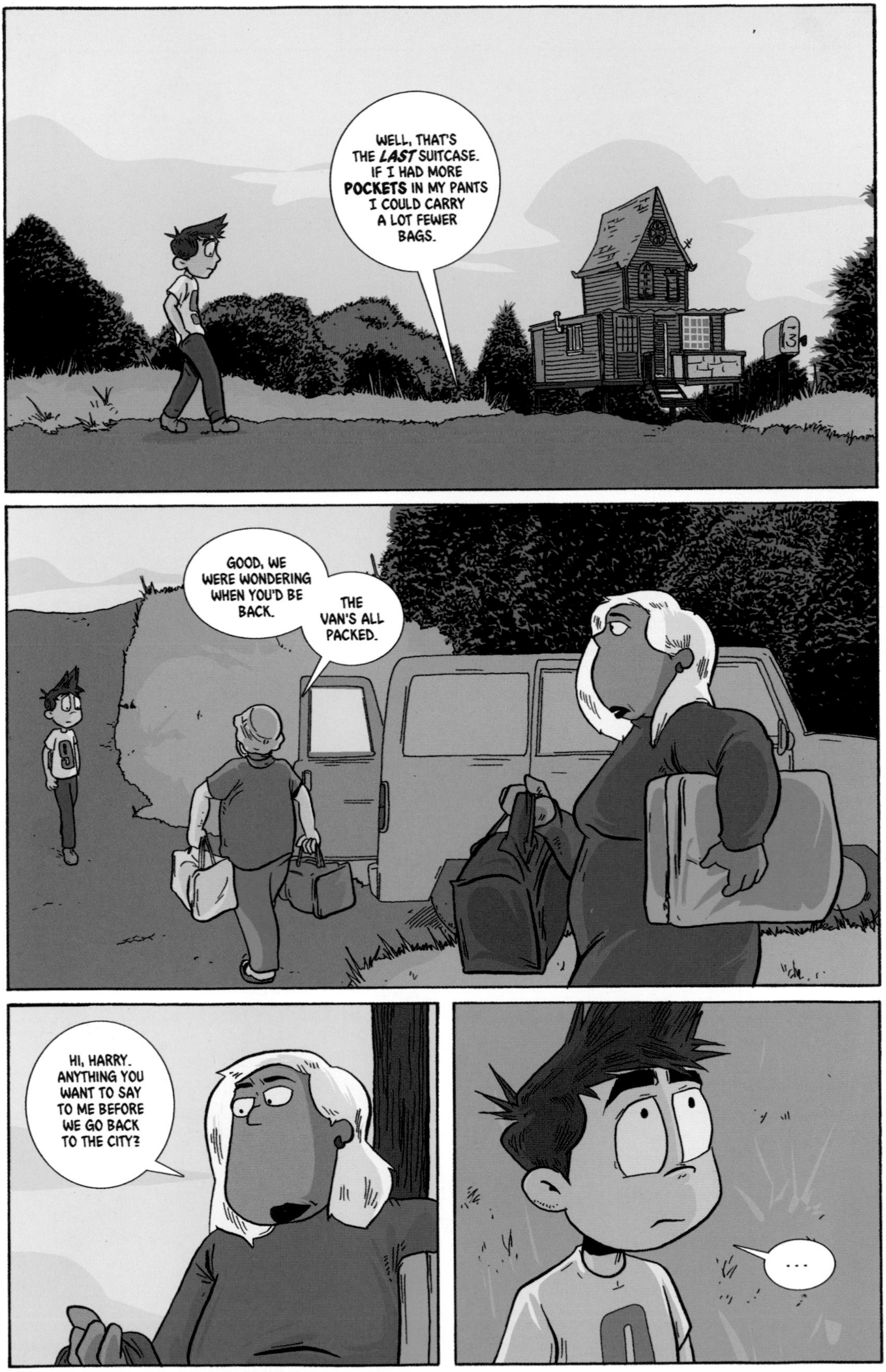
WELL, THAT'S THE ***LAST*** SUITCASE. IF I HAD MORE **POCKETS** IN MY PANTS I COULD CARRY A LOT FEWER BAGS.
GOOD, WE WERE WONDERING WHEN YOU'D BE BACK.
THE VAN'S ALL PACKED.
HI, HARRY. ANYTHING YOU WANT TO SAY TO ME BEFORE WE GO BACK TO THE CITY?
...

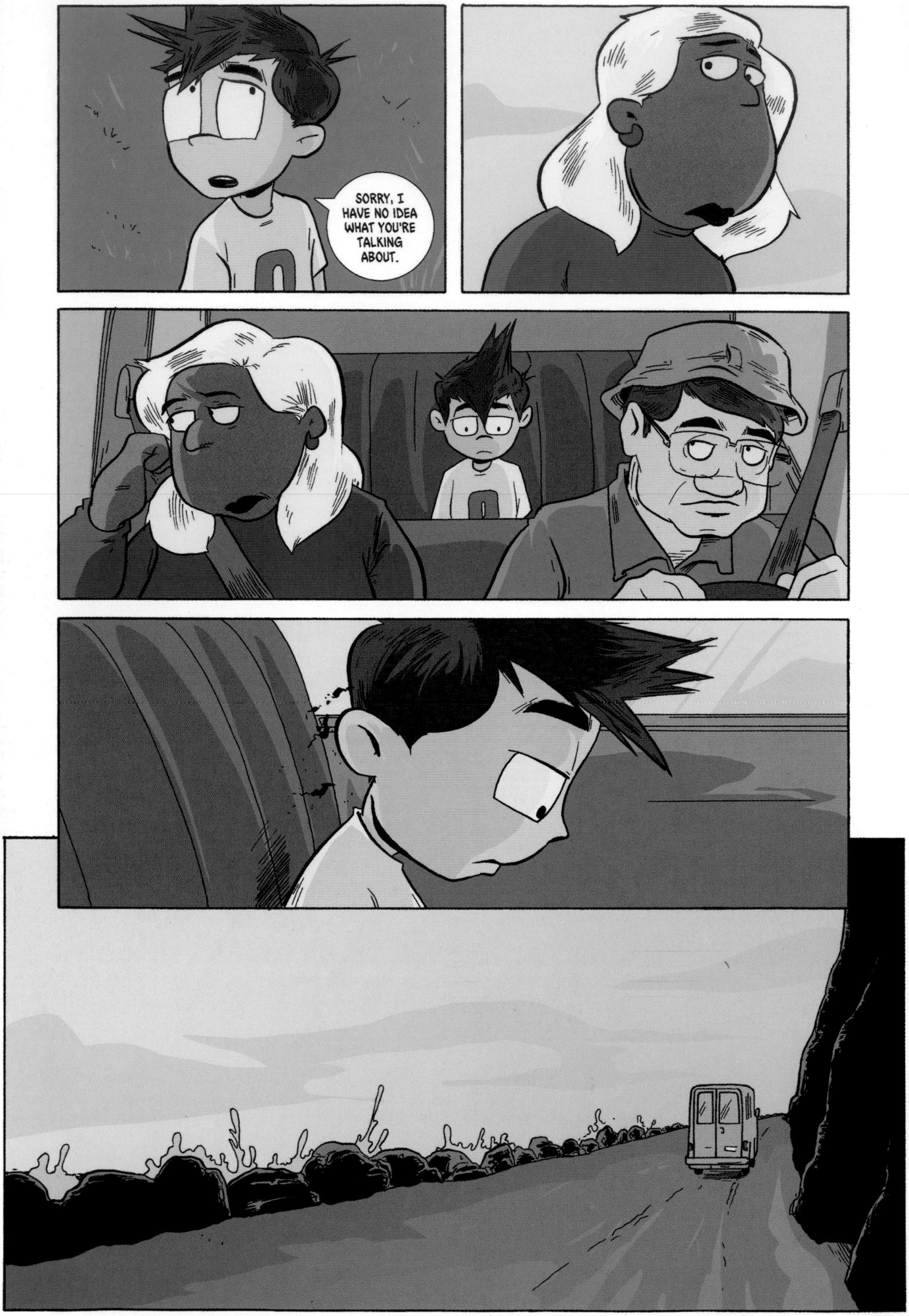
SORRY, I HAVE NO IDEA WHAT YOU'RE TALKING ABOUT.

THE END

Coming in Summer 2022,

the third book in the BLACK SAND BEACH series

Character design doesn't happen overnight. You have to learn what works and what doesn't, find out which angles they look good from and which ones make them look plain weird. So, here are a bunch of early sketches of the kids from Black Sand Beach so you can see how they grew and changed.

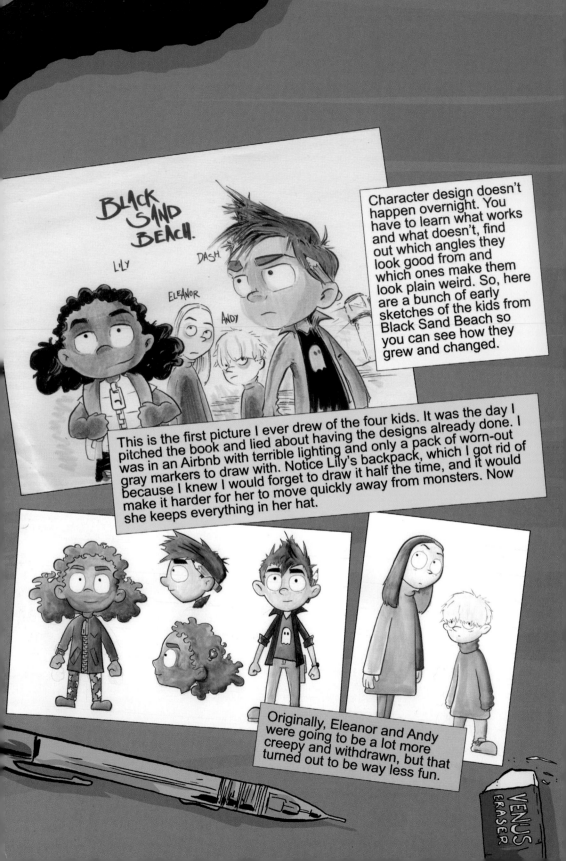

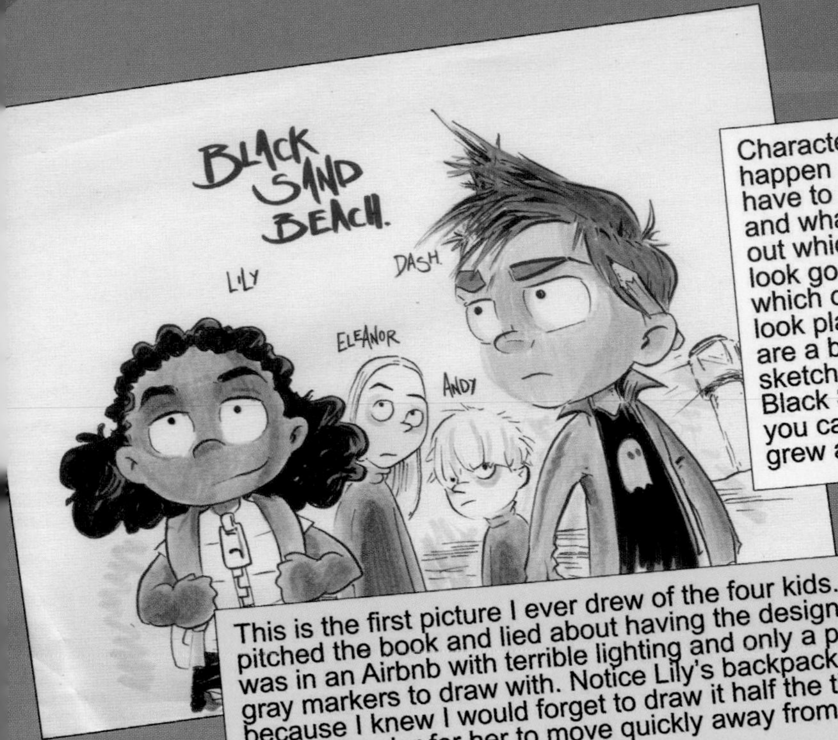
BLACK SAND BEACH.
LILY
DASH.
ELEANOR
ANDY

This is the first picture I ever drew of the four kids. It was the day I pitched the book and lied about having the designs already done. I was in an Airbnb with terrible lighting and only a pack of worn-out gray markers to draw with. Notice Lily's backpack, which I got rid of because I knew I would forget to draw it half the time, and it would make it harder for her to move quickly away from monsters. Now she keeps everything in her hat.

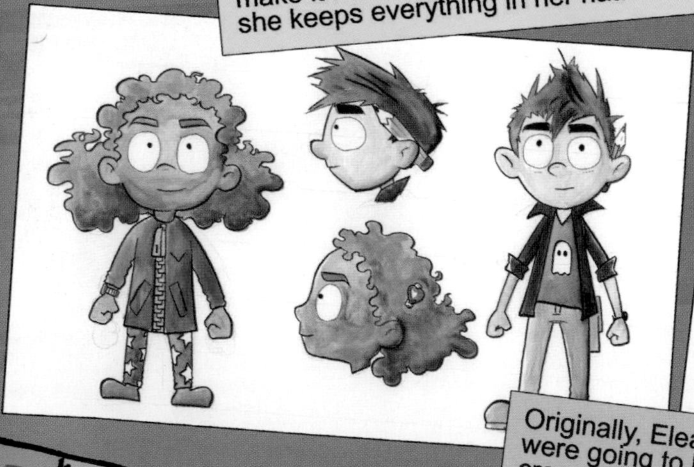

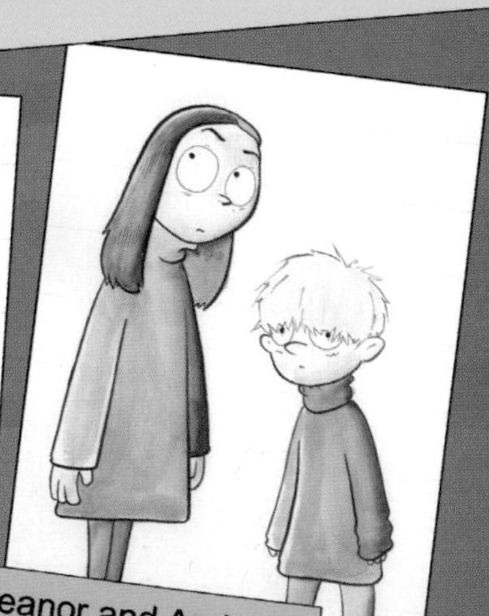

Originally, Eleanor and Andy were going to be a lot more creepy and withdrawn, but that turned out to be way less fun.

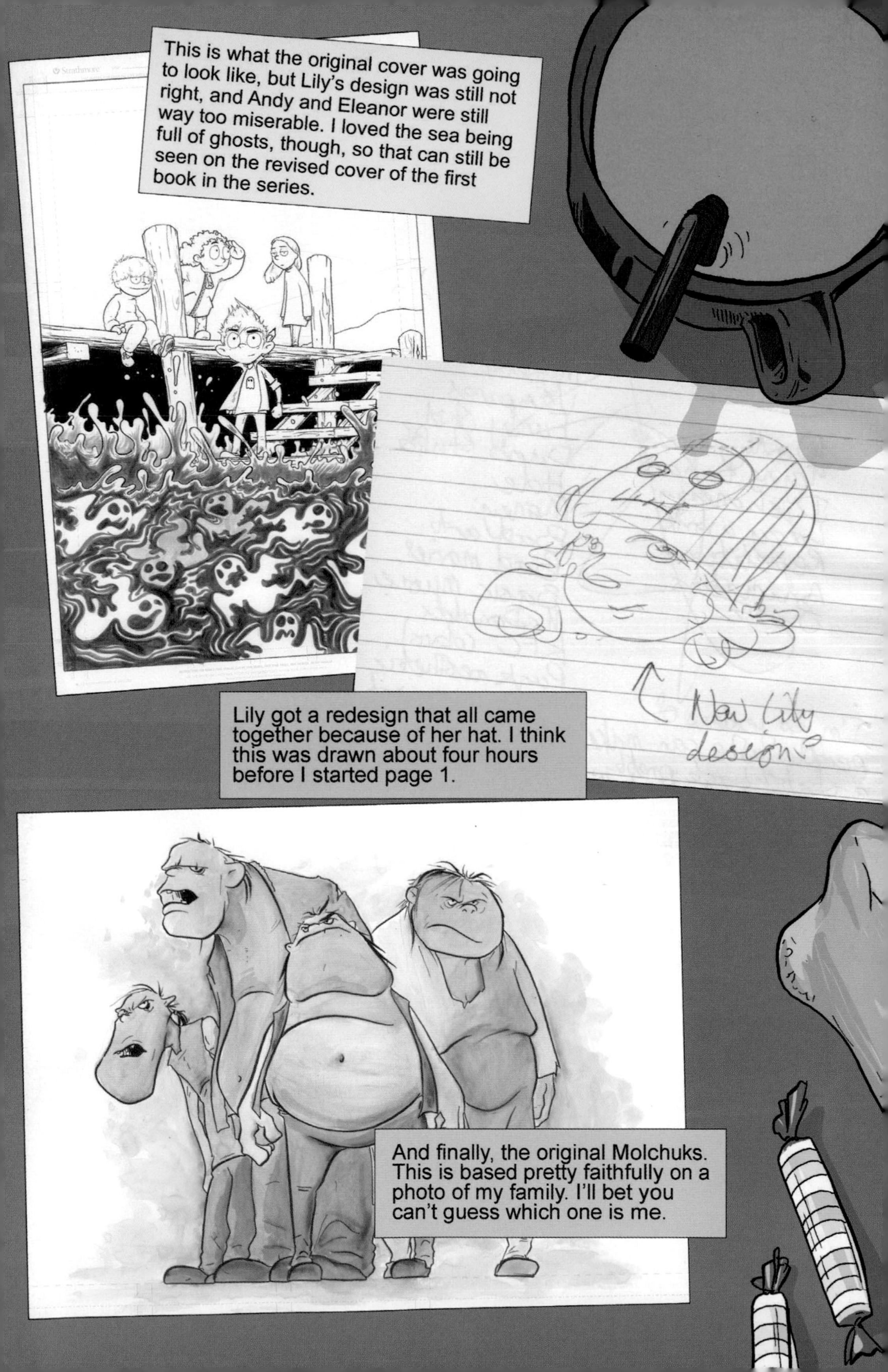
This is what the original cover was going to look like, but Lily's design was still not right, and Andy and Eleanor were still way too miserable. I loved the sea being full of ghosts, though, so that can still be seen on the revised cover of the first book in the series.
New Lily design!
Lily got a redesign that all came together because of her hat. I think this was drawn about four hours before I started page 1.
And finally, the original Molchuks. This is based pretty faithfully on a photo of my family. I'll bet you can't guess which one is me.

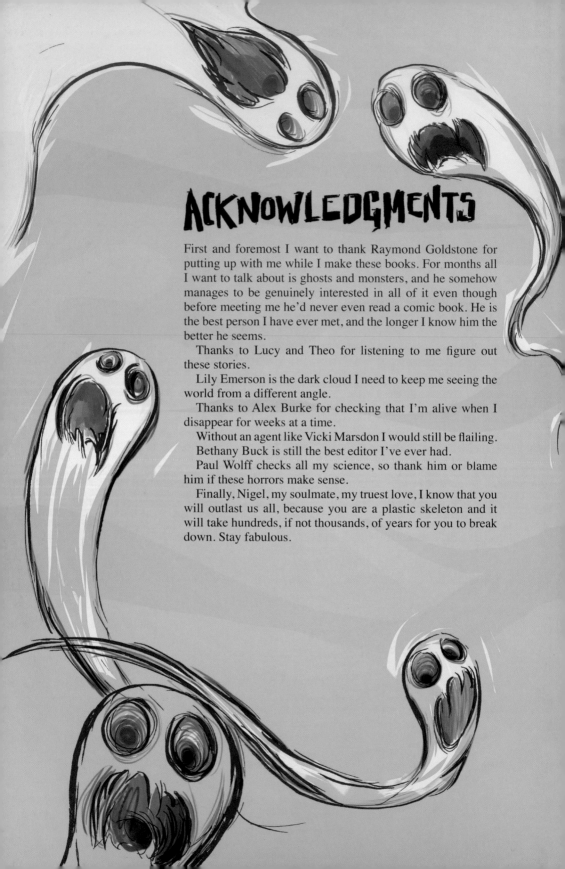

ACKNOWLEDGMENTS

First and foremost I want to thank Raymond Goldstone for putting up with me while I make these books. For months all I want to talk about is ghosts and monsters, and he somehow manages to be genuinely interested in all of it even though before meeting me he'd never even read a comic book. He is the best person I have ever met, and the longer I know him the better he seems.

Thanks to Lucy and Theo for listening to me figure out these stories.

Lily Emerson is the dark cloud I need to keep me seeing the world from a different angle.

Thanks to Alex Burke for checking that I'm alive when I disappear for weeks at a time.

Without an agent like Vicki Marsdon I would still be flailing.

Bethany Buck is still the best editor I've ever had.

Paul Wolff checks all my science, so thank him or blame him if these horrors make sense.

Finally, Nigel, my soulmate, my truest love, I know that you will outlast us all, because you are a plastic skeleton and it will take hundreds, if not thousands, of years for you to break down. Stay fabulous.

RICHARD FAIRGRAY

On the one hundred and ninth day of 1985, the sixteenth Friday of that year, Richard Fairgray was born. In an alternate dimension, Princess Grace was celebrating her twenty-ninth wedding anniversary by watching *The Simpsons* (which, here, would not premier as a short for exactly two more years). Richard is two years older than *The Simpsons,* a fact that has haunted him since he first saw the show.

At age four, Richard wrote his first ghost story, but wouldn't see or meet a ghost for another three years. At age seven he made his first comic book, but wouldn't see or read a comic book for another six years. At age eleven he cooked his family hamburgers, with patties made from scratch, but he wouldn't even try a hamburger until he was in his early twenties. All this to say, Richard has a tendency to make things before he experiences them, so he keeps delaying writing a will. If, as this series predicts, the world is full of terrifying monsters, Richard will surely fall, in which case all his stuff gets left to his roommate's cat, Maureen Thomas.

Richard hopes to one day own the best slide in the world.

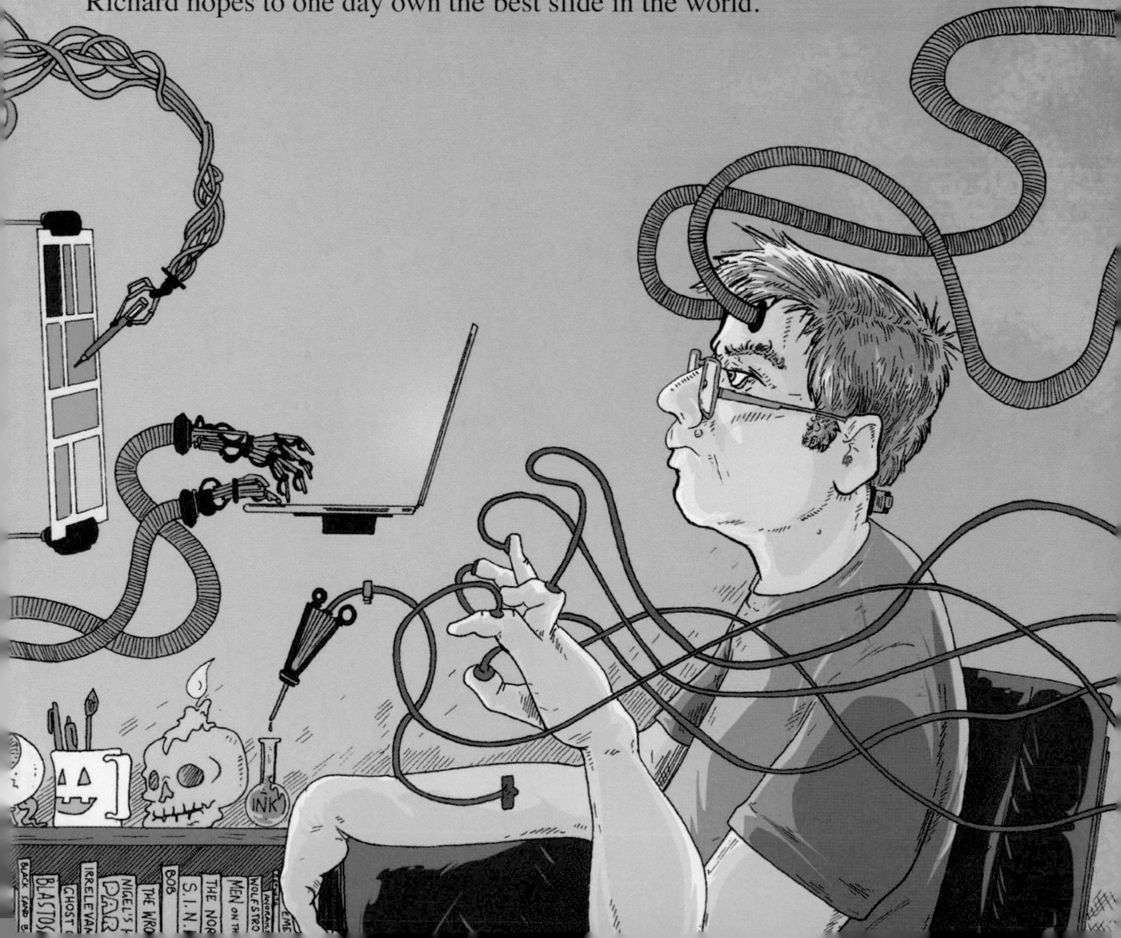
INK
BOB
S.I.N.

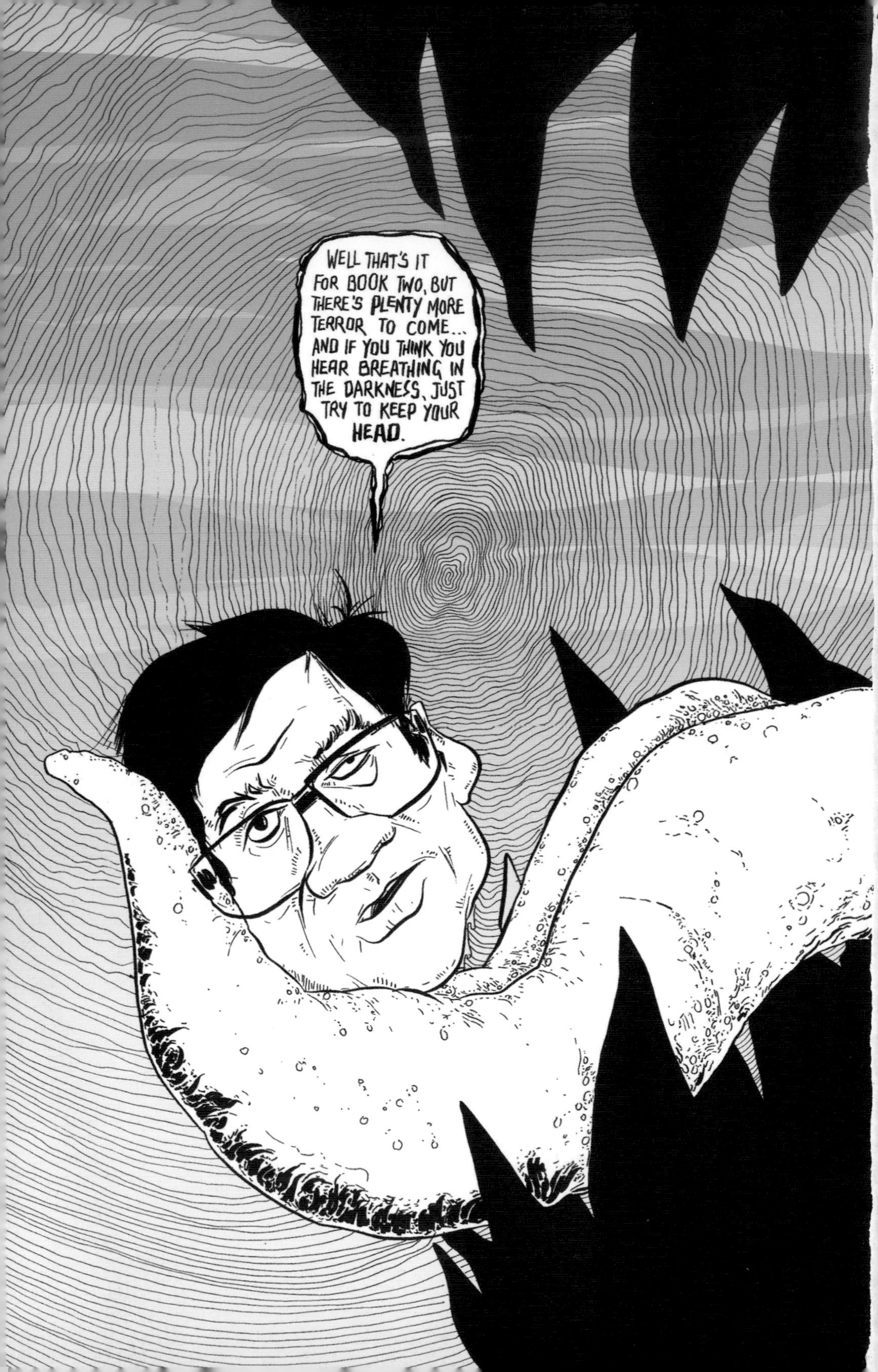
WELL THAT'S IT FOR BOOK TWO, BUT THERE'S PLENTY MORE TERROR TO COME... AND IF YOU THINK YOU HEAR BREATHING IN THE DARKNESS, JUST TRY TO KEEP YOUR HEAD.